I0606698

This was turning out to be much more than the murder of a cop...

"Wow," Joe said, looking at Trinity and Mark in the car. "I think we've a much bigger problem than we originally thought. This may not be a normal cop shooting but the beginning of a terrorist attack in Orlando. I hope not, but it's seems to be headed that way. We have to get this Khan guy and anyone he's associated with. We can't just go in, shut down the ten mosques, and interrogate every person belonging to them, or even anyone who looks like a Muslim. Hell, those three guys look as white as any Irishman with blue eyes and a pale complexion. Speaking of that, Jack, were you able to pull anything from the DNA samples we sent to you from the two dead guys?"

"I was just getting to that, Joe. My guys rushed the test to get it to you as soon as possible. We know how important it is to identify the two dead guys as either Russian or Chechen because it could lead the investigation in two opposites paths. From the samples taken from Mr. Dudayev and Mr. Shishani, both showed that they were Caucasian and the mitochondrial DNA had evidence of the Middle East on the Y-DNA side. There's no doubt that your first guess was right. These guys are both Chechens. To be one-hundred percent sure, it would take us weeks and many more tests, but I don't think you need that to continue this investigation. I'd look for Chechen Muslims if I were you."

"Thanks, Jack. You've confirmed our worst fears."

Joe turned to Trinity and shook his head. "We've got a big problem."

A shootout with terrorists at Orlando International Airport, killing one police officer and wounding two others, thrusts US Coast Guard Lieutenant Joe Traynor and his team of highly skilled experts into the middle of another dangerous investigation. Once the terrorist leader is identified, Joe suspects that he not only had something to do with the Boston Marathon bombing, but that he came to Orlando with the intent of executing another 9/11. In an area rich with prime targets, both military and civilian, Joe's team has to both find the suspect and identify where he will strike—and they're running out of time.

KUDOS for *Never Say Never*

In *Never Say Never* by Daniel J. Barrett, we are reunited with Joe Traynor and his elite team of US Coast Guard investigators. This time, they are chasing terrorists in Orlando, Florida, after a shooting at the Orlando International Airport. Joe is called in because the suspect who shot one cop and wounded two others appears to be Russian. Joe determines that he is not Russian but Chechen and calls in his team to investigate. Joe has to juggle this investigation with his other work, as well as his impending marriage to Julie Chapman, who has a busy schedule of her own, including finishing her second book in her *A Girl's Life Trilogy*. As Joe closes in on the terrorists, Julie is concerned that he live long enough to make her a bride, especially since the danger to Joe and his team seems to be escalating. This is the fourth book in the Joe Traynor and Julie Chapman series for this talented author. And like the others, this one will keep you perched on the edge of your seat, turning pages as fast as you can. ~ *Taylor Jones, Reviewer*

Never Say Never by Daniel Barrett is the fourth book in Barrett's *Conch Town Girl* series. Our hero, Joe Traynor, is a US Coast Guard lieutenant who is in charge of special investigation in southern Florida and The Keys. He mainly works with Russian and Spanish speaking suspects as Joe is fluent in both languages and few in the Coast Guard are. When a suspected terrorist shoots up the airport in Orlando, the local authorities, who have worked with Joe in the past, call him in again because they think the suspect is Russian. Turns out that he is Chechen instead, but Joe speaks that too, so he finds himself heading up this investigation as well. However, this time there is a problem. Joe is set to marry his long-time sweetheart, Julie Chapman, and she wants him to stay alive and out of danger—at least as much as possible. And, in fact, Joe is planning to leave the Coast Guard once his term is up, so this will probably be his last investigation, or so he hopes. So all he has to do is survive a little longer. Good luck with that, especially since the bad guys play for keeps. *Never Say Never*, like the books before it, has the author's unique and informative voice, taking us deep inside Coast Guard investigations and the high-tech equipment used to combat terrorists these days. It's a hard way to make a living, but someone has to do it. *Never Say Never* will hold your interest from beginning to end. ~ *Regan Murphy, Reviewer*

ACKNOWLEDGEMENTS

Once again, thank you to Black Opal Books for making this fourth book in the Conch Town Girl series possible. A special thank you to Lauri Wellington, Acquisitions Editor, and to Faith, Senior Editor, for making Never Say Never the best that it can be. Your dedication and hard work is very much appreciated.

NEVER SAY NEVER

Daniel J. Barrett

A Black Opal Books Publication

GENRE: THRILLER/SUSPENSE/MYSTERY-DETECTIVE

This is a work of fiction. Names, places, characters and incidents are either the product of the author's imagination or are used fictitiously, and any resemblance to any actual persons, living or dead, businesses, organizations, events or locales is entirely coincidental. All trademarks, service marks, registered trademarks, and registered service marks are the property of their respective owners and are used herein for identification purposes only. The publisher does not have any control over or assume any responsibility for author or third-party websites or their contents.

NEVER SAY NEVER
Copyright © 2016 by Daniel J. Barrett
Cover Design by Daniel J. Barrett
All cover art copyright © 2016
All Rights Reserved
Print ISBN: 978-1-626945-41-8

First Publication: OCTOBER 2016

All rights reserved under the International and Pan-American Copyright Conventions. No part of this book may be reproduced or transmitted in any form or by any means, electronic or mechanical, including photocopying, recording, or by any information storage and retrieval system, without permission in writing from the publisher.

WARNING: The unauthorized reproduction or distribution of this copyrighted work is illegal. Criminal copyright infringement, including infringement without monetary gain, is investigated by the FBI and is punishable by up to 5 years in federal prison and a fine of $250,000. Anyone pirating our ebooks will be prosecuted to the fullest extent of the law and may be liable for each individual download resulting therefrom.

ABOUT THE PRINT VERSION: If you purchased a print version of this book without a cover, you should be aware that the book is stolen property. It was reported as "unsold and destroyed" to the publisher, and neither the author nor the publisher has received any payment for this "stripped book."

IF YOU FIND AN EBOOK OR PRINT VERSION OF THIS BOOK BEING SOLD OR SHARED ILLEGALLY, PLEASE REPORT IT TO: lpn@blackopalbooks.com

Published by Black Opal Books **http://www.blackopalbooks.com**

*Never Say Never is dedicated to the Orlando
terrorist attack victims and their families.
They will forever be in our prayers and our memories.*

CHAPTER 1

Hi, Jane. Thanks for coming down for the closing," Julie said to her attorney.

Julie Chapman and Joe Traynor had purchased a house in Tavernier. It was the house that Julie had her heart set on but it was $20,000.00 more than she wanted to spend. The owners compromised, brought it down $10,000.00, and offered to pay all the closing costs.

They jumped on it. Cash out of pocket, right now before the wedding, was at a premium. The mortgage could be paid off over thirty years.

"I wouldn't have missed it for the world, Julie. When is Joe getting here?" Jane asked.

"Soon, I hope. He's out at sea on another investigation but absolutely promised to be here for the closing, or there won't be one."

Both Joe and Julie would own the house equally and both would be on the deed and on the mortgage as well. Julie wanted to make sure that she paid her fair monthly share. She was putting down the majority of the down payment since Joe bought her engagement ring, and he was taking care of both wedding receptions—in New York City and back in Key Largo, the following month. The closing was taking place at the Keys Federal Credit Union on North Roosevelt Avenue in Key West.

Julie looked out the window. "As we speak, Joe is parking his car right in front of the building. Talk about cutting it close."

"Nervous?" asked Jane.

"A little. This is a big deal to me. You know?"

"I know and that's why I'm here. Are we going out afterward to celebrate the closing?"

Julie smiled. "I could use a drink right now."

"Joe walked into the conference room. "Sorry I'm late. I wasn't steering the ship or I'd have been here earlier."

Julie hugged him. "Real funny. How'd everything go, Joe?"

"Fine. There was a little action but it ended quickly. I can't wait for my time to be up," he said.

Joe was thinking about leaving the Coast Guard in the fall when his two years were up. He promised Rear Admiral Jake Barnes that if he were to leave, it wouldn't be until Jake retired. They needed to clean up the Seventh District after the huge scandal that had just happened. Washington was allowing Jake to take care of all the problems and then retire on a positive note.

Julie grimaced. "Keep it down, Joe. We want them to think you'll still be gainfully employed or we won't get the mortgage."

Jane smiled at both of them. She'd been married a while and had to go through the exact same thing in Miami. The only difference was that in Miami, it was a rollercoaster ride of property values. One day a condo sold for $400,000.00 and the next it was being auctioned off for under $200,000.00. Jane and Nick, her husband, bought their house in Coral Gables, only a few blocks from the University of Miami, during the down cycle, and it held its value. Being a commercial real estate attorney for one of the largest firms in Miami didn't hurt at all, and Jane did their own closing and title transfers, saving a bundle.

The mortgage officer, Susan Jacoby, walked into the room, greeted everyone, and took her seat. The former owners weren't there but were represented by their own attorney who'd smile, pick up the check, and be out of there in a half an hour. Julie was sure he'd charge enough to pick up the check. Jane had all the cashier's checks ready for the closing. The final price for the house was $385,000.00 and Jane had the check for the $30,000.00 down payment. Their new house, at 107 High Street in Tavernier, only four blocks from Coral Shoes High School and one block to the ocean, was in a federal-government-designated area with a minimal risk of flood. This house, fortunately, was an "X Zone" and the FEMA flood insurance, although expensive, was the cheapest of all flood insurance at less than $1,500.00 a year. Property taxes in the Florida Keys weren't prohibitive, due to a large commercial property tax base paying the bulk of county and school taxes.

Altogether, their payments came in right at the $1,400.00 per month mark, and both Joe and Julie were ecstatic. The mortgage interest and taxes were tax deductible and made the payment even more affordable. They'd furnish the house over the next year, as they could afford it, especially with two weddings coming up. Julie was also asked to be in Maddy Malone's wedding in Reading, Massachusetts, near the end of the summer, creating another burden with flight costs, hotels, bridesmaid dress, and gifts. Julie was grateful that they had two steady incomes, and her new book would be handed in right before their own wedding.

Jane reviewed all the documents and handed each of them, one at a time, to Julie and Joe to sign. Within the hour, the paperwork was completed. The previous owners' attorney handed them the keys to their new home. They smiled and gave each other a hug and a kiss.

"Julie, are you happy?"

"Very happy. How about you?"

"I'm thrilled for you and, yes, I'm happy, too. I know this was a big deal for you and you deserve it."

"Thank you. That means a lot," she said.

Jane cleared her throat. "If you're through congratulating each other, I've made arrangements for dinner at your favorite restaurant in Islamorada, where I believe all this began many years ago."

They both knew what Jane had meant, Bentley's Restaurant. After Joe had given Julie and her grandmother, Tillie, the tour of his Coast Guard Station at 4:00 p.m. that day, many years ago, Joe asked them if they were hungry. They said yes. So they all hopped into Tillie's Escort and drove the short distance to Bentley's Restaurant, right on Overseas Highway. At ten years old and in fifth grade, at that time, Julie had only eaten at the Waffle House, where Tillie worked, or from the children's menu, when they went someplace else on a special occasion. Bentley's had a children's menu for kids under twelve but Joe said they were all ordering from the main menu. Having only met Joe that day, and knowing how little he was paid as a first year seaman, Tillie glanced at the prices and looked at Joe. He simply nodded "my treat." It was about half of what he was paid every two weeks. He couldn't think of a better way to spend his money or his time. Now they'd bought a house together and they'd be married in a few months.

Jane followed Julie and Joe from Key West and, as they pulled into the restaurant parking lot, they saw Tillie, Jeff, Joan, and Lucy Talbot, and Mark and Louise and the kids. Julie and Joe got out of the car and smiled at Jane. "Surprise?"

Jane chuckled. " I don't get to share a lot of joy being an attorney so bear with me, okay?"

"We love you, Jane. You know that? Right?" Julie said. Joe nodded.

"Yes, I do. Nick was coming to the party but had emergency surgery this afternoon." Jane's husband, Dr. Nick Snyder, was a neurologist at Jackson Memorial Hospital in Miami and was constantly on call for emergency brain surgery due to accidents and crimes. Jackson Memorial Hospital was noted for its emergency surgeries, so Nick was practically living there. Once his full time residency was over, he could live a normal life. A normal life for a doctor was still over seventy hours a week and Jane had known that going in.

All three walked up the steps to the front door of Bentley's and everyone gave all three a hug. As they walked in, Julie had a tear in her eye. "This is so special, everyone. I don't know how to thank you for coming. Joe, did you have anything to do with this?"

"Honestly, no. I didn't have a clue. Thank you, Jane, for everything. You're a great friend," he said. They were seated on the deck, exactly where they ate those many years ago. Joe, Tillie, and Julie ate the same meals they did back then. The waitress brought out a cake for dessert that spelled out their new address with a bride and a groom on the cake. Jane had thought of everything.

Tillie started to cry but Julie turned and hugged her. "Did you ever think everything would turn out like this, Tillie?"

"No, but I certainly hoped it would."

With that, everyone, including the kids, raised their glasses and gave Julie and Joe a toast for their future happiness.

"Does this qualify as a third wedding reception," Julie asked everyone gathered.

Jane laughed. "Only if you want it to, Julie."

෩෨෩

Julie and Joe spent the next month moving their limited furniture and clothes into the new house. Joe was still caught between cleaning up the mess in Miami with the Seventh District and working investigations at Islamorada. At least Joan Talbot was now in charge, and Joe didn't have to walk on pins and needles around Jacob Cramer, the Chief Warrant Officer, formerly in charge of the Islamorada Station.

He was transferred, as a promotion, at Joe's request to Rear Admiral Jake Barnes, to the Port Canaveral Station, reporting to command up in Jacksonville.

Having Joan in command at Islamorada, at least until she retired, was a blessing.

Julie still had a busy schedule. She was just about finished with her second book, *The Middle Years*, as part of *A Girl's Story*, the trilogy she started with *Conch Town Girl* while at Brown University. *Conch Town Girl* was doing extremely well, which generated the second book advance of $30,000.00. At least now, when she hopped into her car, it was a two-minute drive to the high school. She still had to drive because she'd still leave at noon for her grant funded duties at the elementary school in Key Largo and back to the high school for her coaching duties. At least school got out early in May in the Keys so the wedding, now being planned for both places, should go off without a hitch—hopefully.

CHAPTER 2

"Hi, Julie. How are you?"

Julie had barely reached the phone before it stopped ringing. "Hi, Trinity. Sorry about the phone. We've no idea where everything is, including our cell phones."

Trinity Hightower was a detective with the Orlando Police Department. She met Joe and Julie when they were in Orlando last year for a meeting at Hollywood Studios. Production staff flew to Orlando to discuss Julie's new book, *Conch Town Girl*, as being selected for a new movie. Julie and their people were still talking, but Julie turned them down for now, at least until she'd completed her second book, *The Middle Years*, of the trilogy *A Girl's Life*. At the time of the meeting, Joe and Julie needed protection while Joe was in charge of an internal Coast Guard investigation that included Coast Guard personnel and the Columbians in an almost undetected cocaine switching operation.

"Julie, is Joe around? I need to talk to him about a major problem we have up here in Orlando. I think we need his help. At least that's what Chief Roberts said. He told me to call Joe as quickly as possible."

"Joe should be here in a few minutes, Trinity. Will you be at this number or should he call your cell?"

"I'm with Cal Roberts right now in his office. I'll tell you what this is about so he knows it's important but please don't say a word to anyone else. We had a shooting at the

Orlando International Airport. We were following a lead from Boston about a potential terrorist getting off a plane from Logan Airport. Two others met him when he got off the plane, both unknown at this point. Archie Higgins was at the airport with three other officers, in plain clothes, waiting for the plane to arrive. At this point, we don't know what happened, but these three individuals started shooting at Archie and the other officers. Archie had his vest on but evidently he was hit in the head. I'm sorry to say, Julie, but Archie is dead and two of the other three officers were wounded. Two of the three suspects were also killed in the shootout. One of them escaped. Unfortunately, it might have been the guy coming off the plane who escaped. The perp obviously didn't have a weapon on the plane but must have gotten one from the others who met him before leaving the airport. They were just outside the main gate, right after going through security. We've no idea who the two dead perps are but they look Slavic or Russian. We don't know and haven't identified them as of yet."

"Trinity, I'm so sorry for your loss. Archie was a good guy and both Joe and I really liked him. As soon as Joe comes in, I'll have him call you. Why do you need Joe?"

Trinity was now in tears. "We think the two dead guys are Russians, but we're not sure. Joe is fluent in Russian. We don't have anybody who speaks the language or even knows about Russians in the United States. We didn't even know we had Russians in Orlando. In the last hour, after a preliminary investigation, it seems like the Russians have crept up on us. We've almost 4,000 of them in downtown Orlando, alone. We downloaded the 2013 census data by zip code for Orlando. Boy, were we surprised. We were so concerned after the meth takedown that Joe did here in Orlando, that we've been concentrating on drugs not Russians. Who the hell would think there'd be Russians in Orlando?"

"Why do you think they're Russians, Trinity?"

"Someone thought they heard them speaking Russian or something like it. We're only guessing Russian at this point.

We thought the guy coming off the plane from Boston was Russian. At least that's what the FBI told us on the phone and in the email we got with his picture. That's what we believed to be true, anyway. I remember Joe telling us about Cyrillic money wrappers on the money you found in your attic. We know about your run in. Joe told us before."

"I'll have him call you as soon as he comes in, Trinity. Say Hi to Kiki for us," Julie said.

"Thanks, Julie. I'll talk to you later."

As she got off the phone, Julie fast tracked back to Archie Higgins and Trinity serving as bodyguards for Julie and Joe. Both their lives appeared to be in danger back a while ago but Joe still wanted her to meet with the movie people.

"You can't back down from these people," he'd said. "You have to go right at them or you'll never have a quiet moment."

Archie wound up being a friend but Trinity became close to Julie and Joe after Joe saved Trinity's niece, Kiki, from sex traffickers in Miami.

Trinity knew that Joe probably had enough of investigations to last the rest of his life and that he was thinking about leaving the Coast Guard when his time was up in the fall. However, she and her chief were caught between a rock and a hard place. They knew Joe could be helpful in solving this new crisis. Dead officers and two supposed Russians, lying on the floor of the Orlando International Airport wouldn't sit well with the residents of Orlando. They relied heavily on tourism at their theme parks to keep school, city, and Orange County taxes down. Trinity doubted that they could keep this quiet, but if it ended quickly, at least they could contain the damage. A week of issues was better than having tourists worry about family safety. Then they wouldn't come at all, and that would be a disaster.

§§§

Joe walked in the door about twenty minutes later. He dropped his briefcase on the kitchen table and his go-to bag on the floor. Joe always had to be packed and ready at a minute's notice. He'd grab his briefcase, side arm, and go-to bag, and run for the door as soon as he was given orders.

"Hi, Julie. How's the unpacking coming? How's your book? Getting close?"

"Before we begin this conversation, Joe, call Trinity. She and Cal have a big problem at the Orlando International Airport. Unfortunately, there was gunplay. Archie Higgins was shot dead and two other officers wounded. They were chasing what looked like a bunch of Russians."

"Russians? Archie dead? Wow, slow down. Give me a second. Where's Trinity now? When did she call? What's she want with me?"

"Trinity is in Cal Roberts's office. Here's her number. Call her now. She's very upset about Archie. I can only imagine. Call her, Joe."

With a sigh, Joe sat on the arm of the couch and dialed Cal's phone. He popped opened a Sam Adams Oktoberfest beer and took two quick swigs.

"Trinity? It's Joe. Is Cal there? Tell me what happened."

Trinity got on the speakerphone with Cal Roberts, the Chief of Police, listening in. She could barely speak. After all, Archie Higgins was Trinity's first partner as a detective. They weren't best friends but got along fine, and Trinity liked him, in spite of his being gruff most of the time. She helped him solve cases using new technology, and he was very patient with a new detective's mistakes. She still couldn't believe he was gone. She'd just been reassigned to major crimes. She couldn't turn it down, even though it meant losing Archie as her partner. She was sure it would hit her hard once she was alone with her thoughts.

"Hi, Joe. It's Cal here."

"Hi, Cal. Can both of you hear me? Tell me what's going on."

Trinity proceeded to tell Joe about the call from the FBI

in Boston to the Orlando FBI and then on to the police department. "The local FBI, with very limited staff, asked the police to follow a man they suspected to be an associate or friend of the Boston Marathon bombers. At that point, they'd no specific idea who he was. They only wanted him followed. They thought he was Russian but the Boston FBI office was very aware, after the Boston Marathon bombing, that the two brothers responsible were Chechen, not just Russian. They spoke Russian but, in fact, were Muslims. The gentleman on the plane was caught on camera talking to the two brothers in downtown Boston, the previous year. They were cleaning out their records for the trial and started to compile pictures of people, not necessarily known associates of the brothers, but somehow connected to them. They'd no idea who he was but his picture was on file and on the no-fly list for facial recognition, without a name. After the bombing, they never saw him again. Today, they were fortunate to have the picture on file match a man getting on the plane at Logan Airport in Boston, heading on a direct flight to Orlando. He was pale looking, Russian maybe, but other than that, they'd no idea who he was. Scrambling, the calls were made and Archie Higgins and three officers were waiting in the wings to see where he'd go when he got off the plane. Obviously, they were in plain clothes, not in uniforms."

"So, guys, where do I fit in?" Joe asked.

"Can you get here as soon as possible, Joe?" Cal asked. "We really need your help. We'd no idea about the size of the Russian population. We'd no idea about a connection to Boston and either Russian thugs or Chechens. In any case, we've no one with your background in Russian language or ethnic understanding. We know that you know the Russian Mafia inside and out, but we're quite lacking. Can you come up, Joe?"

"I'll see what I can do. I have to call my rear admiral."

"I'm putting Trinity in charge of the investigation," Cal informed him. "Not directly as it relates to the shooting, because Archie was her former partner. But in charge of the entire process, which appears to be greater than its parts. I'll have another detective take care of the shooting. I just split up the Archie and Trinity partnership last week. Archie got a new partner, and Trinity was moved into major crimes. She deserves it, Joe. But now, I feel so bad. I have to think if I hadn't done that, Archie might be alive."

"Think of this, Cal," Joe said. "Both of them could be dead right now and not just Archie." Joe hesitated. "You know Julie and I are getting married in a few weeks, and we just moved into a new house. You're also aware that I'll be leaving active duty, at least as an investigator, in the fall when my commission expires."

"Honestly, Joe, I wouldn't ask, nor would Trinity even suggest it, if we weren't really in need of your services. Hopefully, we can wrap this up within the next week or two at the most. If not, we can turn it over to the FBI but not the murder of a police officer. That's on us, Joe, as you know."

"I hear you, Cal. Let me call my boss and I'll call you back shortly. If I'm allowed to come up, I'll probably hop on a helicopter stationed in Miami, but I'll have to get there first. I'll call you."

"Thanks, Joe. We'll continue to work on this until we hear from you."

Joe called Rear Admiral Barnes and got him just before he left his office for the day. The rear admiral knew about Joe's personal relationship with the Orlando police and how he, Julie, and Trinity became close friends. He was unaware of Archie Higgins's involvement with them as well. He gave Joe permission to spend no more than two weeks in Orlando. They'd a lot to do before the fall, especially since both would be leaving the service and their work would be halted for a short time, anyway, because of the wedding and honeymoon. Joe thanked him and asked him if he could borrow a helicopter.

"Anything else, Joe?" Barnes asked kiddingly.

"Not that I can think of at the moment, sir."

"Be careful, especially with the wedding coming up, Joe. When you get back, we need to go over the list of those in new jobs at the Seventh District. So far so good. You were right about allowing the ladies to move up and be in charge of the stations. You were also right about moving Michelle Bower into George Pagan's spot as head of personnel. She knows the rules better than anyone I've met so far in all my years. She's also memorized every person and position in the District. I personally can't believe it, but she has."

"That's great, Jake. I knew you'd be pleased. I kept hearing how bad the new recruits are and how no one could ever replace the old guys who were retiring. I got news for those people. Our new personnel are better educated, better trained, and fully aware of what they're protecting since Nine/Eleven. All they need is seasoning in the job."

Barnes chuckled. "I fully agree. I've a few new situations that have crept up since we last spoke. We still have problems with drugs in the ranks. Frank Cortez pointed it out to me at our last meeting. He and his staff, in one week, did more than the others did in the last ten years. Of course, they were the problem, as you so gracefully pointed out."

"Hopefully, what I have to do for Trinity and Cal won't take long," Joe said. "I probably have to prove one way or the other that the dead men are Russians and see where that takes us. Trinity and Cal had no idea that there are almost 4,000 Russians living in Orlando. She also didn't realize that there are Russian Orthodox churches and even ten new mosques in their immediate area. It's clear. Things in Orlando are starting to change dramatically. Before, they were trying to accommodate a growing Latino population, but now those groups seemed to have fit in nicely into the fabric of Orlando. It's now the ethnic populations that no one ever even suspected would wind up in Orlando that's cause for concern."

"Well, do what you can and get back here as soon as possible."

"I will, Jake. Thanks again. Trinity and Cal mean a lot to us, and we want to support them."

"I think you already did by getting her niece and her girl-friend back to their family in one piece. God only knows what their life would be like now if you hadn't found them quickly. I'll see you, Joe. Be safe and say hi to Julie for me."

With that, they both hung up. Joe had to pack quickly. He made the call to Cal and Trinity. He needed to make a few calls to Mark and Joan Talbot. He also needed to call his father and brother. It'd been a while. Joe might need Mark, once again, depending on where this led them. Mark was an expert on gangs, mostly Mexican and other Hispanic gangs, but he still proved very useful when they took out the Russians in Miami and had them renditioned by the CIA.

Joe hoped this wouldn't have to be the case one more time. It was getting trickier and trickier every time they needed to clear another hurdle to work under the Patriot Act. It was not as clean as it once was when the Twin Towers in New York City came down. The problems that led up to that were getting even more profound than before. The enemy kept moving and incorporating new ethnic groups that Joe and his team had never had to deal with before.

ᴄᴏᴄᴏ

"Mark, how are you? It's been a while."

"Who's this?" Mark inquired. He was just breaking Joe's ass—as if Joe hadn't done that enough to Mark over the years.

Joe snorted. "You know damn well who this is. What do you have going on? I got a call from Trinity in Orlando. She and Cal Roberts need my Russian expertise, and I might need you on call in case the crap hits the fan. Are you avail-able?"

"Everything here at Dania Beach is fine, but I've been

helping out the rear admiral's transition team in Miami. Does he know you might need me?"

"I just got off the phone with him, and he gave me two weeks and—by extension—he gave you two weeks up in Orlando. He knows we're a team."

"Give me a call when you get there and let me know what's going on."

"Will do." Joe hung up and called Joan Talbot. He was looking for a ride to Miami in her husband Jeff's go-fast boat.

"Joan, how are you?"

She laughed. "What do you need now, Joe? You only call me when you need something."

"Is Jeff around? I need a ride to Miami to catch a helicopter to Orlando. I'm supposed to meet it at our 100 MacArthur Causeway facility. The quicker I get there, the quicker I can get to Orlando. You remember Trinity, right?"

"Of course, Joe."

"They've two supposed dead Russians that were killed in a shootout at the Orlando International Airport. Unfortunately, Archie Higgins was killed and two other officers shot as well. I just got permission from our rear admiral to head up to help them with their Russian, if, in fact, they're Russian. I have to be there ASAP. They're moving the bodies to the morgue. The same morgue that I went to with Tom's daughter to identify his body."

"I've a better idea, Joe. If you have to get there quickly, I've a helicopter coming in from a surveillance mission near Key West. They should be landing in half an hour. If you can be here by then, I'll get it refueled and they can get you up to Miami within the next hour."

"You're a sweetheart, Joan. I'll be there."

"By the way, I imagine that you're aware of this, but Julie asked both me and Jeff to walk her down the aisle at your wedding at Saint Patrick's Cathedral in New York City and the following month at St. Justin Martyr in Key Largo. I've never been so honored. Not only is Lucy in the wedding but we are as well. It would have been different if her grandmother, Tillie, walked her down the aisle, but Julie told me that she asked her to be the matron of honor. We don't know if that's the right title since her husband has been deceased for so many years but Tillie said she wasn't a 'maid,' either." Joan laughed. "You knew about this and never said a thing to us."

Joe chuckled. "First, when Julie told me her plans, she told me not to interfere. I've been told by a good source—two actually including your husband, Jeff, and my good friend, Mark—to do whatever the bride wanted and I'll live peacefully for the rest of our lives. If not, then I was asking for trouble. On a side note, Julie told me that you and Tillie have served as her mothers since she met you when she was ten years old. You made her your babysitter for the kids but, more than that, you made her your oldest daughter, and she said she loves both of you for that."

"You're making me cry, Joe. We were thrilled when she asked Lucy to be in the wedding like she was her little sister. Now this. We're overwhelmed. I'll see you in a little while."

Joe turned to Julie and told her what was going on. He always had a bag packed with a week's worth of clothes, both uniforms and civilian, including his trusty construction boots that he'd had since he was a teenager working for his father.

"Do you want to come to Orlando?" he asked.

"No, I've got a lot to do for the wedding, and I'm still in school until early May. If I'm needed, I'll hitch a ride later, but not now."

Joe kissed her goodbye and left their new Tavernier home to head for his helicopter ride from the Islamorada Coast Guard station.

It was only a fifteen-minute drive. This was the luxury of having a new home close to both their work sites. Joe pulled in and parked next to his still-occupied officer's quarters that he wouldn't give up until he completed his service in the fall. He was forever staying over after a long day and early morning. He'd moved most of his things to their new home but still had the Coast Guard furniture and extra clothes on site, in case of emergencies just like this. He picked up additional uniforms, just in case he had to fill a role for the Coast Guard, Homeland Security, or the FBI, of which he carried credentials for all three organizations.

He walked into the station and went to the commander's office, which now housed Warrant Officer Joan Talbot, a title that she earned and deserved. He knocked on the door and walked in while she was on the phone. She raised her index finger to say just a minute. "Your cab is ready, sir," she said when she got off the phone. "Is there anything else you need? I'm at your beck and call."

Joe smiled at her. "It's only taken sixteen years to hear the 'warrant officer' part."

"Don't let it go to your head, Lieutenant."

Joe came around her desk and gave her a big hug and a kiss. "Thanks for all you do and thanks for being in the wedding, all three of you." He knew that Jeff, Jr. would be taking finals in May but would be there at the June wedding in Key Largo. "I'll have more challenging duties for him, like being in charge of all the kegs of beer."

Joan laughed. "Don't you go corrupting my little boy."

"I think college has already done that to him, Joan." He laughed and headed toward the helipad. "Can you call the Miami facility and tell them we're on our way. They have to hold the helicopter for me. Tell them we're landing at the Orlando police headquarters at their helipad at the main police station on South Hughey Avenue in downtown Orlando. Cal and Trinity will be waiting for me."

CHAPTER 3

Joe made it to the MacArthur Causeway facility in thirty-five minutes, door to door. As soon as they landed, he grabbed his go-to bag and his separate uniform bag, and headed for the other helicopter that was all ready to take off to Orlando.

As he walked toward the helicopter, he looked up and saw Mark waiting for him at the door.

"Joan called me and told me I had to watch you so nothing happened to you before the wedding. Before you ask, yes, Joe, I called the rear admiral and confirmed my working with you. He said it might just speed up the process if I tagged along. He told me to get down here before it left. I hitched a ride with one of my men. I thought for sure that we'd get killed on I-95 South but I'm here in one piece. As you know, I, too, have a go-to bag and all my weapons ready at a minute's notice. I called Louise from the station and she told me to watch you like a hawk, and I will, or she'll never forgive me. So I was told."

"And I'm fine thanks. How are you?" Joe smiled and hopped aboard right behind Mark.

They should be landing at police headquarters in Orlando in under two hours. Joe phoned ahead and told Cal and Trinity when they should expect both him and Mark.

စာစာ

Joe and Mark chatted in the helicopter. They had earphones on so they could talk above the noise. As they were landing in Orlando, Joe pulled his cell phone and called Trinity. He asked her to meet them on the heliport at the police headquarters so they didn't have to go through security at the front of the building. She said she'd go down right now and wait by the side door near the helipad. Joe and Mark got out of the helicopter and thanked the pilot for the ride. As soon as they saw Trinity by the door, they waved for the pilot to leave, and he immediately took off. Joe and Mark had to hold on for dear life because of the turbulence created by the helicopter blades as it was rising from the pad. Trinity beckoned for Mark and Joe to go through the door she was holding open.

As soon as they got to the door, Joe gave Trinity a big hug and a kiss on the cheek. Mark did the same.

"Mark, I didn't know you were coming," she said.

"Neither did I until the last minute. I've been charged with keeping Joe alive, at least until the wedding. After that, he's on his own. Thank God."

Trinity felt bad about dragging Joe up to Orlando, but she didn't have much choice. If he could at least identify the men as Russians or whatever, they'd be ahead of the game. If the investigation was still going on for a while, Joe could go to the wedding and, after the honeymoon, he could finish up if they moved further along in the investigation. "As of now, we had nothing but what we were told by the Boston FBI. They never said anyone would be armed and dangerous and more than willing to kill police officers in the middle of an international airport."

Joe turned to Mark. "It looks like we might be staying at least for a few days. Do you think we can get our old hotel room back? That worked quite nicely when we were here before for Tom's murder investigation and subsequent meth sting operation."

"I'll see what I can do," Mark said.

Back when they were in Orlando for Tom's investigation, they stayed only a few blocks from police headquarters on South Hughey. Joe had used his iPad to look up hotels close to police headquarters and there were three possibilities in the downtown area, only a few blocks away. He had called the Embassy Suites, located less than a mile away at 191 East Pine Street, in downtown. He got a suites room for Mark and himself at a government rate that included breakfast and two queen size beds. They had a living area where they could spread out their equipment to continue the investigation. The room was $148.00 a night for both and had WiFi included. At the time, they left their car in the garage when not in use and walked the mile to the police department in less than fifteen minutes.

Mark made the call, since he still had the hotel phone number on his cell phone. He told them that they were back in town and would like the same room they had previously for at least the next two to three days.

The front desk receptionist said she didn't have the same room but one exactly like it on the second floor, which was also conveniently located next to the breakfast bar. She said they could have it for the same government rate. Since they didn't have a car, they didn't need to pay the overnight parking fees.

Mark accepted and told her that they'd be there in a few hours but to hold the room.

Joe and Trinity walked into Cal's conference room, with Mark following up after his call to the hotel.

"Joe, thank you for coming on such a short notice. It's appreciated. Do you want some coffee or something to eat?"

"Actually, that's not a bad idea. I haven't eaten since breakfast. Please get me anything, a sandwich or whatever and a large regular coffee, cream and two sugars. Thanks."

Mark got the same.

Cal took the lead. "Let Trinity go through exactly where we are, what happened, and what we'd like you to do at this point. She's in charge of the investigation, not of the murder because it was her old partner. She'll be in complete charge of what happens now to find the third suspect. Obviously, the other two were shot dead by our officers."

"Go ahead, Trinity. It's your baby," Joe said as Mark nodded.

"As I told you on the phone, our local FBI got a call from the FBI in Boston. They had a person of interest get on a plane at Logan Airport in Boston headed to Orlando. They never had a name for this individual and all they had was a picture of him standing behind the two brothers. Those individuals had been identified as the Boston Marathon bombers. After the one brother was shot dead and the other taken into custody, everything that could be found out about them had been gathered. That included pictures of individuals who appeared in pictures with the two brothers, either alone or together.

"Subsequently, those pictures have been plastered all over Boston and at every airport in America. Whoever the individual was, he was never identified and seemed to have fallen off the face of the earth until today. He got on the plane and was not identified until the plane had already taken off. While in flight and almost arriving, we were notified by the FBI. Archie Higgins and three officers went to the airport to see who got off the plane. They had his picture and no other information. Subsequently, the airline matched a picture of the individual with a passport that said the person's name was Bronislaw or Bruno Jawarski. He had what appeared to be a valid passport from Poland. He had a street address in Krakow and arrived in the United States last year as a businessman in the technology area. We believe now that he wasn't Polish but a friend of the two Boston Marathon bomber brothers."

Trinity paused and took a deep breath before continuing. "We're not sure about what happened after the plane landed. We know that Jawarski made it to the main concourse, outside the security area. Now, we have camera shots. It appeared that Archie, or one of the other officers, spooked Jawarski, who'd just met two others in the concourse on the way out. It appeared that Jawarski was unarmed coming off the plane, hopefully, but must have gotten a weapon from one of the two he met. From the camera angle, it also appeared that Jawarski and his two companions turned, pulled out their weapons, and started shooting at Archie and his fellow officers.

"From eyewitness reports and another camera, it looked like Archie, even though he was wearing a vest, was shot in the head and died immediately. Two of the other three officers were also wounded.

"The third uninjured officer took out two of the assailants, killing both of them. During this twenty- to thirty-second time frame, Jawarski bolted out the door during the shooting with total pandemonium breaking out with passengers screaming for their lives. Jawarski escaped and we've no idea where he went. We're pulling video from where we believe he headed but, so far, nothing has popped up. That's where we are, Joe. Sorry for the long explanation but I thought, knowing you, that you'd want all the details first before anything else happened."

"Thanks, Trinity. Now, how can Mark and I be of help to you?"

"There's confusion with Jawarski's passport. If he's Polish and the two Boston Marathon bombers were Chechen or Russian, we've no idea who the two dead guys are who are now lying in the morgue. They had no ID on them. They had no driver's licenses, no wallets, nothing. We thought everyone was Russian and that's why we called you, Joe. Can you go the morgue right now to see if there's anything you can identify that might help us? Unfortunately, Archie is there as well. We haven't notified his next of kin yet. Cal will be doing that after we hit the morgue. He's staying here for that, and I'll go with you two to the morgue."

Joe sighed. "Having no ID means only one thing. They were running underground and wanted to stay off the radar. Obviously, causing a shootout in one of the busiest airports in the world exposed them. What kind of guns did they have?"

"We're not sure, the guns don't look quite like ours," Cal said. "Let me go get the weapons right now."

When Cal returned, he handed two guns to Joe. Joe put on a pair of sterile disposable evidence gloves so as not to cause a smudge. He looked at both guns from every angle. "From what I know, these two guns are PR-15 Raguns, semi-automatics manufactured by the Lucznik Arms Factory in Poland. They were copied from a late model Browning design. They've got a fifteen-round box magazine. The cartridge action is a nine-by-nineteen mm parabellum short recoil operated locked breech. In other words, these guns were made for the exact purpose of shooting quickly in a confined or close space. Archie and his fellow officers didn't have a chance. If the one who escaped had a Polish passport, real or forged, his two dead friends probably came from Poland as well on their way to the United States. How they got here and what they're doing here is another matter. We better find out fast or the repercussions could be severe. Not to be an alarmist, but dead terrorists in Yemen have been found with the same guns on them."

"Holy crap. Really? Oh my God," Trinity said. "Let's head to the morgue now. It's getting late and you have to check into the hotel. You'll need a ride from the morgue but you can walk back to headquarters from the hotel tomorrow since it's less than a mile from here. Shall we go?"

Joe and Mark took their bags with them so they could head directly to the hotel after viewing the bodies. Trinity drove with Joe in the back seat of the police car. Mark rode shotgun as they drove to the Medical Examiner's office to identify the perps. It was less than three miles, door to door. They got out, went up the stairs, and met with the medical chief.

The chief greeted them as they walked down the hall to view the bodies. "Good to see you again, Joe. I wish it could be under better circumstances. It's a shame about

Archie. He was a good guy and everyone liked him. At least I did."

"We all did," said Joe.

Cal, Trinity, Joe, and Mark put on surgical clothing and masks as they walked into the room. The two dead perps were right next to Archie's body. Joe asked the chief medical examiner if he could separate Archie from the other two.

The chief nodded. "Yes. Sorry." He meant it.

Joe looked at the two men, lying on cold metallic tables. He pulled the sheets from their heads and looked closely at them. He took a good ten minutes to look at every square inch of both their bodies.

"Well, I can tell you one thing. These two individuals aren't Russian. They're also not Russian mafia."

"How do you know?" asked Trinity.

"First, Russian mafia have tons of tattoos. Each tattoo means something in their criminal lives. Do you see any tattoos on either of these two men?"

"No, not that we can notice."

"Also—to be a little indelicate, Trinity—these men are circumcised."

"So? What's that mean."

"As you know, not only am I fluent in Russian, but I've studied all the former Russian states and their people's migration patterns. These two appear to be Chechen not Polish or Russian as their weapons would have suggested. That's only my preliminary guess. Circumcisions are performed on newborn baby boys for religious reasons. Most Russians are secular and have no religion, due to the communists banning of religious activity. Yes, it's growing back with Russian Orthodox churches appearing everywhere, but it's still a miniscule portion of the population. Jewish and Islam traditions require circumcisions for religious reasons. We can rule out Jewish. Most were banned from Russia and sent to Israel.

"I believe these are Chechen men of Islamic faith. Now, to tie it to Jawarski. They could have come from Poland, as well, but probably illegally as suggested by the guns. I believe you've got a Chechen presence in Orlando along with the Russian population. I downloaded a lot of information already and you've got ten new Islamic mosques in the greater Orlando proper. These men aren't Russian and, in fact, Chechens hate Russians, who've tortured them for centuries. Once we know who these two are, we can then determine why they're here. It can't be good, no matter what the reason, especially if they were also friends of the Boston Marathon bombers. By the way, you know those two brothers were also Chechens."

"How do we find out who these men are?" Trinity asked.

"Well, I've been thinking about it since we took off from Miami. The first thing we do is take their fingerprints and send them to Interpol, after matching their prints to the guns, as well, to make sure they were the ones who fired. Interpol has a Krakow office. If these men were known Islamic terrorists or committed a crime, we will know it through Interpol. I'll call Jack Forest. He's always in touch with Interpol and can get results faster than the FBI, or even Homeland Security. By the way, this will be a Homeland Security issue if I'm right. Next, we need DNA samples from the two bodies."

"What'll that tell, specifically?" she asked.

"It will tell me if they're Chechen or Eastern European with Islamic identifiers." Joe then went on to tell them about the tattoos. "Chechens are Sunni Muslims. Permanent tattoos are considered forbidden in Sunni Islam, but are permissible in Shia Islam. Due to Sharia or Islamic Law, the majority of Sunni Muslims hold that tattooing is religiously forbidden, along with most other forms of permanent physical modification. This view arises from references in the Prophetic Hadith, which denounce those who attempt to change the creation of God, in what seemed as excessive attempts to beautify that which was already perfected. The human being was seen as having been ennobled by God, the human form viewed as created beautifully, such that the act of tattooing would be a form of mutilation. This is however viewed differently in Shia Islam, as is it permitted. That's why I believe they're Chechens, who're Sunni Muslims."

"How enlightening, Joe," Mark said with a grin.

"Too much information, guys?" Joe asked.

"Mark, go away," Trinity said. "We need as much information as Joe can give us. We may not see him for a while."

Joe shrugged. "I also don't believe they're Russians because Chechens exhibit traits typical of European and Caucasian peoples. The Chechen are black-, brown-, and red- or fair-haired, and eyes can be brown, blue, or green. The skin is generally pale. The physical traits of Chechens, which also include being round-headed and taller than average, are typical of the "Caucasian type," which is much different than their Russian cousins. So there, smart-ass," he said, addressing himself to Mark. "I also want Jack to get a genetic test done from their DNA. Genetic tests on Chechens, though sparse and not sufficiently thorough so far, have shown roots in the Caucasus as well as strong connections to and influences from the Middle East, as well as Europe. As is the case with many other Caucasian peoples, Chechens are connected with the Middle East on the Y-DNA side, but closer to Europe in terms of mitochondrial DNA. In humans, mitochondrial DNA can be assessed as the smallest chromosome coding for thirty-seven genes and containing approximately 16,600 base pairs."

He paused for a quick breath. "Human mitochondrial DNA was the first significant part of the human genome to be sequenced. In most species, including humans, mtDNA is inherited solely from the mother. This will prove beyond a doubt that they're Chechens, and then we can lead the investigation one way versus another."

Trinity blinked and stared. "Have you always been this way Joe? I'm in shock."

Mark just shook his head.

She patted Joe on the arm. "Thank you. We'd no idea

what was involved in this. We thought it would be a simple go get the guy who killed our cop. But what you're saying is, if I read you right, if these are Chechens and radical Muslims, we could be in serious trouble. Right?"

"It's more than just a Polish guy who got on a plane and landed in Orlando. It doesn't bring Archie back or the others from being shot. But it could prevent something very bad from happening in Orlando if this leads to where I think it might. You need to contact your local FBI and have them meet us in your office tomorrow. If we're lucky, we can find out who the dead guys are and maybe point us in the right direction. By the way, Chechens speak both Russian and Chechen fluently. Chechen isn't that far removed, and I understand Chechen, not as well as Russian, but okay. It's like living in Montreal where French and English are spoken fluently by everyone."

"I guess you're right, Joe." Trinity grinned. "The least I can do for you two is take you to dinner. Ribs, right boys?"

CHAPTER 4

Joe had the medical examiner put together a package of fingerprints from both bodies. He took DNA samples from them as well. In addition, they took pictures of both bodies including those sensitive areas that Joe thought might prove that they were in fact Chechens. Joe knew that Jack Forest would give him crap about the circumcision pictures but he thought it was the clear-cut reason, along with no tattoos that separated the two from being Russian. Joe also sent Jack pictures of both guns as well with a printout he downloaded from the web of the guns' capabilities and where both were produced in Poland. He also had Trinity download the picture they received of Jawarski to see if Interpol in Krakow could identify him as well.

Joe opened his phone and hit the number three button to get Jack up in Virginia. Obviously, Julie was number one and Mark number two, with the rear admiral right behind at number four.

"Jack, it's Joe. How the hell are you?"

"What the hell do you want? I thought I could leave early today but not if you call."

"I'm fine. Thanks for asking. Julie is well and Mark is right here. He says to say thanks for asking about him as well."

"What do you want?" Jack said again with a smile in his voice.

"I'm in Orlando with Trinity and Cal Roberts and Mark as well. We were called up to check out a shooting in the middle of the Orlando International Airport, only a few feet from the theme park buses. Nice, huh?"

"So what do you need?"

"I believe the two dead guys who shot the cops are Chechens, but I got called up here because everyone believed they're Russians and, tag, I'm it when it comes to the Russians. If they're Chechens, Orlando may be in for a world of hurt, Jack. Can you help me?"

"Of course," Jack said, no longer kidding. "Dead cop, huh? Not good, Joe. Not good at all."

"I need you to run fingerprints from Krakow, Poland, through Interpol and take the DNA samples and do a genetic test to make sure that they're Chechens connected with the Middle East on the Y-DNA side.

"Also see if their fingerprints match any crimes in Poland and take their pictures and see if they match any police reports. I'm also sending you the picture of the guy who got off the plane. He was carrying a Polish passport with the name of Bronislaw or Bruno Jawarski. He had what appeared to be a valid passport from Poland. He had a street address in Krakow and arrived in the United States last year as a businessman. We believe now that he wasn't Polish but a friend of the two Boston Marathon bomber brothers. They were Chechen."

"Really? Wow," Jack said. "This is a lot more complicated than I thought."

"I'm afraid it might be. Those guns used to shoot the cops are manufactured in Poland and the same models have been found on dead terrorists in northern Iraq. I can't say any more, but I think Homeland Security and the FBI better be brought in. Also, if there's a connection to Poland, or with Chechens in Syria and Iraq, I'd better call my friend, Mike Hanley. He's still stationed in Miami, and he could get us some overseas help as well. I know he's in charge of the Caribbean, but I'm sure he can point us in the right direction. Theme parks here in Orlando scare the crap out of me, Jack. There are also several large military installations in Orlando, including the Naval Air Warfare Center Training System Division inside the Central Florida Research Park at the University of Central Florida, right in the heart of Orlando."

"I can see why. I'll start right now and see what I can get. Poland is six hours ahead of us, making it close to 11:00 p.m. I don't know whom I'll get but I'll contact my friend in France and let him handle it from there."

"Thanks, Jack. You're the best." With that, they hung up and Joe called Rear Admiral Jake Barnes.

"Jake Barnes, here," he said.

"Sir, it's Joe. I'm up in Orlando with Mark Silva, as you know. Thanks for the bodyguard."

"Nice touch, don't you think? I don't want to be responsible for holding up any wedding plans so he'll be shadowing your rear until that date."

"Yes, sir. I hear you, sir. But we've what looks like a very big problem on our hands. Not Coast Guard but could be if it includes the ports but definitely Homeland Security and the FBI. It looks like we might just have some Chechen Muslims landing in Orlando today killing Archie and wounding two other cops. Two of the supposed Chechens are dead, and I asked Jack to do some DNA testing and use his Interpol connections to see if we can identify the three individuals. Evidently, the most dangerous one, the one coming off the plane, escaped during the shooting."

Barnes laughed cautiously. "It's never cut and dried with you, Joe. Is it?"

"This one isn't on me, sir. I was invited up to help and got dropped into the middle of a potential Homeland Security issue, especially with major military installations right in Orlando and theme parks right down the road."

"I understand, and I can't think of anyone better to be dropped into the middle of it than you and Mark. I'll make some calls to Washington and give them a heads up. At least for now, before it can be handed off to the proper authorities, I want you on top of this, Joe."

"Yes, sir. We'll do our best." With that, he hung up, hopped into the police car with Trinity driving and Mark in the front seat.

"What did he say, Joe?" Trinity asked.

"He said he'd make some calls to Washington. Trinity, I think this is going to be much bigger than anyone ever thought."

CHAPTER 5

Trinity dropped Joe and Mark off at the hotel and waited for them to check in and put their bags in their room. Joe actually liked the convenience of the second floor versus their old room because of the ease of getting in and out of the hotel and the fact that they were on the same floor as the free breakfast buffet. They signed in, went up one flight of stairs, turned left, and their room was the first door on the right, room 211. It was easy to remember. Joe hit the toilet quickly and Mark followed. They went downstairs and out the front door to Trinity's car. Trinity asked them where they wanted to go, thinking barbeque all the way but was surprised at the request for the Cuban Restaurant, only a few blocks from the hotel. She pulled in front of the restaurant after a one-minute drive, parked, and locked the doors once they were all out of the car.

"Let's go, guys. You looked starved."

"We are," they both said.

"I've never had Cuban food, guys," Trinity said.

"Really? Well you're in for a treat," Joe said.

Trinity chuckled. "Growing up, it was soul food all the way and then barbeque, barbeque, barbeque. This might be a nice change."

As they walked through the door, the obviously Hispanic dinner crowd stared at all three of them. Joe and Mark had on their plain clothes but it was clear that Trinity was a cop with her badge fashionably displayed on the belt of her pant suit. Her gun was securely tucked in her holster under her left arm. Joe and Mark, when in plain clothes, simply tucked their weapons in their belts behind their backs. Joe and Mark had the latest version of Joe's former service weapon that he gave up when he left the Coast Guard. The weapon was a P229R DAK, which was the standard pistol of the Department of Homeland Security and the US Coast Guard.

The P229R was compact in size, with a choice in firepower of 9 mm, .357 SIG, or .40 S&W. Joe got the .40 Smith and Wesson version while Mark had the .357 SIG. These weapons were extremely accurate, very durable, and very reliable. It was an overall exceptional duty weapon. It held twelve rounds and both Mark and Joe had used their guns on numerous occasions since Joe came back to the Coast Guard after several years' absence.

Joe explained the menu to Trinity, asking her likes and dislikes. "Did you like spicy food?"

"No."

"Do you like black beans and rice?"

"Yes."

"Chicken or beef?"

"Chicken."

It went on for a few minutes and Mark suggested several items that Trinity agreed to try. They ordered *Ala Carte* so she could sample everything. As soon as the food was served, they all dug in. Trinity had a white wine and Joe and Mark were already on their second Cuban beer, Hatuey.

"Good?" Joe asked her.

"Yes, very. I'm not surprised. All the ingredients are familiar to me, except for some of the spices. Nothing is really hot, but I'll bet you can order it as hot as you like. Right?"

"Yes. I'm not a real hot freak but Mark is Mexican and has a galvanized stomach. He can eat anything. If it were me, I wouldn't leave the bathroom for a week."

"Great visual, Joe," she said, smiling. "So how are the wedding plans coming along?"

"Very well, thank you. And yes, I'm doing everything I've been told to do so far. A happy wife is a happy life, so I've been told. You're coming to the wedding down in the Keys, right? I don't expect you to come to St. Patrick's Cathedral in New York City, but you're invited, as you well know."

"Never say never, Joe. But with this now happening, I don't see how I can make it. By the way, the invitation is for a guest and me. Right? Does that have to mean Kiki?"

Joe knew Kiki, Trinity's niece and goddaughter, from her rescue in Miami from the sex traffickers and then afterward when they spent some time together at the Coast Guard condo at Brickell Plaza.

He smiled. "Are you trying to tell me something, Trinity?"

"Well, I met someone at school."

Trinity was finishing her doctoral program at the University of Central Florida in Orlando and was also teaching several police-related classes several nights a week. She had one busy schedule but seemed to enjoy it and had one very strong goal to be the first female chief of police for Orlando. Being African American had nothing to do with it, being a woman did. Before helping her get her niece back after Cal Roberts's call, Joe had decided to check on Trinity Hightower to see if she was legitimate and trustworthy. She was all that and more.

∽∾∽

At that time, it was great of Cal Roberts to promote her, and both Joe and Julie thought highly of her after meeting her in Orlando. She did an admirable job in shadowing Julie and Joe for the weekend. They became friends, but being friends didn't make her qualified. So, back then, one of

Jack's first duties, when he arrived at the Coast Guard condo, was to do a thorough search on Trinity Hightower that included her professional and personal activities.

Joe knew that she was twenty-eight years old and single. She wasn't seeing anyone at that time, but it looked like she was now. It was evident from their meeting and conversations up in Orlando that education, her job, and her family, were everything to her. Jack's quick investigation, back then, gave Joe even more respect for her and her abilities than he'd had before. He was pleased to have her on this team, as long as she kept her emotions intact. She did a wonderful job backing up Joe and the team, which had led to the successful recovery of her niece and her niece's best friend. Trinity became close friends with Julie and then with Joe.

Trinity, now twenty-nine, was the youngest daughter and the first police officer in her family. Joe knew that. She had a master's degree in Criminology from the University of Central Florida. After graduation as salutatorian from Colonial High School in the western part of Orlando, she received her bachelor's degree in Criminology and immediately afterward went full time for her Masters. Upon completion, she attended the Orlando Citizen's Police Academy and was immediately hired upon completion of the program. She was ranked first in her class.

She was in the Doctoral Program in Public Affairs, which was an interdisciplinary program drawing from the strengths of faculty in Criminal Justice, Health Management and Informatics, Public Administration, and Social Work. The Criminal Justice Track prepared her for academic positions in colleges and universities, as well as research and leadership positions in public, nonprofit, and private agencies. Joe hadn't known that and was surprised. She'd chosen police work over all others.

Joe read the report on the doctoral program at Central Florida University. It stated that the doctoral program included a dynamic mix of an interdisciplinary faculty with students of varied backgrounds, which created a stimulating environment to examine contemporary organizational, institutional, and community problems and issues. Graduates possessed the theoretical, analytical, and ethical foundation to produce new knowledge that impacted policies and programs and enhanced institutional and community performance. *She wants to contribute to changing society's thinking about criminology. Wow. That's one hell of a challenge.*

She was now a member of the adjunct faculty at the university, in the Criminology Department. She specialized in examining crime, criminals, and justice policy. She taught courses in leadership, crime analysis, juvenile justice leadership, and police leadership. Joe knew none of this and was enlightened. He knew that Trinity was promoted as a detective in the violent crimes section, taking the place of Jim Butler

Joe also found out anecdotally that there was skepticism in the department because the detectives had their own favorites to be promoted from the ranks and because she was an African-American female. They simply dismissed her as being a token. Over the last six months, she closed more cases with Archie Higgins, her partner, than anyone else in the division. She used her education and high-tech skills to close in on murderers, drug pushers, and, her specialty—sex trafficking of young females. After a while, the squad members asked her for her assistance in their cases. This pleased Joe. She rose above her circumstances and proved everyone wrong. Joe believed that about himself.

↜↝

"So, Trinity. Who's the guy? Level with us," Joe said, smiling from ear to ear.

"If you must know, I've been seeing a visiting professor at the university. His name is Dr. Eugene Whitcomb, professor of English literature from Scotland. He'll be here for a two-year term and is teaching a full load in the English literature department. His father is one-hundred-percent Scottish and his mother is one-hundred-percent Nigerian, who immigrated to Glasgow, Scotland, many years ago. They met when his father had an accident and was in the emergency room at the Glasgow Hospital when this nurse from Nigeria took care of him."

"Great story. It sounds like Louise's parents love story. Right, Mark?"

Mark looked up and had been paying no attention whatsoever.

"As a matter of fact, it sounds like Mark and Louise's romance." Joe went on to tell her about Ken and Antoinette Harding, he being from England on vacation to Miami when he fell in love with this half-Irish, half-Cuban girl. Joe told Trinity they were married shortly after he returned from England. He went home to pack and went back to Miami to be with her. "Mark and Louise met at the Hard Rock Café in Hollywood where she was a waitress when he walked in with his buddies."

Mark smiled. "Joe, we can't all pick our wives out when they're ten years old in fifth grade in elementary school, you know?"

Joe was about to say something but just glared at Mark. Joe sort of smirked but looked like he wanted to punch Mark.

"I thought this was about me, you guys? I forgot about the ten-year-old-girl pickup, Joe." She laughed. Joe and Mark both laughed.

"As I was saying before I was so rudely interrupted," she said. "Gene and I met at a faculty brunch at the beginning of the spring semester, only a few months ago but I like him very much. He's not a snob. I don't know what he is but he's certainly intriguing and worth my time. He's half white and half black but that doesn't seem to faze him. It must be different growing up in Scotland than in the United States. My parents were skeptical at first but once they met him, they really liked him. He's just a regular guy with a doctorate, and he's certainly not pretentious. I thought he might not like my police background but it didn't seem to concern him. So, at least hopefully, for the next year and a half, I might just be tied up," she said, smiling.

"Well, Trinity, that's great. Are you going to bring him to our wedding?"

"I have to bring Kiki or she'll never forgive me. She's in awe of Julie, especially about her story and her ability to rise above her circumstances. No offense, but, there are very few white people in our lives, who've made a difference to us. As you know, Joe, we're forever in your debt."

"Trinity, that's the farthest thing from our minds. We're friends and will remain lifelong friends. Whenever you call, we will be there, and I'm sure it's the same for you."

"Amen to that, brother." She laughed. "Do you want to meet Gene?"

"How about after this case, so he doesn't get shot?"

"The same goes for you two as well," Trinity agreed. "Mark, are you alive? You haven't looked up once from your plate since we got here."

"What? I'm hungry and tired. There's just so much sweetness between you two that I could probably get diabetes."

Joe chuckled. "You'll get it anyway if you keep eating like that. Let's get the bill and get out of here. I've calls to make. I'm sure Julie wants to know exactly what's going on, and that I'm safe. You people have her worried to death about me."

"All in a day's work, Joe. All in a day's work." Mark said.

෴

They got back to their room at the Embassy Suites Hotel on Pine Street, after saying goodbye to Trinity when she dropped them off. They unpacked their meager belongings. At least they had their dress officer's uniforms for Archie's funeral, if they were still there by then. They wanted to stay, especially Joe, because Archie had helped both he and Julie out when they were at the Hollywood Studios for Julie's meeting about her book. It didn't seem that long ago. Joe went into his room and called Julie. Mark did the same to call Louise.

"Julie? Hi, it's me. How are you?"

"Probably a lot better than you. How's Trinity?" Julie asked.

"She's trying to keep it under control, but I think she's going to lose it pretty soon. She's been crying, I can tell, but she hides it well. Archie was her first assigned partner when she made detective. They weren't partners for long, about six months, but you never forget your first partner. They were as different as night and day, but they got along fine, as far as I can tell and from what Cal Roberts told me. It's just that she was ready to move up to major crimes, even though Archie had years on her. He didn't have her strategic mind, but they certainly liked each other."

"Amazing how people of such different backgrounds can get along so well. Trinity and I became very good friends in such a short time as well."

"Bonding over the potential loss of her niece probably made you closer because of your empathy to situations like that after what you went through growing up."

"Probably true," she said.

"I don't know how long Mark and I'll be here. It's not going to be a Russian thing. I think the perps are Chechens but they still speak Russian as their main language along with Chechen. Tomorrow, we'll go through a list of things we need to do and then see where we are. Don't worry, Mark is watching me like a hawk."

"Joan told me already. I didn't have anything to do with you being watched over but it's not a bad thing, as far as I'm concerned. The more the merrier until the wedding."

"You too, huh?"

"Yes, me too. I love you. Got to go. Got testing to do in the morning and another planned career day for tenth and eleventh graders. We're finishing the first year of the grant and have to resubmit for year two, so we'll be quite busy. Call me tomorrow and every day after until you're home."

"Yes, dear. I love you, too."

When they hung up, Joe went into the kitchen area to pop open a beer. They'd stopped at the Beverage Mart on the way back and he got his twelve-pack of Oktoberfest and some snacks. It was early and he and Mark would watch television for a while and then hit the sack. As they'd learned over the last many years, eat when you can, sleep when you can, because you never knew what would happen. Mark finished his call to Louise. This was not her first rodeo so she was used to Mark coming and going, depending on emergencies. This was kind of different because it had nothing to do with either Mark or Joe, but they were buying in and that meant that Joe would have to call the rear admiral and ask him for anything he might need to assist in way of time, money, people, and equipment. Jake Barnes always cooperated with them because they got results and made the Coast Guard proud of their accomplishments. Joe was starting to believe that this was bigger than a shootout at an airport but might have national significance if it wound up involving Chechen Muslims. *God forbid.*

CHAPTER 6

Joe and Mark went down to the breakfast buffet at 7:00 a.m. They were dressed in everyday street clothes because they weren't sure how the day would go. Deep down, Joe knew that Trinity was a wreck and was trying her best to keep a calm demeanor.

They finished breakfast, and started to walk to police headquarters, less than a mile from their hotel. Joe had called Jake Barnes as soon as he got up at 6:00 a.m. and let him know exactly what was going on. He told Jake that they'd have a better idea of what direction they'd be headed after the day was over. They were waiting for information from Jack Forest that would determine what direction the investigation would take. Joe also knew that Jawarski couldn't have just disappeared into thin air. They needed the video camera data from all around the airport, especially down near the Disney Magical Express Terminal, which was in the main terminal, Level 1, where buses took families to their resort hotels. There were several spots for police cars and for handicapped accessibility.

They needed to head to the airport and check in with security to see if Jawarski hopped on a bus headed for the resort hotels or hopped into a car. There was massive confusion but the confrontation and gunfire took place near the terminal entrance. Mark had picked up Joe at the terminal on a previous investigation, parking in a police parking spot. It would save a lot of time since security was right around the corner.

❧❧❧

Axmad Khan just barely escaped. Arzuh had handed him the gun just as they passed outside the security line coming into the flight takeoff area. Axmad saw the men rushing toward them, and he immediately fired at the first guy, hitting him in the head, killing him instantly. Arzuh took out one of the others, shooting him in the leg. Arzuh then shot the other guy in the shoulder before the fourth officer, hiding behind a dividing wall, shot him dead.

The officer then shot Elbek in the back as he was turning to run away. In the meantime, after Axmad shot the first man in the head, he took off for the outside door with his gym bag in hand. He traveled lightly but needed what he had on him, including his passport under the name of Bronislaw Jawarski of Krakow, Poland. He placed his PR-15 Ragun in his pocket and headed out the door. Evidently, the two Chechens with him, Arzu Dudayev and Elbek Shishani, were dead. At least they had no ID on them. Axmad was sure they'd be identified sooner rather than later, but all he needed was enough time to get to his mosque in Orlando.

The two dead Chechens had come to meet Axmad, after he cleared the plane and outside the security area, while another member of their cell drove around while waiting for a call to pull up right outside the Disney Magical Express Terminal and pick them up. *Well, that won't happen now.*

The buses were loading up with families but the bus drivers were meticulously checking bus passes for each family to make sure that the passengers were going to the right hotel. Each bus went to different hotels. *Well, that takes care of that.* He ran down the sidewalk and up the hill and got into the first taxi he saw. He gave him directions to downtown Orlando. From there he'd call his van driver and have him pick him up and take him to the safe house. This operation, other than getting two Chechens killed, was well planned. This would put a crimp in the plans once everyone was identified, but it wouldn't stop Axmad from pulling off what he had hoped to be the next biggest thing. *Praise Allah.*

☙❧

Jack and Mark cleared security at the front of police headquarters and headed up the stairs to meet with Cal and Trinity. As they walked into Cal's conference room, they saw that the meeting was already packed. Joe and Mark knew most of them from the previous operation. The chief was already there with his three deputy chiefs who were in charge of investigative services, special operations, and community policing and patrol services divisions. Trinity sat at the other end of the table with two detectives from the Violent Crimes Unit, who reported to the deputy chief of investigative services. The three chiefs were there when Joe read Jim Butler his Miranda rights. He was the dirty detective who was charged with Tom Jones's murder and hauled off to Homeland Security in Miami. Joe and Mark nodded at everyone and sat down. To say the least, they were underdressed for this meeting.

Cal Roberts, Chief of the Orlando Police Department, started the meeting by thanking Joe and Mark for their help. Everyone at the table nodded in agreement. He described the scene at the Orlando International Airport. He told his deputy chiefs what Joe and Mark had already done and, if they were right, this could be a major problem for the Orlando area. He explained what that meant.

"Jawarski hasn't been apprehended as of yet," he added. "The deputy chief will be in charge of the murder investigation, but Trinity Hightower will be in charge of any potential terrorist threats that may arise from the situation. Joe and Mark are on loan from the Coast Guard for a short period that I hope can be extended, but I won't count on it. Please keep that in mind, Officers, and use their knowledge as quickly as you can. They won't be here long. As a matter of fact, Joe is getting married in a month, so please keep him safe."

Joe laughed. "Not you too, sir?"

"Don't think that I haven't been given the third degree by everyone, including a direct call from your rear admiral," Cal mentioned.

"Direct call from my rear admiral?"

"Yes, Joe. You're to remain safe and sound and surrounded by as many men as we can gather. We heard about your last incident running through the rear door of the drug warehouse in Miami, shooting the only perp trying to escape," he said.

"Can't argue with you then, huh?" Joe asked.

"No. Next order of business. As soon as we get a lead on the two dead men, we can move forward. Joe, Mark, and Trinity will go to the airport and start looking at video to see if we can discover what direction Jawarski was headed. From there, we will involve our deputy chief and detectives from the major crimes unit."

He paused and took a deep breath. "I'd like to say a few words about Detective Archie Higgins and the other three officers, two of whom were shot in the line of duty. The third is to be commended for taking out two of the three suspects. He was unharmed but will be placed on inactive duty until Internal Affairs and our independent psychologist clears him. The other two are still at the Orlando Regional Medical Center. The wounds received by the two officers, one in the shoulder and the other in the leg, were immediately taken care of as they were rushed into surgery. They should make a full recovery, but they'll be out for some time."

The deputy chief of investigations, and Archie's boss,

cleared his throat. "As you know, our rank and file is extremely pissed off that one of the suspects got away. I don't want any vigilantes running around out there. If anyone gets a lead, we need to know it right away. If the suspect is a Chechen, we've a very big problem. We have major targets down here in Orlando and please keep that in mind. Don't just go after one individual without thinking about the ramifications for everything else. Sorry for the diversion, but I just wanted to get that off my chest."

The chief nodded. "I'd like to have a minute of silence for Archie and his fellow officers who were shot yesterday."

After the silent period, the chief continued. "Let me give you Archie Higgins biography so you'll know what kind of officer died yesterday in the line of duty. Archie was thirty-seven years old. He was divorced from his wife, Leigh. They had no children. They were married for five years and she now lives in Tampa. We'll notify her as next of kin along with his parents. We don't know if he had a significant other but, if he did, we will include that person in the process." He shook his head in dismay. "Archie was a good cop for fifteen years. He was a beat cop for the first seven years and an outstanding detective for the last eight. He and Trinity closed the most cases of any team in the department's history. He had the ability to sift through meaningless data and pull it together to prove cases. He lived to be a cop. It probably cost him his marriage, like a lot of our fellow officers." He looked down at his notes a moment, to regain his composure. "He lived in the downtown area in a condo complex and he was Catholic. His father, Martin, age sixty-five, and mother, Joyce, age sixty-three, are still alive and members of St. James Catholic Cathedral, right down the street. We believe that the funeral will be held at the Cathedral with the bishop saying the funeral Mass with several of his fellow priests. As Archie was killed in the line of duty, he will receive the highest honor we have, posthumously.

"If he'd had an immediate family—wife and children—

he'd receive an automatic promotion, posthumously as well. Instead, the department will start a scholarship program at the St. James Middle School for those children who'd like to receive a Catholic education, but can't afford to do so. We will hold a viewing right here in the lobby of police headquarters, on Friday from 4:00 p.m. to 9:00 p.m. with a procession on Saturday from headquarters to the church with a funeral Mass at 10:00 a.m. All of this is solely based on the approval of Archie's mother and father. I also understand, he has a ton of aunts and uncles, cousins, and several godchildren. We understand that he was a role model for his family and will be missed."

Joe looked at Trinity and saw tears forming in her eyes. He nodded to her and she wiped the corners of her eyes with a tissue. She was holding up, but for how long?

"Just a short time ago, I asked Trinity if she could be the point person for the funeral services for her old partner," Cal said. "She said she would but she's not Catholic. Is there anyone here who'd be able to contribute to the tasks at hand?"

Inconspicuously, Joe raised his hand. "I've dealt with a similar situation. I'm Catholic and so is Mark. However, the Mexican Mafia murdered my boss up in Albany, Ted Simmons, when I was with the Albany Coalition for Families. The family was Methodist, but it made no difference. Here, there's a bigger difference, in that we've a police officer killed in the line of duty. Last night, I downloaded from the web all the protocols necessary to hold a proper viewing and funeral service, including a graveside ceremony for an officer slain while on duty. There will be thousands of police officers showing up Friday, so, if you want, Trinity, Mark, and I to handle the event, we should put our heads together now, while we're waiting for the results from our Coast Guard lab under Jack Forest, up in Virginia. Cal, are you in agreement?"

"I'm in complete agreement, Joe. Anyone else have any other ideas or suggestions?"

Everyone at the table shook their heads. Joe, Trinity, and Mark excused themselves as the team pulled together and divvied up the different parts of the investigation that included the shooting, the killing of a police officer, the escape, and the potential terrorist threat. Joe, Trinity, and Mark would work around their duties until the funeral was over. They needed to head to the cathedral, talk to the bishop, head to the Benton Funeral Home and Crematorium, on Michigan Street, and arrange for the wake at police headquarters, utilizing the funeral director's services. This was the same funeral home that had handled Tom Jones's wake and cremation.

CHAPTER 7

Joe, Trinity, and Mark went to Archie's parents' house to give their condolences. Archie's father, Marty, met them at the door and hugged Trinity.

Joyce came in from the kitchen. "Trinity, how are you? We know how much you cared for Archie. Thanks for coming."

Trinity introduced Joe and Mark and told Archie's parents how she and Archie had been Joe and his fiancée, Julie's, security detail when they went to Disney.

"Nice to meet you," they said.

"The reason we came by, as well as to give our condolences, is to ask your permission to give Archie the special funeral that he deserves as a police officer who was killed in the line of duty. I've been assigned to be in charge of the arrangements as well as Joe and Mark. As you know, I'm Baptist but both Joe and Mark are Catholics and offered to assist in the arrangements. They're also here on loan from the Coast Guard to help in the investigation and bring the other responsible parties to justice. As you know, two other of our officers, Lenny Bannister and Fred Stein, were shot along with Archie. Jermaine Marsh, the third officer along with Archie, had killed two of the three suspects. We're now waiting for information to be supplied to us by the Coast Guard. Joe and Mark aren't only friends of mine and Archie's, but they're the top two criminal investigators for

District Seven of the Coast Guard which covers all of Florida."

"Gentlemen, thank you for your help. It's greatly appreciated," Marty said. "We will fully cooperate with the police department, not only to give Archie his due, but to honor those others who were shot on duty, as well as all those participating in the investigation."

Trinity ran through the main arrangements with Archie's parents. Not that the arrangements were difficult but they had to fit a very tight schedule to accommodate the thousands of police officers who'd attend from across the state and the country and for others who'd come to pay their respects and to honor Archie.

"A careful coordination also means a safe one. Having a terrorist on the loose could also mean a second attack right at the church or during the funeral procession. We want everyone to be safe. We're coordinating with the media through Sergeant Beverly Fitch, the spokesperson for Chief Roberts. She'll also coordinate all our efforts with the mayor's office that will also fully participate. We believe there will be many state officials, congressmen, and at least one of our Florida Senators, coming to the funeral. Sergeant Fitch will coordinate TV, Radio, Facebook, Instagram, Twitter, Flickr, YouTube, RSS Feeds, as well as Pinterest."

Marty laughed. "Trinity, we can hardly do email, let alone know what the hell all that stuff is."

"At least I know how to use an iPad and do email," Joyce said, smiling. "I'm just learning how to download videos and work the Internet. Marty can't even spell Internet."

"The procession from headquarters to the church, the funeral Mass, and the graveside ceremony will all be recorded, and we will give you as many copies as you wish for your friends and family. It's the least we can do, Mrs. Higgins."

"Please, Trinity, call me Joyce. We certainly know you well enough for that."

"Thank you, Joyce," Trinity said.

They left to meet the bishop, head to the funeral home and the cemetery, and then talk to Jermaine Marsh who killed the two terrorists. He was on desk duty until he met with the psychiatrist and internal staff. They thought that would be a good starting point to see if there was anything specific that they might have missed. When the information came in from Jack Forest, if anything, they wanted Jermaine to look at it as well to see if anything else jarred his memory.

"Let's go, guys. We got a lot to do today," she said.

ⱷⱭⱷⱭ

First thing, they headed to the funeral home to speak to the funeral director who'd be in charge of the actual funeral services and Archie's cremation. Joe and Mark had met him previously when he'd handled Tom Jones's arrangements through Tom's daughter, Claire Murphy. They stopped only for a few minutes. It was less than ten minutes from Archie's parents' home. Everything was set for the Friday night wake at police headquarters. The funeral director would decorate the lobby in somber tones on Friday after-noon and have everything ready for the viewing, starting at 4:00 p.m. Those in the funeral procession from police head-quarters to the church would be there by 8:00 a.m. on Sat-urday morning.

This schedule was picked precisely so that downtown Orlando traffic would be dissipated by the time everything was ready to roll, allowing room for the visiting officers to attend. The procession would start at 9:00 a.m. and proceed to the Cathedral for the 10:00 a.m. funeral Mass. From there, only the family, and a few dignitaries, would head to the graveside ceremony and then back to the Cathedral school building where a reception would be held at 12:30 p.m., ending at 2:00 p.m. Saturday afternoon.

Next, they went to the cathedral to meet with the bishop to ensure that everything from a religious point of view was addressed. Trinity let Joe and Mark handle the Catholic funeral Mass. The cardinal made the school gymnasium available. Volunteers would decorate the hall appropriately and would, at no charge to the family, supply assorted snacks, baked goods, and treats for the children, along with appropriate drinks for adults and children. Trinity thanked the Bishop.

"I've known Archie for a long time," he said. "He was a fulltime parishioner. He also said that Archie, at the time of his death, was seeking an annulment of his marriage to Leigh, even though he was not seeing anyone at the time. He just wanted the ability to maintain his status as an active church participant and receive Holy Communion, even though he was divorced. It was a point of honor for Archie and he wanted to please his parent as well, who are also fulltime parishioners."

From there, they headed to Greenwood cemetery and made sure that everything was in its proper place and that it not only could hold the family, but also accommodate any dignitaries who wanted to attend as well. They had to go to the hospital and talk to the two wounded officers, Lenny Bannister and Fred Stein, and they were meeting Jermaine Marsh later to describe how all the events went down at the airport, from his perspective.

They wanted to find out anything they could about the man who'd escaped. They also had to go back to the hotel where Joe and Mark were staying, so that, in private, they could fully review all the procedures that Joe had downloaded concerning a line of duty death.

෴

Before they went to the airport, they made it back to the Embassy Suites Hotel by 2:00 p.m. They picked up three submarine sandwiches and drinks for a working lunch at the hotel to discuss the funeral arrangements. Trinity parked right in front of the hotel and placed the police car placard in the front window. After they went in, Joe went up to the receptionist and told her that it was their car and they'd be in their room on the second floor for a few hours. Early that morning, Joe had mentioned to the hotel manager to expect a full house for a few days due to the pending funeral arrangements on Friday and Saturday. The manager thanked Joe and told him that he could conveniently park their car in front just out of the way. They headed to the room and sat at the small breakfast nook and ate their lunch.

"Guys, I've copies of everything we need to make sure we do to have all the arrangements run smoothly," Joe said. He handed sheets to Trinity and Mark, and then he started to read a few of the beginning pages out loud. "Law enforcement officers pledge to serve the public good and put their lives on the line daily. When they pass away, whether from circumstances in the line of duty or otherwise, their funerals should reflect honor and respect for their service and dedication. Perhaps you've witnessed one of these sad occasions, when an entire city can come to a standstill as a lengthy funeral procession, with full police escort, winds its way to the cemetery. Often such a funeral, especially for a line-of-duty death, will draw thousands of uniformed officers from across the country. Their demonstration of honor, unity, and brotherhood is a sight never to be forgotten."

He paused, took a breath, fighting for composure. "'Departments and precincts often have unique traditions. For instance, the last radio call may include a mention of the officer's background, length of service, and circumstances of death, or it may consist of a few simple words, usually ending in, 'Gone, but not forgotten.' The information presented here is intended to be helpful to the officer's family, friends, and department. Our purpose is to outline the funeral traditions for police and other law enforcement officers. We'll also list helpful resources that give more detail.

"'The starting point for planning an officer's memorial service is the final wishes of the officer, if they are known. Law enforcement departments that plan ahead for these occasions are wise to ask each officer to write down exactly what's desired at a memorial. These directives can include the designated department representative, like Trinity, choice of music, pallbearers, clergy, interment, and any other details the officer cares to designate.'"

They'd asked Archie's parents and Archie had made no requests. His parents didn't believe he even thought about dying in the line of duty. Trinity was making notes and would suggest, after the funeral, that all officers be required to have this information on file, in their personnel records in case of such a tragedy.

Joe considered a moment. "Trinity, can you call Beverly and see if there are any funeral arrangements listed in the file?"

"Sure." She went ahead and called Sergeant Beverly Fitch at police headquarters and got her on the line. "Beverly, can you look at Archie's personnel records to see if there is any information in the file on his final wishes?"

"Sure. I'll call you right back."

Trinity's cell phone rang about ten minutes later. "Hi, Beverly. What did you find out?" She turned and said, "Nothing in the file," to Mark and Joe as they nodded that they didn't think there would be. "We're at the hotel if you want to join us in reviewing all the upcoming plans," Trinity told Beverly. "Afterward, we should come up with a police force plan to include a questionnaire filled out by each individual officer, in case of his or her untimely death, killed on duty or not."

"I agree. I'm packing up and will head over in about thirty minutes."

They took a break, rather than restart the process and waited for Beverly to arrive.

While waiting for Beverly, Joe ran down the stairs to the hotel business office and asked them to make another copy of the protocol document for Beverly. They made several more just in case they needed additional copies for the chief and his staff.

Joe got back and they finished their lunches just as they heard a knock on the door. Trinity opened it after looking through the peephole. "Hi, Beverly. Come on in. We waited for you before we started again."

Trinity told Beverly what had occurred to date.

"That's great, guys," Beverly said. "I've been busy on the social media scene, and I've got all the bases covered. I've called and met with the mayor's office and their staff will handle the dignitaries if we handle the large influx of police officers that we expect to show up Friday afternoon."

Joe started to read the documentation again, beginning where he'd left off after Trinity had updated Beverly. "'With the officer's directives taken into consideration, the family must be consulted.'"

"We did that earlier today," Mark said.

"'Their wishes outweigh the traditions of the department. It's vital that all options for honoring the fallen officer be presented to the survivors. They need to know not only what'll be done according to tradition, or what's always been done, but also what can be done to memorialize their loved one. It would be a sad situation for the family to learn, after the service, that they could have had a last radio call, but it wasn't part of the department's tradition.'"

Joe paused, cleared his throat. "Archie's parents told us to do whatever we could to honor Archie, and we will do everything in our power to ensure that we cover all the basis."

"Joe, thank you and Mark for helping Trinity and me," Beverly said. "It's one thing to be a police officer, but another to be a female police officer. You two being Coast Guard, FBI, and Homeland Security officers helping out, gives us a lot of credibility."

"We want no recognition at all," Joe assured her. "As a matter of fact, we have to keep a very low profile on this because, if it turns out to be a federal case, we need to be as undercover as we can possibly be. Please no accolades coming our way. You two are in charge and deserve all the credit for arranging this funeral service and for finding Archie's killer. We hope it's no more than that. It scares me to think that it is, though."

He started reading again. "'The family can select those elements of the service they wish to have included. For example, tradition might call for a three-volley salute to be offered at the cemetery; the family may decline because the sound of gunfire would be too traumatic. A 'twenty-one bells' ceremony can be substituted. Again, survivors should understand the options presented but not be pressured into including any tradition. The family of the deceased must be notified before the press, always in person and (if possible) by the chief, the senior chaplain, and a designated department representative, who'll become the family's liaison. The family liaison will stay with the family until no longer needed."

Trinity nodded. "That's covered. The chief notified Archie's parents immediately and they called all their relatives. The chief appointed me to run the funeral arrangements with you, Joe, and you, Mark, and to fully coordinate everything with Beverly, who's a genius with social media."

Mark glanced up from his notes. "We need shrouded badges or at least piece of black tape or cloth placed horizontally across the badge and flags lowered to half-staff. At the time of the funeral, we can use black bunting to display on the station and a cruiser."

Beverly went into the other room and ordered the badges from the funeral home that had an overnight connection to get everything in town before the public viewing.

"'Most departments assign a member to be the designated family liaison,'" Mark said, reading from the protocol document. "'It's especially important for one person to act as the family's single point of contact with the department, and it's preferable that this person knows the family. Support should be made available to the survivors twenty-four hours a day, for as long as needed for up to a year after the funeral service. This support also includes transportation, especially immediately after the notification and at the funeral services.'

"Trinity that's yours," he said.

"Got it," she said.

"Other responsibilities that can be taken on by the department include assigning a twenty-four/seven watch of the survivors' home until after the funeral, shifts on casket watch, who'll stay with the body around the clock until the funeral, a color guard for the funeral, ushers for the service, and pallbearers to carry the casket or cremated remains. Be sure to ask the family if they'd like to request certain people for these roles.'"

"The chief already assigned two police cars to park outside both Archie's condo and his parent's house, 24/7, until the entire events is concluded," Beverly said. "It will also cover all day Sunday and Monday after the services. The funeral director will transport Archie to headquarters by three p.m. Friday where the entire lobby will be prepared in an appropriate manner.

"Full military-style honors will be available, starting with a casket watch. The duty of those who have the high honor of casket watch is to stand vigil during the wake or viewing. A team of two takes a fifteen- to thirty-minute watch, beginning thirty minutes before the viewing and ending thirty minutes after, one at the head and one at the foot of the casket, facing each other. A second team relieves them every fifteen to thirty minutes. Like many departments, we won't limit the casket watch to only the wake or viewing, but we will stand guard twenty-four/seven until the funeral Saturday morning."

"This is interesting. I don't think we knew this," Trinity said, locking at the document. "'Those assigned to the honor guard include the casket watch, pallbearers, and color guard,'" she read. "'All of these functions require up to eighteen people, with experience or training needed for those responsible for standing guard, carrying the flags, folding the flag that drapes the casket, and performing other duties.' Beverly, do we have this in place?"

"No, we don't but we're a quick bunch. I'll call the chief and get all this in place, ready by Friday afternoon."

"Thanks, Beverly. You're the best," Joe said.

Trinity continued reading. "'An area of confusion for all of the uniformed services seems to be, "When do I remove my hat?" The answer is, "when entering the funeral home or church unless you're a pallbearer or member of the honor guard or color guard." They may wear their hats at all times. Others put their hats on when they go back outside. The other question is whether to salute the casket indoors with hat on or off. Protocol seems to contradict itself here: "Don't wear your hat indoors, but don't salute unless you're wearing your cover."'"

"I'll put an 'Etiquette List' together as soon as I get back and include that so the chief can distribute it to everyone associated with the ceremonies," Beverly said.

"The following suggested order of events would be appropriate for a formal, full-honors funeral," Joe said. "First, the honor guard designee escorts the family to the Church, meeting up with the casket at the front of St. James Cathedral. The chief is advised to start the ceremony. At this point, the honor guard—casket detail, pallbearers—performs its duties. They accompany the casket to its place of honor, and the color guard presents the colors. After this ceremony, the funeral service itself begins."

Joe went back to reading the document. "'Following is an example of the order of events for a religious services: invocation, prayer, opening remarks/greetings, special music, scripture reading and clergy remarks, speakers including the mayor, local elected official from district, state or Federal officials, family representatives, police union representative, department representative's friends, the eulogy, ending music, closing remarks, twenty-one bells ceremony, bagpipes play Amazing Grace, and then the final radio call ceremony. Then the Color Guard retires the colors and the bagpipes play as the pallbearers remove the casket and then dismissal instructions.'

"Just remember this is a Catholic ceremony and the Mass takes precedence over all the above," he reminded them. "The bishop said he'd follow the police protocol during the Mass and Holy Communion. He'd be in charge of all the movements in and out of the cathedral. He'll bring in ten other priests to direct the flow of the Mass and help move along the program. The Mass will start at 10:00 a.m. and will end by 11:30 a.m. for the benefit of Archie's relatives and not for campaigning by public officials. They still have to have a graveside ceremony at Greenwood Cemetery and then back to the church hall for the reception. He made that very clear. Right, Trinity?"

"Very clear. We're to follow the bishop's instructions to a tee just like we would if my father was in charge as pastor of his Baptist church," she said.

Joe nodded. "Thanks." Then he went back to reading. "'Finally, the honor guard's duties continue during the pro-cession to the cemetery and the interment, with each de-partment following its own procedures. The procession will only include the immediate family including Archie's aunt and uncles, nieces and nephews and a few select dignitaries including all the priests and the Bishop. We will have police cars from across the state blocking each and every corner until we hit the cemetery. Its only about a mile, so it won't be that bad.'"

"Thanks, Joe," Trinity said. "So in conclusion, I think we've everything covered so far. It's a lot more than we probably expected but doling out the duties really helps. Again, thank you, Beverly, for everything, and Joe and Mark, thank you as well."

"Well, we aren't done, Trinity. We need to head to the airport to get the tapes and see what actually happened and wait for Jack Forest to get back to us to see if we can catch the guys who started all this. We will get them, I promise you that," Joe said.

Chapter 8

It looked like the funeral arrangements were all set for Archie. Everything had to work like clockwork to get all the details into play. They did a good job putting everything in place. They met with the chief and explained what was required. He did his part and coordinated all his fellow officers to participate in one form or another. Beverly met with the mayor's staff, and they were in good shape as well. They couldn't determine how many officers and dignitaries would show up from across the state and nationally, but there would be enough security on hand, hopefully, to prevent anything from happening.

All the politicians knew their roles. The bishop called the mayor's office and the congressional and senatorial offices to make sure about seating arrangements at the church. The long-term church ushers, along with the added priests, would serve a dual purpose to ensure that the bishop's wishes came first. Those wishes only had concerns for Archie's parents, his other relatives, and St. James's own parishioners who'd be attending the funeral Mass and graveside ceremony.

Because this was high profile and everyone was concerned about security, all the dignitaries would meet at the church a half hour before the procession from police headquarters would arrive at the cathedral. All the black armbands showed up on time at headquarters and were distributed. Today was Thursday and nothing would be happening before 4:00 p.m. on Friday, when the first visitors to the wake would arrive. The family would be there at 3:00 p.m. Joe, Mark, Trinity, and Beverly would be there as well, with Chief Roberts and the mayor. Only a select few would be there at the beginning of the wake. The chief and mayor were presenting Archie an award for bravery, posthumously, just to the immediate family. It would include Archie's ex-wife who'd be in attendance. She never remarried and always got along well with Archie's parents. They knew Archie's job was just as responsible for the breakup as Archie and Leigh.

℮℈℮

Joe's cell phone rang. It was Jack Forest. "Hey, Jack. What's up?"

"Got some good information for you. It's been a very long day, especially with the time differences in Poland and here. But it looks like we've identified all three men. It wasn't easy but we got the information."

"Hold on a minute, we have to pull over. We're on our way to the Orlando International Airport to see what the tapes show from the shooting. Trinity, pull over. It's Jack."

Trinity pulled to the side of the highway right outside the exit ramp to the airport. She turned the car off so they could hear Jack. She took out her pad and pen and so did both Joe and Mark. Joe put the speakerphone on. "Okay, Jack. Go ahead."

"First, the guy who escaped did have an official Polish passport in the name of Bronislaw Jawarski. He's in fact a Polish citizen. He's thirty-five years old and received his citizen papers three years ago. Joe, you were right. He's Chechen. His real name is Axmad Khan and he's a Muslim. Axmad is Chechen for Ahmed. He was allowed to change his name from Axmad Khan to Bronislaw Jawarski immediately after he received his citizenship. He then applied for a Polish passport under his new official name. He arrived in Krakow ten years ago at age twenty-five. So this must have been building for some time. He was considered a businessman in the import/export of electronics. He was supposedly in Boston on business but that's where the trail ended until he was spotted in the photograph with the two Chechen brothers."

He paused and they could hear papers rustling in the background as Jack continued. "The two dead individuals were Arzu Dudayev, age forty, and Elbek Shishani, age thirty-two. Those two weren't Polish citizens but were known felons in Krakow, both arrested twice for assault and battery and armed robbery. They both had lengthy jail sentences in Krakow. They apparently got out last year and also disappeared. They obviously entered the United States illegally and were the two individuals who met Khan at the airport. They never changed their names so Interpol was able to match the names and the pictures you sent of them at the airport. They too were Chechens, according to their arrest records. They were deported back to Chechnya upon their release. They had to have known Khan in Krakow to pull this off in Orlando. I dug a little further and found that Khan was born in Grozny, the capital of the Chechen Republic, Russia. It's still debated whether the Chechen Republic is still part of Russia or not. The biggest difference is that ninety percent of Chechens are Muslim and are a major part of all Muslin Jihadist terrorist activity around the world."

"Wow," Joe said, looking at Trinity and Mark in the car. "I think we've a much bigger problem than we originally thought. This may not be a normal cop shooting but the beginning of a terrorist attack in Orlando. I hope not, but it's seems to be headed that way. We have to get this Khan guy and anyone he's associated with. We can't just go in, shut down the ten mosques, and interrogate every person belonging to them, or even anyone who looks like a Muslim. Hell, those three guys look as white as any Irishman with blue eyes and a pale complexion. Speaking of that, Jack, were you able to pull anything from the DNA samples we sent to you from the two dead guys?"

"I was just getting to that, Joe. My guys rushed the test to get it to you as soon as possible. We know how important it is to identify the two dead guys as either Russian or Chechen because it could lead the investigation in two opposites paths. From the samples taken from Mr. Dudayev and Mr. Shishani, both showed that they were Caucasian and the mitochondrial DNA had evidence of the Middle East on the Y-DNA side. There's no doubt that your first guess was right. These guys are both Chechens. To be one-hundred percent sure, it would take us weeks and many more tests, but I don't think you need that to continue this investigation. I'd look for Chechen Muslims if I were you."

"Thanks, Jack. You've confirmed our worst fears. Did you hear all that, Trinity and Mark?"

Trinity answered first. "Yes, Joe. Jack, thank you. There's no one here, or anywhere else, who was at our disposal who could makes these determinations so quickly. Joe, we have to meet with the chief and let him know what we found out. I'm in charge of this investigation after the funeral services and we need a jump-start to find these guys. I think we need your specific strategic planning techniques, if you will, to make sure we're headed in the right direction, both legally and procedurally. Are you game?"

"Let me say goodbye to Jack first. Jack, thanks again. We may need some more information from you if we run into more guys down the road that look like Chechens. We probably need to do the same research on each one we find. If you don't mind. Can you also see if the pictures of the three Chechens show up anywhere else in the news, on television, the internet, or anywhere else so we can actually identify them as terrorists? Right now we're guessing. It's a good guess but we need to be very sure before we go down that road."

"Sure. I can do that."

Thanks, Jack."

With that, they both hung up and Joe turned to Trinity. He shook his head. "We've got a big problem."

❦

Trinity drove into the Orlando International Airport and parked in a police parking spot right outside the terminal. It was a short walk to the security office.

Joe went first. He headed up to the receptionist at the security desk and gave her his Homeland Security credentials. Mark had his out as well and Trinity flashed her Orlando detective badge to the young lady at the desk.

"We'd like to speak to the head of security, please," Joe said.

"What's this in reference to?" she asked.

"It's Homeland Security business, so if you wouldn't mind, please, we need to speak to the manager. Who's in charge?"

"Mitch Stewart is head of security at the airport. He's not in the office but he's here somewhere. Let me text him on his phone."

Mitch got the text and texted back that he'd be right there. He was meeting with a few of the TSA staff to swap information on potential threats. He was back at the security office door in ten minutes. "Hi, I'm Mitch Stewart. How can I help you?"

"We're here to look at the videos on the day of the shooting involving the Orlando Police Department. If you don't mind, can we go inside to discuss this?"

Mitch smiled. "Sure. I'm sorry. Forgot my manners."

Joe introduced himself, Mark, and Trinity. "By the way, do you know Brian Murphy? He's the chief accountant for the Walt Disney World Airport Division."

"Of course, I know Brian. He's in charge of our budgets and paychecks. Everyone knows Brian," Mitch said with a smile. "How do you know him?"

"His father-in-law Tom Jones was a very dear friend of mine. I met his wife Claire when she was just a teenager. Tom was my first chief petty officer when I joined the Coast Guard and we became life-long friends. Mark's too."

"How does the Coast Guard get involved in this?" Mitch asked.

Joe sighed. *Same question, different day.* "My credentials, as well as Mark's, are three-fold. First, we're both lieutenants in the Coast Guard in charge of criminal investigations on the Florida coast. Second, we carry FBI credentials, and, thirdly, we carry Homeland Security credentials. All three entities are under the umbrella of Homeland Security."

"I didn't know that."

"No one seems to ever know that." Joe laughed. "We're also a member of the Coast Guard intelligence division, and this shooting looks to be more than a tragedy of two officers being wounded and another dying. This shooting has national implications concerning terrorism. I wish I could say more, but I can't at this point. Can we review all the tapes for that day? We need to look at several hours before and several hours afterward. Specifically, from when the flight from Boston landed at the terminal to when one of the perps fled?"

"Let me get the log book of where and when the Boston flight landed. I've been told the gentleman who got off the plane was met outside the security barriers, almost outside the facility before the shooting began."

Joe nodded. "That's our supposition as well, but we want to be sure and see as much of what went down as possible."

"It's going to take some time gathering all that. Can you come back in an hour? I'll stay and help you identify each area of the airport he walked through."

"Sure, we'll grab something to eat and make a few calls. Is there someplace we can park ourselves without roaming the halls with our guns exposed? I think we'll make your passengers a little nervous."

"Why don't you get something to eat right upstairs, and you can use our conference room to eat and make your calls. I'll set it up with the video screen and a computer and you can use that as well."

"Thanks, we'll do that. Guys, let's get something to eat. It's going to be a long day."

CHAPTER 9

After their break, Joe, Trinity, and Mark came back to the airport security office to wait for Mitch while he gathered all the video feeds from the various concourse cameras where the Chechens traveled. They waited in the conference room. Mitch walked in.

"Mitch, did you get our stuff?" Joe asked.

"Got every video from the time Jawarski got off the plane from Logan to when he ran out the door at the terminal."

"Actually, at the exact time he fled out the door, did you get videos outside to see where he went?" Trinity asked.

Mark was checking his emails. He still had a job to do back in Miami. He then looked up and focused on Mitch.

Mitch nodded. "I did indeed."

"Let's see those first," said Joe.

Mitch had all the videos set up to play on a large LED television. He had ten separate feeds all from the exact moment that Jawarski ran out the door.

"As you can see, he ran out the terminal door and up the hill. Three cameras on the north side picked him up as he was headed to Terminal A. It's quite clear he was headed for transportation. Buses, taxis, and limos are located at the Terminal A commercial lane. See, he's coming into view right here," Mitch said.

They all watched the cameras as Jawarski came into

view. He hopped into a Diamond cab and the driver pulled out immediately. The taxi was number forty-seven. They couldn't see the license plates because of the angle but it was clearly marked on the side of the cab as number forty-seven.

"Best news yet," Trinity said.

Mitch immediately called Diamond. He had all the numbers for the transportation companies at his fingertips. He spoke with the dispatcher on duty. The dispatcher went to the logs and found that cab forty-seven, just after the shooting took place, pulled out of the airport and took a passenger to the Florida Mall at 8100 South Orange Blossom Trail.

The cab driver was called at home. "Yes, I remember dropping a guy off at the front door of Macy's at the Mall. He looked kind of foreign but he was very light skinned and very tall. The toll was $35.00. The guy was in a big hurry and didn't wait for the change. He gave me a $50.00 bill. I remember those kinds of tips."

Joe had the picture of Jawarski on his phone. He emailed it to the driver.

"Yeah, that's the person I picked up and dropped off at the Florida Mall."

"Mark, can you stay here and see what else you can find on the rest of the downloads from the moment he walked off the plane until he left? Also, someone had to have been picking them up because, at that terminal door, the only transportation is for the buses to head to the guest hotels. Look outside from the time he arrived to the time he left, and see if anyone pulled up or even kept circling, like the driver was waiting for someone. I remember we did the same thing but you were able to park in the police parking spot when I got back from Nashville. Trinity and I are heading to the Florida Mall to see if we can pick up Jawarski getting out of the taxi and maybe see where he headed."

Mark simply nodded. He and Joe had been together so long, they knew what each other thought. If he could tie a vehicle outside the terminal to someone picking Jawarski up outside the Florida Mall, they could nail him much sooner than expected. All it took was one screw up to get caught. They had found the meth warehouse up in Nashville simply by having their drone follow Michael Johnson, the bagman, who never once changed cars. He drove his own car everyplace, including for deliveries and pickups. Some criminals were very smart, but some certainly weren't. Johnson wasn't. Mark hoped that Jawarski fell closer to Johnson.

೭౨౬౩

It was exactly nine miles, door to door, from the airport to the Florida Mall on Orange Blossom Trail. Trinity parked right by the door at Macy's. A mall cop came out who didn't know that Trinity was driving a detective's police car. It was kind of hard to miss if he was paying any attention at all. Trinity showed him her badge and the police placard, and he backed off.

Joe pulled out his iPhone, found the directory to the mall, and called the security office. He said they'd be there momentarily. Trinity and he walked to the office. Joe flashed his Homeland Security credentials and Trinity raised her detective's badge for all to see. They asked for the manager. Joe explained that it was a matter of national security and, without speaking, handed over what he had written out as to what he needed. The manager read the request, looked at both of them, and waved them into his office. He went to the videos and pulled out the feeds for the exact time and date, written on the paper, for all the entrances and for the main doors. "If you need the feeds for every camera in the mall, it may take a week to get them."

Joe nodded. It was not like the airport where security was always on high alert. Mall security was quite a few steps below TSA.

They went through the video feeds and the manager

pulled up the cab at the moment he arrived in front of Macy's. They saw Jawarski walk in to Macy's. The manager then pulled the camera feed immediately inside the door and saw Jawarski walk into the main promenade and turn to the right toward Dillard's. It was no more than a few minutes' walk, door to door. He then pulled the feeds for the outside entrance to Dillard's and, after about ten minutes, they saw Jawarski head toward a white van that had just pulled up outside the door. He hopped in and was long gone. There were no markings on the truck and the license plate seemed to be covered by dirt.

Joe sighed. *So much for a quick arrest. Back to square one. Where the hell did he go?*

Trinity got printouts of the feeds for the front of Macy's for the arrival and all the shots they could at Dillard's, both inside and outside, for whatever it was worth. They knew that Jawarski was now loose in the main part of Orlando, but why?

"Trinity, it looks like we might have just hit a dead end," Joe grumbled. "That's if Mark doesn't find anything on his end. Let's go back and see what he's got, if anything."

Neither one felt very well about the wall they just hit. *Oh well.*

❧❧❧

Trinity and Joe got back to the airport and walked in while Mark was just finishing up with the feeds. "Find anything?" Joe asked.

"Found something, but not sure. Come here you two and look at this." Mark went back and forth, following the video cameras outside the building. He started watching the feeds as soon as it was established exactly when the plane landed and the passengers started to depart into the chute up to the lobby area. He was now concentrating on the outside of the building over a fifteen- to-twenty-minute time span.

"Watch this," he said. "The two Chechens who were with Jawarski walked through the terminal A door, level one, about the same time the plane landed. They must have walked into the terminal from somewhere else."

As they continued to watch, about fifteen minutes later, a white van began circling the terminal area and making U-turns back out to the main road. That happened several times.

Then Mark pointed to the screen. "There's Jawarski running up the hill and there's the white van. See? It appeared to stop for a pickup, and it looked like, when Jawarski took off, the driver of the van hit the gas, made a quick U-turn, and headed out. He didn't come back."

Trinity turned to Joe. "Think it's the same van we picked up at the front of Dillard's? It certainly looks like it. Mark, can you see a license plate number?"

"No, it looks like it's covered with dirt."

"I don't believe in coincidences," Joe said. "It's got to be the same van. If they don't dump it, and if it's not stolen, we may be on to something, guys."

They spent the next half hour and watched the actual gun battle in the terminal, frame by frame. It was almost like the execution of Archie Higgins. As soon as they saw that they were being followed, the Chechens pulled out their guns and shot Archie dead. It was a good thing that Jermaine Marsh took out the two other Chechens, or they'd have all been long gone.

"Let's head back, talk to Jermaine, and see if he can add anything else," Joe said. "Let's see if there was anyone else on the Chechens' side that we didn't pick up. Jermaine certainly kept his head, especially with such a surprise attack. The other two cops, Lenny and Fred, are very lucky to be alive today."

CHAPTER 10

As soon as Axmad got to the Florida Mall, he called Hamzah Umarov to pick him up outside Dillard's. He'd glanced at the list of store names on the display as soon as he entered the promenade area. He told him to pick him up as soon as he could. Hamzah only knew him as Axmad, not as Bronislaw or Bruno Jawarski. Hamzah had been driving around the airport and then decided to head for the safe house. Axmad was beside himself. Nothing went as planned. He almost got killed. He was glad he saw the first cop out of the corner of his eye. Arzu had just handed him his gun. He had it in his hand ready to put in his coat pocket but, instead, turned and shot the cop dead. Axmad didn't realize that there were three others there. Unfortunately, Elbek and Arzu weren't quick enough. Axmad saw them get shot, and the other two cops got shot as well.

He ran like hell out the door and up the hill to the other side. He thought he'd be better off, and he had more places to go if he was followed. He saw the van coming for him but didn't want to chance a shootout in that confined space. He could have cared less how many he killed getting on the buses. He had a mission first and had to get out of there. He saw the cab and hopped in. Fluent in English, Russian, Polish, and Chechen, he had no trouble directing the driver to the Florida Mall. Unlike the others, he always had a plan B. Head to a mall and get lost in the crowd. You could always meet up later if you were alive. He preselected the mall because it was close to the safe house and in a not-so-nice neighborhood where people didn't question others. He'd fit right in. The mosque was only a few miles away.

He greeted Hamzah in Chechen and told him to drive. He'd met Hamzah when he was a child in Grozney and, then again, a while ago in Krakow when the mission was planned. He knew that, of all those who vowed their loyalty, he could trust Hamzah the most. He was the grandson of Dokka Abu Usman, one of the first Chechen Islamic militants in Russia in the mid-1960s. He was a martyr for Islam and his grandson was raised that way since he was a child.

They drove quietly to their non-descript safe house on Eighteenth Street, near Nashville Avenue, in the heart of Orlando. The mosque was a few miles away on Old Winter Garden Road. It would have been a long walk but nothing compared to what he had to endure growing up in Grozney. The Russian army attempted full-scale genocide against the Chechens for years. Axmad and his family hid in the mountains and went from there to Moscow to Krakow where he became a Polish citizen. Everything was planned since he was a child. He followed wherever Allah took him. Allah was his home, his ideal, and his mission. Nothing would stop him.

They pulled into the driveway and Hamzah unlocked the front door. It was time for prayer, and they did that before anything else. They'd be meeting their imam later that night. The Sunni branch of Islam didn't have imams in the same sense as the Shi'a, an important distinction often overlooked by those outside of the Islamic faith. In everyday terms, the imam for Sunni Muslims was the one who led Islamic formal prayers, even in locations besides the mosque, whenever prayers were done in a group of two or more with one person leading, usually an imam, and the others following by copying his ritual actions of worship. An appointed imam most often gave the Friday sermon. All mosques had an imam to lead congregational prayers, even though it might sometimes just be a member from the gathered congregation, rather than an officially appointed person.

There was also a big difference in imams. There were those who were peace loving and those who wanted to rule the world. Money had been wired to Hamzah for this mosque for over two years through a Cayman Islands Bank. Hamzah and the Imam had been taking a private plane down to the Cayman Islands several times a year, loading up their briefcases with cash. It was now payback time.

⌀⌀⌀

Joe, Mark, and Trinity made it back to headquarters to meet with Jermaine. After their brief visit, it was clear that Jermaine had nothing else to tell them about that moment.

"It was instinctive," he said. "It was kill or be killed. As soon as I dropped the two Chechens, I dove behind a pillar and saw bullets whizzing by me. I lifted my head up and saw one of the shooters go through the outside door. My immediate thought was for Archie and my other two fellow officers who were shot. Archie was already dead by the time I reached him. I called the shooting in and took care of Lenny and Fred before the ambulance got there. I took my belt and tied up one of the officer's legs and then grabbed the other's coat and tied off his shoulder. It seemed like a lifetime to me but I know it was only a matter of minutes before my fellow officers and the EMTs came through the outside door. At that point, there was mass confusion, and I lost track of the third shooter." He cleared his throat. "I apologize."

But all three told him that, under the circumstances, he was a hero.

"Jermaine, that's valor under fire, and we thank you for what you did," Joe said. "If you hadn't gotten those two, we'd have no leads whatsoever." He leaned closer and lowered his voice. "This is going to be a Homeland Security issue at the highest priority."

They went in to see Chief Roberts. Joe owed a lot of calls to a lot of his own Coast Guard staff. He'd finish up with what he had and hoped that they'd have enough to work on while he went home. Joe and Trinity stayed for the meeting. Mark walked back to the hotel to pack. He would leave right after the funeral. He wasn't really needed at this stage, and he was falling behind in his own work with the rear admiral. Not only was he still working at the Dania Beach Station, but he was also helping out with the transition to a new management team that was reconstructed after the last internal problem. The rear admiral was making dramatic changes to staff, with Joe's help, and it looked like both of them would be leaving in the fall. Mark still had a few years left because he signed up for the Coast Guard at the latest age of twenty-seven. He and Joe were now equals as lieutenants, and Mark was planning on staying until retirement. The Coast Guard was Mark's life, and it had saved his life from going downhill in San Diego. He was now a solid citizen, family man and looking forward to retirement in a few years. He was taking courses now to get a degree to fall back on when he retired.

Joe was smart, Mark thought. He got his bachelor's degree in the Coast Guard and then left to get his MBA at Rensselaer, and then came back at a much higher level than when he left. He told Joe that he'd grab dinner with him, finish up paperwork tonight, and then help out with Archie's funeral arrangements. He'd leave right after the graveside ceremony. He wouldn't come back for the reception at St. James School.

Trinity and Joe said goodbye to Mark and headed for the chief's office.

"Trinity, Joe, what's going on?" the chief asked when they walked in.

"We've a lot to tell you, chief," she said. "We're making progress. We found out that Jawarski got into a cab at the airport and it brought him to the Florida Mall. He left there in a white van with no markings and the license plate was covered with dirt. That's was probably intentional."

"Good work, guys," he said.

"We identified all three as Chechen's through Jack Forest," Joe reported. "All indications are that they're Chechen Muslims. There aren't supposed to be more than two hundred in the country legally, but I don't believe that to be true. In fact, they speak Russian as their second language to Chechen, but they're as far removed from Russians as you can get. We also now know there are ten new mosques in Orlando. Muslims are, by their very nature, religious and good people. These guys aren't. We believe they're terrorists. If they are, we believe that there will be a major event in Orlando. We need to get Jawarski before anything else happens. However, I have to leave for Miami, as well. I've got lots of stuff going on that I have to clean up before the wedding. I'll be back as soon as you need me, especially for the Russian and Chechen interrogation if he's caught. Trinity has a handle on this and you're in good hands. She was invited to our wedding in New York City but this obviously comes first. She can come to wedding number two in Key Largo in June. Is that okay, Trinity?"

"I hope we get him, and whoever, before then, Joe. I want to go to New York City," she said.

With that, they left the chief's office. Joe and Mark needed their officer's uniforms cleaned and pressed, both sets. Joe decided he would also leave with Mark after the graveside ceremony. They were going to rent a car to head south. They could get a Coast Guard vehicle from the Port Canaveral Station but then they'd have to get it back. Joe didn't want to have to speak to Jacob Cramer who was now in charge of that station. Frank Cortez took the position in charge of all security for the Seventh District in Miami. They needed him there a lot more than at an outpost like Port Canaveral. The rental car would be delivered to them by Enterprise after the ceremony and they'd head out.

Tomorrow, they'd make their calls, do more research on the Chechens in Orlando, and then head to the wake by 3:00 p.m. They'd assist Trinity and Beverly, up to, and including, the graveside ceremony. They wouldn't go to the reception afterward at the church hall but would instead head home—for now. They'd be back when needed.

But Joe and Mark had a wedding to attend.

CHAPTER 11

It was now Friday morning. Joe and Mark went down to the breakfast buffet at the Embassy Suites Hotel. At least they were eating well. There was so much going on in both their lives that the only time either of them relaxed was at breakfast. They were dressed down once again. Joe had his old work boots and jeans on from his old construction days with his father back in Troy. Mark was similarly dressed. They'd go to police headquarters and meet with Trinity for any last minute funeral arrangement details and to see if there were any breaks in finding Bruno Jawarski. They decided to stick with the Jawarski name for now. The name Axmad Khan, if released, could cause a panic in the city.

Everyone thought it would be better to put out the BOLO on the white van, smeared license plate, and white perps in their early forties or late thirties. Joe and Mark didn't expect much from the BOLO. If they found an abandoned van, it might be more rewarding to track that down to where it was stolen to give some kind of idea where Jawarski might have gone in the city. Maybe there was a neighborhood or even a mosque in the vicinity that they could hone in on for the investigation.

They knew they couldn't go knocking on mosque doors or even talk to local imams, or it could look like targeting, even though it would be. Mark even related that, as a Mexican-American, if it looked like a duck and quacked like a duck, it was probably a duck. When he was younger, he was targeted so many times in San Diego that he knew most of the police officers by name. They knew he was a gangbanger but could never prove anything until they finally did. Thank God for the Coast Guard. It was either jail or the sea. The sea changed his life around. He knew all about targeting and how to do it so they wouldn't be accused of it, even if it were true. It had worked over the years for Joe and him when taking down drug runners and their connections.

After their meetings, Joe and Mark would head back to the hotel, change into their dress uniforms, and be back early for the viewing at police headquarters. They'd help Trinity and Beverly move the crowd along and help introduce mourners to the family. It was almost like what Joe and Mary Lynch, his old girlfriend in Albany, had to do for Ted Simmons' family, when Ted was killed in a car crash that was later determined to be no accident. Ted was the president of the Albany Coalition for Families, where Joe worked while uncovering a national money-laundering scheme involving the Mexican Mafia.

Joe and Mark had to meet Trinity, Beverly, and the chief for 9:00 a.m. Joe was sure that, knowing Trinity, she'd probably already have been there for several hours.

They walked the mile to the station, checked their guns at the security checkpoint, and walked up to the chief's office. They saw Trinity, who pointed to the conference room next door. She silently asked them if they wanted coffee and both shook their heads. Mark hardly drank any and Joe had more than enough as usual. His Dunkin' Donuts breakfasts were legendary wherever he went.

"Joe, Mark, welcome," said the chief. "Trinity went over what you already told us last night just to jumpstart the conversation. Anything new?"

"Not from this end," Joe said.

Mark, as usual, simply nodded. He was a man of few words.

"I do want to bounce a few things off you, though," Joe added.

"Whatever you can think of will be fine with us. We're kind of stymied for now."

"Let's revisit who the perps are. Two are dead Chechens. Jawarski is Polish by citizenship but Chechen by birth. The three are from Grozny, the capital of Chechnya. We can assume that the driver of the white van is probably Chechen as well. The three identified were in Krakow, Poland. One came here legally through Boston, that being Jawarski. The other two were released from prison in Krakow and were sent back to Chechnya, at least that's what we believe. We believe those three were Chechen Muslims. That leaves out any connection with the 4,000 Russians living in Orlando. They're secular or Christian, not Muslim. The Russians hate the Chechens, and vice versa. I don't think we have to spend manpower looking in that community. We should be looking in the Muslim community. Since there are supposedly less than 200 Chechens in all of the United States—but I believe there are a lot more—I'll bet it would be fairly easy to spot a tall, Caucasian, light-skinned blue-eyed, round-headed Chechen coming out of a mosque. I know that's profiling, but under the Patriot Act, it appears to be okay or understood to be a non-issue after all that's happened."

Joe paused to gage his audience and got a series of nods. "From the pictures, it looked like he got into a midsize Ford Econoline van," he continued. There must be hundreds of them in Florida. I couldn't tell the difference in the model years, but those vans have been around since the 1980s. This one in the video looked older, maybe late 1990s. We should go to Florida DMV and get a full list of all Ford Econoline vans on the road, from the 1990s up to maybe 2010. It could be just beat up and not old. Let's start with Orlando first and Orange County second. I don't think they'd buy or even steal a van outside those parameters. Let's get a map of Orlando, a large one. Then, let's put a red pin where each of the ten mosques are located. Put blue pins where the white Econoline vans are registered in Orlando or Orange County. It might give us an idea about the neighborhoods where the Chechens are now, where they move around, or even go to religious services. I can work on this at home, in Excel, and send it back to Trinity. At least it's a start."

The chief smiled. "Joe, that's a very well thought out idea. We'll do that. In addition, the BOLO went out already but maybe not to your liking. We'll change it to include the other information and then reissue it."

"Sounds good," Joe said.

As usual, Mark sat there and simply nodded his head.

〰️

They were done with their meeting and walked back to the hotel. They ate subs they'd gotten on the way. Joe called Julie. She should be on a break at her school right about now.

Julie picked up immediately. "Joe, I'm headed to Key Largo School for the grant project, and I have to be back for track practice. Lucy's participating in track this year to build up her strength in cross-country. Great things are expected of her and maybe a scholarship from Miami."

Joe started to think about how close Julie was to the Talbot family. Julie and Lucy had gone full circle from Julie babysitting for Lucy and her brother, Jeff, Jr., and later coaching her cross-country and track teams to having Lucy in her wedding, along with Lucy's parents giving her away. All of this connection began many years ago when Joe, Mark, and Joan Talbot walked into Julie's fifth grade classroom for career day. They represented the Coast Guard that day but Joan represented more of a mother to Julie from then on. Joan had given Julie what Julie's grandmother, Tillie, couldn't—a perspective of growing up in a new, changing world. Tillie loved Julie and raised her, but Joan led Julie through her formative years to womanhood with the kind of advice that only a mother could give. Tillie grew up in the '50s and '60s but did the best she could.

"Are you there, Joe?" Julie asked.

"Sorry. I was daydreaming," he said.

"About what?"

"Life in general. Your life in particular," he said. "That's great about Lucy. I just wanted to let you know, I'm not overstaying my welcome up here. Mark and I are heading out after the graveside ceremony. I'll be back to Tavernier later Sunday afternoon. I'll stay at Mark's overnight on Saturday then go to Miami to meet Jake on early Sunday morning. He said he wanted to talk to me, no matter the day or time. I think there's something special happening that I don't know about. I'll fill you in when I get back."

"Just be careful and call me from Mark's. Tillie and I are going to 9:00 a.m. Mass at St. Justin Martyr, Sunday. I have to talk to Father Schmidt about the Key Largo wedding on June twentieth. I'm really glad we already did our six-month Pre-Cana counseling to get married. That takes care of the St. Patrick's wedding as well. However, we will need the license for New York that will be the official marriage license. We'll get two Catholic Church marriage certificates as well, one from St. Patrick's and one from St. Justin Martyr." She laughed. "Maybe we can put all three over the mantle in the living room."

"Well, you can't say you weren't officially married, can you?"

"Nope."

"I got to go. We're heading over to the wake. I'll call you before we leave tomorrow. Love you," said Joe.

"Me, too," she said and they hung up.

❧❧❧

They took a taxi back to police headquarters shortly before 3:00 p.m. so they wouldn't get their uniforms wrinkled walking the mile. The cab dropped them off out front just as the funeral home was delivering Archie's body to the lobby. Archie's parents and ex-wife were already there. The chief was talking to them with Beverly and Trinity by his side. From the looks of the small gathering crowd, it appeared that Archie's other relatives were coming in the side door for the pre-ceremony to honor their nephew, cousin, and godchild.

Joe and Mark moved over near Trinity and stood at her side. The ceremony was short and the chief presented honors to the family on behalf of Archie. He announced to them about the scholarships to St. James Catholic School for those less fortunate. Archie's parents and relatives were deeply moved by the gesture. They shook hands all around with those officers participating and thanked them profusely. Joe noted that they seemed to be in a trance, as if it wasn't happening. Perhaps after the final call at the graveside, they'd release their pent-up emotions. It was clear they were trying to stay strong to honor Archie.

The wake went smoothly, with a few thousand mourners showing up, including officials and police officers from around the state with several from across the country. Archie's parents took several breaks. Archie's ex-wife stayed in the greeting line for the entire time. There was an office set up for food and beverages for the family, especially for the children who came. They were restless and Archie's cousins took the kids home a little after 6:00 p.m. They told his parents that they'd be coming early in the morning and they'd get someone to watch the kids so they could participate more fully. Archie's parents understood. Archie had been a handful growing up.

Just after 9:00 p.m., the honor guards closed the doors, since the line started thinning out a little after 8:30 p.m. The guards allowed everyone waiting at that time to pay their respects and politely told the others who were now showing up that the funeral procession would begin at 9:00 a.m. on

Saturday if they cared to come back. The funeral Mass would begin at 10:00 a.m. in the cathedral.

Joe and Mark stayed until the end. Everyone was tired. Trinity told them to wait so she could give them a ride back to the hotel. They said their goodbyes to the family and proceeded to the parking lot.

"Long day, guys," Trinity said. "Did you eat?"

Joe nodded. "We had a sub for lunch. Can you stop on the way back so we could grab another one? Maybe we can grab a few beers as well. Want to join us?"

"Thanks, but I'm beat. I'm heading home. I've got washing to do and I have to iron my uniform. I never got back my other ones from the cleaners. I completely forgot," she said.

Joe laughed. "Maybe you should live out of a hotel for a while and get all the amenities that we obviously enjoy."

"No thanks. I'll pass." She stopped at the sub shop and the 7/11 on the way. At the hotel entrance, Joe and Mark thanked her, got out of the car, and headed for their room. They'd eat and hit the sack. They needed to have an early breakfast and head for the procession, funeral Mass, and graveside ceremony. Then, they'd be on their way home, when the car rental showed up. The agency promised it would be there by 2:00 p.m. and they'd park out front and give the keys to the receptionist at the front desk. By this time, Joe and Mark were like old friends with the staff. Joe also put $50.00 on the room desk for the maid and handed an envelope to the downstairs staff with a hundred dollar bill and a big "Thanks" from Joe and Mark. They'd be coming back, probably after the wedding, and wanted to be remembered. They'd be remembered.

ᏨᎢᏨ

Joe and Mark got up early, ate at the hotel, and arrived at headquarters at 8:00 a.m. They got a taxi again for the same reasons. They were packed and their luggage was down at the front desk. The staff promised them that when their rental car arrived, they'd load the car with their luggage, lock it, and keep the keys at the front desk. They couldn't ask for more.

"Chief Roberts," Joe said when they arrived at the police station. "Trinity, good morning."

As usual, Mark nodded in agreement. They were intentionally early and they were fully armed. There would be plenty of armed officers in the procession and at every street corner, but if someone wanted to get to the honor guard, the family, or Archie's body, there was no doubt it could be done. Vigilance was the word of the day.

Joe, Trinity, Mark, and Beverly had their day's funeral plans in their hands, and they addressed each issue in sequence. They stood by themselves to the side, and everyone knew, exactly down to the minute, the schedule of events right up to the ending of the graveside ceremony.

The procession started at precisely 9:00 a.m. It took forty-five minutes to go about a mile to St. James Catholic Cathedral. The casket, draped in the American flag, was brought up the front steps by the pallbearers—all policemen—placed onto a rolling cart, and pushed to the altar. The body was always placed feet first toward the altar, as if the person was walking into church.

The bishop met the procession at the foot of the altar and began the funeral Mass. Several honorary guests spoke. The chief and mayor spoke, but everyone seemed to break down when two eighth graders, a boy and a girl, from St. James spoke on behalf of Archie's alma mater. There wasn't a dry eye in the place. The Mass ended with a Catholic blessing, and Archie's body was placed in the waiting hearse to be taken to Greenwood Cemetery. Protocol for full honors was followed throughout the trip, with every corner blocked off by police cars, not only from Orlando but also from across the State of Florida. There were several from adjacent states as well. The bishop said his prayers at the cemetery and greeted the family for the final time.

Joe and Mark got a ride back to the hotel from Trinity, and Beverly joined them for the ride. The two women were needed back at the reception and would meet the chief immediately after dropping off Mark and Joe. When they pulled up to the Embassy Suites, an obvious rental car was parked in the "no-parking zone" right by the front door.

"Somebody's going to get a ticket," Beverly said, smiling. "Guys, thank you for everything that you've done."

Trinity seconded the statement.

"Trinity, you know we will be leaving in a week for New York City. You're certainly invited, as you know. If you come and can't get a room at the hotel, call Julie and you can probably just stay at Julie's publisher's apartment with several of the bridal party and Tillie. It will be crowded, but nicely crowded. If you can't make it, you're definitely coming to the June wedding in Key Largo. You and Kiki and your boyfriend can stay at our new house. We will be taking a quick second honeymoon to Key West for a few nights."

"Thanks, Joe. I think I'll be here still on the investigation, but I'll be there for June's wedding," she said. "I'll send you the file for the mosques and the vans as soon as I get the information. You said that Jack Forest will continue to see if those three pop up in any pictures or films. Can we still call him if you're not around?"

"Of course. He knows you, so just call him at any time. Just let Mark and I know what's going on at all times. It can't interfere with the wedding, or Julie will kill me, but we can work around it still."

Trinity had met Jack down in Miami when her niece Kiki and her friend, Glenda Davis, were kidnapped. Jack was instrumental in finding information that led to her and her girlfriend's whereabouts and rescue.

Mark and Joe gave both Beverly and Trinity a kiss and a hug. They went into the hotel, got the keys from the front desk, and unlocked the car. They waved goodbye just as Trinity was pulling out of the hotel entrance. They were going home.

CHAPTER 12

Joe and Mark arrived at Mark's condo on North Ocean Drive near Fort Lauderdale in Dania Beach. It was almost 2:30 p.m. by the time they left Orlando. It was close to 7:00 p.m. when they arrived at Mark's. It was a four-hour drive with a stop for a quick bite.

They unloaded the car. Mark's wife was working at the Hard Rock and her parents were watching the kids. When Mark opened the door, MJ jumped into his arms. Jennifer, now that she was getting older, simply hugged him. She seemed to be more affectionate to Joe since he was her god-father. MJ went over and hugged Joe as well. Louise's father was sitting on the couch and her mother, Toni, was in the kitchen.

She hurried out to greet them. "Hi, guys. You hungry? I made lasagna, and it's still warm in the oven. I made garlic bread as well."

"Will you run away with me Toni?" Joe asked.

The kids giggled.

"She's too old for you, Joe," Jennifer said.

"I am not! I'm mature and that's a good thing. Right, Ken?" She glared at Ken, her husband, as if to say, "You better have the right answer."

He smiled. "A happy wife means a happy life."

"You, too, Ken?" Joe said. "Wow. No wonder your so meek, Mark. Louise learned from the best."

"Let's eat." Mark ignored Joe's comment and headed for the kitchen. "Any beer?"

Ken nodded. "I ran down to the beverage store and bought Sam Adams Oktoberfest. Is that okay?"

"I knew you liked him better than me!" Mark growled.

Joe grinned. "Why not? I'm much more loveable and I'm actually able to carry on a conversation with almost anyone, Mark."

"Stuff it. Let's eat."

They headed to the kitchen and devoured almost half the lasagna and all the garlic bread. It was a good thing Toni had fed Ken and the kids before they arrived. Louise always ate a sandwich before she left for the evening shift and usually got something at the Hard Rock around 9:00 p.m. By the time she got home, there would be no evidence of lasagna or garlic bread. Toni always cleaned up after babysitting. After she cleaned up and gave MJ his bath, she read to him and said goodbye to Jennifer.

Jennifer was getting older and didn't want to be bothered. Toni kissed Mark and Joe goodbye. Ken waved and headed out the door. Mark was officially in charge, at least until Louise came home. He knew his place and Joe knew what would be expected of himself after the wedding. God knew he heard enough about it from both Mark and Louise.

Mark and Joe stayed up until Louise came home from work around midnight. She came in and gave Mark a very meaningful kiss. Joe knew what that meant. She then turned around. "Joe, how are you?"

"Fine, just fine. Can't wait to go home, though. I have to stop and see the rear admiral on the way back to Islamorada. He wanted to speak to me, he said. But I've no idea why. We're both leaving in the fall around the first of October."

They talked for about a half hour, and Joe headed to MJ's room. He got his spot on the floor in his old sleeping bag. Louise gave him several pillows. "What time do you want me to set the alarm for, Joe?"

"Around 6:30 a.m. if that's okay. I have to be at the rear

admiral's before 9:00 a.m. It will give me some time with the kids before I leave and get some breakfast. Do you have an iron handy? It feels like I've been living in my uniform. This is the last time I can wear it to meet the boss and it goes then back to the cleaners when I get back. It's all I got left. We really should have more dress uniforms, you know?"

"Well, I take care of Mark's. It's my job, he says. I don't see Julie doing it, though."

"Me neither. Goodnight."

ℛℛℛ

The alarm rang on the dot of 6:30 a.m., and Louise popped her head into MJ's room to let Joe know. He headed for the shower first. He did his bathroom routine and at least had one last clean pair of underwear and socks. He buffed his shoes with a rag he carried with him. Louise had set up the ironing board and left the iron on the board unplugged.

He went into the kitchen and made coffee. The kids would be up shortly. This was almost like home. He'd been here so many times. He took out the bacon and eggs and bread from the breadbox. He'd make scrambled eggs, bacon, and toast for him and the kids. The coffee was already on. Louise would be up shortly.

She got up to say goodbye to Joe and then would go back to bed until ten or eleven a.m. She'd get her chores done and get back to the house to start dinner. It was an odd schedule, but it'd worked for the family for a long time. Joe needed to leave so the family could get back to their routine. He knew what a routine meant to him. He'd been called anal retentive by so many people, especially Mark and Julie, that he never let it bother him anymore. That was the way it was.

He said goodbye and hopped into the rental. He'd drop it off when he got to Islamorada and then would get his own car back. Sometimes, Joan would loan it out, if he wasn't around. He hadn't been around a lot and he was unsure at this point where he'd be at any given time. He could always get a ride with Julie.

∽∽∽

He made it to District Seven Coast Guard headquarters on Brickell Avenue around 8:45 a.m. He had the rental so he'd let the guard at the gate know that he'd be using his usual spot in the lot with a different car. Joe put his business card in the window just in case there was a problem. He headed up the front stairs to the security checkpoint and then up to the rear admiral's office. It seemed like months since he'd been back, but it was actually only a little more than a week. He'd been spending more time in Miami than in Islamorada because he worked side by side with Jake Barnes, changing the face of the Seventh District before they both left the service. Jake was retiring and Joe was moving on—at least he thought he was. He wondered what was so important that he had to meet with Jake before heading home, especially on Sunday morning.

"Rear Admiral Barnes," Joe said, entering the office. "I'm at your service, sir."

"Joe, welcome back. How's Julie?"

"Hopefully not mad at me. The wedding is coming up, sir."

"I know. My wife and I'll be there, as you know. Two weddings, huh? You'll never be able to say you weren't married officially, Joe."

"I know. That's all I hear, sir. Mark said to say hello. He'll be down to see you tomorrow. He still has some things to do at the Dania Beach Station and will be here by noon tomorrow. He said that he and Frank Cortez had some security items to clear with you before implementation."

"Good, I look forward to it. But that's not why I wanted you to stop on the way home. It won't take too long. I believe I may have an opportunity for you that may have long-term implications. Care to hear what I have to tell you, Joe?"

Joe smiled. "Of course, sir. As Ross Perot used to say, 'I'm all ears.'"

"Still a smart-ass, Joe?"

"I didn't want to disappoint you, sir."

"You didn't. Please sit down. This will take a while to explain." Jake waited until Joe took a seat. "As you may remember, after our busting up the Columbians and arresting our own Coast Guard thieves, I knew you were thinking about leaving the service when your time expired in the fall. You said you'd stay to help me right-size District Seven by putting in good, honest people, who can be trusted. We're doing that, thanks to you, your friends, and my insistence that I wanted to be the one in charge for the cleanup, since everything happened on my watch. However, Joe, I don't want to lose you, so as I said before, we have two choices that would keep you in the Coast Guard and moving up the ladder at a pace that you're comfortable with. I know that you're getting married to Julie." He laughed. "Hell, who wouldn't?"

"I do want you to go to Washington and see my boss, the admiral in charge of the entire East Coast. He could pretty much offer you any job you wanted, but you probably won't get away from the investigations that you and Mark are so good at. I already discussed it with him, and he wanted you on call for emergencies like you just got up in Orlando for terrorism, national security, or other major problems, which you're so well qualified to handle. That probably won't suit your needs but, as a favor to me, I'd like you to go to talk to him, anyway, when you get back from your honeymoon. Your short honeymoon, I may add," he said with a smile. "If I only have you for a few more months, I'm going to work you to the bone, newlywed or not. You can hate me later."

"Sir, I'll be glad to go see the admiral, but you hit it on

the head. I've been shot at so many times over the years, since I was just a kid. I don't want to keep doing it. The odds aren't in my favor. I don't want to leave Julie a widow before our life together even begins, you know?"

"I know. So I've got another suggestion that we also discussed, but this may be a reality, after all. I know you also don't want to be involved with the FBI and Homeland Security, even though you do carry those credentials."

"What is it, sir?" Joe asked.

"You're thirty-four, almost thirty-five correct?"

"Yes, sir."

"You could use some administrative experience for what I'm about to suggest."

Jake went on to explain the position that he'd spoken to Joe about at the Florida Keys Community College in Key West would be open by October first. "The officer in charge is going to be transferred to another position up in Virginia, very similar to this one. This position I told you about in the Military Education Office, at the Florida Keys Community College, has a dual title of Lieutenant in the Coast Guard and Vice President for Institutional Research. You'd have a dual reporting system. First, you'd report to me, or to my successor, for the military aspect, and second, to the president of the community college. You'd also be a member of his official cabinet. Barry University also operates out of the same site for four-year degrees, master's degrees, and PhDs as well. Joe, we send our military, all branches stationed in Florida, for further education and degrees to both institutions at the same Key West campus. It's no different than how you got your degrees from Miami Dade College, the Coast Guard Academy, and then RPI for your MBA."

The rear admiral cocked his head and studied Joe a moment before continuing. "If you took the job, liked it, and excelled, you could wind up as the superintendent of the Coast Guard Academy. It wouldn't take as long as you might think. Well," he said when Joe said nothing, "what do you think, Joe?"

"Would I be able to continue my education and get a PhD while I'm there?" Joe asked.

"I'm glad you asked," Jake said. "I already took the liberty of calling the president of Barry University, at the main campus located in Miami Shores. He's a friend of mine. It's only minutes away from here at Brickell. Barry University offers a Doctor of Philosophy in Leadership and Education Specialization in Higher Education Administration. You'd need fifty-four additional credit hours added to your MBA from Rensselaer, and that includes the six credits needed for your dissertation." He handed Joe the brochure from the university. "This shouldn't be difficult for you. You could specialize in either Russian or Spanish, or both, as it relates to higher education for new immigrants. Most of your classes would be at the community college or online, and you'd have to meet every now and then on their main campus with your assigned advisor. If you stayed in South Florida, you could name your own ticket at Barry University. However, I'd like to see you eventually wind up at the Coast Guard Academy as superintendent. The superintendent is usually a rear admiral like myself. It isn't out of your range, by any stretch of the imagination. I'll bet, in five to seven years, your qualification, education, and experience would be more than needed for the job. You'll have to be promoted several times from lieutenant, to lieutenant commander, to commander, to captain, and then to rear admiral—lower half. You'd be promoted to rear admiral, lower half, the day you were promoted to superintendent of the Coast Guard Academy. Of course, Julie's input would weigh heavily on your decision. That would be especially true if she continues to grow as an international writer. What do you say, Joe?"

"Well, first I'm honored that you think that highly of me, and I'd never let you down. The only problem that could occur is if I'm continually called back for investigations that could interfere with the job and my PhD, as well. However, it's certainly well worth checking out. Can I meet with the

Barry University staff and ask questions, and the same at the community college? You certainly have peaked my interest. My only other concern is that, upon your retirement, the new rear admiral for District Seven could have an entirely different opinion."

"Joe, that's why I want you to go meet the admiral after your honeymoon. He'll appoint my successor and, with my recommendation, he'd ensure your status as I just outlined. He knows what you've done for us ever since you got back. He wants to meet you to see what makes you tick and see if he can convince you to stay as well. I did a pretty good sales job when I was there. He told me that, quite frankly, if I didn't have you and your friends helping me with the personnel cleanup underway, it wouldn't have happened with me in charge. Trust me. I know what I'm talking about."

"I do trust you, sir. I also want to thank you again for everything you've done for me and Julie and for my friends," Joe said. "I'll think about this and get back to you."

With that, Joe turned, saluted, and walked out. His head was spinning. He had to discuss this with Julie. It was only days before the wedding, and he didn't want to cram her mind with more things to worry about. However, this was a good thing that would keep them both in the Keys for a long while.

Chapter 13

Trinity came into headquarters on Sunday. She slept restlessly all night and was up by 6:00 a.m. She was going to attend services at her father's church at 10 a.m. Marvin Hightower had been the pastor for the last thirty years, before Trinity was even born. Her mother, Mavis, ran the choir for the same length of time. It had been a while since Trinity had been there, and her parents let her know that they'd noticed. Church was important to both her and her family, but her life sometimes got in the way. Finishing her PhD, teaching at the college, and working as a fulltime detective took its toll on her church going activities.

Trinity's two sisters were as different as day and night. Trinity was the youngest, just turning twenty-nine a few weeks ago. Her sister, Hope, now thirty-six, and the oldest, married very young and had Kiki with her husband, Quentin Lonell. He left her right after the baby was born. They'd believed that he just couldn't take the pressure. He was a jazz pianist and traveled the country with a quartet. He wound up in Miami, near South Beach, playing at a few jazz clubs. Only after Kiki, Hope's daughter, was kidnapped with her best friend, did Trinity find out the real reason that Quentin left home. He'd found out that Hope was cheating on him with his best friend and he didn't believe that Kiki was really his daughter. That all changed when Joe led the charge to save Kiki from sex traffickers in Miami. Once

Quentin looked at Kiki and saw his own reflection in his daughter, he knew she was his, and now they were back to talking. Hope had finally admitted to Trinity what she'd done. Trinity kept that secret to herself at the request of Quentin.

Faith was the second oldest of Trinity's sisters at thirty-four, married to Antoine Lawrence, age thirty-five, and a very well-respected software engineer in Orlando at a new high-tech company. They had two daughters ages six and four. They attend her father's church to this day. She'd take over mother's music ministry one day. It was tough for Trinity to keep up with Faith, who was a stay-at-home mother and spent many hours a week at the church.

Thank God we have Hope to make me look like a saint. At least I'm worth saving, according to my mother. Thank you, Hope.

Trinity was working quietly at her desk. It was now around 9:15 a.m. and she had to leave soon. Being late was worse than not being there at all, according to her father.

"Trinity, what're you doing in here today?" asked Chief Roberts.

"I could ask you the same," she said. "I'm getting information on the white van and where they're located in relationship to the ten mosques in Orlando. It's a shot in the dark, but we need to start somewhere. I found out that two white vans were stolen in the last week. I have to find out the make and models. We're looking for a Ford Econoline van model in the late 1990s or early 2000 to 2010. We will pinpoint where the owners are located in relationship to the mosques and see what that brings us. Joe gave me Jack Forest's phone number and told me to call for whatever I needed. God, those three guys, Joe, Mark, and Jack are the best."

"Yes, they are. Unfortunately, we will lose all three soon when Joe gets married in New York City. Mark and Joe's brother are best men, side by side, and Jack will be at the wedding as well. I hope we don't lose momentum on this. I don't have to tell you how important it is to get a cop killer off the streets, let alone the ramifications it has to people flying in for vacation. I also don't want our men acting like vigilantes out there. That could spell a worse disaster. We don't need to be clubbing Muslims over the head, dragging them into headquarters as suspects. I was just thinking about it. At least you and I are African-American so, hopefully, the public won't think the worst of us as being biased. Joe has a very difficult time being a white Irish officer in this day and age. At least he can prove himself, since he's fluent in Spanish—Mexican infused Spanish, I may add—as well as Russian. Having Mark as his best friend doesn't hurt either."

"It's too bad those thoughts have to surface. Joe is one of the finest men I've ever met. He put his life on the line for my family, and nobody will ever know."

"We will," said the chief. "And that's all that matters. If you need me, call me at home. We're having a cookout. Come on over if you want. Estelle will be happy to see you." He laughed. "That's if you don't mind being seen with your boss."

"Well, there's that." She smiled and laughed as well. They left together. Trinity had fifteen minutes to get to church.

ℝ℞ℝ

After church, Trinity came back and downloaded all the Ford Econoline vans registrations for Orange County for the years 1995 through 2010. She put the information into an Excel document. She didn't know how to get the driver's licenses for the owners. But just having an address for the vans would be a good start, and she could have Joe pinpoint the locations in relationship to the mosques. However, as Joe had told her, getting the driver's licenses helped in identifying potential people who'd have driven the van as it left the Florida Mall and the airport. She knew that Joe would be busy on his first day back, so she called Jack Forest on his private cell.

"Jack, Hi. It's Trinity Hightower."

"Hi, Trinity. Joe said you might call. I called his cell but it's off. I think he might be sleeping and Julie must be out. What can I do for you?"

"Can I ship a list of Ford Econoline vans to you and have you get the registered owner's driver's license and picture. I don't know how you and Joe do that, and I'm afraid to ask," she said.

"Don't ask, Trinity. How many vehicles are we talking about?"

"There are 175 Ford Econoline vans model years 1995 to 2010 in Orange County and fifty-eight specifically in the City of Orlando. Two of the vans were stolen in the county but none in the city in the last month. So, maybe, just maybe, we can get lucky. Joe told me how he identified the driver of the white pickup truck that ran Tillie off the road. Joe said he had a white arm and that started the elimination process. Here we go again. It's a fine line when we start targeting but a police officer was killed and two others shot. I believe all bets are off when it comes to any question of propriety. Do you know what I mean, Jack?"

"Joe had to do it to match the owner of the pickup truck. He knew he was white. Are you going to look for middle-eastern names and faces as owners of the vans?"

"Specifically, I want to look at names and faces of owners who live within the vicinity of any mosques. If those names produce a Muslim, so be it," she said.

"Send me the list. I have the program I ran for Joe back when we were looking at the white pickup truck. It's actually better that we will be doing this on Sunday, when either nobody will be at DMV or they'll have such a limited crew that they'd never be able to pick up a blip on the screen. It will take me about two hours. I'll send the file to you by 3:00 p.m. and then you email it to Joe. He said he'd do the matrix right away, when we discussed it previously, and get it back to you. I know they'll be in Tavernier for a week and then they'll be heading to New York City on Tuesday before the wedding. I don't know how they'll pull it off but, somehow, I suspect it will go as smoothly as it can. That's just their nature. It's a thing to behold," Jack said and laughed.

"Thank you, Jack. You guys are great. I don't know what we'd do without you. You never hear cops talk that way about the FBI."

"Don't forget, I'm not FBI, but Joe and Mark are Coast Guard Lieutenants and carry credentials for both the FBI and Homeland Security. If they can't get it done, nobody can."

Trinity waited around, ate her lunch, and saw the email come in from Jack. It was a huge file with all the data they needed. Trinity could sort it but Joe was an expert in Excel and in strategically looking at the data that made everything stand out and become clear. It was his gift to her. It would take her hours and he'd spend less than an hour and get it back to her. She could then place the pins on the map and have names and faces to go with the vans and the mosques. She didn't know what the story would be, but it had to be better than what she now had—nothing.

Chapter 14

Joe got the file at home in Tavernier and told Julie that he'd only be tied up for an hour or so. He downloaded all the data from Trinity, which included the 175 white Econoline vans in Orange County. Jack got Joe the registered van owner's driver's licenses and matched the addresses from the van registrations to the driver's addresses. There were about twenty discrepancies between addresses. Of the twenty, Joe searched and found that ten were corporations that had moved locations. For the ten others, Joe had no idea. That had happened to Joe when he was chasing down the same information up in Nashville. People moved and never changed addresses either on their license or their vehicle registration.

Of the 175 vans, 100 of them were registered to corporations, which didn't help the cause. Of the remaining seventy-five vans, fifty of them were registered to individuals at addresses in the city of Orlando. Of the fifty individual vans, thirty of them had addresses that were less than two miles from a mosque. That wasn't as revealing as Joe might have thought because Orlando wasn't that big in size or population. Orange County was big, but not the immediate city itself.

So, at first, he'd concentrate on those vans owners who appeared to have something in common with the two deceased Chechens and the third one who got away. Did any of the thirty owners look like they were Chechens? That was the next step. Of the thirty owners, fifteen were dark skinned and could potentially be Muslims, ten were clearly white and, of those ten, only two or three looked like they could be Mediterranean or even Middle Eastern. The remaining five were clearly Hispanic, but you never knew. However, Chechens didn't look like Muslims. They looked like blue-eyed Irishmen, so he'd spend more time looking at what appeared to be white male owners to see if there were any distinguishing marks or ethnic signs that he could find, like enlarged heads or height that appeared taller than average. They'd have to start by studying the actual licenses, the pictures and the information recorded on the license. They needed to run credit reports to see if and where they worked. Some vans were individually owned, but single individual contractors, plumbers, electricians, or even a carpet cleaner could own the vans.

Of the 100 vans registered to corporations, three were actually registered to corporations owned by mosques. Joe thought that might be a good place to start. Two of the three vans were owned by mosques which were located only two miles, in each direction, from the Florida Mall in Orlando. The third van owned by a mosque was in northern Orange County, far removed from the scene.

Joe couldn't do any more with this information other than to point out interesting facts. He compiled a list for Trinity to think about. Those included: (1) look at the two vans owned by the local mosques. See if there are any distinguishing marks or if the license plates are covered with mud. (2) check out the thirty drivers who individually owned white Econoline vans and had addresses close to the ten mosques. (3) compile reports on the ten white drivers, of which two or three could be Chechens. The names could have been changed or Americanized. Follow up and drive by all the addresses. He jotted down a few more thoughts and added them to the list. If worst came to worst, they could go to whitepages.com and check out Chechen names on a list compiled by Joe. He downloaded Chechen men's first and last names, which were equivalent to Smith and Jones in Chechen.

Joe forwarded the information to Trinity and cc'd the chief and Jack Forest. He asked Jack to follow up with credit reports on all thirty individuals near the mosques, especially to look at the ten white owners who could be Chechens. Joe also asked him to continue to look online to see if the two dead terrorists or Jawarski's pictures could be found in print or in any videos produced. Just a few weeks ago, an Englishman had been identified as the murderer in the video where he cut off innocent people's heads in the Middle East.

If they found any information, there was no question about the Patriot Act being in play. As of now, they had the murder of a cop and the wounding of two other officers. At this point, this was a local matter and couldn't involve the FBI or Homeland Security unless they had proof that it was a terrorist act.

෭ඔ෭ඔ

Right before he'd left Jake's office in Miami, Joe promised the rear admiral that he'd go to Washington DC to meet Admiral Hartnagle after the wedding. He decided to go before the wedding to get it over with. He was able to get a flight out of Miami at 7:00 a.m. on Tuesday morning, landing at Reagan National Airport later in the morning. He was told that a member of the Coast Guard would meet him at the baggage carousel upon landing. He was promised that he'd be back in Miami by Thursday evening.

He and Julie had a lot to do before the wedding. Logistics was a big problem, heading to New York City with wedding gowns, Coast Guard uniforms, and baggage sent ahead to the publisher's apartment. Julie's publisher, Sarah Atwood, told her to ship her items directly to their headquarters, and they'd personally delivery everything to the apartment as soon as it arrived. That would be a big relief for Julie.

No one was scheduled to use the apartment the week before the wedding, so they could have it at any time that week. They'd be flying into JFK on the following Wednesday afternoon. The most important thing they had to do was pick up their wedding license at city hall on Thursday morning. Sarah Atwood made the appointment with the mayor's office directly, so the wedding license could be taken care of swiftly. Joe thought to himself that Julie must be very important to Sarah for her to go to those lengths to help out. Sarah would be attending the wedding with her husband, Bennett, but it appeared to be more than just a courtesy. Sarah and Bennett Atwood were considered heavy hitters in the New York City world of book publishing. If they liked you, you'd go far. Julie had only met Sarah's husband once, but he was enthralled with Julie's first book, *Conch Town Girl.*

At the time he told Julie that they had two young daughters but when they hit their teen years, he'd definitely offer them the book. Sarah had agreed as well and actually offered her the contract as she was leaving Brown University with her MFA degree.

Julie also had to hand in her completed manuscript for her second book, *The Middle Years,* on Thursday morning, right after they got their wedding license. Tillie would be coming with them as well. Julie really needed her to help coordinate everything and keep her in check. Tillie was extremely level headed and had always been there for Julie, whenever she was needed. She never volunteered, never butted in, and never gave an unasked opinion. Julie loved that about Tillie.

Joe met his contact as soon as he arrived for his luggage.

The man said he was parked right outside the door in a military police parking spot. After all, it was Washington DC, and this was an ongoing routine for visiting guests. It was good to be the king, Joe thought and laughed to himself. The last time he was in Washington DC was in 2008 for President Obama's inauguration. They drove up from Miami, which was a long trip. Today, he was met in style and the trip from the airport to Coast Guard headquarters was less than five miles away. Depending on traffic, it could take fifteen minutes to an hour going across town.

They started out going north on National Airport Access Road toward Smith Boulevard. They took the George Washington Memorial Parkway North for less than a mile and merged onto I-395 N/Southwest Freeway North toward Washington, crossing into the District of Columbia. They stayed straight and got onto I-695 S/Southwest Freeway North and merged onto South Capitol Street SW toward Nationals Park. They quickly turned right onto Potomac Avenue SW and then slightly right onto R Street SW. They finally turned left onto Second Street SW, which required gate access. They immediately pulled up in front of 2100 Second Street SW, which was on the left.

When they arrived at Coast Guard headquarters, Joe thanked the driver and walked up the stairs to security. He'd be meeting Admiral Kenneth T. Hartnagle in a few minutes. Evidently, Jake had put together a full itinerary for Tuesday, Wednesday and early Thursday morning. Joe would have a direct flight back to Miami on Thursday, arriving around 5:00 p.m. He'd be back home no later than 6:30 p.m. depending on traffic heading to the Keys. Today he was meeting all day with the admiral. Over the next two days he'd be meeting with the deputy director of the FBI and deputy secretary of Homeland Security. He was having dinner with Mike Hanley, his CIA friend from Miami who was in town, at Joe's request, to discuss a possible presence of Chechen terrorists in Orlando.

That should kill the better part of an evening.

"Admiral it a pleasure to meet you."

"Likewise, Lieutenant Traynor. My pleasure. Please come in. Would you like some coffee or something to eat? I thought we could grab an early lunch around 11:30 a.m. at the officer's club if you don't have any other plans."

"No, sir. No other plans. I'm here specifically at your request. I've met you once before, sir."

"When was that, Lieutenant?" the admiral asked.

Joe thought that he was very formal and very different from Jake Barnes, his own rear admiral. Joe wondered how Jake got along with Hartnagle. He'd ask him when he got back. "It was in 2008, sir. It was right before President Obama's inauguration. My partner Mark Silva and I were called in to develop intelligence from chatter in Spanish over the lines. Mark and I worked as a two-man team, passing along our findings to the high command. We were told that you, sir, at the time, served as the principal advisor to the Secretary, regarding intelligence matters. We made a presentation to you on some extremely delicate intelligence that we discovered over the lines in Spanish. We passed it on to you, sir, directly. At the time, I didn't speak Russian and the transmissions were both in Russian and Spanish. Now, of course, I'm fluent in both, which would have been extremely helpful back then."

"I do remember meeting you, Joe." The admiral seemed to relax a little. "I went over your dossier, and I'm quite impressed. I forgot that you're fluent in Spanish and Russian, written and verbally, and with cultural and historical background in both. That's quite impressive. May I summarize some of your efforts on our behalf, and you can correct me if I'm wrong."

"Yes, sir. Please do."

"During your first tour from, when you were eighteen to twenty-eight, you served with honor and decided to leave the service to obtain your MBA, which you did with honors from Rensselaer Polytechnic Institute. From there, everything seemed to have started clicking with you. You stopped a national money-laundering scheme that included the Mexican Mafia. It ended with the death of the son of the Mexican Mafia general and three gangbangers in the offices of the president of the Albany Coalition for Families. You received the second highest honor given by the Coast Guard, the Coast Guard Commendation Medal with a Ribbon. It's the highest award issued for heroism, not involving combat with an enemy outside the country, by the United States Coast Guard. That's quite an achievement, Joe."

"Thank you, sir."

"Then after you rejoined the Coast Guard, you took down the Russian Mafia in the Keys, the so-called Dixie meth distributors in Nashville, the Columbian cocaine cartel in Miami, and our own Coast Guard crooks. Then you caught the Haitian sex traffickers in Miami, and you're now in the middle of what appears to be terrorists in America sitting in Orlando. Plus, you solved the murder of Tom Jones, one of our own. Is that all correct?"

"Yes, sir. That pretty much sums it up."

"I guess what I'm saying Joe, is that you've done more in the last two years than most officers have done during a thirty-year career. You're to be commended, and that's why Jake wanted me to talk to you to see how we can keep you around after your tour is up in October. I know you're staying to help Jake Barnes clean up the mess in District Seven but I'd like to see more of you. Jake is retiring. You've more to offer. Can we at least start there, Joe?"

"Certainly, sir. I must tell you, though, that I'm here specifically at the request of Rear Admiral Barnes, for whom I have great respect."

"I understand that, Lieutenant. Let's head to lunch. We're meeting a few of my direct staff reports and, after lunch, I'd like to hear more about the potential terrorist issues in Orlando. Tomorrow, you'll be meeting with the Deputy Secretary of Homeland Security, Martin Sutherland, and in the afternoon, you'll meet with Deputy Director of the FBI, Stephen Sandberg. Do you have plans for dinner, Joe?"

"Yes, sir. I'm meeting with a personal friend of mine for dinner at 6:00 p.m." Joe didn't want to tell him about his connection with Mike Hanley of the CIA in Miami unless he had to. Mike flew up just to meet Joe. He knew that Joe was going to ask him to pull a few strings to see what he could find out about the three Chechens and if he'd heard anything about Chechens in America. Joe wanted to go to Philip's Seafood Restaurant on the southwest waterfront of Washington DC, but they'd just recently closed permanently. Mike recommended meeting Joe at Hank's Oyster Bar in DuPont Circle, one of the best seafood restaurants Washington had to offer. Joe loved oysters and Mike said it was his wedding treat.

Joe went through lunch, informing the admiral and his staff about his experience, history, education, and language and cultural skills. They wanted to know how a kid from Troy, New York, could be so successful outside his comfort zone. Joe told them about his baseball career and how it taught him to be his best under trying circumstances. He related the story about walking the best opposing batters so he could pick them off first base.

They laughed.

"But my best attribute is respecting myself, my fellow Coast Guard members, and especially the enemies that I have to confront. I've never underestimated anyone because I've been underestimated and it made me that much more aware and stronger."

The assembled officers simply nodded their heads and showed great admiration for this young man who'd become someone, in the Coast Guard or not.

When they came back from lunch, Joe went through everything he knew about the Orlando threat. He went through what the next steps the Orlando police needed to take while he was away getting married. "With the permission of my rear admiral, of course, I'll go back to help if they find any leads, especially if they need my strategic skills or Russian language skills. I am also fully up to speed now on Chechen culture and the difference in language idioms that could prove very different if I get the opportunity to question the suspects down the road."

"How did you develop your strategic skills?" Admiral Hartnagle asked him.

Joe went through the same speech he'd given Jake about his somewhat photographic memory that was more than just memorization. "My memory skills had key word components that allow me to instantaneously recall specific facts and figures with quick precision and recall. I can also memorize numbers to decimal point efficiency, just as I remembered the VIN numbers on the white truck that belonged to Julie's father during the Russian Mafia investigation."

Joe's meeting that afternoon was more about the admiral getting to know Lieutenant Joe Traynor and what Rear Admiral Barnes described as the new intelligence needed to make the Coast Guard a world-class organization on the cutting edge to ensure the safety of the United States.

To that end, Admiral Hartnagle was very impressed with Joe and he'd call Jake at the end of the day.

Joe excused himself to head to the hotel to check in, clean up, and meet with Mike Hanley at 6:00 p.m. He'd take a taxi to DuPont Circle, about a twenty-minute ride from his hotel.

CHAPTER 15

Joe arrived at Hank's Oyster Bar just before 6:00 p.m. Mike was sitting at the bar having a beer. He saw Joe coming in the door in the mirror and turned around and waved him over. "Joe, what's your pleasure?"

"A beer will do. What do you have? Guinness on tap?"

"Yup."

"I'll have the same," Joe said and sat down on the stool beside him.

"Well, here's to you, Joe, from one Irishman to another on the verge of getting married. May your soul already be in heaven an hour before the devil knows your dead."

"Any wedding toasts?" Joe asked.

"Sure," Mike said. "There are four things you must never do: lie, steal, cheat, or drink. But if you must lie, lie in the arms of the one you love. If you must steal, steal away from bad company. If you must cheat, cheat death. And if you must drink, drink in the moments that take your breath away."

Joe laughed. "Fine toast. Are we drinking or eating tonight?"

"Both. I already got us a booth and I already ordered a dozen oysters each. Your favorites I may add—Wellfleet oysters from Cape Cod. Then a bowl of chowder and a whole belly clam roll for each of us. How'd I do?"

"Will you run away with me before I pledge my love to someone else?"

"You already did that, buddy. And, I may add, you're marrying up," Mike said with a smile.

"No shit," Joe said.

They dug into their grub and finished every last bite of it. "What'd you have to do, take out a mortgage?" Joe asked.

"Pretty close. I may have to break into one of your Halliburton attaché briefcases for a few hundreds to cover us. You certainly took care of your guys down in Islamorada, didn't you?"

"I believe we slipped you a few hundred thousand as well for a simple one-way taxi ride to hell for the Russians."

"And the Mexicans, the Columbians, and the Haitians, anybody else, Joe?"

"Yes, as a matter of fact," Joe said quietly, "I need to talk to you about the Chechens in Orlando. I believe we've got a terrorist problem within our midst. Can we talk after dinner? I need you to call in a few favors from you CIA compatriots overseas, especially those messing with terrorists. I need confirmation on three men, who we have pictures of, who were involved in the airport shooting. We need to see them in pictures or videos working directly with terrorists so I can slap down the Patriot Act and have you ship them out. Where can we talk?"

"Let's go around the corner. There's another out of the way bar where no one will bother us. You can tell me all about it then."

"Sounds like a plan."

❧❧❧

Joe made it back to his hotel after dinner and the meeting with Mike. Mike Hanley was as strong a friend as Joe had, even though they didn't see each other a lot. They had each other's back, and that was no small achievement, considering what they were involved in. Not everyone knew about Mike Hanley. The exception was Mark, Jack, and the rear admiral. On many an occasion, Joe stepped into one of Mike's investigations to handle the linguistics, either Spanish or Russian, or both on many an occasion. They could count on each other. Both being one-hundred-percent Irish also led to their bonding, especially around St. Patrick's Day when they were both in Miami on that day. Mark usually was the designated driver for the day. He'd bring Joe back to his house because it was closer and then he'd dump him in MJ's room for the night. Joe never said anything the next day, but Mark knew. Joe owed him.

❧❧❧

"Julie, Hi. Do you have time to talk?"

"Sure, Joe. When are you getting back?"

"I promised you that I'd be back on the flight into Miami at 5:00 p.m. from Reagan. I should be home around 6:30 p.m. by the time I find my car and get out of the airport. Remember, we're fifteen miles more south now than you were in Key Largo."

"I know. I miss you. How was your meeting with the admiral?"

"It was fine, and I met his staff. He wants me to stay on but as we talked about it, I'd only stay if I could take the academic route through the Florida Keys Community College position. I'm getting too old to get shot, and I know you wouldn't be happy about it either. How was your day?"

"I'm just about packed and ready to UPS all my wedding stuff up to Sarah. Thank God, she offered that to us. I can't envision getting on a plane with everything. I picked up Tillie and she'll be here until we leave. She's a great help and I probably wouldn't keep everything straight without her. I finished the book, *The Middle Years*. I'm hand delivering the manuscript to their office next Thursday after we get our marriage license at city hall. I emailed it to her, anyway, to be safe. By the way, I've good news for you. Do you want to hear it?"

"Of course."

"I just got my first royalty statement from Sarah and an attached check. I sold 103,191 books, with a $2.00 royalty fee attached to each book, equaling $206,382.00, minus the two advances they made to me, totaling $60,000.00. I'm looking at a gross check of $146,382.00, before taxes. After taxes of thirty percent are taken out, we will net $102,467.40. Not a bad wedding present, huh?"

"Wow! Are you kidding me? Julie, that's fantastic. That certainly eases the burden of making a decision about the movie rights for *Conch Town Girl*."

"Well, as a matter of fact, as you know, I've got an offer for $600,000.00 for both books. Now, the second book is complete, and we can collect on that too, if we want. This is a joint decision, Joe. I'd never be here in this position if it weren't for you."

"Thank you for saying that, but that's not true. You were always headed for greatness."

"Do you want some more news that will knock your socks off?"

"What could be more dramatic than what you just told me?" he said.

"I think that Tillie has a male friend in the wings. She hinted that she'd like to invite a Mr. Ed Lansing to the June wedding at Saint Justin Martyr's. Evidently, he lives in Key Largo. He just retired this year as an engineer for the City of Pittsburgh and bought a house in town. He's a month younger than Tillie. His wife died a few years ago. He's Catholic, a regular churchgoer, and met Tillie at Mass. And afterward he volunteered at the food bank. He has two married daughters, Elizabeth, age thirty-eight and Melissa, age thirty-five. They live in Pittsburgh. Each of the daughters has a little boy and a girl. So he's a grandfather four times over. He's also a regular for breakfast at the Waffle House, especially, it seems, during Tillie's hours. What do you think of that, Joe? My grandfather George, died six years before I was born and you could count the number of dates Tillie's had on one hand. I guess my pending marriage changed everything."

"Is that the second or third 'Wow' during this conversation. I don't know what to say. I'm really happy for her, if she is, and it sounds to me from this conversation that she is. How do you feel, Julie?"

"Well, I'd like to meet him before the wedding next Saturday in New York City, but that's not going to happen. I talked to her about it and all she said was, 'never say never.' I think she likes this man a great deal. We'll just have to wait and see."

"Julie, I have to go. I'm happy on all counts if you and Tillie are happy. That's all that matters to me, other than you worrying about me getting shot. I promise you it won't happen. I'll see you Thursday night, early."

With that they both said "I love you" and hung up.

Joe got to bed early. He wanted to be sharp but he also wanted to call Trinity early tomorrow morning to see if there was any news.

⌘

Joe got up at 6:00 a.m. as soon as the alarm went off. Ten minutes later, he got the wake-up call. He started the little coffee maker, as bad as it was. At least it would wake him up. He took his shower, dressed in his full uniform, had his coffee and his daily constitution, and left for headquarters. He walked to the building. It was less than a mile from the hotel. He checked in at security and was in the admiral's waiting room by 8:00 a.m.

He'd called Trinity at 6:30 a.m. to see if there was anything new. They spoke for about twenty minutes, and Joe told her he had to head out for a meeting at the admiral's at

8:00 a.m. The only news in Orlando was a church bombing that night at 2:00 a.m. It was the New Bethel AME Church in downtown Orlando, one of the oldest African-American churches in Orlando. The pastor, Reverend Elijah James, was a close friend of Trinity's father, Marvin Hightower, the pastor of the First Baptist Church of Orlando. Her father called her at 3:00 a.m., as soon as he heard, and woke her up out of a sound sleep. Her boyfriend Gene was there at the time. She got the news and headed in early. When Joe called her on her cell, she'd already been there for two hours.

They hoped that it wasn't a startup of another white supremacist attack on African-American churches. There hadn't been one in ten years. Back in the early 1960s and 1970s, attacks were regular occurrences. Trinity hoped that racism in America was a thing of the past. But every now and then, racism raised its ugly head. She wanted to make sure that her police department wasn't painted with the same brush as the Ferguson, Missouri, Police Department. Orlando had gone through a very similar problem back in the day and made every attempt to bring the department into the twenty-first century. Trinity's promotion, although questioned at the time, was a shining example as to how Orlando had grown as a community. Now, it didn't look like a black and white issue but, like a lot of large mainstream American cities, it was now a multicultural problem, with new emerging populations like Russians and Muslims putting down roots in their community. It was a new America.

Joe told her to keep him informed. She'd gotten the matrix and the questions, and she was reviewing the information today and would start the ball rolling. She'd been given a task force of five detectives and ten patrolmen to start the investigation to find the Chechen leader. Someone else was looking into the murder of Archie Higgins but, at the end of the day, even though Archie was her former partner, she'd help in finding his murderer. Her main task was to stop any potential terrorist attack from happening in Orlando. That was what she was charged with by Chief Roberts, and she was going to see it through. Now, she had a church bombing investigation to look into, to see if there was any connection.

ೲ

"Lieutenant Traynor, I'd like you to meet the Deputy Secretary of Homeland Security, Martin J. Sutherland."

"Sir, my pleasure," Joe said as he sat down at the table. "As you know, sir, I carry credentials for the Coast Guard, Homeland Security, and the FBI, since we're all under one roof. At any given time, I've used all three together and separately to make an arrest or get information."

Sutherland nodded. "When we set that up, we thought we might be able to get rid of the backstabbing that happened between agencies. There have been a few successes like you but many failures. How do we make it work? You seem to be a prime example, Joe. May I call you, Joe?"

"Of course, please do," Joe said.

Joe didn't want to be the poster boy for cooperative agencies, any more than he wanted to be the poster boy for the Spanish-speaking community in Albany when he worked for the Albany Coalition for Families, which seemed like a million years ago. He simply gave evidence of the cooperation between agencies, how it worked, and how people who liked each other actually got along. He wanted nothing to do with Homeland Security, other than to carry its badge when it was convenient and appropriate. He felt the same way about the FBI. He could live with just being a Coast Guard guy.

They spoke for most of the morning, with the deputy secretary and his staff taking notes furiously. They too were intrigued by Joe's skills, not only with languages and culture, but were intrigued by his use of drones to pinpoint and target the bad guys.

That must have gone on for an hour before lunch. *They really should get out of their offices more.*

The admiral took Joe to lunch with his staff, and Joe could barely eat between questions. It was as if they'd had no idea what it was like out in the field. The only time he showed his temper was when one of the staff laughed about Katrina and New Orleans. Joe almost bit his head off and told him, in no uncertain terms, how poorly the African-American citizens of New Orleans were treated by American military forces. Not the Coast Guard, who were considered the only saviors of New Orleans, but by every other thug organizations disguised as government agencies. The admiral noticed Joe's temper and was not surprised. Evidently, Jake Barnes told him directly not to piss Joe off, because he'd tell you exactly what was on his mind. The staff member would long remember the short, but to the point, confrontation at lunch with Joe. The admiral admired Joe's passion, and, at that point, knew that headquarters would be a waste of his talents.

Joe spent the afternoon with the deputy director of the FBI. He couldn't wait to get the hell out of there. At 2:00 p.m. he was drained and just wanted to head to the airport. The admiral kept the afternoon meeting to a minimum, knowing that Joe had to make the plane. He shook Joe's hand. Joe picked up his luggage at the front of the admiral's office and had a car waiting for him right at the front door.

"Joe, I haven't had that much fun over a few days in a long time. I remember myself at your age, and I didn't have one-tenth the balls or integrity that you've shown me here at headquarters. Jake was right. You're a keeper. Can we continue to talk before your October commitment comes due?"

"Of course, sir. I'd be happy to. Thank you for taking the time to meet with me and to set up these other meetings. It's been enlightening, and I hope that I lived up to your expectations."

"Joe, you more than lived up to my expectations. Jake was right. You're the real deal. My staff member almost crapped his pants when you laid into him about the treatment of the people of New Orleans. I was surprised at your passion, but I shouldn't have been. Let's talk some more. Best wishes for your wedding day. Please get home safe and sound. From what I hear, that's not always an easy thing with you."

Joe laughed. "Goodbye. Thanks for everything." He headed out the door.

✑✑✑

"Jake, it's Admiral Hartnagle as if you didn't know," he said with a laugh.

"How did it go with Joe Traynor?"

"As you warned me, Jake. He's the real deal. Let's see if we can keep him in the Coast Guard somewhere. It would be a tragedy for this country if we let him go without a fight."

"I agree, sir. Let me know what you want to do. I think he'd take the community college job, get his PhD, and take over as superintendent of the Coast Guard Academy. He could do that in a heartbeat with the right support in place, sir. I'm leaving. He needs you, admiral."

"I agree. We'll talk more."

They said goodbye.

✑✑✑

Joe's plane got into Miami right on schedule at 5:00 p.m. By the time he got his gear and got to his car in the long-term lot, it was around 5:30 p.m. The sixty-five miles, door-to-door to Tavernier would take all of an hour if there was no traffic. There was always traffic, but Joe was headed home and ready to get married. He was starting a new chapter with the woman he loved and would love for the rest of his life. Up to now, not much mattered in his life until Julie told him she loved him. That was all he needed. *Tillie's got a boyfriend. Who'd have thought that would happen at this point in her life?* He laughed and headed home.

CHAPTER 16

As soon as Joe got back to Tavernier, he gave Julie a big kiss. He did the same to Tillie as well. He forgot she'd be at their new house until they left for the wedding.

Joe told Julie that all his meetings went well, but he wasn't going to commit to anything before they had a long chat after the honeymoon.

He then called Trinity. She didn't want to keep him long, but as soon as he called, she wanted to tell him about the second bombing of a Christian Church in Orlando the night before.

"Joe, the bomb squad went through the first church with a fine-toothed comb. They said it was definitely a bomb that went off that caused the fire and the church was totaled. They found the bomb fragments, and there was nothing special, but they did notice that there was chlorine gas found on the scene near the center of the blast. Reverend Elijah James, the pastor of the New Bethel AME Church, is totally distraught. Joe, who could have done such a thing? I thought we were well beyond white-supremacist attacks on African-American churches. Two in two nights is two too many. At least there were no casualties, thank God. The second church destroyed is Bell Chapel African American Church, not far from New Bethel. We're checking the source of this bomb as well."

"Did you say that the first bomb had remnants of chlorine gas on the premises?"

"Yes, why?" asked Trinity.

"I don't want to be the bearer of bad news, but these two bombings may be related to the Chechens being in Orlando. They probably want the Orlando police to suspect white supremacists, but it may just be a diversionary tactic, Trinity."

"How so?" was all Trinity could get out of her mouth.

She was now at a total loss for words. How much more qualified was Joe and his team than her own police force? It might just be staggering, she thought. *God, I'm glad he's on our side.*

"Here's the reason why, Trinity. Previous footage captured by an Iraqi bomb disposal team showed plumes of thick orange gas emerging from a detonated roadside bomb. The team told the BBC it was diffused 'dozens' of chlorine bombs left by militants, which it says were used more as a means to create fear than harm. In Iraq, Syria, and other places in the Middle East, they have resorted to this new method. They're putting chlorine inside these homemade roadside bombs, which is toxic for those who inhale it."

Joe sighed. "It was not the first time claims emerged that they used bombs filled with chemical agents. In October last year, Kurdish officials and doctors said they believed toxic gases had been released in an eastern district of Kobani. Tikrit, Saddam Hussein's hometown, was overrun by militants' rapid advance across northern Iraq in June last year. They used chlorine gas on the people living there. This sounds a lot like those used in Iraq."

"Joe, we're so screwed."

"Not necessarily, Trinity. I don't have to be there for you to continue to search out and find these terrorists. Your police force just needs to be diligent at all times. If there's another church going to be bombed, you can bet it will be an African-American church. Quietly let them know and be vigilant until you find the perps. I'm waiting for Jack to see if he found any pictures online tying the three Chechens. If he does, it could help everything. I also met with a friend of mine in Washington who was going to do a little snooping with his friends working in the Middle East. I can't say anything more at this time. I'd keep the possible bombing ties quiet for now. You never know if the Chechens have people on the payroll with direct ties to the authorities. Just let it leak that it could be white supremacists for now. No need to give away our potential hand to anyone. It won't do us any good and could help them. Keep it to yourself for now, Trinity."

"What do I tell the chief, Joe?"

"Tell him to call me on a secure phone. You can certainly be in on the call. There's a method to our madness. We want to flush them out without setting off a shit storm, if you know what I mean. If the public gets a hold of this, we could be in for a world of hurt with no answers. It wouldn't look good for anyone. Is Beverly Fitch up to speed at this point?"

"I believe so. But, Joe, she doesn't know anything that's going on other than 'It's an ongoing investigation so she can't comment.' That won't last long, especially with Fox News and the other channels clamoring for more information on Archie's murder and now the two church bombings in two days. It doesn't look good, Joe."

"I hear you. Have the chief call me with you there. If I hear anything from Jack or my other source, I'll let you know."

Thanks, Joe." They hung up.

⁌⁍

Joe walked back into the kitchen to grab a beer. Julie could see that he was stressed. He looked like he always looked when he was one-hundred percent on an investigation but this was different. This wasn't his investigation, and he had to let it go for at least two weeks. She knew that Joe trusted his friends, but he always had to be on top of everything.

"Julie, I have to call Jake in a little while. I need to let him know what's going on and how I'm leaving things before we go to New York City. Just as he said that, his cell phone rang. It was Jack Forest.

"Hi, Jack. Any news?"

"Nothing yet. We can't find any pictures online of any of the three guys, so that's no help. What did you make of the information from the vans and driver's licenses? Were any near any of the mosques?

"As a matter of fact, two mosques actually own Econoline vans so Trinity will follow up. There are a good number in the city itself, so she'll have her assigned officers start checking out the owners and the driver licenses that matched. There are a ton of commercial vans so that will take a lot longer. Trinity was just assigned a staff of five detectives and ten assigned officers in patrol cars. They'll be looking for any white vans near the mosques as well as go to the residences that popped up that matched both the van registrations and the driver's licenses of the owners. Other than that, she has nothing else."

"I'll keep checking for videos to see if any of the three Chechens pop up anywhere. I guess I'll be on call until the wedding. You're getting there Wednesday, right?"

"Yes, we'll be flying in Wednesday with Tillie and staying at the publisher's apartment. We'll all have our cells, if one of us doesn't pick up. We will be getting our marriage license on Thursday morning, and Julie has to go to her publisher's to drop off the manuscript for her second book. Thank God, that's out of the way. Your rooms are on the same floor at the Waldorf Astoria. Everyone else will be there Friday morning. The rehearsal dinner is at Luigi's around the corner from the apartment."

"If we don't speak before then, I'll see you Friday."

"Thanks, as usual, Jack," Joe said.

❧❧❧

Julie, Joe, and Tillie packed everything that was to be shipped. Joe had to go to the main UPS headquarters in Miami Friday morning to make sure everything went out on time to get to the apartment by Wednesday. Julie would be more relaxed once her wedding dress was packed and gone. Tillie spent extra time to make sure that nothing would be wrinkled when it arrived.

The phone rang. It was Mike Hanley. "Joe call me on your secure phone," he said and hung up.

Joe's phone was a SAT phone that he used in all his investigations. He went into the bedroom and closed the door. "What's up, Mike. Good news?"

"We've a video of Axmad Khan in an jeep with his rifle raised over his head in celebration. This video was run simultaneously with the videos of Bronislaw Jawarski walking through the Orlando International Airport. We used facial recognition software, and all the main facial identifiers appear to be the same. It's at least a ninety-five percent match. Unless he has an identical twin brother, I'd say they're one and the same. The video we found came from Yemen."

"That's great but frightening news, Mike," Joe said. "I'll definitely have to pass this on now as a Homeland Security issue involving the Patriot Act. I'll call my rear admiral first and then Trinity. Did you hear about the bombing of two African American churches in Orlando during the last two days? I think it's a diversionary measure. They found chlorine gas on the premises after the bombing. That seems to be their calling card."

"Joe, as you know, I can't participate in-country, but I'll have my men and resources ready if you need me to participate outside international waters. You know the drill."

"I know the drill. This is going to weigh heavily on me during the wedding, but I have to let it go. I'd never be forgiven if I bowed out now for an investigation, especially since Julie knows I'll probably leave the Coast Guard when my time expires. I'll ask the rear admiral if Frank Cortez and his folks, along with Mark's men, could join forces in Orlando with Trinity and her team. This also could be an FBI call, but that would mean more time, which we may not have. Any more bombings and this will open up to national scrutiny, if it hasn't already."

"Well, just remember, I'm here if you need me."

"Thanks, Mike, it's appreciated."

"Joe, are you all right?" Julie asked when he hung up.

"I will be, but I have to call Jake and then Trinity and let her know that this will be a federal investigation, not just the murder of a police officer. Mike found video evidence of the escapee's involvement in Yemen. I promise to let it go after my calls. I won't let anything interfere with our wedding, Julie. I promise."

"Thank you, Joe. That means a lot to me, as you know. I only plan on getting married once, and it's a pretty big deal."

"I know and I appreciate that," Joe said. "But aren't we actually getting married twice?"

Julie didn't think that was as funny as he did.

"Sorry," he offered.

CHAPTER 17

Joe called Trinity back right after he spoke to his rear admiral.

"Trinity, my contact outside the country identified Jawarski in a video in Yemen. I called my boss, and I'll be seeing him first thing tomorrow. I have to go to Miami to ship Julie's wedding gown and stuff at the main UPS headquarters. I'll drive over to see Jake right afterward. Trinity, this makes this a Homeland Security issue and not just the murder of a police officer. I asked my rear admiral to put Frank Cortez in charge until we get back. He said he'd try, but the FBI may have jurisdiction at this point. If it does, I can't wiggle my way in if I'm in New York City getting married. Mark and I carry all three credentials, but Frank does not. He's strictly a Coast Guard guy. He's certainly qualified but has no standing at this point. I'll call you from the rear admiral's office when I get there. At that point, we should let your chief know exactly what to expect. I'll be home through Tuesday and then flying out of Miami with Julie and Tillie early Wednesday morning for the wedding."

❧❧❧

Joe dropped off the gown and Julie's wedding stuff along with Tillie's outfit and luggage. They'd get on the plane on Wednesday with very limited luggage. Each would have a carry-on bag and Joe would have his uniforms in a garment bag, just to be sure. He didn't even want to think about the ramifications if the rest of the UPS shipment didn't arrive on time. He headed over to Brickell and Coast Guard headquarters. After going through security, Joe met Rear Admiral Barnes in his conference room with Frank Cortez, Warren Anderson, Jeremy Lock, and Jean Gold—all Frank's security team who'd moved from the Port Canaveral Station to take over security in Miami for District Seven. Also included was Chief Petty Officer Michele Bower who took over all District Seven personnel from the forced-retired George Pagan. She was promoted to Warrant Officer with the move. Joe was quite pleased. Captain Bert Jennings, who'd been there before the shakeup of staff, was still second in command to Jake and still chief of staff.

Joe said hello to everyone, and Rear Admiral Jake Barnes took over the meeting. "Tell us what you have, Joe. I know you have to get back to pack for the wedding. Becky and I'll be there early Saturday morning. I get to fly up in a Navy jet. After thirty some odd years, it's about time I got a perk," he said and smiled.

"Nice," said Joe.

Joe went through everything he had, including his suspicions about the two church bombings. He told him the chief's plans and how Trinity was in charge up to this point, which would change with the new information leading to a Homeland Security issue. He told the assembled staff that she'd been assigned five detectives and ten patrol officers in police cars still looking for the van. Joe hadn't mentioned looking for the van near the two bombings. He'd hoped that Trinity and her crew would have thought of that themselves.

"Can I put Trinity and Cal Roberts on the phone, sir. Trinity said they'd be standing by for the call," Joe said.

"Sure, ring them up," said the rear admiral.

Now that they were on the phone, introductions were made, and Joe asked Trinity for a rundown. He deferred to her and didn't want it look like he was going over her head by asking the chief questions. His rear admiral could do that peer-to-peer but Joe was sensitive about this. It was her partner and she was the first female detective in charge of a major investigation. That was, up to now.

"Joe, we immediately looked at videos near both bombings. We saw a partial white van. Couldn't tell what kind but we did get a low picture near the bumper but it had mud on the license plate. We don't know if it was parked there and belonged there or was driven by the perps. We'll keep going until we find something."

"Get the partial number to Jack Forest," Joe told her. "He can do miracles with those plates." He summarized how they found the two Russians driving around Tillie's apartment in Key Largo. "We only had partial plates but Jack has a logarithm that could arbitrarily place numbers where they'd be missing and then attempt to find a similarly registered Ford Econoline van, especially in the greater Orlando area."

Chief Roberts came on. "Joe, that's great news. We could use a break right now. We don't want the FBI taking over, but we may have no choice. If you could be put in charge when you get back, that would be great."

Jake spoke up. "Cal, that's what we plan on doing but sometimes plans don't work out. We'll just have to wait and see. Everyone knows that Joe may be leaving the service when I do, so they may not want a so-called lame duck in charge. I'm just saying, not that it will happen that way, but it could certainly go that way, and we couldn't balk at it. We've got no control."

"I understand, Rear Admiral, but just do your best. That's all we ask."

"That we will do," said Jake.

Joe summarized where they were, what his expectations were while he was away, and what each in the room, other than the rear admiral, could be doing while he was gone. "When I get back, depending on the situation, I'll be glad to reenter the fray, so to speak."

Jake thanked him for coming and told Frank Cortez and his crew to be on call in case they were put in charge. If not, they should still head up toward Orlando and to be ready if called. "I'll be on the phone with my admiral, Homeland Security, and the FBI."

The meeting broke up and Joe headed to his new house. He was relieved that something would be going on during his absence, but he knew that if he said a word about it, Julie wouldn't be a happy camper. He was probably more afraid of Tillie's reaction than he was of Julie's. He'd tread lightly from here on out until after the honeymoon and they were home. Then he was back on duty and on call for whatever transpired. They'd had an agreement that she'd never interfere with his duties, even though he'd most likely be leaving in only a few more months.

⌘

The phone rang early Saturday morning. It was Trinity. "Joe, it's Trinity, Did I wake you?"

"No, Trinity. I had to get up to answer the phone anyway," he said with a chuckle.

"Funny. Very funny, Joe. I got another bombing but this was too close to home. They bombed my father's church last night, just about the same time as the others. They also killed someone this time."

"What happened?"

"The firemen and the bomb squad found a body in the rubble. It was Leon Jenkins, my father's only employee. He was in charge of maintenance, and he was an all-around handyman. He was fifty-six and had been with my father and mother the day they started the church. My parents are devastated."

"How did they find out who he was right away, and how did he die? Was it from the explosion, the fire or something else?" he asked.

"He wasn't near the explosion at the time nor was he burned. It appeared to the bomb squad that he died from inhaling something. I mentioned what you told me to the chief. I called him as soon as I heard, and he told them to check for chlorine gas exposure. They said that Leon's eyes, throat, and lungs looked like they were damaged. There was also a pungent, irritating odor coming from him that smelled almost like bleach. That's why they think he was exposed to chlorine gas. They took his body immediately to the Orlando Regional Medical Center's Level One Trauma Center. The chief asked them to immediately test for poisoning levels, even though he was determined to be dead by the EMTs."

"Trinity, this will only reconfirm what we already suspect. It's three bombings of African-American Christian churches in Orlando. Unfortunately, it was your father's church among the three. Homeland Security must keep this relatively quiet. Let the world think it's racially motivated and not a terrorist attack at this point, or you'll have worse panic on your hands than you do now. I believe these three bombings are a diversion for something even bigger coming down the road. We need to stop them now, Trinity. Put teams around every mosque in town and near all the African American Christian churches. Fifteen officers may not be enough, but Homeland Security will bring in everything they need. Unfortunately, Archie's death will be put on the back burner for now, unless you can get Jawarski under lock and key for premeditated murder. If you can do that, you may have first priority for trial. I'll ask the rear admiral to ask our Coast Guard attorneys for a definitive ruling. It may not matter. Homeland Security and the FBI trump almost everything else," Joe said. "I'll tell Julie, so expect a call from your friend. I'm so sorry for your loss. I'm sure Mr. Jenkins was your friend as well."

"He was. He was very loyal to my family for all these years. I have to get the people who did this. It can't fall to the wayside. It just can't, Joe."

"I'm here if you need me, at least through Tuesday, Trinity."

"Thanks, Joe."

Joe just shook his head. There was nothing he could do at this point but pray. Joe's mother, Veronica Traynor, always believed in the power of prayer. *I hope your listening from heaven, Mom.*

CHAPTER 18

Axmad and Hamzah left the safe house for a quiet meeting with the imam at the mosque that was less than a few miles away on Old Winter Garden Road. It was the first meeting for Axmad with the imam at the mosque. When he'd arrived in the country, they first met at the safe house and planned the bombings of the African American Christian Churches. Axmad had planned this wisely to divert attention from his arrival to a potential race war in downtown Orlando.

African American churches hadn't been burned in Orlando in decades. Now with African American officers on the force, Axmad was certain that these bombings would completely overtake the shooting of their fellow officers. Ferguson was a hot topic and would buy them the time they needed for their real intentions.

Hamzah had been a mosque member for the last few years, ever since he arrived. He'd tested all ten of the new mosques before settling down with this one. Imam Abu Malik was a youngish forty-one years old and, at times, displayed great disdain for the United States. Hamzah worked his way up to meeting the imam and, over time, became a close confidant. Hamzah appeared, to the imam, to be a genuine believer and was thought to be the son of a very rich man back in Chechnya. That came to fruition. Hamzah gave large donations to entrench himself into the fabric of the community. He was viewed as a philanthropist who had dedicated himself to the Islamic faith.

Unbeknownst to the community, he and the imam also took trips to the Cayman Islands on a private plane, coming back with a suitcase full of hundred-dollar bills. The imam believed that Axmad was Hamzah's relative and had been wiring money to Hamzah for this mosque for the last two years through a Cayman Island Bank. A million dollars in cash greatly influenced the imam's decision making, especially since half went directly to his support. Imam Malik was fully aware, at that point, that Axmad and Hamzah were supported by terrorists. He, himself, had been radicalized many years ago in a New York City mosque as a new twenty-five-year-old immigrant. When the heat got too hot after Nine/Eleven, he migrated to Orlando and had established this mosque with money supplied by his New York City brethren.

Axman and Hamzah entered the rear of the mosque and went directly to the imam's office. They quietly shook hands and started a conversation. Axmad knew that he had the imam exactly where he needed to be to supply complete cover for his operation in Orlando. He had an active cell ready to go at any time. They'd been recruited starting the day that Hamzah arrived. They'd been fully financially supported by Axmad and were given low-level jobs at a small furniture store right around the corner. They catered to the growing community by importing furniture, soft goods, and other home decor items that made them feel like they were back in the Middle East.

The cell consisted of ten men beside two other young men, just recruited at the mosque. The more educated ones became salesmen in the store. One was a bookkeeper, and four worked the delivery truck. Unlike American businesses, who worked off the books to hide income from the IRS, this small store reflected sales and income appropriate for a growing Islamic community who relied on the store for their own ethnic goods. The store grew without any advertising, except within its own community and close-knit neighborhood. Hamzah was an up and coming twenty-four-year-old businessman who gave jobs to his own community members.

He joined the local chamber of commerce and was highly thought of in his own Islamic community. No one would ever have guessed that he'd eventually attack the United States at one of its most prestigious military installations, the Naval Air Warfare Training System Division, right at the Central Florida Research Center.

"Axmad, when are you planning this attack and exactly where? The church bombings will only hold off the police investigators for so long before they figure out that it's a diversionary tactic," stated Imam Malik. "I don't believe that they'll give up so readily on the shooting and killing of one of their own police officers. Pitting black and white interests against each other can only go so far. Regardless of what you may believe, all ethnic citizens of the United States, regardless of what's happening now, want their children to grow up in a free society, whatever that brings. I'm not saying you're wrong, but don't underestimate the people. Far more want the United States to continue than those who don't. I hate this country and I do want to see it grow only under Islam, but I'm a realist."

Axmad had never been spoken to like this before. He'd not tolerate insubordination from anyone, even the imam. "I believe you give these infidels too much credit. They're so caught up in their own personal lives that they can't see what's happening around the world. They'll lose. It's inevitable," he said.

He was beside himself at this point.

"I'm sorry that I upset you, Axmad. Perhaps you're right," the imam said.

He was used to being in charge, but now felt very afraid of the two individuals sitting in front of him. What they were proposing was the mass killing of thousands employed at the naval facility.

" I thought about what we needed to do to attract the attention of the world. We need to let the United States and the world know that they're unsafe, as long as they don't follow Sharia Law. These infidels will cower once they see what we're capable of doing. We need to kill as many soldiers as we can to strike fear into the United States. Going after women and children only seems to hurt our message. Going after military bases right in the heart of the country will prove our superiority. Sitting on only forty acres in Orlando, at the University of Central Florida, is the Naval Support Activities Division or NSA for short. This will be our target."

He took a breath and leashed his temper. "There are about 1,000 scientists, engineers, contractors, and support personnel employed there. They spend over a billion dollars a year. NSA Orlando has approximately 120 active duty military personnel, and 2,200 civil service personnel serving on or near NSA Orlando. NSA Orlando also serves a community of 3,200 Joint Services Reserves, 48,000 military retirees, and 350 military families in the area of Central Florida. If we hit them here, we hit them hard and put a real dent in their ability to take us out. This division, besides training for air warfare, develops training systems for military personnel in undersea and surface operations.

"I believe that setting off our chlorine bombs throughout this facility would prove to the world that we cannot be stopped. I looked at the Central Florida Research Park, and I'll bet there are thousands working right in that area at any given time. That's where we will change the world. I'm picking the third shift when everyone is working diligently at their desks late into the night. The chlorine gas bombs we place there will be much bigger than what we've already done. Getting the gas into the air conditioning vents could prove fatal to everyone near where we set the bombs off. If we only get one bomb off, it will still kills hundreds, if not thousands, in minutes. This is where we will hit America, in its heart. Praise Be to Allah."

❧❦❧

Monday morning, the situation in Orlando was declared a national priority under Homeland Security and the FBI. Rear Admiral Barnes made his connections to his Admiral, Kenneth T. Hartnagle, in Washington who, in turn, notified the headquarters for both Homeland Security and the FBI and, specifically, through FBI Deputy Director, Stephen L. Sandberg, and Deputy Secretary of Homeland Security, Martin J. Sutherland. They all commented that what Joe Traynor predicted would happen looked most likely correct. They wanted to put Joe in charge of the operation, since he carried all three credentials but Joe was getting married. His partner, Mark Silva, would also be attending along with Rear Admiral Barnes, up in New York City. Joe would be back in Islamorada in late May. Rear Admiral Barnes presented Frank Cortez's credentials as the new director for security for the Seventh District. He stated that there was limited comparison to Joe, and even Mark, but he certainly would move the investigation forward until Joe and Mark got back. Jake also recommended a task force that included local FBI agents, Chief Roberts, and Trinity Hightower. "Joe Traynor thinks very highly of both Roberts and Hightower, and they should be fully involved."

Both deputies agreed, made a call to the chief, and said they'd call a meeting for that afternoon in Orlando.

Frank Cortez and his staff, including Warren Anderson, Investigator IV; Jeremy Lock, Detective; and Jean Gold, Coast Guard Military Police Officer would stay at the same hotel that Joe did previously. Jean would get her own room and the others would share. They'd keep a separate room set up for meetings. The FBI agents would select their own accommodations. They were always like that. They wanted to be alone. Jake had faith in his men but wanted the next few weeks to move quickly so Joe could be back and in charge. That was how much faith he had in Joe's abilities.

Everyone got to Orlando on time and met in Chief Robert's office. Joe was not leaving for New York City until Wednesday morning, so he was attending by phone as well as Mark up in Dania Beach. The head FBI agent attempted to run the meeting but Frank Cortez had been around the block before. He stepped in and showed the FBI agent the letter from Washington appointing him as the temporary leader of the task force until Joe Traynor assumed the reigns. On speakerphone, Frank asked Joe to summarize everything that had happened to date.

Joe mentioned that the Coast Guard was doing clandestine work up in Virginia but wouldn't discuss it with the group. Enough said. Frank knew exactly what was going on. Joe would also talk to Trinity after the meeting. He'd called her prior to the meeting to discuss the situation and told her how to act in front of the FBI. He'd had the same discussion with Chief Roberts.

They were still looking for the white Econoline van. Trinity was given ten more street officers to go with the ten already in police cars and five detectives. She understood the significance of the issues. She'd be tracing down all the vans that were flagged as being close to the mosques and following up with the two vans owned by the mosques. She'd have another officer follow up on the commercial vans until something hit. There were a lot of vans that had sole owners but were commercial by nature and included plumbers, electricians, and other small businesses, including florists and pizza delivery vans.

She'd get as much video from businesses around the bombed out churches as she could and send the feeds to Jack Forest. He'd run all the videos simultaneously to see if a pattern of movement could be picked up. Trinity didn't bring up the fact that Joe thought that the church bombings were a diversion and not the actual target.

Joe also told her, in the separate phone call after the meeting, to make a personal visit to Marshall Tillman at Hollywood Studios. He didn't want him finding out what was going on at the last minute. He wanted Tillman to keep it quiet for a while and start spreading the word around that there might be terrorists in the area and to do double duty on the security front. Joe wasn't sold on any problems with the major theme parks because of their intense security measures but he didn't want to take any chances. He knew how much security there actually was in all the parks from their meeting a while ago with Julie being offered a movie contract for her first book, *Conch Town Girl*.

"Joe, I know I won't make your New York City wedding at Saint Patrick's Cathedral, but I want you to know I'm thinking of both you and Julie on your wedding day. I'll definitely be there for the June wedding in Key Largo. Until we see you when you get back from your honeymoon, please be safe. Don't worry about our investigation. Hopefully, nothing major will happen when you're not here and, if it does, we have it covered. Best wishes," she said.

Joe thanked her. "I'll email you, step by step, what I want you to do while I'm gone, along with anything else you think of. I most definitely want you to contact Marshall Tillman. I'd never forgive myself if anything happened at a theme park. I've read a lot about the Chechens, and their real targets across the world are military personnel and to kill as many soldiers as they can. As soon as I get back, I'll put a chart together of every military installation in the greater Orlando area. This is also a destination point for re-tired military veterans and their families. It is also a not-so-well-kept secret that a lot of military research is done in the Orlando area only miles away from all the major theme parks. If there is an attack on a military base, it could affect tourism in the Orlando area for years to come."

CHAPTER 19

It was early Tuesday morning.

"Mr. Tillman, this is Detective Trinity Hightower of the Major Crimes Division of the Orlando Police Department. Joe Traynor asked me to call you and set up a meeting to discuss something with you."

"Yes, Trinity. I remember you very well. You and Archie Higgins were assigned to Joe and Julie when Julie came up for her meeting with the movie people from our Burbank office. I'm very sorry to hear about Detective Higgins. That must have been quite a shock to you and your fellow officers. Does Joe's request have anything to do with that incident?"

`"In a way it does. I really don't want to discuss anything over the phone. Is there a time, sooner rather than later, that we can meet, preferably today?"

"That important, huh?"

"Yes, sir. It is," said Trinity. "I'll be coming alone for the meeting, sir. You can take that to mean that this is under the radar and coming from Joe directly."

"Joe and Julie are getting married next weekend, Saturday, May twenty-third, right? I know that Claire Murphy asked for time off to go to the New York City wedding with her husband, Brian. Saint Patrick's Cathedral, right?"

"Yes, sir. The wedding is at noon on May twenty-third. Joe and Julie will be in New York on this Wednesday. His rear admiral and Mark Silva and his family and Jack Forest, whom you probably don't know, will also be attending. Can I meet you at your office at 1:00 p.m. today, sir?"

"Yes, that's fine. I'll have lunch ready for you when you get here. You know that my office is in the same building where you stayed when you were shadowing Joe and Julie?"

"Yes, I know exactly where to go. I'll be pulling up in an undercover white Ford Taurus. That's undercover if anyone believes that an unmarked Ford Police Interceptor, that looks like a Ford Taurus, is undercover. Can you let the guards know that I'll be there?"

"Sure, no problem."

"Thanks. I'll see you then," she said.

They hung up.

Trinity had a series of meetings with her detectives and the two police officer teams, ten assigned to cars and ten assigned to the street. Each of the ten would be assigned to the cars and dropped off to knock on doors to look for white vans that popped up on the report. They would be backed up by the assigned officers in the cars and one detective for every two cars assigned. They had hoped to run down all the vans near the mosques. Trinity would handle the two actually owned by two separate mosques. One was in the north end near the county line and she would do that first. She would concentrate on the one owned by the mosque in the city near the Florida Mall. After talking to Joe and clearing it with Chief Roberts, she was going to let out the picture of the two dead terrorists and not Jawarski/Khan.

It was inevitable that some news reporters would obtain their pictures, and God knew what they would do with them. At least if someone came forward and said they saw the two individuals, it could start the ball rolling. Joe told her that, under no circumstances, was she to release the picture of Jawarski because they wanted him to think he got away clean. It was a long shot at best, but worth a try for the time being. The release would simply state that the two individuals were killed in a gun battle in the Orlando International Airport and the police wanted to see if the public could identify either one of the two dead individuals. Nothing was to be released about their ties to terrorists.

഍ഌഉ

Trinity arrived at Hollywood Studios a few minutes early and the guard, who was waiting for her, raised the gate and let her go to the administration building and park in a visitor's spot. She walked into the building and was greeted by Claire Murphy, Marshall Tillman's administrative assistant. Claire met Trinity at the same time that Marshall did when they came for Julie's meeting. Trinity knew that Claire was Tom Jones's daughter. Tom was Joe's mentor and was murdered in Orlando.

"Trinity, it's good to see you again," said Claire.

"You, too. When are you going to the wedding?"

"We will be flying into JFK around noon on Friday. There's a direct flight back and forth. Sometimes you can take advantage of Walt Disney World and Universal Studios being right here. You have a meeting with Marshall, yes?"

"Yes, I do. Joe asked me to speak with him concerning a potential dangerous situation. I can't talk about it other than to Marshall directly."

"Well, let's not wait. Please follow me up to his office. He's at his desk and he ordered lunch for both of you. I hope sandwiches are okay with you?"

"Absolutely. Most of the time, I never get a chance to eat. This is a treat," Trinity said.

They walked into Marshall's office, and he got up from his desk to greet Trinity. "Good afternoon Trinity. It's great to see you again. I have lunch ready. Why don't we eat and then go outside where it's nice and quiet with no possible interruptions."

"Sounds good. Claire, thanks for seeing me to his office.

It was good seeing you again. You have to tell me how the wedding went. Here's my cell number. You have to call me and let me know every detail. I was supposed to go but I'm tied up here. I'll be going to the June wedding in Key Largo instead."

"I won't hold back any details, and I'll take plenty of pictures to share with you."

Claire closed and locked Marshall's office. He and Trinity went into his conference room and ate in silence. They did a little chitchat during the meal but both were busy, obviously, and wanted to finish lunch and go outside for their discussion. Marshall thought that if Joe wanted this meeting to happen, it must be very important.

"Let's walk down to the pocket park around the corner," Marshal said after they finished eating.

Trinity turned to Marshall. "You must keep this confidential and only share with your other park administrators and the heads of each security unit. Joe trusts you, or I wouldn't be here. None of us want a tragedy to happen if it can be prevented. I also cleared it with Chief Roberts, who knows that I am talking to you. The deputies in charge of both the FBI and Homeland Security do not know I am talking to you. I hope that is very clear?"

"Crystal."

"You must know Joe by now. You met with him previously. He is a straight shooter and will not allow anything to happen if he has anything to say about it. What I am about to tell you has been turned over to the FBI and Homeland Security. However, it will be administered by one of Joe's closest Coast Guard allies, Frank Cortez, until Joe gets back from his honeymoon. In the meantime, there is a task force put together to keep a lid on this and to hopefully bring it to a conclusion before Joe gets back.

"Now, you have my attention," Marshall said. "What the hell is going on?"

"Because of Joe's conclusions, we have discovered there are Chechens in Orlando at this very moment. The two identified individuals, who were killed in the airport after killing Archie, are Chechen nationals. The person who escaped was a naturalized Polish citizen from Chechnya as well. He was seen with terrorists in Yemen last year. We have a picture that Joe secured through his sources. We also believe that the three African American church bombings were done as a diversionary tactic to cause trouble between the races here in Orlando. Trust me, it's working, and we are unable to say what we believe really happened and why. We are looking for the escaped Polish citizen, who is really a Chechen by birth. He was picked up in a white Econoline van but we were unable to identify the license plate. We are working through the registration process for all those kinds of vans in the greater Orlando area. However, Joe wanted you to know so you could take special precautions here at your park in case you are a target and please pass it on to the others. He doesn't believe that Chechens would land in Orlando unless they specifically wanted to target some significant site in Orlando. We have no specific knowledge of any attack or plans for an attack but Joe was emphatic that if he was in their shoes, and he has done extensive research on the Chechens, that their targets would be military installations and not theme parks, but you never know and that's why I am here"

"You never know," Marshall agreed. "That's a lot to digest but we continually prepare for an event like what you are talking about. It's never one-hundred percent preventable, but we have our own undercover staff throughout the parks looking for suspicious individuals on a twenty-four/seven basis, seven days a week. We are vigilant in that pursuit. It has not escaped us that anything can happen at any time and Joe is absolutely right to let us know. He is also probably right that if they plan an attack it will be to kill military personnel. That has been their mission in the past. Trust me, we are on top of these issues every waking moment. We don't want to panic the public, but it's better to know and keep our eyes open at all times. I'll call an emergency meeting of all the heads of security at all the parks and the administrators."

Trinity thanked Marshall, walked out of the office, and said goodbye to Claire. Trinity wondered how anyone could do such terrible things to totally innocent people. Vigilance was the name of the game, and Joe was right. This was the right place to go immediately. He didn't care what the FBI or Homeland Security thought about his reaching out. Trinity knew through her and Joe's experience that they never moved quick enough to prevent anything, but were always there taking over after it happened. She hoped this would not be the case here. She was now only a regular member of the task force but she was assured by Joe that when, and if, he got back on time, her role would expand. He told her he needed her. That was good enough for her.

She headed back to the office and called Joe on the way. He wished her well and she did the same. She hoped the next two weeks went smoothly and that nothing more would happen on her watch. It might not officially be her watch, as of now, but she felt an obligation to help find Archie's murderer and stop anything else from happening. It was a big challenge.

CHAPTER 20

Julie, Joe, and Tillie arrived at JFK right on time, early Wednesday afternoon. As they picked up their bags from the baggage claim, Julie noticed a young man standing by the luggage carousel holding a sign that said *MS. CHAPMAN*.

Joe grabbed the bags coming off the track and placed each one, side by side, next to Tillie. As he was doing that, Julie went over to the young man. "Are you waiting for Julie Chapman?"

"Yes. I'm supposed to meet a Ms. Julie Chapman, her fiancé, and her grandmother. Are you Ms. Chapman from Key Largo?"

"Yes, I am." She decided not to go into the move to a new house in Tavernier.

"Your limousine is double-parked right outside these doors. So we'd best hurry so that the driver doesn't get asked to move by the police. May I take a few of your bags, miss?"

"Of course. Most of our luggage was forwarded to the apartment already," she said.

He nodded, grabbed two bags next to Tillie, and waved the three of them to the door. He opened it and nodded toward the waiting town car. Julie noticed that it was the same driver that she and Joe had when he was here after his father's surgery.

She said hello and the driver was flattered that she remembered him.

The young man opened the trunk, carefully placed the luggage in, and then hopped into the front passenger seat, after closing the door for Julie and Tillie. Joe got in the back on the other side.

"This ride will take about forty-five minutes, door to door," the driver said. "In the refrigerator, there are drinks and snacks, courtesy of your publisher, Sarah Atwood. She also said to tell you that the apartment's refrigerator is fully stocked, and she said to tell Joe she bought him a case of Sam Adams' Oktoberfest."

"I love her already," Joe said as he smiled at Julie and Tillie and thanked the driver and the young man for picking them up.

He grabbed a few sodas, handed the drinks to Julie and Tillie, opened a bag of chips, and passed it around. The bag of peanuts and the four-ounce drink on the plane hadn't quite done the trick.

They pulled up out in front of the apartment about an hour later. Traffic coming into New York City was a little heavier than usual. The Yankees were home that night, playing Baltimore to end a three game series. Sam the doorman greeted them as they went through the door. The young man unpacked the trunk and placed the bags inside the opened doors.

All three thanked the driver and his assistant and asked if they'd be driving them for the wedding. They said yes, but Sarah had a special surprise that they couldn't tell them right now.

The driver smiled. "You'll be surprised when we come to get you for the wedding on Saturday, though."

"I can hardly wait," Julie said. "Thanks for not spilling the beans."

"Sam, you remember my fiancé, Joe Traynor?

"Yes, ma'am, I met him when he was here with you before."

"And I'd like to introduce you to my grandmother, Tillie Carpenter. She's my matron of honor."

"That so nice," he said and meant it. Tillie wasn't that much older than Sam. "Mrs. Carpenter, it is an honor to meet you. I hope you enjoy your stay and, especially, I hope you enjoy the wedding. This is supposed to be the best weekend of the spring this year in the city. It's Lieutenant Joseph Traynor now, is it not, sir?"

"How did you know?" Joe asked.

Sam laughed. "I can't say, sir. It's under the doorman's code of honor. My lips are sealed, sir, as it may."

Joe smiled and looked at Julie as if to say, "How the hell did he know that?"

She returned the smile. "I told Sarah and she must have taken it from there."

They made it up to the apartment on the tenth floor, the same one Julie used previously. The luggage was placed in the living room to be separated later. Sitting in the corner of the room were all the UPS packages sent from Key Largo on the Friday before. All were accounted for, and Sam handled the delivery, signing off on each package.

Julie immediately went to the large box holding her wedding gown and veil, opened it, and looked very pleased. "It's in perfect shape, Joe. I could care less about the rest of my stuff. I'm now a happy camper."

She and Tillie, together, unfolded the items and placed both on special velvet hangers that were packed with the gown. They hung it up in the bedroom that would be used by Julie. Tillie got the other room and Joe would sleep on the couch tonight and Thursday, in deference to Tillie. He'd move to the Waldorf Astoria on Friday and meet his friends who would be arriving throughout the afternoon and staying at the same hotel.

"Ladies, if you don't mind, let's see what in the refrigerator." He looked. There were several cold bottles of beer on the top shelf and the rest of the case on the floor near the sink. There was a fruit plate, a vegetable platter, and a platter of cut up sub sandwiches for their lunch. Joe was in awe. Julie smiled and shook her head.

Just then, the phone rang. It was Sam. "You have a very special guest coming up to the apartment Ms. Chapman."

There was a knock on the door and Joe opened it. It was Sarah Atwood, Julie's publisher. "I wanted to greet you upon your arrival and meet Mrs. Carpenter," Sarah said. She walked into the room, gave Julie a hug, and shook Tillie's hand. She smiled and said hello to Joe.

"Thank you. Thank you," Julie said. "Thank you for everything you've done for us. I just can't thank you enough."

Joe and Tillie nodded in agreement.

"Can I join you for lunch? I've one hour before my next meeting at our offices."

They sat at the kitchen table and Tillie was amazed at how well respected Julie was in the eyes of her publisher.

"I think that having Tillie, as the matron of honor is one of the nicest things I've ever heard of," Sarah told them.

"Julie's good friend, Maddy Malone, will be the maid of honor," Tillie said, "with me as the matron, as well, and both Joe's brother, Pete, and his best friend, Mark Silva will share best man duties.

"All my items that were shipped arrived safely and Sam was wonderful," Julie told her.

"I couldn't wait for Saturday," Sarah said. "My husband, Bennett, and I are looking forward to a wonderful afternoon that day."

Just about an hour later, Sarah excused herself and said she had to run. She gave all three hugs and left for her meeting.

"What a wonderful person," Tillie said.

"None of this would have happened if she wasn't my publisher," Julie said. "Goes to show that your first choice is usually the best. Between Joe's father getting the bishop of Albany and the cardinal to perform the wedding, along with my own pastor, is more than I could have ever wished for."

They unpacked and had dinner early at Luigi's around the corner. Julie wanted to make sure everything was set for the rehearsal dinner Friday night. The hostess greeted them at the door and had all the staff come over to greet Julie and be introduced to her grandmother. The chef and owner walked out and gave Julie a hug as well. Tillie was absolutely amazed at the friends that Julie had made during the short time she was here previously. She simply shook her head and smiled.

They got home and went to bed early. Everyone was exhausted. Joe sat on the couch, had a few beers, watched Jimmy Fallon for his monologue, and fell sound asleep. They'd a lot to do on Thursday. They had to get the wedding license from city hall in the morning at an appointment set up by Sarah. Then Julie had a meeting at Sarah's office to hand in her second book, *The Middle Years*.

ↂↄↂ

The driver picked them up early Thursday morning and headed to city hall. They waltzed in and got their wedding license. They went to Saint Patrick's Cathedral and dropped it off at the rectory. They didn't need to see the Cardinal. The priest in charge of weddings took the license and placed it in their wedding folder. Everything was set for noon on Saturday.

"Bishop Harold Humphries will be coming in late Friday afternoon and he said he'd join us for the rehearsal dinner at Luigi's," the priest said.

He was one of Joe's father's best friends growing up, and they'd remained friends for almost sixty years. They had time so Tillie walked around and toured the cathedral. She was quite impressed by its long history. Joe had bought her a pair of rosary beads when he was here with Julie. She wanted some postcards to send her friends and an official 2015 Catholic Missal from Saint Patrick's Cathedral. She got her prized possessions, and they headed to Julie's publisher's offices. She had her manuscript with her, and she wanted to officially hand it personally to Sarah.

They arrived around 1:00 p.m. and walked into headquarters. The receptionist told them that Ms. Atwood would be with them momentarily. Sarah came out of her office, walked to the reception area, and asked Julie, Joe, and Tillie to step into the conference room. Assembled was her entire staff, who clapped as they walked into the room. Julie was blushing from ear to ear. Sarah presented her and Joe with a wedding gift, beautifully wrapped. Sarah said that if Julie opened it, they'd have it shipped to their new home in Tavernier. The gift was a beautiful sterling silver place setting for eight. Julie stared in amazement as she unwrapped the gift. Both her and Tillie had tears in their eyes. Joe stood in the corner. His eyes started to glisten as well. He turned and used his index finger to quickly brush his eyelids, hoping that no one would see him.

"Sarah," Julie said, and then named each of the staff members individually, "I thank you from the bottom of my heart. If you read my book, you'd know that we aren't use to people giving Tillie and me anything. Hopefully, as we move forward together, I'll be able to help others as well. I'm so pleased that I've such good friends in New York City. I'd have never dreamed this in a million years."

Everyone was teary eyed and Sarah handed Tillie and Julie napkins. "Joe?"

He waved a hand. "No, I'm good,"

"Let's cut the cake," Sarah suggested. "It's not wedding cake. It's more of a pre-wedding cake but it looks absolutely delicious."

All at once, the cake was cut and handed out. Sodas were poured and passed around the room. They all toasted Julie and Joe.

"Oh, by the way, here's my new manuscript before I forget it," she said.

Everyone laughed.

They spent the rest of the day walking around town. Tillie bought a few souvenirs. They were near the Empire State Building and they went to the top so Tillie could use her new camera that she bought for the wedding. "I haven't had this much fun in years, guys," she said.

ↁↂↁ

Everyone invited to the wedding made it in by late Friday afternoon. They were all invited to the wedding rehearsal but most thought it was best to keep it as intimate as they could and only those actually in the wedding went to the church and to Luigi's afterward. The bishop went through the ceremony procedures and the cardinal stopped by to shake Julie and Joe's hands and to introduce himself to the wedding party attending the rehearsal. Later that evening after they got back to the apartment, Joe said goodbye and headed for the Waldorf Astoria. His friends were meeting him in the bar, and they promised to get him back to his room at a decent hour. Joe remembered how they all showed up for Mark's fortieth birthday party at the Hard Rock in Fort Lauderdale, a while ago. Joe could still remember the pounding headache attached to a very good time. This time, it was his big moment and he vowed not to screw it up.

Back at the apartment, Julie had called the Waldorf Astoria and the room was booked and ready for thirty-one guests for a very expensive $300.00 a plate wedding brunch. New York City was not cheap and as Joe's father said, "It only costs a little more to go first class."

Joe didn't think his father knew what the hell he was talking about. After all, $10,000.00 for a luncheon wasn't "a little more to go first class." It was a hell of a lot more.

Julie and Tillie went through the guest list. Everyone was in town and attending the wedding. There was Joe, Julie and Tillie; Joe's father, John, his brother, Pete, and

Pete's girlfriend, Tanya. Mark, Louise, Jennifer, and MJ were here. Maddy Malone and her fiancé, Kevin White arrived on time. Joan and Jeff Talbot and their daughter, Lucy, were also here. Joan and Jeff would walk Julie down the aisle and Lucy, who was like Julie's little sister, was also in the wedding. The entire wedding party, including Bishop Humphries, were all here. Father Schmidt from Saint Justin Martyr's Church in Key Largo was also here.

Jack Forest arrived from Virginia. Brian and Claire Murphy, Tom Jones's daughter and son-in-law were here. His parents were watching their kids back in Orlando. Unfortunately, Trinity Hightower and her boyfriend couldn't make it because of the situation in Orlando but she'd said she'd be there for the June ceremony in Key Largo.

Maddy's father and mother arrived. Dan Simmons and his girlfriend, Samantha, took the train down from Albany. Johnathon Mills and his wife, Francine, went on the train with Dan and would return the same way. Rear Admiral, Jake Barnes and his wife, Becky, would arrive early Saturday morning by navy jet to LaGuardia. Jane Swanson had to come alone because her husband Nick Snyder was on call at the hospital. Julie's dean, Gerald Spaulding, from Brown University, and his wife, Maureen, were friends with Sarah and Bennett Atwood and they'd be staying with them and arriving at the wedding together. Father Schmidt would stay at Saint Patrick's rectory and he'd come to the reception at Luigi's as well. The cardinal would only be at the wedding itself and would drop in at the wedding reception at the Waldorf Astoria. His duties, as Cardinal of the Archdiocese of New York were overwhelming. He had three other events that day. He couldn't be busier if he was running for President of the United States. His favorable rating was higher than the president's anyway, Julie thought.

She and Tillie closed their notes and went to bed. Tomorrow would be the most important day of Julie's life. She hoped Joe felt the same. She knew he did.

CHAPTER 21

Joe got up at 6:00 a.m. It was Saturday morning and he couldn't sleep. They didn't stay late at the bar last night, but he just tossed and turned all night long. They stayed at the hotel, which was a very smart thing to do in New York City. Sir Harry's was named for a legendary explorer. The hotel website stated that the bar "was a clubby and companionable Manhattan mainstay where friends unwind with premium libations such as the in-house invented Rob Roy or Waldorf Sunset. Located just off the main lobby, the lounge offers traditional club ambiance with an elegant bar and seating around checkerboard tables."

Around 10:00 p.m., all the guys attending the wedding, or who were actually in the wedding, showed up. They'd just gotten back from the rehearsal dinner. Julie went to the apartment with her bridal party and with the other women guests, who came from the hotel, whom were invited for a 9:00 p.m. get together.

At the hotel, Jeff, Mark, Jack, Dan, Pete, Maddy's father Art, Johnathon, Brian Murphy, and Joe's father John, along with Bishop Humphries and Father Schmidt, all showed up as planned. They drank until midnight, and then they gradually broke up around 1:00 a.m. Having a bishop and the parish priest drinking with them kept them in check. However, both clergymen could hold their own as the guys found out.

I've been worse, Joe thought.

Actually, he was quite pleased with himself. He even had bar snacks and a sandwich before heading up to his room. No Oktoberfest on tap but he'd had plenty of bottles, one after another, shoved at him by his friends and family.

Julie got back from the rehearsal dinner to the apartment around 9:00 p.m. Waiting for her in the lobby were the women wedding guests not part of the bridal party. Sitting in the lobby were Pete's girlfriend Tanya, Claire Murphy, Maddy's mother Marilyn, Jane Swanson, Dan Simmons' girlfriend Samantha, and Francine Mills. The hotel gave them a car and driver to get to the apartment. The rear admiral's wife Becky wouldn't be in until the morning.

Sam held the door open for Julie as she walked into the lobby with Tillie, Louise, her children, Maddy Malone, Lucy and Joan Talbot. As they entered the apartment, Sarah and Maureen Spaulding, the dean's wife, were already there. It was as close as Julie would get to a bachelorette party. Sarah had the entire party catered. Everyone left around 11:00 p.m. except for Julie and Tillie. The bridal party would be back at 9:00 a.m. for pictures and the ride to the church in the limousine.

෨෩෨෩

All the women in the bridal party showed up at 9:00 a.m. Sarah's limousine picked them up at the hotel. They didn't need two vehicles, one from the hotel and Sarah's. The videographer and the photographer showed up at 10:00 a.m. after the ladies were almost dressed. They took group photos and photos of just Julie and her grandmother, alone. MJ started to get fussy. After all, he was the only "guy" at the apartment. He was the ring bearer and his sister, although older, would serve as the flower girl. Both were in the wedding and had to be in the pictures, according to both their mother, Louise, and Julie. MJ didn't have to get ready until the photographer needed him. He sat around in jeans and watched TV, eating fruity pebbles and drinking orange juice. They were set around 11:00 a.m., all the pictures were completed, and Julie was ready to leave. She was not used to such fussing.

They went down to get in the limousine that brought the ladies from the hotel but sitting in its place was a brand new Rolls Royce, ordered by Sarah for the trip to Saint Patrick's Cathedral. Julie was shocked. The wedding party looked around at each other to say, "Wow, what class."

Julie thought it was a little over the top but there were no complaints. It took almost a half an hour in traffic to get to the cathedral, and they parked right out front at the steps of Saint Patrick's. She'd enter the front of the cathedral around twenty minutes to noon. They'd have pictures taken of the ladies at various stages upon entering the church. The photographer excused himself and went back to wait for the bridegroom and his groomsmen.

౭౩౭౩

One of the reasons why they picked the Waldorf Astoria Hotel was that, not only was it one of the finest in the world, but it was close to the cathedral. Joe and the guys, after meeting in the lobby at 11:00 a.m., would go out the front door of the hotel, start down Park Avenue for a block, turn left onto East Fifty-First Street, and then left onto Fifth Avenue, and they were there. It was two blocks door to door. After the wedding—depending on the weather, and it was a beautiful day—they planned on walking back to the hotel, hand in hand followed by the wedding guests. Joe thought that would be a nice touch. They arrived and immediately went to the rear of the church, off to the side of the altar in an alcove where the groom and his ushers would wait until the music began. Joe, Mark, and Jack were in full Coast Guard officer dress uniforms.

The photographer took their pictures and went back to

the front of the church to watch the bride go down the aisle.

At precisely noon, Julie and her bridal party stood in line. The wedding guests were already seated in the very front of the cathedral, equally on both sides of the aisle. Father Schmidt, Bishop Humphries, and Cardinal Reagan were waiting at the foot of the altar. Joe and his two best men, Mark and Peter, were waiting on the right side of the altar. The "Wedding March, Canon in D" started.

Leading the procession were the two bridesmaids, Lucy Talbot and Louise Silva, followed by Jack Forest, a groomsman, and then Jennifer Silva as the flower girl and MJ Silva as the ring bearer together. Following them, Maddy Malone as maid of honor and Julie's grandmother, Tillie, walked together down the aisle. Both Joan and Jeff Talbot accompanied Julie. Both would be giving Julie away to Joe at the altar. Everyone turned and marveled at how beautiful she was.

Julie had chosen an empire-waist bridal gown. It was a classic gown design with the empire waist cinched just below the bust line. It was considered a timeless dress with a skirt beginning close to the ribcage. This dress featured a straight versus full skirt for a slender, streamlined silhouette. The empire-waist dress was popular among women who wanted to capture a bit of the old-world style that was reminiscent of romantic fairy tales. When choosing the dress, Julie believed that this was her fairy tale come true. Even though she was being married at Saint Patrick's Cathedral in New York City, she also wanted to emphasize her tenth generation Conch background. Her lineage went back to the time of the birth of the United States. Walking down the aisle with people she loved to be married to the man she'd always loved was her dream come true and the happiest moment of her life.

Joan and Jeff Talbot bowed to the clergy and handed Julie to Joe. They both turned to face the altar, hand in hand. Joe was more nervous than Julie. She was as calm as he was nervous.

She smiled at him. "What're you doing the rest of your life, Joe?"

The gathered guests picked up on the inside joke and laughed.

"Hopefully, I'll be with you," Joe said, and he meant it.

Catholic weddings were highly traditional and followed a set standard, rarely deviating from the religious customs. The ceremony consisted of biblical readings, a sermon, the exchange of vows and rings, and the Prayer of the Faithful, followed by additional prayers. The ceremony always took place within the church—never outdoors. It was considered a public event, and the entire Catholic community was encouraged to participate in the liturgy. A very important element of a Catholic wedding ceremony was the Sacrament of Matrimony, which Catholics believed was a route toward God's grace.

After the processional, the official ceremony began with a greeting by the priest to the bride and groom and their guests. The priest's greeting, or in this case greetings by a priest, a bishop, and a cardinal, was followed by prayers, readings from the Old and New Testament, a psalm, the "hallelujah," and a gospel reading. Tillie, Maddy, Pete, and Mark all read from the scriptures.

All three clergymen gave a sermon, which contained personal references to the bride and groom. Julie's priest, Father Schmidt, went on a little longer than the others, praising Julie and her grandmother. The bishop commented on how lucky Joe was to be marrying such a beautiful young woman, especially since he knew him as a kid growing up in Troy. "You did good, Joe," he said.

The cardinal simply said, "Joe and Julie, thank you for continuing your Catholic faith in this way. Please continue to do so in your long journey together."

Both the videographer and the photographer were well placed to capture these moments. Joe and Julie seemed to be oblivious to their movements around the ceremony.

Finally, Joe and Julie turned to each other. The cardinal,

then the bishop, and the priest all said, "Julie Chapman and Joseph Traynor have you come here freely and without reservation to give yourselves to each other in marriage?"

They both answered together, "Yes."

"Will you honor each other as man and wife for the rest of your lives?"

"Yes."

"Will you accept children lovingly from God and bring them up according to the law of Christ and his Church?"

"Yes," they answered.

"Since it is your intention to enter into marriage, join your right hands and declare your consent before God and his Church."

"I, Joseph Traynor, take you, Julie Chapman, to be my wife. I promise to be true to you in good times and in bad, in sickness and in health. I will love you and honor you all the days of my life."

"I, Julie Chapman, take you, Joseph Traynor, to be my husband. I promise to be true to you in good times and in bad, in sickness and in health. I will love you and honor you all the days of my life."

The cardinal, bishop and priest, together, blessed their rings and then Joe and Julie declared their consent.

Joe placed the wedding ring on Julie's ring finger "Julie, take this ring as a sign of my love and fidelity. In the name of the Father, and of the Son, and of the Holy Spirit."

Julie followed, placing the wedding ring on Joe's ring finger. "Joe, take this ring as a sign of my love and fidelity. In the name of the Father, and of the Son, and of the Holy Spirit."

The General Intercessions, called Prayers of the Faithful, followed, and then, since the sacrament of marriage was being celebrated within Mass, they began the Liturgy of the Eucharist. The congregation, including the bridal party and anyone else in the church, received Holy Communion. To conclude the Mass, the priest issued a final blessing and then Father Schmidt said, "Joe, you may kiss the bride."

With that, the Mass was ended. "Go in peace," the cardinal said.

The assembled congregation said, "Thanks be to God."

Then the recessional started and "Ode to Joy" began. Joe and Julie, arm-in-arm, walked together as man and wife out of Saint Patrick's Cathedral. The assembled guests and church visitors followed them. Joe and Julie and the bridal party formed a line at the front steps of the cathedral. They kissed, hugged, and thanked everyone coming through the line, including ordinary church visitors. After twenty minutes, they went back into the church for formal pictures. Then everyone, all thirty-one guests, also entered the altar area and were photographed as one big family. The videographer captured not only the pictures but the words coming from the guests as well. "What a wonderful, thoughtful wedding" was heard.

Joe turned to Julie. "Could we have a few special pictures with Rear Admiral Barnes?"

"Of course.

Joe also wanted a picture of him with Mark, Jack, and the rear admiral in full military dress. He also got pictures of the cardinal, the bishop, Julie, and with Tillie and Father Schmidt. Joe got a very special picture of his father, John, with his close friend Bishop Humphries with his brother, Pete, and a second picture that included Tanya, Julie, and Tillie as well.

For hating picture taking, Joe felt good about these. Those pictures would all hang in their new home in Tavernier. Joe also got a separate picture of the rear admiral and his wife, Becky. He would have that framed and sent to them as his present to them.

To everyone's surprise, except for the guests', Joe and Julie walked out of the cathedral, down the stairs, and started walking, hand in hand, to their reception at the Waldorf Astoria, two blocks away. Maddy held Julie's train all the way to the hotel. New Yorkers were shocked and delighted at the scene happening in front of them.

It was truly an "Ode to Joy" moment.

They walked into the lobby of the hotel and everyone there, including staff and guests, began to applaud. More pictures were taken in the lobby. It was as if thirty-one people completely took over the hotel, and no one seemed to mind. They walked back to their party room. The guests were now seated and the band began "Here Comes the Bride" for the first time today. "Ladies and gentlemen, I give you Mr. and Mrs. Joseph Traynor. How about a big round of applause for Joe and Julie," the bandleader said.

They stopped and gave each other a big hug and kiss, to the delight of everyone in attendance. They walked to their table and someone started tinkling the glasses for another kiss. They complied. Joe wished that his mother could have been here for this. She would have been happy and very proud that he married Julie. He thought that Julie's mother would be looking down on her today as well. Annie Chapman missed a lot. Tillie did a remarkable job in raising her only granddaughter.

After Julie and Joe's first dance together, to Joe's favorite song by Van Morrison "Have I told You Lately That I Love You," Joe danced with Tillie and Julie danced with Joe's father, John. There wasn't a dry eye in the room.

CHAPTER 22

The wedding reception, as small as it was with only thirty-one guests, was a great success. The band played right up to 5:45 p.m. and Julie and Joe had one last dance before they shut down. They'd gone to everyone individually and thanked each for coming all that way to their wedding. Everyone said they wouldn't have missed it for the world and were honored to be one of the select few in attendance. There were only a handful of actual wedding gifts and they were manageable. The event manager had the few gifts placed in their honeymoon suite.

Julie had several envelopes that obviously had money or checks inside. She had a special handbag that Tillie had given her just for that purpose. They'd open each in their room later on. It was near 6:30 p.m. by the time everyone said their goodbyes. All but the Atwoods and Spauldings were staying at the hotel. Many set plans to meet up later in the evening for a drink or a light dinner. The buffet set up by the Waldorf Astoria staff was exquisite with something for everyone. Julie cut the cake made by the pastry chef from the hotel and everyone had ample. The staff wrapped up the few remaining pieces and took that to their room as well.

Both were exhausted and overwhelmed. Julie simply wanted to take a shower and a short nap. They planned on staying in their honeymoon suite for the evening. As part of the package, they were having a late dinner in their room, complete with a bottle of champagne. Joe had settled up with the banquet manager. He wrote a check for approximately $10,000.00 that included the room, food, gratuity, champagne toast, wine, beer, and soda for the kids, and the cake.

Specialty drinks were up to the individual and everyone bought what they wanted. Joe paid the band separately. He thought what a blessing it was that Julie just got her royalty check. He also wondered if they got any monetary gifts to offset the costs.

He knew how costly it was for everyone to go to the wedding with flights, hotels, transportation, and extra food costs, especially for Mark, Louise, and the kids. Whatever they got, Joe asked Julie if it was all right to take some of the money and put it into Jennifer and TJ's college fund that had been set up by Mark just last year.

"Of course," Julie said. "That's a wonderful idea."

They said their goodbyes and walked to the elevator.

As they got to their room, Joe inserted the key, turned to Julie, and lifted her up into his arms to walk her across the threshold. He didn't do that when they moved into their house and he felt like a jerk. He'd not forget this time.

"Joe, how romantic. Are you sure you can lift me? I had a lot to eat, you know," she said, smiling.

"Of course, I can lift you for at least, hopefully, the next ten feet into the room. After that, you're on your own." He glided into the room and unceremoniously dropped her on the couch.

"Thanks, Joe. Too much?"

He smiled "I want to save my energy."

"Oh. In that case, I better shower. It's been over eight hours in this dress."

She headed into the bathroom and took her time. She came out with a towel wrapped around her and one on her head to dry her hair. "What a cheap joint," she said. "At least I got a nice robe at the Ritz Carlton in Miami."

With that, Joe smiled and handed her a carefully wrapped box. "Look inside, Julie."

"What's this?" She opened it quickly and pulled out the softest robe she'd ever seen. It had the Waldorf Astoria logo on the pocket. "Oh, my God," she said. "What a terrific, thoughtful gift." She dropped her towel, to Joe's delight, and put on the robe. "I guess I should thank you personally, Joe."

With that, she took his hand and brought him to the bedroom with a huge king size bed. Joe barely had time to take off his uniform. He hoped that he didn't smell that badly himself. They came up for air about a half an hour later. Joe excused himself and headed to the bathroom. She could hear the water running and then stop, and then Joe ran back to the bed.

"I'm ready for a cleaner second chance, Julie." He laughed and took her in his arms. "I love you, Julie Chapman, or Julie Traynor, or Julie Chapman Traynor or whatever hell name you choose."

"Me too, husband."

He filled her one more time, more slowly this time, more tender, and with as much love as he could gather. They came at the same time in crashing waves of ecstasy. Julie came and kept coming for the next few minutes. She grabbed him across his back and kept pulling him into her until she cried out one last time. "My God," she said. "That was truly memorable."

Joe was spent. He couldn't move a muscle. They held each other and fell asleep. Joe heard someone knocking on the door. He turned to the clock and it was now 9:00 p.m. It was room service with their scheduled dinner and champagne. Joe flew to the door and told the waiter that he'd be just a minute. He pulled on his pants, took his wallet and took out $20.00 to hand to the waiter. The trolley was pulled into the room and matching chairs were set up for their meal.

The champagne was uncorked and left in a chiller. Joe

turned to the older man, who smiled and said, "Congratulations."

Joe handed him the $20.00 and he thanked him profusely.

Julie peeked out of the room. "Is he gone?"

"Yes, put your robe on and come on out. I'm starved."

"Starved for what, sailor?"

He laughed. "Well, both the food and you are still hot. What would you prefer?"

"Let's eat and then we can go from there." She walked out in her newly acquired Waldorf Astoria robe, and it was obvious that she had nothing on underneath.

"Now, this is the way the rich and famous eat dinner, I'd imagine," he said.

"Sure, Joe. Pass the champagne."

❧❧❧

They were up by 8:00 a.m. Joe made coffee from the room coffee maker. It was okay, not great. He went by the door and picked up a note that said there would be a special breakfast in the same room that held the wedding reception from 9:00 a.m. to 11:00 a.m. for all wedding guests. The invitation was from Peter, Tanya, and Joe's father. *How nice,* he thought. He told Julie and they hurried up and got dressed.

"Later, Joe. I'm too tired," she said.

Joe knew what she meant. They thought it might be a good idea if they were there to greet the guests as well. The regular hotel buffet started at 11:00 a.m. and cost $98.00 a person. It would have been too late for most of the guests who had to get to the airport or train to head home.

They came down the elevator and walked through the lobby, meeting several of the guests, including Jake and Becky Barnes, Mark and his family, and Jack Forest. As they walked into the room, Tillie was already at the table and half the guests had already arrived. There was a hot and cold buffet. The kids had cereal and juice. People were getting in line to pick out various breakfast items. Waitresses walked around filling coffee cups and presenting various types of teas to the ladies. Joe and Julie sat with his family and Tillie at the same table. Tillie couldn't wait to fly back home with Father Schmidt and the Barnes on the navy jet. Most everyone had flights after 2:00 p.m. Checkout was at 11:00 a.m. but Joe and Julie had a late checkout for 1:00 p.m.

John stood after everyone walked in and made a toast to the new bride and groom and everyone clapped. There were a few off-color remarks from Joe's friends, not unexpected. Julie smiled, gave Pete a wave, and told him that he'd be in the very same boat very soon from everything she saw. He started to blush. Tanya laughed and punched him.

Around 10:30 a.m. everyone was done, and all they had to do was go pick up their luggage since checkout was now automatic. Look at the bill and let it go. It was all paid for as part of the wedding package.

Joe and Julie said their goodbyes and gave Tillie a kiss. Joe hugged his brother, Tanya, and his father, not knowing when they'd see each other again.

"By the way, Julie, did you see the *New York Times* today? Your wedding picture and write-up is in the bridal section," Tanya said. "I got five papers to bring home. I'll frame one and send it to you."

"Thanks, Tanya, that's great." Julie asked Joe to pick up several papers in the lobby newsroom and they'd read the article when they got to the apartment.

The car service came for Julie after they called. With the *New York Times* in hand, they hopped into the town car around 1:30 p.m. The presents were placed in the trunk with their luggage. Last night they'd opened the presents, which were very thoughtful and elegant gifts especially chosen for their new home. They opened the envelopes and were very surprised by the generosity of their guests. They didn't expect much from those few attending the wedding. Their presence and the cost to get there was more than sufficient. However, when Joe added up the cash and checks, they received almost $12,000.00 of which $4,000.00 was in cash. That made him nervous. Joe's father gave him $2,000.00 in cash plus the breakfast. His brother and Tanya gave them a $1,000.00. Tillie gave Julie a check for $2,500.00, which brought a tear to her eye and Joe's as well. The rear admiral and their friends gave similar gifts. Jack and Mark each gave them $500.00. That was a lot of money for Mark, considering the expense incurred for a family of four, and to be in the wedding as well.

They decided that on Monday, after they got back to the apartment, they'd open a savings account at the Bank of America, right around the corner from the apartment. Julie would be back to visit Sarah at some point, and she could use the funds as needed when she was in New York City. There were plenty Bank of America branches in the Florida Keys as well if they needed to tap into the savings.

ᴇᴏᴇᴏ

Later that day, they went over their plans for the week. They'd stay in the apartment all week, thanks to Sarah. They'd fly to Miami International Airport on Sunday afternoon from JFK and they had a car reserved for the trip home. On Monday, they'd open a bank account down the street and walk around to get their bearings. They'd take a cab to Saint Patrick's Cathedral afterward to thank the priests and staff for making their wedding day memorable. They didn't want anyone picking them up. They would UPS the gifts and her wedding gown on Tuesday so everything would be in Tavernier when they get home. The dress would go directly to Tillie's apartment and she'd immediately get it cleaned and repacked for next month's wedding at Saint Justin Martyr's in Key Largo.

Julie wanted to see a few Broadway plays and she let the cat out of the bag by presenting Joe with two tickets to Yankee Stadium for Friday's game against the Rangers at 7:05 p.m.

Joe looked at the tickets. "Wow, Julie. What a wedding present." The tickets were each $164.02 for seats in Section 113 right behind the Yankee dugout on the first base side, row thirty, seats three and four right at the end. "I can get up and go get beer and hot dogs without hitting anyone," he said.

"I know, Joe. That's called research."

She laughed. He did too. Little did he know that he was to stay in his seat during the bottom of the third inning because the Yankee announcer would congratulate them on their recent wedding last Saturday at Saint Patrick's Cathedral. Julie had already emailed the Yankees the picture of them walking out of the cathedral, all smiles, hand in hand. At breakfast after the wedding, Julie told everyone to turn on the game and record it for them. The rear admiral was quite impressed by Julie's ingenuity.

They planned to have dinner on Thursday night at Sarah and Bennett Atwood's home. Sarah was bringing in a few friends from the publishing world to introduce Julie and her two books. She'd also mention the possibility of a possible movie to the guests. Sarah might have mixed business with pleasure, but she more than made up for it with her extreme hospitality and true friendship and kindness she showed to Joe, Julie, and Tillie.

The rest of the week, they'd hang around and not plan a thing. They ate two nights at Luigi's, her home away from home. She felt comfortable with her New York City choices and that made all the difference to Joe.

On Sunday, they were looking forward to heading home. It had been a long twelve days from when they flew in on that Wednesday before the wedding. Joe was antsy. He did two loads of wash in the basement of the apartment building. He read a book for the first time in a long time. Julie mostly slept, ate, and relaxed. There was a lot of lovemaking, and that was obviously expected and enjoyed thoroughly.

The limousine pulled up at noon to bring them to the airport on Sunday. They took a taxi to an early Mass at Saint Patrick's before leaving. They walked back and had breakfast on the way. They were already packed when Sam called up to tell them the car was there. He and his assistant loaded the car, gave Julie a hug, and shook Joe's hand. Before leaving, Julie called Sarah at home and thanked her again for everything she did for them to make this the most memorable week of their lives. Sarah was quite touched. Living in New York City, things like a simple thank you never happened, or happened so rarely that you took notice.

They made it to JFK by 12:30 p.m. for their 2:00 p.m. direct flight to Miami International Airport, arriving around 7:00 p.m. They'd be home in Tavernier by 9:00 p.m. after stopping to see Tillie on the way. Joe had to be back in Orlando no later than Monday night. Joan got him a flight into Orlando on a navy plane out of Key West. Mark and Frank would meet him at the terminal when he got in. Navy jets arrived at a different area than commercial flights.

Joe really didn't want to be in on this investigation, but he'd promised Trinity and Chief Roberts that he would. He'd be in charge of his last investigation ever, he thought. He wasn't tired as much as he was tired of all this negative energy. He wanted to head back and stay in Tavernier with Julie, raise a family, and simply be happy. Every investigation that he was on, someone got hurt or killed. Every investigation he did was high profile with everyone second-guessing everyone else when there were no answers for what was happening.

He was really thinking about taking the position at the Florida Keys Community College and where that would eventually lead. Getting his PhD would only add to his credentials. However, at this point, he was more interested in Julie's success than his own. She was just coming into her own at a very young age. He wasn't sure if he was peaking, but it started to feel that way. He wanted the best for Julie. He loved her that much.

Please let the investigation end peacefully and let me go on my way.

CHAPTER 23

Joe said goodbye to Julie and headed for the Key West International Airport around 11:00 a.m., on Monday morning, May twenty-five. The honeymoon was over and he had a few months until his last day in this job. Hopefully on the first day of the college year, he'd be taking over the reins of the military division of the Florida Keys Community College, as well as serve as vice president for Institutional Research and Grants on the non-military end. If approved, and he believed it would be after talking to the rear admiral, he'd also be starting his PhD program at Barry University at the same time. He would take all his required courses this semester to see how it would go with his two full time jobs. After this investigation, Joe was just about one-hundred percent set on taking the job that would be offered to him, as he was told.

He had to be back for the second wedding ceremony for June twentieth in Key Largo at Saint Justin Martyr Catholic Church. He and Julie also had to fly up to Boston, toward the end of the summer for Maddy Malone and Kevin White's wedding in Wakefield, Massachusetts, at Saint Joseph's Church. It looked to Joe like the whole world was Catholic at this point, which he knew not to be true. Julie would be Maddy's matron of honor.

Joe would now drive to the Islamorada Coast Guard Station and Joan Talbot would bring him to the Key West airport. It was eighty miles from Islamorada and about an hour and a half to get there. The navy plane would arrive around 1:30 p.m., refuel, and leave with Joe at approximately 1:40 p.m. The flight would take one hour and twenty minutes in the air and another fifteen to twenty minutes to taxi around the Orlando International Airport. Joe would get a jeep ride from the military side over to where Frank Cortez would be picking him up with Mark at the main terminal. It would be closer to 4:00 p.m. before they could head out and get to the Embassy Suites Hotel to meet.

The military jeep pulled up right next to Frank Cortez, who was parked near Terminal A. Joe took his bags out of the back of the jeep, thanked the driver, walked over, and tapped on Frank's window. Mark was sitting in the front passenger seat and nodded at Joe as soon as got into the back and closed the door.

"Hi, guys," Joe said. "Were you waiting long?"

"Not really," Frank said. "How was your trip?"

"Good and uneventful. The wedding is behind me so it's back to work. Yippee! Hi, Mark. A man of few words."

"I really missed you, Joe. What's it been about a week?"

"A little longer but not much."

"How's Julie holding up from the wedding?"

"Planning the next one in June. You guys are coming. Right?"

Both said yes and that was that. Frank pulled out and headed into traffic to get back to the hotel. They'd be meeting Trinity at 6:00 p.m. in the lobby. They'd head out to dinner somewhere close. Joe wanted a full update on everything that had happened. He had to wrap his head back around the investigation. He hadn't had one thought about it since he left for New York City thirteen days earlier. He had a way to compartmentalize just about everything. He'd bring the investigation back to the forefront and then start to remember exactly how everything came down before he left. He'd add all the new stuff they found out while he was gone and then see where those things took him.

They made it back to the hotel with time to spare. Joe hopped into the shower and changed into his jeans, T-shirt, and old work boots back to his Troy construction days. The boots were almost twenty years old and worn but comfortable. When out of uniform, this was his uniform. They walked down to the lobby and met Trinity. Joe was surprised. Next to Trinity stood Cal Roberts to welcome him back. *That was very nice of him. Or is something else brewing?*

✌✌

"Hi, Joe. Welcome back," Trinity said. "How was the wedding?"

"Great, you're coming in June, right? You too, Cal?"

"We wouldn't miss it for the world," Cal said. "Estelle and I haven't been to the Keys in twenty-five years. After the reception, we're going to take a mini-vacation and head to Key West. It's Estelle's idea."

"So I heard recently," said Joe, smiling. "Trinity, the wedding was great. Julie has both the video and photos, which will be developed by the time June rolls around. She'll loop the video on a widescreen television under the tent and play the complete wedding and reception from New York City. Saint Patrick's Cathedral was gorgeous and what a great place for a wedding. Julie said she'd call you this week to tell you all about it. That's if you have time," he said.

"I'll make time."

With that, they headed out to the chief's car at the front door.

"By the way, Claire Murphy called me this week and forwarded your wedding pictures to me. The wedding pictures were beautiful," she said.

"I thought, if you don't mind, we could head to my house for a cookout," the chief said. "Estelle made ribs, chicken, collard greens, cornbread, and mac and cheese. I also have plenty of beer. I'll bring you back after dinner."

"Sound good? Sounds great," Mark said, followed by Joe, Trinity, and Frank.

They made it to Cal's house in twenty minutes and pulled up in the driveway. Estelle and the kids greeted them at the door. She grabbed Joe, gave him a hug, and told him congratulations on the wedding. She hugged Trinity as well and shook Mark and Frank's hands. "Please come in. Everything is ready and we're set up in the backyard. I'm boiling the corn right now."

They walked through the living room to the kitchen and out the backdoor. They remembered the backyard from their first visit to Cal and Estelle's house. Joe had to tell Cal that he had a dirty cop on his hands.

After they ate, Cal said, "Trinity, please tell the guys where we are right now and then Mark and Frank can fill us in. Joe once you're up to date, help us figure out where we head next."

Trinity had her envelope and a three-ring binder on her and started to pull out pictures and reports and placed everything in front of her. "Guys, we've done a lot of running around and not getting anywhere. The church bombings are bad enough, but if there's something bigger planned, we haven't enough manpower to run several investigations separately. We've got the shooting in the airport, the three bombings we'll keep as one investigation, and then a final one if there's a bigger target. I've been reviewing all the film. I feel like I'm an NFL quarterback looking at next week's opponent's previous games to decide how we'll put together a game plan. I've noticed one thing, though, that stood out to me that no one else has seemed to notice."

"What's that, Trinity?" Joe asked.

"We've got three separate pictures of a white older Ford Econoline van with no name on the sides. That doesn't mean it's not a business. From all the pictures, including at the airport, at the Florida Mall, and at the last church bombing—my father's church, I might add—all the license plates are covered up with mud. That's obviously so no one can get the number. But no one has pointed out to me the remnants of a sticker in the back right van window that's evident on each van at all three locations. I believe that ties the van to all three investigations and that it's the same van. I blew up the sticker in each case but it's barely readable." She handed pictures of the same van, taken at three locations, and from all angles and then a picture of the sticker blown up to maximum size without losing complete definition.

"So, obviously, the sticker was partially removed from the window but it looks like either they were in a rush or didn't think it would show up anywhere," Trinity continued. "From looking at the sticker a million times, I think it's about four inches square. On the top of the sticker, I believe it says 'Oran' with the rest scraped off the name. I believe it's Orange and begins the words Orange County, which is our county for Orlando. The middle is wiped out but the bottom still has 'fill' that's readable with part of a number eleven, scraped about an inch and then three. I'm guessing, Joe, that it's a municipal sticker for Orange County Landfill and the partial number is the number recorded for the van to dump in the city dump over on Young Pine Road going out of the city."

"Trinity, that's an unbelievable find," Frank said. "Can we go to the landfill and check records to see if the van is registered to dump there?"

"I don't know. I just thought of that while waiting for you in the lobby with Cal."

"If this pans out, Trinity, you're a freaking genius," Mark said.

Joe smiled at Cal and nodded his head. "Trinity, do you have that picture of the sticker in your phone so I can send it immediately to Jack Forest?" he asked. "We've got software that helps us reconstruct old pictures and attempts to fill in what's missing by analyzing the differences between lines and the end of the document. It calculates what it believes should be in the empty space. It won't tell you the missing numbers but it will tell you the accuracy of your guess, and I believe your right. Send it to Jack right now. You've his email address."

"I do and I just sent it."

Joe called Jack immediately. He never left his office before 9:00 p.m., girlfriend or no girlfriend. "Jack, Hi. I see you got back all right from the wedding."

"I did. Lots of fun. Hated to go back to work. I'll be there in June too with my new friend."

"I can't wait to meet your new friend, Jack," Joe said, laughing. Mark told him to tell Jack, that Louise couldn't wait either.

"Trinity just sent you a sticker, four inches square, to reconstruct quickly, as best as you can. It doesn't have to be perfect but it's the best lead we got right now. What do you say?"

"Reconstruction of documents and digitizing the results is time consuming if there isn't a lot to go on. Let me look at what you sent me and, if it's in good shape, we can do it in an hour. I'll call you," Jack said.

With that, Joe hung up and finished dinner.

He went through the steps they needed to take. First, he had to be formally put back in charge of the investigation and Frank removed but he didn't want that to happen. He'd be leaving the Coast Guard in October and Frank was a lifer. This would give Frank more credibility, if it was resolved, and possibly the promotion he needed with a pay grade to help send his kids to college. "Frank, let's keep you in charge for now. I'm better in the background in this one because, if we find the Chechens, I'll have to stick with them as I'm the only one who speaks the language. While that's going on, whoever is in charge of the investigation may have to run three separate plans and keep on top of it. I can't do that and keep on top of the Chechens. I'll call Rear Admiral Barnes to tell him my reasons, and he can make the calls to the admiral in Washington and to the FBI and Homeland Security. Trinity, we still need to keep an eye all the mosques, so you've got your men doing that. Mark needs to keep on top of the bomb squad to sift through the remains and make absolutely sure that each bomb had chlorine gas attached. Trinity, your father's church, with the killing of Mr. Leon Jenkins, has to have the chlorine element causing Mr. Jenkins death, or we will be running down another rabbit hole. Mark stay on top of that. Cal, you need to keep a lid on all three separate investigations and to make sure that it doesn't get out about a potential terrorist threat. I don't want to leave it like a KKK bombing of African American churches, but for now, that's our best explanation to the public."

Trinity's phone rang. It was Jack. "Trinity put me on speakerphone if you guys are by yourselves."

She did.

"Can you hear me?" Jack asked.

"Yes, go ahead," Joe said.

"I sent the photo through our digitizing process. Although it's not one-hundred percent positive about what I'm saying, it's close enough to move forward. The sticker appears to be an Orange County Florida municipal landfill sticker. A partial address that I brought up seems to be 'Young Pine something.' I can't make out if it's a street or road. It also has a registration number and four numbers. Can't make out the rest but from the length of it and the size of the print and spacing between the numbers, it appears to have eleven numbers for the sticker number. It starts 'one-one-four,' then misses the next seven numbers and ends in a three. I'm sure if there's an actual record being kept for the associated vehicles and registration numbers, you'll be able to reconstruct it for a white Ford Econoline van. That's what you told me. Right, Trinity?"

"Yes, that's what I said."

"Tomorrow morning as soon as they open, let's get down to the landfill and pull the records and then see if there's any video of cars and trucks pulling in," Joe said. "If the van was commercial, they had to be dumping large items like furniture and fixtures, mattresses and box springs. Those vans couldn't hold the weight of a construction site waste. You couldn't continue to put cement blocks or debris in it. That would obviously go in some sort of pickup truck or dump truck. We'd be looking for commercial waste materials that were relatively large and non-construction."

They headed out after thanking Estelle for a wonderful dinner. Mark especially loved the ribs and asked for the recipe. He gave her Louise's email address for her to send it. As they were leaving, Joe said, "Cal, that was one hell of a find for Trinity. I never thought to even look at an old scratched off sticker. I'd have found it, maybe after five or six reviews, but she's so sharp and on top of things. I hope this leads us somewhere. I believe it will."

"I do too, Joe. I hope it's sooner rather than later. I should have resigned when I told you I was going to after you caught our detective in the murder of Mr. Jones. I wanted to right then but this has to lead somewhere."

CHAPTER 24

Trinity picked up Joe, Mark, and Frank at the Embassy Suites, and they headed out. Just to be on the safe side, the chief got a warrant for all the records, pictures, and video, if any, for the Orange County Landfill, located at 5901 Young Pine Road, Orlando. The chief also called the Orange County Commissioner to let them know that the murder of an Orlando police officer now led them to the Orange County municipal landfill and needed their cooperation at the Water, Garbage, and Recycling Department that ran the landfill. He told them that his team would be there by 8:00 a.m.

They arrived just at 8:00 a.m. and walked into the manager's office. He was already aware that they'd be coming. He'd assigned one of his clerks to pull records and work with the team for as long as needed. The first item on the agenda was to see if they could isolate the sticker number that matched a white Econoline van. Then they'd look to see when the last time they came to the landfill and see if there was any video of the van and anyone in it. Matching the license plate with the landfill sticker and then to the Florida vehicle registration was the goal. That would get them the owner of the truck and see if it was commercial or a residential vehicle. Getting pictures of what the van dumped and who was dumping there would also prove invaluable.

From the partial landfill sticker numbers of one-one-four, missing the next seven numbers and then a three at the end, they started to look. There were over 5,000 stickers issued and any vehicle, identified as a truck, which included vans, was considered commercial, regardless if it was privately owned. With those numbers, Joe was able to set up an Excel spreadsheet and import commercial vehicles with those first three numbers and ending in a three. There were over 300 that met that category. The sticker numbers also were coded to separate various truck types including pickup, vans, and dump trucks because the rates were different and the loads were much different. Vans had the three at the end of their sticker number. Pickups had a four, and dump trucks—eighteen-wheel, six-wheel, long-bed, etc.—split into several categories that took up the rest of the zero through nine numbers. Joe did a reverse pickup on the sticker numbers, starting with the last number and flunking out all the threes. There were twenty-seven "threes." Joe then separated the vans by the make and model that included Fords, Dodges, Nissans, and other makes. There were seven Econoline vans in the group. Three of those were newer models leaving four to check.

"Joe, that's amazing," said Trinity.

"Not really when I've done this a million times across a wide array of splits. Hell, we did it for boats, planes, cars, and that's how I found out Julie's father was still alive."

They went in and checked the four Econoline vans that were built prior to 2012. Of those, two were in the name of a plumbing company, and one was an electrician. Evidently, they only dumped old fixtures, wiring, and smaller items. They weren't in the remodeling business. Large and small contractors seemed to use pickups and dump trucks to dump their waste materials into the Orange County Landfill. The last van was owned by the Old Winter Furniture Store, on Old Winter Garden Road in Orlando. They went into the records and saw that they had dumped a week earlier. They went to the video for the day recorded and there was an

Econoline van checking in at the office. They claimed a used mattress, box spring, metal frame, and a beat up old dresser. They moved the van to the appropriate area and, from the video, Joe and his team saw two men open the back door and remove exactly what they'd claimed. After closing the door, they saw that the license plate was still covered with dirt but the sticker on the back right window, partially scratched off was in the exact same spot as the van from the bombing scene. They didn't need the license plate if they knew who owned the vehicle. They now did. They took the video, isolated the picture of the sticker, and immediately sent it to Jack Forest. He knew they were heading to the dump that day so he stayed around up in Virginia in case they needed him. They did.

Jack called Trinity back on her cell phone. "The picture of the sticker that you sent yesterday, and the captured video today, once I isolated it and placed it over the top of the other one, matched exactly. It matched all the scrapes and matched the exact numbers and print, line for line. You have your vehicle," he said.

"Well, that's a good start to the day." Trinity then said, "Let's go to DMV again and sort out all the vehicles owned by Old Winter Furniture and get the official VIN number and registration and make sure the vehicle is owned by the company."

Joe nodded. "I'm going to ask Jack to go online to the Florida Department of State and see who incorporated Old Winter Furniture in Orlando. That should be interesting." He called Jack and gave him what he needed.

Within fifteen minutes, Joe's computer dinged with an email. He opened it and found there were the incorporation papers for the company. Hamzah Umarov incorporated it, at age twenty-five, as president and treasurer with Alvi Bisolta, age thirty-two, as vice president and secretary. It was incorporated in 2012.

"Are those Chechen names as well?" Trinity asked Joe.

"Let's look online." Joe went to Google and typed in a

request for names of Chechen men. Up popped four or five different searches. "It looks like both first and last names for both men, are Chechen. What's the closest mosque to Old Winter Garden Road? You know that ninety-five percent of Chechens are Muslim, right?"

"Yes." Trinity then looked at her notes. "How about the mosque less than a few miles away on, guess what, on Old Winter Garden Road. Convenient. The store is only a few miles from the mosque."

"Well, I think we're starting to isolate where we need to focus. Bronislaw Jawarski, AKA Axmad Khan, has to be near the mosque on Old Winter Garden Road, somewhere near the furniture store, or in a safe house somewhere near either one. Does that seem reasonable?"

Mark, Trinity, and Frank all nodded their heads.

"Let's go back to police headquarters and talk to Cal," Joe said. "There's a bunch of things we need to look at in order to get closer to this case. Actually, there are still three cases, including Archie, the bombing, and a potential threat. That's three as far as I'm concerned. First, we need everything we can get on Umarov and Bisolta and the furniture company. We need to find out who works there, who drives the van, who the customers and suppliers are, and then we need to find out exactly what's happening at the mosque. Who's the imam and how or does he fit into this investigation? We need to pull financials on everyone we see. Did they pay taxes? How can a twenty-one-year-old finance a new company? How long has he been here? What's his connection to the community? Finally, we need to think about if there's going to be a terrorist plot against anything in Orlando. We need to look at military bases, installations, think tanks, and anything else related to the federal government. That's what they're after, I believe. They didn't kill Archie and shoot at the police in a major international airport for no reason. They had to escape if they were planning something for Allah. They don't run away. They want to be martyrs. So there was a reason that Jawarski took off like a bat out of hell and left his two other men. They were expendable. That seems to be clear."

CHAPTER 25

Back at the station, they met with Cal Roberts in his conference room.

"Have your rooms been swept for bugs recently? Joe asked the chief.

"Yes, because of the incident with my dirty detective, I have it swept every week, including all my direct reports."

Joe had previously told him about the *Super Sweep 2000s,* which were devices used by all the military services, including the Coast Guard, law enforcement, and private investigators. He ordered one for the chief from Jack Forest, using the funds taken from the previous drug bust. Joe also paid for the training for the chief, who wanted to learn how to use the device, and his immediate staff, including Trinity Hightower.

This counter surveillance probe/monitor provided five of the most desired sweep functions in one package. An RF probe was a device which allowed electronic test equipment to measure radio frequency oscillation, "RF," in an electronic circuit. The RF probe sniffed the environment for hidden phone, room, or body bugs, remote signals, computer, fax, or telex transmitters, video transmitters, pulsed tracking transmitters, and even wide-band, frequency-hopping, or burst bugs. Then very low frequency, "VLF," probe tests were done on AC outlets, phone lines or suspicious wires for very low frequency carrier current signs. The phones in the rooms didn't have to be physically touched to do this. The perpetrators could tap into a phone without even putting their hands or equipment onto the phone. After a sweep, the alarm monitor guarded against new devices brought in, remote control activation, or someone tampering with the equipment.

"Joe, we've kept the devise plugged in ever since we got it. We still run weekly updated tests and look at printouts just to be sure. This place is now officially clean, thanks to you and Jack."

"No problem. What Trinity is about to tell you needs to be kept quiet, regardless of the press trying to cover a so-called race war," Joe said. "Trinity broke this case wide open with what she found. It would have taken me days and maybe weeks to hone in on what she picked up immediately. Tell him, Trinity."

Trinity went through all the steps that brought them to the Orange County Landfill and the van they found that was owned by a Chechen furniture company just down the road from a mosque. "We still need to find Jawarski, but this will help us hone in on where we should be looking. Joe is also running reports on the owners and the company and even the mosque, quietly."

"What do you hope to find, Joe, or Trinity?" Cal asked.

"We hope to find Jawarski, stop any pending terrorist attacks, and arrest a murderer of a cop." Trinity was emphatic about that and everyone knew it.

"Joe, are you aware that we've been experimenting with two small drones? Our tech staff went away for a week to learn how to operate the equipment. Should we use the new technology to spy on the store?"

"I wouldn't. Something could happen if this is your first venture into drones. We've been using drones for ten years, and it took that long to perfect what we needed to do. Cal, read about the UCLA football coach who was on *60 Minutes*. He explained they work well now, as long as they didn't continue to run the drones into the goal posts. If you

ran a drone into the building, it could be over for us catching anyone," Joe said.

"Okay. It was just a thought."

"We don't need the drones. What we need is to find all
the real estate in the names of the owners of the furniture
store. I'm sure that Jawarski isn't camped out at the store or
delivering furniture. That's a cover for their cell. He's hiding in a safe house owned by the owners or by someone involved at the mosque. Of that, I'm almost positive. Why
don't we wait to hear from Jack? In the meantime, I want
Frank to drive by with Mark and take as many pictures of
the store and the mosque as they can without revealing
themselves. Also, I'll go to Google Earth and see how isolated the building are and see what other buildings we can
find near the store and the mosque so we can place cameras
if feasible. Depending on who the owners are of the sur-
rounding facilities, we might want to place devices without
their knowledge late at night. I'm also sure that there will be
an attack on some military facility somewhere here in Orlando. We need to deeply research everything we can find
on a military basis and notify those installations of a potential attack. I need to go through my rear admiral to the admiral in Washington to Homeland Security and the FBI. As
you know, Frank is still in charge, allowing me the freedom
to move around and find out what I can, as quickly as I
can."

Joe went through his checklist and read to everyone present: owners of store, properties in name of owners, background on owners both financial and otherwise, citizenship,
sponsors into the country, payroll and employees, who they
were and where they lived. Were they citizens or on visas or
here illegally? They needed to pull company tax records,
W-2s and 1099s. Who were the customers and suppliers?
Any donations? Any foreign banks involved? Large cash
deposits by the store or the mosque? Who was the imam
and what was his background and financial status?

Jack was working on everything he checked off. Joe

didn't believe that a twenty-four-year-old man could pull everything off for the last three years without backing. Was his family rich? Where'd they come from? Were there any relatives in Orlando or in the United States?

They left the chief's office and Joe, Mark, and Frank headed back to the hotel and then to lunch. They'd be on hold until Jack got back to them. Trinity went to her office and met with her team. At this point they were in the dark and frustrated that nothing had come of this investigation into the murder of a cop. They were tired of being attacked on the street by people who didn't think they were doing anything about the bombings of African American churches or attempts to find the racist organizations responsible. None of the top brass had told the troops anything at this point, and Trinity was in the cross hairs as the wonder girl who'd done nothing so far except help run a really nice funeral for a fallen cop.

She spoke to the chief, who had told her to give them some information but nothing about what they'd just discovered. They were on the verge of breaking the case wide open but didn't want any potential vigilantes roaming the street in police uniforms.

She walked into the conference room on the first floor where her expanded team was now assembled. It had been exactly four days since she met with them. They weren't happy and they just stared at her as she walked into the room.

If the chief was there, it might help her in the short term but, in the long term, she'd come off as a token and not as a competent leader and detective. She certainly wouldn't have the support of the rank and file if she hid behind the veil of secrecy.

The other problem was there were FBI and Homeland Security members as part of the task force who were also unaware of what was going on. Joe told her that was deliberate because they'd slow up the investigation, or so he believed. He told Trinity that'd be on Frank and him in the long run. He said he could live with it since this would be his last investigation.

He wouldn't speak for Frank but he was on board as well. Time would tell.

Trinity looked right at Beverly Fitch, the chief's spokesperson. "Let's begin. I know how frustrated you all are," she said, as she looked at every individual in the room. "However, this case isn't just about a murdered cop. You know it and I know it. We aren't in charge anymore. This is a national and international crisis. I'm not allowed, or at liberty, to say much more at this point. Let me say, yes, three churches have been burnt to the ground, including my own father's church. It's hard for me to look him in the eye as well, since his friend was also murdered in the incident. Yes, murdered. Regardless of how we look, or how incompetent we look in the papers, we're to continue our investigation into the murder of our officer, Archie Higgins, and the shooting of two other cops. We're to continue to sift through the rubble of three churches to find as much evidence as we can. We're to continue to look for Jawarski as a murderer.

"We're placing in the paper the pictures of the two deceased men who were killed by our officer. We know who they now are. You don't. But we want the public to come forward to help in the identification, if possible. We want to run this like any normal investigation. I can tell you from my heart that this is no normal investigation and, hopefully, it will end without any additional tragedy.

"If you hear anything from any of your snitches on the street or from the public, please gather it and give it to me. That's all I can say for now. I know that 'trust me,' doesn't ring true, anymore. God knows, I feel the same some days. But please trust me, the chief, and your senior officers that we know what we're doing and it's in Orlando's and the country's best interests that we move ahead with caution. Thank you."

Trinity turned and headed back to her office. The rumblings subsided. She hoped that for now, at least, it would give them some breathing room. That's what they needed. Time.

CHAPTER 26

Hamzah had two young men, whom he'd radicalized from the mosque. They were not in the cell. He had them apply for and receive positions with the cleaning crew at the Naval Air Warfare Center Training System Division inside the Central Florida Research Park at the University of Central Florida. Both men had been citizens for over ten years, arriving before 2005. The two young men were only ten and eleven years old when they arrived from Poland with their parents who'd immigrated to Orlando. Both sets of fathers were professionals. One was a certified engineer and the other was a family doctor who came to work with new immigrants in the area.

Back then, being Muslim was a rarity and an oddity but there was limited pressure since they were thought to be Polish. The two sons, now twenty-five and twenty-six, were citizens and had clearance. Both were high school graduates from Orlando schools and both were seemingly honorable people. They both had their associate's degree from a local community college and were willing to start at the bottom while going nights to get their four-year degrees. They were vetted, even though they held low level cleaning jobs and worked the midnight shift. They told the human resources department that they wanted to attend college days and work nights. None of the parents knew that both had become radicalized at their mosque on Old Winter Garden

Road. They were concerned about their newly acquired religious fervor and faithfulness to their imam but not to the point of worry. They believed that their imam, Ibu Malik, was a good man, a man of God. They didn't know that he too had been radicalized many years ago in a New York City mosque as a new twenty-five-year-old immigrant. They also didn't know that he left New York City after Nine/Eleven, migrated to Orlando, and had established this mosque with money supplied by his New York City brethren. They also didn't know about his trips to the Cayman Islands to feather his own nest.

The two young men were considered good workers, attentive, prompt, always on time, and always did their work as required. They were polite and considered good, valuable employees who'd gradually rise in status at the facility as they continued their education and training. Little did they know that they were constantly taking pictures of everything in the facility on their iPhones and worked their way into the engineering area where weapons were tested and blueprints and diagrams were available, just sitting out, waiting to be photographed. Security was very lax, to say the least.

Axmad met the two young men at the mosque in the imam's office, late at night. He explained the importance of their mission and their target. He wanted them to be as dedicated to this mission as they appeared to be dedicated to their imam. Axmad had plans to take the imam out when the attack took place so he couldn't be compromised or taken for interrogation. The attack would be an attack on America and the Homeland Security officers wouldn't be kind to him if they found out about his involvement. Jawarski would also take out the two young men as well. He was not worried about Hamzah. He had no local ties. He'd pay off his cell members and have them spread to the four winds. Axmad and Hamzah would work their way back to Chechnya, in due time, through Mexico.

If you could cross the border going into America, he

guessed it would be easier going the other way.

The furniture company and all the property owned by Hamzah were small potatoes compared to the millions of dollars they had in their war chest. By the time Homeland Security would get to the furniture company, the only one left holding the bag would be Alvi Bisolta, the vice president and secretary on the corporation papers. He knew nothing of this attack. He really believed that they were hiring Chechens for good jobs and helping their mosque at the same time. Alvi's family had moved many years ago to the United States and became Americanized, to Axmad's disdain. By the time Homeland Security got around to anything, Axmad, Hamzah, and the active cell members would be gone. Imam Abu Malik and the two young men would be dead, and Alvi would be left holding the bag, if found out. As Axmad believed, they'd never be found out because Americans were soft, weak, and scared of the unknown. They'd sit back and let things happen because they were always justifying everyone's point of view. *What hogwash*, he thought.

In Chechen, Axmad said, "Men, we will put fear into the hearts of every American. An attack on this facility, right in the middle of a major university campus, will show the world that Allah is great and they must bow before him. We aren't targeting students. That's bad publicity if we want to get more members. We're targeting scientists and weapons workers who design killing machines to take out our brother Muslims. We will use chlorine bombs, that will poison and suffocate everyone in this building, by placing chlorine gas devices in the air conditioning units. The blast will spread the gas immediately and pass through all the vents in the building. Within minutes, the death toll will be huge. We may be talking about the same size as Nine/Eleven, as dramatic as that was. This won't be dramatic but just as lethal, to let them know that we don't need fanfare, and we can attack America's military whenever and wherever we want. That will wake them up.

"What you're going to do is to learn to assemble pieces of these bombs during the day and bring them into the facility, piece by piece. After the assemblies are armed, the bombs will be remotely activated using a cell phone call to each one simultaneously. There will be a ten-minute delay to make sure that wherever we are, we will have time to clear out. I suspect that I'll be within a very short distance from the building, well within the range for activation. You'll have time to prepare. Every day, you'll bring in an item that will never be suspected as having any potential threat. Most of the parts will be undetected and made of ceramic or super strength plastic. On the last night, I will hand you the activated chlorine gas materials and cell phone through a back door that you will have already deactivated.

"We will have ten bombs that must be separately armed with a cell phone wired to the explosive. Each package of chlorine gas explosives is less than a pound. The one of you who opens the door will pick up a gym bag with ten separate packages. On that night, you will set the explosive into the assembly and turn on the phone. You will place them back into the air vent and leave as soon as you can. We know that if assembled properly, all will work. Even if half work, we should kill as many as we can with ten."

Axmad paused and looked each man in the eye. "Be here every night before your shift and after your classes. We don't want to raise any attention as to your involvement. Just tell your family that you're studying to be an imam. What can they say? They know you've turned very religious over the last year. They've no knowledge of this event. Am I correct?"

"Yes. No one knows about this except you and our imam."

Little did they know there was a terrorist cell under Hamzah. Now the imam was becoming more and more worried. He knew that his life would be uprooted. He was radicalized but becoming less so. He thought that he needed more prayer to ask Allah if this was what he wanted. Where would he go? He wasn't married. He couldn't be, knowing that his fate would lead to his death. But he liked Orlando. He liked this life. He liked being the religious leader of his people. He liked being looked up to and praised. *Maybe being weak isn't so bad,* he thought. *Do I really want this to happen? What'll happen to these two young men and their families?* He knew what would happen but really was torn on what to do. Obviously, he liked having a half-million dollars in the bank and another few hundred thousand in a safe deposit box that no one knew about.

If Axmad could be stopped and even killed, could the imam stay and continue? That would be nice but he didn't believe it would turn out that way. He was sure that if Axmad didn't make this happen then Hamzah would. They were cut from the same cloth. Within a short period, there were two murders, two other cops shot, and three churches burned down. He was sure that the cops weren't stupid and, eventually, it would lead to a mosque door. Maybe not his right away, but eventually it would. He needed to figure out exactly what side of the ledger he was on. He didn't have much time.

The way Axmad looked at him and talked to him, the imam didn't believe that when it was over he'd be kind to him. *I need to do something. But what?* His back was against the wall. He didn't believe in seventy-plus virgins meeting him as promised. An educated man would never believe that. He needed to read up on the Naval Air Warfare Center Training System Division to see if they could actually pull this off. There was no sense worrying about it if it couldn't happen.

After downloading information from the internet, he read that the Central Florida Research Park was located at 12424 Research Parkway in Orlando on the east side of the city. It was eighteen miles away from the mosque on Old Winter Garden Road. They had to take Fl-408 E/E West Expressway for fifteen miles and then merge onto Challenger Parkway for about a mile. Then they had to travel another two miles, first turning onto Ingenuity Drive to Science Drive, to Technology Parkway before turning right onto Research Parkway. It was down about a half a mile. It was far enough away that no one would ever connect this mosque or its people with the attack. Most of the mosques in Orlando were nearer to the research park.

As Abu Malik read further, he discovered the size and breadth of this naval facility.

The purpose of the Division, besides training for air warfare, is to develop training systems for military personnel in undersea and surface operations. It is located inside the Central Florida Research Park at the University of Central Florida. Naval Support Activities (NSA) Orlando and located inside the Central Florida Research Park. NSA Orlando is only forty acres in size and is the smallest United States Navy base in the world.

Presently there are about 1,000 scientists, engineers, contractors, and support personnel employed by the NAWCTD Orlando. The funding for 2011 was approximately 918.6 million dollars. NSA Orlando has approximately 120 active-duty military personnel, and 2,200 civil service personnel serving on or near NSA Orlando. NSA Orlando also serves a community of 3,200 Joint Services Reserves, 48,000 military retirees, and 350 military families in the area of Central Florida. There's no temporary housing on base at NSA, Orlando, due to its size. You can contact the housing office for details and directions on several long-term-stay hotels.

Because of its small size NSA Orlando doesn't have many of the things you might find on other bases, such as schools, barber shops, or a commissary. All of these traditional base amenities can, however, be found within approximately twenty miles of the facility. There are no inpatient medical facilities on base at NSA, Orlando. Medical and dental care was provided by local civilian medical facilities. There are also no Navy Federal Credit Unions on base, but there are several in the Orlando area. Due to the base location, be aware of hurricane season, which runs from June through November. If you're due to arrive on base at NSA Orlando and a hurricane is predicted in the area, contact your sponsor before arrival as evacuations may be in progress.

NSA Orlando is only located thirty-five miles away from Disney World, Epcot, Sea World, Universal Studios, and other major theme park attractions so you and your family will find plenty of things to see and do. Orlando is a major tourist destination and, as such, has excellent restaurants, shopping, hotels, and many other family friendly attractions, as well as a healthy dose of night life for adults.

Well, Axmad seemed to pick a winner, Malik decided. In only a short time, could two young men, working on the midnight shift, kill thousands of naval employees using chlorine gas bombs in the air ducts of this facility? Malik supposed that it could happen, but it might be a grandiose plan by someone never before in the United States. However, he thought, Axmad had the backing of his terrorist group with millions to spend. Maybe he could.

Malik knew he was a recipient of that funding, as well as those in his mosque. There were new programs for new immigrants, job fairs, housing, food, clothing, and furniture from Hamzah's store. This was no small operation. Axmad was right. If he pulled this off, America would be shocked and scared of the future. The imam needed to decide soon. He didn't kill anybody, but he was as responsible for two deaths already, just as much as if he pulled the trigger or bombed a church.

CHAPTER 27

It had taken Jack several days to get back to Joe with answers to the questions he'd posed. Not only did Jack get information about the finances and structure of the furniture store, he did research on family histories as well.

"Joe, where are you?" he asked after Joe picked up the phone.

"We're back in the hotel. I'm with Frank, Mark, and Trinity. What do you have for us?"

"It's lengthy, Joe. So grab a pen and a lot of paper. I'll email the answers to you but I think you should hear it verbally, as well, so there's no wrong interpretations."

"Frank, Mark, Trinity are you ready?" They all nodded in agreement. "Go ahead, Jack" Joe said. "Everyone's ready here."

"First, this is a conspiracy in the first degree. I also believe that there are several individuals who can be charged with murder after the fact, even though they didn't pull the trigger, at least in the case of the cops. They may all have been involved with the church bombings. I won't speculate on that. Let me give you a little background on Hamzah Umarov. He's twenty-four years old and was on the incorporation papers of the Old Winter Furniture Store, Inc. as president and treasurer at age twenty-one. He'd just arrived in Orlando from Chechnya and he's been an exemplary candidate on his way to citizenship. He started the company, has hired members of his own community, and was nominated by the local Chamber of Commerce as Employer of the Year. He's raised thousands of dollars for the local school and the mosque he joined and sits on a bunch of committees for the chamber. He's donated a ton of money for education programs for kids at the mosque and opened a tech center for unemployed adults. Nice cover, don't you think?"

"What's next?" Mark said.

"According to my buddies in the nameless three-letter agency, Hamzah is the grandson of Dokka Abu Usman, a major Chechen Islamic militant in the 1960s. Umarov is the Russian version of Usman, which is Muslim. I checked all his financials and he's loaded. He has a six-figure company checking account balance and several corporate certificates of deposit in the company's name. I also did some checking, by way of Chechnya to the Caribbean, to see if there were wire transfers and there were. There were transfers every month for the last year into a personal account in the name of Hamzah Umarov. There have also been transfers from Hamzah to an imam named Abu Malik. Does that ring a bell?"

"Yes, he's the imam for the mosque on Old Winter Garden Road," Joe said.

"Well, as of now, he has a personal liquid net worth in an account at the Cayman National Bank in excess of $500,000.00."

"I guess we now see collusion, don't we?" said Frank and Trinity at the same time.

"Yes, and that's not all. Our imam friend is now forty-one years old and had just arrived in New York City when Nine/Eleven happened. He immediately landed in Orlando and started this mosque. He was only twenty-five at the time and built the mosque, which is incorporated as a 501C3 nonprofit religious organization. With further digging, I discovered the mosque was built from donations of $1.2 million dollars, all from individuals. Nice, huh?"

Joe snorted. "Yeah, unless you get caught."

"Now, I did some further checking. I wanted to see if anyone was running down to the Caymans from Orlando recently. So I went to all the local small independent airports and checked for flights. Guess what? There was a flight every month from Kissimmee to the Caymans on the first Monday of the month. Not surprisingly, there is no record of payment for those flights but the flights obviously had to be recorded for FAA purposes. Joe, or someone, you need to go to this airport and check the video for April sixth, the day after Easter this year. Pull the video and see who was in the plane heading out. I'm pretty sure it was Hamzah, but I'll bet our good friend the imam was with him."

Joe turned to Trinity and shook his head. She smiled, as if to say "Is there anything he doesn't know how to find out?"

Jack paused for a quick breath. "Next, I went to the Florida Department of State and pulled all the corporate records. In addition to Hamzah, there is a Alvi Bisolta named as the vice president and secretary of the corporation. I pulled the tax records as well, and they had over $3.0 million in sales and a profit before taxes of $227,592.00. They paid the corporate rate and I've a copy of the checks that were attached to their filings for both the Federal and the State of Florida. They also collected over $210,000.00 in sales taxes on the sale of furniture, bedding, mattresses, and other sundry items. Their Better Business Bureau rating is A-plus-plus. You can't do any better than that."

Trinity sighed. "I guess they've been planning something for a very long time, but what? What can it be, guys? I've got no idea."

"By the way," Jack continued, "they employ ten other Chechens, besides Hamzah and Bisolta. Four of the ten deliver furniture and take old stuff to the landfill. I'll bet those will be the guys on the video at the landfill. Don't treat them lightly. They could be members of a terrorist cell right here in Orlando. At least Jawarski is surrounded by like people. Four others are sales staff and the last two men work in the office. One is the bookkeeper and the other expedites the purchases, inventory control, and payments. I've got all their names, social security numbers, and every one of the twelve, including the bosses, paid their taxes for the last few years at least. They're good citizens all around, as far as the world knows."

Anything else, Jack, as if that's not enough?"

"Well, I also checked records of property ownership. Would you like to know where Jawarski might be hiding?"

"Holy shit! Really?"

"I shit you not!" Jack said, joking. "I've been a busy bee over the last two days. May I continue?"

"Yes, you may," Trinity said and put her hand over Joe's mouth. "Christ, Joe, let him finish."

"Christ? Trinity, I'm telling your father."

"What can he say? He doesn't even have a church anymore. Remember?" she said factiously.

"Boy. Have you changed from that nice little Baptist girl we met only a short while back."

"Live with it, pal," she said, laughing. "I really want to get these bastards. You've got no idea how much I want to get these bastards."

"I hear you. Me too."

"Are you two done now?" Jack asked. "I checked property in the names of the mosque, in all the names of everyone employed by the furniture company, and in the name of the furniture company itself. The ten workers don't own homes. From their addresses on their tax filings, they all rent because there are no interest or tax deductions for property tax. The mosque is tax exempt but I pulled their nine-ninety form from last year, just filed, and they own the mosque property, the house that the imam lives in, and two other parcels of income property a few blocks from the mosque. Both are small single-family homes. They have to pay tax on the two properties because they aren't part of the mosque mission and are income-producing properties. I've got all the addresses ready to send to you. Hamzah owns his own home and an apartment house with ten units. Guess who lives there? All the ten workers at the store live in the building. Another coincidence, don't you think? Alvi Bisolta is married, with two kids, and is older. He has a house in the suburbs away from Old Winter Garden Road. I think he's nothing but a figurehead and has no idea what's going on. That's just my opinion.

"So let me summarize. I believe that Jawarski or Axmad Khan is living at the mosque; or in one of the two income-producing properties owned by the mosque; or in the apartment building, doubling up with one of the workers; or with Hamzah and/or Bisolta. If I were a betting man, I'd shake down the imam who could be ripe for the picking or at least completely cover the mosque, the two houses, or the apartment building to see if Jawarski pops up. This should be sooner rather than later. I've got a feeling they are planning something big. It's been a few weeks already, and I don't think we've got much time left. Do you, Joe?"

"As usual, I believe you're one-hundred-percent right. Guys, what do you think?"

They all agreed and thanked Jack for what seemed like an incredible amount of information in such a short time. Joe needed to contact the rear admiral, who'd forward the information to Washington to distribute. Joe believed that, with Frank in charge and with Joe and the team, they could take down Jawarski soon with what they learned. At least if they tied up everyone associated with Jawarski, he might not have enough manpower to pull off what he thought would be inevitable.

"Thanks, Jack. Once again, you're remarkable."

"Seriously, guys, please stay safe," Jack said. "Take these guys seriously. They already murdered two people, injured two others, and burned down three churches, all in a matter of a few weeks. Be safe."

With that, he hung up.

♥♥♥

After the call, Trinity invited the chief to the hotel to tell him everything that was going on. As she did that, Joe called the rear admiral to tell him of their breakthrough and what they were going to do to flush out Jawarski and the rest of the cell. They'd ask the chief for twenty-four/seven coverage of the mosque, the two houses, the furniture store, the vans leaving the store every day, the apartment house, and both houses owned by Hamzah and Bisolta. It was only a matter of time before Jawarski would pop up for a meeting. Joe was deciding if he and the team should go right after the imam at the mosque. The man seemed to be a weak link. He was paid off but might fold if confronted. It could save time and lives. Maybe he knew what the next target was. Joe doubted that Jawarski or Hamzah would give up their plans. They were doing it for Allah. Jawarski was a murderer and Hamzah was a generational militant going all the way back to his grandfather's heroic efforts against the Russians.

At least Joe understood the culture and the language. Every minute he had, he listed to Chechen language tapes supplied by Homeland Security. The language was not that much different from Russian but the expressions were as different as someone from New York versus someone living in the sticks of Georgia. They spoke the same language but words and phrases could mean entirely different things to different people. Joe also needed to continue to look at military installations in the greater Orlando area. However, he was pretty sure that he knew where they would strike. At least, he could make a fairly educated guess.

Chapter 28

First things first, thought Joe. They got the pictures at the landfill and picked out two guys from the furniture store dumping mattresses and old furniture. Those pictures were placed on the wall of their Embassy Suites room along with pictures of Jawarski and the two dead Chechens. Trinity had the dead Chechens pictures cleaned up as best she could so they looked like they were only sleeping and had Beverly Fitch put the pictures in the *Orlando Sentinel*, the *Orlando Times*, and the *Orlando Weekly*.

They wanted people to come forward if they recognized the two individuals. There was no reference about why they wanted them found. That was a little risky, but they didn't want anyone to know any of the connections that they were looking into.

Jack also had gotten the driver's licenses and registrations of all vehicles for the individuals at the store, as well as the imam. They downloaded both the vehicle information and the pictures of matching drivers and placed those pictures under the ones they had up on the wall. They matched the two from the landfill and discovered they were the moving truck employees, but there was something about them that didn't seem right.

Joe thought that maybe it was just him. A lot of Eastern Europeans and Middle East people didn't smile in pictures.

It probably made them look tougher in that part of the world. They'd simply transferred their non-smiling looks to Orlando.

"Who wants to go to the airport and see what new videos we can find?" Joe said. "I have to go to flash my credentials. Mark, how about you going with me? Frank, I don't mean to take over. Please let me know if I step on your toes. I'm not used to not doing what I want when I want, and I'm sorry."

"Joe, do whatever you want. I know who's in charge here. I've no qualms about that whatsoever. Thanks for keeping me in charge. It's appreciated. Do what you want. Trinity and I'll be meeting with her detectives, patrol officers, and the street cops in a half hour at headquarters. The chief will be explaining what he wants from them and reconfirming that Trinity is in charge. Right, Chief?" he asked as he turned to look at him.

The chief was engrossed in all the data they uncovered since Joe got back and started to work with Jack Forest.

"We better head out," said the chief. "Frank's right, Joe. I'm going to lay it on the line to our men. We need to be on top of this and have it end as soon as possible. I'm getting heat from every direction. Being incompetent and looking incompetent are two different things. I'll be perceived that way anyway until this is solved. It goes with the territory. The men I handpicked with Trinity have my backing, and I believe there will be no leaks from them. I hope so at least. We've too much riding on this. Joe, are you going to confront the imam directly? If you do, you'll need backup."

"I'll let you know as soon as I have my evidence written down and in place. I want to make sure all of it's solid. Then I think we need a raid to take out the imam, not in the mosque but at his house. Then, depending on what he has to offer, we will immediately take down the store personnel, all of them, as soon as we need to. That leaves finding Jawarski and anyone else he has recruited that's not at the store. That's what worries me. We don't know if we're rounding up everyone. I don't think we are and that scares me. You know?"

Cal grimaced. "I didn't think about that or see that coming. I thought we found all of them, but you make sense. We can't leave it to supposition. We have to make sure we have everyone. How do we do that?"

"I haven't the vaguest idea, but I'll work on it," Joe said.

Mark and Joe headed to the airport. Mark also wanted to see if he could fly drones from there if he ever needed to do so.

⚬⚬⚬

The airport was around twenty miles southwest of Orlando, located on Dyer Boulevard in Kissimmee. From Pine Street, they merged on I-4W to US92W/US-17S US-441S to exit 80 on the left. From there, they turned right onto West Vine Street/US-92W/US-17S/US-192W. They continued to follow West Vine Street for two miles. Dyer Boulevard was on the left and the gate to the airport was easy to find. It took about a half an hour in traffic. They pulled up in front of the main building and parked. They left their Homeland Security card in the driver side windshield. Mark and Joe walked into the building and asked for the manager's office. The front desk receptionist asked them why they were there, and Joe simply showed her his credentials. Immediately, she called the manager's office, and he came trotting out.

"May I help you gentlemen?" he said.

"I hope so," Joe said. "Can we speak in private please?"

The manager showed them the way to his office. "What's this about?" he asked.

Joe didn't waste any time, as usual. He went through what he had. "During our investigation, we went to all the local, small, independent airports and checked for suspicious flights. Guess what? There was a flight every month

from the Kissimmee Airport to the Caymans on the first
Monday of the month for the last six months or so. We
stopped looking after six months. Not surprisingly, there's
no record of payment for those flights but the flights were
obviously recorded for FAA purposes. We need to specifically check the video for April sixth, the day after Easter
this year. Please pull the video so we can see who was getting into the plane heading out and who came back on the
same plane."

"Yes, sir. Let me go get my key. The videos are locked,
just like regulations require," the manager said.

"Do the regulations require regular monthly cash payments as well? Mark growled. "Do you want us to check
those as well, as long as we're here?"

There was no answer and the man ran to get the videos.
Mark and Joe could tell that he'd cooperate as long as they
kept this quiet. He came back, popped the videos into the
player, and hit the button. He knew exactly what they were
looking for and why. He had the pictures of two men getting
onto the plane with the pilot already seated in the cockpit.
They carried an aluminum briefcase with them. Joe and
Mark both knew immediately that the two men were Hamzah Umarov and Imam Abu Malik. They asked for a copy
of the video and a print of the frame. The manager also
showed them the video of the men coming back the same
night with the same briefcase. They got pictures of that as
well.

Joe turned to the manager. " I can hold you as an accessory to murder or as a known terrorist. I can have you renditioned to any place I want. Do you understand me? How
much did you get from them for hiding the flights?"

The manager cringed. "I got $1,500.00 on the days they
flew, about $8,000.00 in total."

"Would you like to live a long life, not in jail, but instead
continue to enjoy your family?"

"Yes, sir."

"Here's what I expect from you. I expect you to take

$10,000.00 in cash and give it to your children's school. You have kids. I know this because we already checked you out. You're to get a receipt for tax purposes, but you'll never be getting a tax break. You'll mail that receipt to the address on my card, immediately. You'll check in with us every week to the phone number on that card. If there's a terrorist attack within the next month, you'll be the first one I go after because of your greed and pure stupidity. What the hell were you thinking? Did you help train the Nine/Eleven Muslim pilots down here in Florida to hit the twin towers? Do you understand me?"

The manager stood there, blinking, and slowly his pants began to get wetter and wetter. "I promise this will never happen again. I wasn't thinking, and I'm an asshole. I'm sorry. I'm really sorry."

"See that it doesn't," Joe said.

With that, he and Mark walked out with what they needed. Right before they left the hotel, Joe had a thought. He asked for duplicate pictures of everyone on the wall. He wanted to see if he could meet the head of the navy installation on the campus of the University of Central Florida. He and Mark had to head back going east but it was still only forty miles door to door and it was early. He thought a warning today might stop whatever could possibly happen, or at least discuss with the security team at the facility the potential of anything happening. How prepared were they for a potential terrorist attack? Were they prepared externally and internally as well?

Joe thought that it would be easier as an inside job than attacking the forty-acre campus externally. There were no fences that he could see from Google Earth, but you never knew.

How the hell would they attack from the outside and how many men would they need? If it was internal, they could hack them and either destroy or steal all their highly classified documents.

Joe couldn't wait to get there. It was just one more thing

on his long checklist. He hadn't called Julie in a few days. *Some honeymoon*, he thought.

ℰᔆℰᔆ

The Naval Air Warfare Center Training System Division was inside the Central Florida Research Park at the University of Central Florida. It was located at 12424 Research Parkway in Orlando on the east side of the city, about eighteen miles from downtown Orlando, headed to Cape Canaveral. They were now in Kissimmee and had to head northeast, retracing the twenty miles down on the west side or Orlando and then head east about eighteen miles. It would take about forty-five minutes to get there. They stopped at McDonalds on the way and grabbed lunch. It seemed like they hadn't eaten since he got back to Orlando. Their motto of "eat and sleep when you can" went to the way side which wasn't good. Being hungry never helped the thinking process. They grabbed two extra chocolate shakes and guzzled those down as well.

They got to the guard station at the front of the NAWCTSD and Joe gave the guard both their credentials. He told him that he needed to see Stephen Slater, Rear Admiral Lower Half, who was in command. The guard took the information and called the commander's office.

The commander picked up and asked to speak to Joe. "Lieutenant, how can I help you?"

"Sir, this is a Homeland Security matter and an FBI matter as well. I carry three credentials, including lieutenant in the Coast Guard. I can't speak to you over this intercom but please call Rear Admiral Jake Barnes in Miami right now. He doesn't know I'm here, but he'll tell you that if I'm here, it's important, sir." Joe added the "sir" for the man's ego. He never needed to call Jake that. He did it out of respect. He gave the commander Jake's private phone number.

"I'll be a few minutes," the commander said. He called

Jake and was quite surprise about the seeming clout that the young man at the front gate had. He told the guard to let Joe in and told him where to park.

Joe and Mark smiled at each other. "Well, that went okay."

They went into the building, past the check-in area, and they were told to go to the rear admiral's office. They walked in the door. Joe held out his hand. "Thanks for seeing us without any notice. I believe it's important enough, sir."

"What's up," the commander asked.

Joe told him. He went over everything they had to date. "Are there any targets more viable than the one we're sitting in right now?" he asked the rear admiral.

"This is the navy's think tank and weapons designer for the entire navy and the marines on the East Coast," the rear admiral told him. "I can't think that any national guard unit or any other facility would be more important than this one to protect."

With that in mind, Joe said, " That's why I believe these Chechens are willing to die for the cause and blow this facility to kingdom come. I think it would be very difficult to bomb this massive forty-acre facility from the outside. However, once in here, I'll bet that, because of the sophistication of the people here, you just don't hire anyone, regardless of the job. Therefore, I believe it would be easier to get someone inside here to do damage, even though you're as heavily protected as you tell me."

The rear admiral thought for a moment before speaking. "We're secure but that means next to nothing in today's world. What was safe ten minutes ago may no longer do the trick. We've hundreds of PhDs running around here, just keeping our technology protected, but the facility itself, I don't think we've done as good a job. We're on a forty-acre open plot of land in the middle of a large university. I'm not speaking out of school here, I don't want anything to happen to the thousands of people who work here every day from top to bottom. Everyone is important here. Trust me, I've thought about this every waking moment. I'm scared to death. Rear Admiral Barnes just told me that you're no bull shitter or alarmist. He said to listen to you carefully because you've taken on your share of bad guys and won. That's a hell of a record at your age."

The rear admiral seemed to be in his fifties, admiring Joe who was twenty years younger.

Joe winced. He was not doing this for kudos. "I know that, in today's age, this might not be politically correct but I know what I'm looking for. I'm looking for specific Chechen identifiers, or if not that, men who are obviously Muslim. Not everything is obvious to everyone but I'm well aware of who I'm targeting. I need to look at every face in your HR system of those working here. We'll ignore all the females and all those who are either African American or Spanish. I can then import your photos into my Excel spreadsheet and I've got a program that has facial recognition software. If there's no match, then I'll look at each man to see if I recognize the features I'm looking for."

"Isn't that profiling?"

"Yes, but specific to a terrorist plot under the Patriot Act which isn't RICO or under the jurisdiction of local law. Only Homeland Security under the Patriot Act guides me. I can do this legally, or at least I'll have support for it."

"Okay, let's head down to HR. I'm sure they won't be happy, but what the hell," the rear admiral said.

They went through the online files. They downloaded the files, and Joe sorted them through his system. He threw out everyone who didn't fit his profile and was left with over 1,000 individuals. He then looked at age groups and sorted it by anyone under forty years old, thinking that, if anyone was radicalized, it must have been in the last several years and they had to be young. He was left with fewer than 500 names and faces. He then went by years of service and suspected that anyone there since before Nine/Eleven was probably okay at least for the first run through. He was now down to under 300. He then went by occupation. It would be hard to believe that a PhD would be involved, because it took so long to get the degree. Anyone that old, in a cell, had to be in a sleeper cell. When considering the Chechens in the furniture store, that didn't seem probable. None of those were here longer than ten years, well after Nine/Eleven. He now started looking at people, comparing them to those he had at the store, and Jawarski and the imam. There were no matches but after programming in the features he wanted to stand out, he noticed a large drop off in numbers. He was now down to twenty-seven individuals who were at the facility for less than ten years, didn't have a PhD, were younger than forty, and had features compatible to Chechen men. Those features included very pale skin, large heads, and above-average height, which couldn't be seen from the picture but was taken from the records afterward. He got the files and had copies made. He'd have Jack run all twenty-seven through the system and see what popped up. He sent the now manageable files to Jack for a thorough check. That check would include the same procedures Jack used for the others at the store.

Joe thanked the rear admiral and asked to speak to the head of security. He met with him, let him copy the pictures Joe brought with him, and asked him to do a thorough shakedown of the facility. Joe told him to do an unplanned fire drill and look into every nook and cranny in the building.

"It might be inconvenient," Joe said, "but not as inconvenient as having thousands of employees gassed. The chlorine bombs that blew up three churches and killed one individual were related to terrorists in Yemen and could be used here in Orlando and specifically at this site."

Joe also asked him to call all the other military installations in the greater Orlando area and place them on alert. The rear admiral and the security chief thanked Joe and Mark as they left the facility. There was a very important confrontation planned with the imam tonight.

CHAPTER 29

They made it back to the hotel. Joe owed Jake Barnes a call, especially after visiting the naval facility. He also needed to speak to Julie. He'd only called her once since he got here. He'd been that busy, but it was no excuse after only being married a little over a week and a half. Mark called Louise as well to find out what was going on. He also had to speak to the rear admiral since Mark had a direct report to him as well while still managing the Dania Beach Station. Frank was still with the chief and Trinity but he called and said he was heading back to the hotel. Trinity was headed home to freshen up and rejoin them for the confrontation later that night at the imam's house.

ಲ

"Julie, Hi. How are you?" Joe asked.

"Who's this?" She chuckled. "Do I know you? Why are you calling me?"

"I'm really sorry, Julie, but this has been a living hell since I got back to Orlando. We're about to crack the case wide open within the next few days. We have to be careful or Jawarski will wind up in the wind again to kill more Americans."

"Sure, use that line on me again so I'll feel bad. Only kidding," she said.

"I really *am* sorry. Have you unpacked everything? Did all the presents arrive? How are the wedding plans for Saint Justin's?"

"Don't worry about me, Joe. I know you're under pressure. I just hope you get back here in time for this wedding. It means a lot to Tillie and me and to her friends. I sent out all the invitations. The large tents are secured and will be delivered Friday afternoon. The food has been ordered and the Waffle House will make up 125 dinners as their donation to the food pantry. I've ordered kegs of beer, soda, and boxes of wine. This will be as lowbrow Conch as we can get. The ladies church auxiliary, led by Tillie of course, will have all the side dishes prepared and ready for Saturday, the twentieth.

"I'm finishing up classes and the grant project, and I've had graduation things to take care of for those heading to college. I have to make sure all the financial aid forms and their scholarships are in place and all final transcripts sent to the colleges. I'm getting a lot of help from volunteers, including Lucy and the track team, Jan Marino from my fifth grade class at Key Largo School, and from Gary Myers and his principal's staff. So, things are falling into place. I've been getting some nice calls asking if we're really donating all the wedding gift proceeds to the church's food bank and second hand store. I don't want to get into the fact that we're sitting on more money than we've ever seen before but I explain that's what we both want to do and they think it's great."

"Well, for my two cents, I do too," he said.

"I'm still getting pressure from Marcia Manning from Burbank about the movie rights. I told her I started the third and final book in the series. I didn't tell her I'm almost half way through. She wants to buy it still and, whenever I'm ready, they're ready to go. It's been green lit as they said before. My head is spinning, Joe," she said. "By the way, a member of the cleaning staff at Key Largo School has just been diagnosed with a brain tumor. She's only thirty years old. Her name is Juanita Lopez and she has a five-year-old daughter named Bella in kindergarten. She's a single mother with no relatives. We think she's Cuban, but we're not sure. I met her at a PTA meeting. She's a very nice woman and loves her daughter. I also ran parent classes to show them how to use the iPad given to their kids and how to work with the kids to only go to appropriate educational websites.

"Bella is so cute. I taught her to use the iPad from the grant. They all get to take an iPad home. She's a wiz. Her biggest problem is, that at home, they speak only Spanish so her English needs work, but she's improving. Juanita doesn't have long, according to the prognosis. I know because we've become friends. Joe, we don't know what'll happen to Bella if Juanita doesn't make it. Can you find out about her father when you get back? Maybe we can find him in time so Bella doesn't wind up in foster care or worse."

"Sure," he said. "Can you quietly, and I mean extremely quietly, get me all the information you can on Juanita, including, birth date, social security number, place of birth for Bella, her birthday, and anything else. I'll have Jack search records to see if we can come up with a father's name on the birth certificate or a name on a wedding license, church or civil. We'll search DMV for driver's licenses and car registrations. We can do the same search we did to find your father, Julie. If that's what you want."

"That's what I want you to do, Joe. I don't want Juanita fighting for her last breath and worrying about what happens to her daughter."

"As soon as I get home, I'll work on it. Better yet, why don't you get all the information you can and you call Jack. I'm sure he'll have no problem doing it. He does have to justify everything he does but I wouldn't worry about that if I were you. So far, since I've known him, he's had no problem getting anything he needed. When you're the best at what you do, the brass tends to look away at the small stuff.

Call him. Julie, I love you. I have to go. Frank just got back. Trinity will be here shortly."

"Say hi to Trinity and tell her I expect her at our wedding. If she can't find a room, tell her she can stay at our new place. We'll be away for a few days after the wedding anyway, in Key West. See you when I see you. Hope it's before June twentieth."

ↄ৲ↄ৲ↄ

Frank walked into the suite. He had a bunch of subs with him, a twelve-pack of Oktoberfest for Joe, and another twelve-pack of Coors. Frank liked Coors. Mark would drink anything.

Joe grabbed a beer. "We just ate at McDonald's a while ago, but thanks. We'll eat again. Won't we, Mark?"

Frank's team, all the way up from Miami, would get their own beer. They'd been working on the church bombings away from Joe, Mark, and Frank. Frank hadn't even seen them in two days. After their investigation at the churches, they would be sent home. There were now more than enough FBI agents running around doing the same thing.

"Of course," Mark said with a smile. "Is it free? I'll eat anything if it's free."

Joe laughed. "He's not kidding."

Just then Trinity walked in. "So, what do you have for us, Joe? Any breakthroughs other than what we have? We're going to visit the imam tonight, right?"

"Yes, we are and we confirmed that the imam and the owner of the store flew back and forth to the Cayman's on April sixth, the day after Easter. We also read the riot act to the airport manager for taking cash from them and not recording the flights. The flight was recorded for FAA purposes and that we knew. The born-again manager will be making a sizable contribution to the local elementary school and forwarding the receipt to us, so he can't take a tax deduction. He also has to pay extra for a laundry bill for pissing in his pants after we told him he was going to be renditioned as a terrorists. Right, Mark?"

"You're correct, sir," Mark said as he was downing half a sub.

"Well, that ties the imam to corruption, I believe. Doesn't it?" she asked.

"It's enough when added to his half million dollar Cayman account," Frank said. "But we need him to talk about where Jawarski's been stashed. Without that, we've got nothing. What else do we need?"

Joe went through the checklist with him. They'd visit the imam tonight and have all of Trinity's officers ready if they got an address for Jawarski. They'd raid the store as soon as they needed to do so, after meeting the imam.

Jawarski was slippery. They had to give him that. They also would question the imam about any pending terrorist attacks that he knew about. Was there anything in the works already? Was Jawarski needed to complete any mission that had already started? Was there another cell or anyone else involved that they didn't know about? Joe continued to ask those questions that had no answers right now. Hopefully, they'd get those answers and break up any potential attack down the road. This needed to end with an arrest, quietly, and Jawarski needed to be held with a death sentence hanging over his head for the murder of a police officer.

⌘

It was late May so it starting getting dark around 7:30 p.m. since day light savings came back in March. They planned on arriving just after dusk to knock on the imam's door. They weren't sure if he'd be home, at the mosque, or simply out. The officers had been watching the store, the mosque, the apartment house, Hamzah's house, and the two houses owned by the mosque. The imam's pattern suggested that right after sunset prayers, he'd leave the mosque and go home to dinner. There was no one there. He wasn't married and had no children that they could determine. He could have a whole family back in Chechnya, for all they knew. They were positive he didn't have one here. Maybe that was why he was gathering cash in the Caymans—to go home.

Trinity called her teams and the team at the imam's house told her that he arrived home only minutes earlier, right on schedule. To Joe, that meant, since he wasn't breaking a pattern that he probably never thought about, that he was unaware that he was being investigated and shadowed. That was good. There would, hopefully, be an element of surprise. When Joe hit him right between the eyes with what he had, Joe would watch his eyes and body language. If they were wrong, it could lead to a lawsuit, professionally and personally and could label him and all those around him as anti-Muslim.

Joe didn't need to leave his current assignment with a large blemish on his record. He was looking forward to his potential new job at the Florida Keys Community College. Even if he didn't stay in the Coast Guard, he could still do all those things that he was told about by the rear admiral. He had the experience, the education, and was fluent in two languages. He could hook on somewhere. He wanted to do the job that was recommended to him by Jake Barnes. He'd love, with Julie's okay, to wind up as the superintendent of the U.S. Coast Guard Academy up in New London, Connecticut. He could serve for a few years and then move on to another position with a major university of his choosing.

It was fun to dream, he thought. He also went back to Julie's request. Was her interest in Bella Lopez that of a teacher interested in her student's welfare or something more? She was kind of cryptic, not revealing anything more than her request. Joe had to start thinking about kids, now that they were married. Julie was twenty-five but he was thirty-four. If they were to have kids, and Julie wanted kids, he knew that for a fact. She wanted three kids. She'd told him so. He was well aware that the clock, for him, was ticking. He better sit down with her as soon as he got back. Hopefully, he'd get back and not wind up as another statistic in the war on terrorism.

CHAPTER 30

Trinity drove her undercover car with Joe in the shotgun seat. Mark went with Frank in his Coast Guard vehicle. The Orlando police officers assigned to watch the house were set in place at all four corners of the imam's house. There were also coverage at all the other identified buildings but they were told to wait unless something major happened and there was massive movement from those facilities, especially if anyone spotted Jawarski.

Trinity, Joe, Mark, and Frank got out of the two vehicles, and Joe went first. He rang the doorbell. He saw movement through the front door into the kitchen in a straight line to the back of the house. The imam got up from his chair at the kitchen table and moved toward the door. He opened the door with the chain still on.

"May I help you, gentlemen," he asked. "I'm in the middle of my dinner." He didn't seem to be fazed by four people standing at his front door. Joe suspected that he was used to people gathering in his office and home, at all times of the day, since he was the spiritual advisor to his mosque.

Joe introduced himself, Trinity, Frank, and Mark. He introduced himself as an officer with Homeland Security, Trinity as a detective with the Orlando police department, and Frank and Mark as his associates. The man needed no further explanation. "Imam, we need to speak to you immediately. We can speak freely here or if you prefer at Homeland Security headquarters in downtown. It's your option, sir," he said.

"What's this about?" the imam asked.

"May we come in, sir? I've a warrant for your arrest, even though I don't need one to talk to you. If you prefer, I can just place you under arrest under the Patriot Act, sir. What do you prefer?"

"Please come in. I've nothing to hide. I need to put my dinner back on the stove. Would that be all right?"

"Yes, certainly," Joe said.

They waited for the imam to come back to the door and show them to the living room. The officers outside had listening devices and video equipment, in case the imam called anyone to warn them. "Please come in and sit down. Now, can you tell me what this is all about?"

"Sir, I believe you already know what this is about. We've got enough evidence against you to either arrest you for harboring a fugitive and as an accessory before and after the fact to murder in the first degree of a police officer that includes the death penalty. In addition, we have you in a money-laundering scheme, tax evasion, and all the funds you had in the Cayman National Bank are now in our possession. Trinity, how much did you have Jack Forest transfer today?"

"Five hundred thousand dollars, more or less," she said.

"Imam, we also have you on video leaving and coming back on a plane from the Kissimmee Airport to the Cayman Islands with another known terrorist. You were carrying a Halliburton money briefcase on April sixth, the day after Easter. Would you care to comment on any one of these situations that I've just presented to you?"

"I want my lawyer, sir."

"Well, you made that easy. Under the Patriot Act, sir, you've no access to a lawyer. You've also entered the country with an expired visa in 2001 residing in New York City. You left New York City after Nine/Eleven and came to Orlando, and you were funded to the tune of millions of dollars to establish this Chechen-based mosque. We believe—and even if we aren't sure, it doesn't matter—that you're a member of a Chechen terrorist cell established as a sleeper cell. It now looks like you've been activated and you, sir, are caught red-handed. Anything you want to say before you're hauled off as a terrorist?"

"I'm the imam for this mosque. I'll be missed. You can't get away with this. I've got rights."

"You used to have rights but not anymore, sir. Trinity, please cuff the imam. We'll transport him out through the back. Our van is waiting for us. Just like the van that picked up Jawarski after he murdered a heroic police officer in the line of duty. You've got one chance, and one chance only. If you don't believe me, here is the number, and I'll dial it, for the Deputy Secretary, Martin J. Sutherland, of Homeland Security in Washington, DC."

Joe dialed the number and the deputy secretary came on the phone. As they were headed to the imam's house earlier, Joe had called the rear admiral and told him what he'd planned. He asked him to call the deputy secretary and to be by the phone when he called close to 8:00 p.m., which it now was. Jake told Joe that he had a lot of balls but if this worked, it could save a lot of lives.

The imam's head was spinning when he got off the phone with Mr. Sutherland. In very direct language, the deputy secretary told him that he'd be renditioned out of the country to a place not far from where he grew up. He told him that he'd love Romania this time of year but he'd only see it from a two-foot secured window. Imam Malik looked at Joe. "I'll talk, but you need to protect me." He sighed. "I never wanted any of this, never."

"But you took the money, didn't you?" said Mark and Frank at the same time. They had no sympathy for the imam.

Trinity was now in charge. It was her investigation. They wanted a murderer caught as well as to stop a terrorist plot if there was one. "Tell us exactly what you know," she said.

"I was seduced by Hamzah Umarov. I didn't know he was the grandson of a Chechen Islamic Muslim terrorist, from the 1960s. I only learned this two nights ago from Axmad Khan who you call Bronislaw Jawarski. Jawarski is staying in our second house's basement down the street. He threatened me just the other night. I really believed that Hamzah was taking care of the mosque and me personally because he was religious. I didn't know he was the grandson of a terrorist from Chechnya. He's been a model citizen and had won awards from the Chamber of Commerce. He'd given millions to the mosque and our people. He'd sponsored job programs and hired our own members and made a life for them. Little did I know," he said.

Trinity snorted. "This misremembering the facts seems to be your strong suit. From our research, you were a known critic of the United States. We downloaded some of your speeches since you've been here. You were on a minor watch list because of your hate speech and because the government is now sensitive to the Muslim plight in America. Even though you had an expired visa, they left you alone so as to not stir up anything. However, now that we see you've been involved in a future terrorist plot, we don't give a shit about your rights. We care about the rights of those you plan on murdering, you scumbag."

Everyone looked at her with new eyes. She was pissed. She didn't forget about the African American churches being burned or about Archie.

"You going to rebuild those churches with your new found wealth?"

"Yes, if I have the chance."

"You won't have the chance, but your members will as a good faith measure. It's about equal to what you got in tainted blood money over the years," She growled. "Now what's the plot—when, where, and how? We don't care why? How do we get Jawarski from the basement, other than blowing him to kingdom come? We can send him to the afterworld as quickly as Allah, if you want."

Now Joe was surprised. He smirked.

Trinity immediately called all her men in their positions. She told them to go ahead and raid the houses and where Jawarski would be. She told them to get to the apartment building, the mosque, Hamzah's home, and the furniture store. She told them not to enter the mosque but simply stay back and wait to see if anyone would come out. It was after prayers and the mosque's night education and training programs would also be ended. "Now tell us about the planned attack."

Imam Malik told the assembled team that Jawarski was planning on attacking a naval installation in the Central Florida Research Park. He had two men planted inside who'd release the chlorine bombs after they arrived for their midnight shift. "If Jawarski isn't at home, he's preparing the two men for the mission," he said.

"Who are they," Joe asked.

"They're two young men who've been radicalized by Hamzah, mostly, and then by Axmad Khan. I now understand that Hamzah did ninety-nine percent of the brainwashing but when Axmad came here, it was like they were meeting God. Axmad told them it was God's plan and Praise Be to Allah for their mission. They were good young men who've been unduly influenced like I was years ago. You may not believe it but I do now like, but not love, America. I see what can happen over time as our members are mainstreamed and become citizens of this country. I'm not wrong but I believe now I'm not right, either. I know I won't be allowed to stay in the United States but I wish it no harm. I was afraid for my own life and the lives of these two men and their families if they didn't carry out this mission." He gave Joe the addresses and phone numbers for both families. The two men still lived at home.

"Let's go to their houses, and if they aren't there, we will pick up their parents and bring them to the naval installation to see if they can talk them out of it before it happens, or at least get everyone out of the building," Mark suggested.

"Joe, there are as many on the night shift as the day shift, right?"

"Yes, but if we call right now before they start their shift, they may panic and kill everyone on both shifts as one comes in and the other leaves. We've no choice but to head there. Imam, we've already been there yesterday and warned the rear admiral of a potential attack. I'll call the rear admiral now but not to evacuate just yet. We want to catch all of them, including Jawarski. What're their names?"

"The two men are Pawel Wysocki and Tomasz Symanski," the imam said. "Like Jawarski, they too lived in Poland before coming here. That's why they thought he was one of them. They traveled the same paths, supposedly. We know they didn't. Back then, the parents knew there would be discrimination in 2005, right after Nine/Eleven. It was still fresh in everyone's mind across the world. They got out of Chechnya just as the Russians invaded. They wound up in Poland and immigrated here. Both fathers are professionals. Martyn Wysocki's fifty-five and is a family physician in a group practice in Orlando. His wife is Anka and she's fifty-two and a housewife. They've got two other children. Stefan Symanski, Tomasz's father, is an engineer with the City of Orlando. He's fifty-four and his wife Halina's fifty-three and a housewife as well. The two wives are sisters, making the two boys first cousins. The Symanski's have no other children. The two families came over together. They're as far from terrorists as you can get. They've no knowledge that I know of, that their two sons are on the verge of mass murder. Here's their address."

Joe pulled out his pictures of the twenty-seven men identified as potential terrorists that worked at the naval facility. He spread them out. Each picture had a folder and a name with their background inside. Joe went to the pictures of Pawel and Tomasz and looked at the imam. "Are these the two men that are planning to bomb the facility?"

The imam looked at the pictures. "That's Pawel Wysocki

and that's Tomasz Symanski. They were in my office many times with Jawarski and Hamzah, planning the attack and how to construct the chlorine bombs, bringing in one piece at a time to put into the air conditioning vents. They were to put the chlorine gas in last, with cell phones, smuggling all of it onto the premises. They were going to go through a backdoor and they would be handed individual packs of chlorine gas and cell phones to trigger the bombs. All they had to do is connect it to each cell phone and, when they left, all they had to do was hit a number on speed dial on each of ten phones in a row. Evidently, Jawarski had all ten phones programmed to his. He'd be hitting the button. I'm afraid of what'll happen to me and to the families, if this mission is accomplished. I don't think he'll let any of us live. Khan and Hamzah probably already have plans to leave the country. I heard them say something a week or so ago about Mexico, but that was it. Nothing else."

As he was speaking, and as everyone was speaking, Frank had recorded everything since they got to the front door. There would be no wrong interpretation about water-boarding or torture. This was a clean as it got, and Frank immediately uploaded the video to the deputy secretary, Jake Barnes, the FBI, the chief of police, and to Jack Forest up in Virginia, in case they needed addition background on the two families to make sure the imam was telling the truth.

Joe thought for a moment. "I'll call the rear admiral, but if they evacuate before everyone starts their shift, while the others were leaving, Jawarski and the two young men may panic and kill everyone. If the two men arrive on their shift, it probably means the bombs aren't armed yet. So we don't need to panic. If they don't come in, we need to evacuate the premises. We've no choice but to head there, as I've said. Do you fully understand the situation?" he asked the imam. "If we stop this now, you'll be treated much differ-ently than if they succeed. No matter what, you're gone from the United States. If you so much as pick up a phone, no one will ever see you again." *No one will ever see him again anyway but he doesn't have to know that.* Hope was a wonderful thing.

They put their heads together. Joe would have Homeland Security pick up the imam immediately. They were waiting for Joe's call after he talked to the deputy secretary. The imam would be held in secrecy until they completed all their tasks. Trinity and Joe would head for the naval facility with a team. Word was coming in from Trinity's teams that they got Hamzah at his house. They got the others at the apartment house and they were headed to the suburbs to get Alvi Bisolta. He'd be held as a material witness. They thought, after all their investigation, that Bisolta was nothing more than an older patsy but he would come in handy if he were to be told that he'd suffer the same consequences if he didn't cooperate. He had the only family.

Word also came back from Trinity's team that they knocked down the door to the house and the basement to find Jawarski, but he was not there. Joe had the imam call the parents just to see if they were home. Neither was at home and it was only around 9:30 p.m. They weren't suspicious. There was no need to be. The parents and the sons were probably unaware of what was going on. The calls put the imam in a slightly more favorable light. He'd better hope that this was stopped completely with no tragedies. They had until midnight when the shifts changed when Wysocki sand Symanski were to begin their cleaning shift. Joe had told the rear admiral what was going on and said to call him back if anything happened up in Washington. He also told the facility commander to specifically keep an eye on all the doors in the back and to make sure that if there were an early handoff through an unalarmed opened door to let him know. He told him that they were on their way and to have the guards ready to let them in.

They headed out. There was nothing left to do but head to the Naval Air Warfare Center Training System at the University of Central Florida's research park about eighteen miles from where they were. At this time, with Trinity's siren and flashing lights going strong, they'd make it under fifteen minutes. Before reaching the park, they'd pull up like nothing was going on and continue on to see the rear admiral, as if it were a routine matter.

Mark and Frank left at the same time to go and pick up the parents. They'd try to convince the fathers to call their sons and tell them that their mothers were together and had an accident and the sons needed to meet them at the Orlando Regional Medical Center's Level One Trauma Center. Trinity assigned four SWAT team officers, fully armed and with the pictures of the two men and Jawarski, to stand near the emergency room entrance where they told the sons to go. If that didn't get them there, nothing would. They hoped that Jawarski wasn't with them.

They didn't believe he would be, but the SWAT team should do the trick with the hospital security team who'd been notified of the plan. It was a decent plan for now but could change as the night grew closer to midnight. Joe could care less if Jawarski was killed or not. Hopefully, if he was dead, this might end quicker before the radicalized men continued on their path of destruction. Joe wouldn't be too sad if the other two got it as well, as long as they saved thousands of lives. Joe thought it was time to pray. This was the most intense investigation he'd ever been in. Other criminal investigations were individually treacherous but thousands of lives would be on the line if he failed this time. No more Nine/Elevens, they all vowed.

CHAPTER 31

It was now close to 9:30 p.m. Joe and Trinity arrived at the gate of the naval facility. The same guard was there and waved them in. They parked in front and walked up to the rear admiral's office. Joe introduced Trinity to Stephen Slater, the rear admiral.

"So, we're it, huh?" he said.

"We believe so," Trinity said. She went through all the steps involved up until now that led to this conclusion. "Right now, two of Joe's men, both Coast Guard, are gathering up the Wysocki and the Symanski parents to bring the fathers to the facility and the mothers to the hospital in case the sons show up there. We need the fathers at this facility as an intervention if the young men show up for work in order to complete their mission.

"Right now, we believe the sons are running around with Jawarski until they have to be here at midnight for their shift. We had the imam call the parents to see if the sons were home, and they weren't. We left it at that. Mark and Frank are picking up the parents. The imam believes they are totally innocent of what their son's may be planning. We also have the fathers making a call to the son's cell phones, telling them that their two mothers have been in an automobile accident and that they should meet them at the medical center. The logic is there, since the mothers are sisters. If that works, we can get them before they get to work.

That's if Jawarski isn't with them. If he is, we have a SWAT team at the hospital to take down all three if necessary."

She paused for a breath. "Have you done a complete and thorough search of the facility and are all the doors secured with cameras?"

"Yes," he said, "the doors are secured and cameras are at each one. I have my security staff, all federal officers, alerted to this potential threat. I say potential because, as of now, we haven't found anything."

"We've got less than two hours before they start arriving for the midnight shift," Joe said. "Trinity's officers will be undercover at each intersection to spot Wysocki and Symanski, if they come. We have the license plates and vehicle descriptions for both. The officers also have their pictures. They will let us know if they're spotted. We haven't blasted it all over the police radios because we still want to keep this a quiet as possible. We don't want panic. Nine/Eleven was obvious and out in the open. It was clearly an attack on America. This potential attack at a military installation might not be viewed in the same light, so we need to keep a lid on it."

Joe paused and considered. "Can we look around the facility with the security team. We want to know where the two men will be working tonight."

Slater walked then down the hall to the security office. " Let's head to where the two men's scheduled rounds begin. They have specific duties every night and everything they have as waste is incinerated at the end of the shift. No trash leaves the facility, due to national security."

Joe walked into the first area where they were to start their duties. He asked about egress and cameras near the first set of rooms to be cleaned. The exit door was less than 150 feet from the first room. Joe asked the security team to unscrew each air conditioning vent cover in each room. There was no need for hot air heat in the building. They used forced air for cooling and electric heat for the two weeks in the winter when it was required. It took about twenty minutes to unscrew every vent cover in all the rooms going toward the exit door.

Joe knew he'd be doing his own search even after they did theirs. He had his bag of tools with him when he entered. The main tool was a VIS-MINI-CAM Duct Inspection Camera that Jack Forest had sent to him a few days earlier. When it arrived, he showed Trinity what he'd planned to do regardless of what the navy did in its own inspection. As it turned out, all they did was take off the vent covers and look in for about three feet.

Joe's camera featured a one-hundred-forty-degree wide-angle view, in full color, with two bright light LED's for long-range illumination, and a twenty-five-foot extendable push rod insertion. It also had a spring-mounted camera head for easy maneuvering around corners. It had a long battery life so there were no electric wires, and it captured both video and still images. It also had a thirty-two-foot cable and a 100-foot extension. He had everything he needed to see if there were any bombs placed in any ducts in this section. He was hoping that he had at least one here. If there were more than one, then this was the area that the chlorine gas would be dumped into the building and carried throughout. He suspected.

There was nothing in the first few rooms but as he got closer to the emergency exit, he noticed that the ducts started to bend around the hallways creating spots where no one could see anything with the naked eye. Joe inserted the camera in the next to last office space and moved it around the bended duct. Sitting there, about five feet in, was a stand-alone box about a foot long and rectangular and four or five inches tall. It had a long string attached that was basically invisible to the naked eye because it was dark with no lights. The navy inspection didn't include anything more than a flashlight and no one would have noticed a string in the duct. To Joe, it was obviously placed there to pull the box toward the opening. Whatever it was, it should fit through the vent opening because they probably got it in that way. Joe tugged the box slowly. He pulled it out and noticed that there was no cell phone attached or any explosive material that he could see. He was getting nervous and asked security what they did under these circumstances.

At least they were prepared. They ran back to security and got a special lead-lined container that was used to transport any suspicious materials away from the facility. They'd take it out immediately and have their own bomb squad open it and see if it was armed. Joe believed it was not, at this point, but it would be soon.

It was still not time to start evacuating the facility. Only if the two men didn't show up for their midnight shift would they do so. Then they felt that something was going to happen. If they did show up on time, Joe thought it meant that they hadn't armed the bombs yet. They would be held and confronted as soon as they walked in the front door. They would be brought to a conference room and be placed face to face with their fathers. Hopefully, if that happened, it would save the day.

If they didn't show up, everyone would head to their cars and immediately head away from the facility. Those using public transportation would head to the nearest bus stop where naval buses would pick them up and move them to safer ground. There was an extensive plan in place. It was never used in a real live situation before. It would be used now, if they didn't show up. If they didn't show up, those coming in for the midnight shift would go back to their cars and leave. After midnight, those coming in late would be stopped a block away and turned around. Each vehicle had a parking sticker attached to their bumper. It was the best they could do for now. Joe wondered if Wysocki and Symanski would show up with Jawarski.

⁓⁓

"Mark, did you get to the parent's houses?" Joe asked.

"We're now at the Symanski house. The Wysocki's didn't go so smoothly. I almost had to arrest them. They didn't believe us and kept asking for a lawyer. I called the deputy secretary just like you did for the imam, and the parents finally started to understand that this was a national crisis and that their son was now involved in a potential mass murder. We showed them all the evidence, and we called the imam, already placed in lockup over at Homeland Security. He told them the truth about their boy. They were shocked."

"Will they help with the Symanskis?" Joe asked.

"They say yes."

"Okay. It's getting late, Mark. How's Frank?"

"He's fine. This is a little new to him. Hell, it's new to me as well, but we're holding up. We will take the fathers to the naval facility and the mothers to the hospital in case they show up there. Then they can talk them down after the SWAT team arrests them. Having them there could prevent bloodshed. I don't like using the mothers but this could prevent a catastrophe. The fathers will come in the backdoor of the naval facility before 11:30 p.m. We will put them in a conference room."

"I think this will prevent a catastrophe, guys," Joe agreed. "We're now in the process of checking to see if the bomb we found is armed. If it isn't, that's great. It probably means they will show up on time and the other bombs, if there are others, will be still unarmed. At least we have, hopefully, prevented a terrorist attack."

"With any luck, we will drop off the mothers at the hospital, protected by the SWAT team, and bring the fathers to the facility," Mark said. "We'll be there no later than 11:30 p.m."

"We'll see you then. The rear admiral is getting his own security team together with a sniper, and they'll be strategically placed outside the building toward the back. There is no way any handoff will be coming from the front unless they try to drive a car through the gate and hit the building.

They would only kill themselves, so we don't believe that will happen. The security team is getting dressed in dark clothing, head to toe. It looks like they are fully prepared. I hope they are, at this point. Lives depend on it. Mark, get here fast. Let Frank know what's going on before you both arrive."

CHAPTER 32

Upon arrival, Frank and Mark's vehicle was escorted around the back by armed guards. Both fathers were in the back seat of the vehicle. They hurriedly rushed the fathers through the backdoor and down the hall to the conference room. Mark quickly left, drove back around the building, and parked in the front of the visitor's lot, in case he needed the vehicle quickly. It was parked right in front of Trinity's unmarked car.

He walked through the front door and nodded at the security team. They pointed to the rear admiral's office, and he ran down the hall. Now in the room were the two fathers, Martyn Wysocki and Stefan Symanski, with Frank. They'd already placed the mothers into the hands of the SWAT team at the hospital. They were fully protected and wouldn't be placed in danger if Jawarski showed up with their sons. Anka Wysocki and Halina Symanski were in tears when they arrived. They were given sodas and something to eat to, hopefully, keep their minds off what was coming. Joe and Trinity walked into the room containing the fathers and closed the door.

"We really appreciate you being here under these very trying circumstances," Joe told the fathers. "We know it's hard to believe that your sons are involved in a terrorist plot that appears to be moving quickly. If they arrive for their midnight shift, we will move them into this conference room with you so you can talk with them. Security will pat them down and make sure that they're unarmed before putting them into this room. You'll have ten minutes to talk to them and explain the consequences of their actions. Just to warn you, if they arrive here for their shift, it means they got here, regardless of the fact that they got the call about their mothers being in an accident and in the hospital. If they come here, it means that this plot is more important than their own mothers. I want to make that clear. If they don't arrive here on time, and they don't go to the hospital, we believe that all the bombs they placed in this facility are armed, and we need to evacuate. If that happens and if they're with Jawarski, they'll be considered combatants and terrorists and will probably be shot on sight if found. You understand exactly what I'm telling you, correct?"

Martyn Wysocki stared at Joe in disbelief. "It's very hard for us to believe this is happening. We arrived in the United States when they were ten and eleven years old. We wanted a better life for our children. We were persecuted in Chechnya, and, like a lot of our friends, we emigrated to Poland and then to Orlando. We've been here ever since. We are and always have been good citizens. Yes, citizens. We're married to sisters. How can this be happening? Our sons are Americans. Why do this? We don't understand."

"Unfortunately, your sons haven't had your trials and ordeals, in order to judge what's right or wrong. You're good citizens, and so are your wives. Your imam isn't. He's a crook and is in this country on an expired visa. He knew that Jawarski and Hamzah were radicalizing your sons, and he did nothing about it. He also had a private offshore bank account in the Cayman Islands. I say 'had' because we have it now. He also knew that Jawarski burned down the three churches. We don't know if your sons were involved in that, but if they were, they're up on a charge of murder along with arson in the first degree. A maintenance man was killed in the last church bombing by inhaling poisonous chlorine gas. We believe they've been radicalized and will show up here on time for their shift. They need to put in the chlorine gas and attach the timers to activate the bombs."

Stefan Symanski shook his head sadly. "We don't believe in terrorism. We're good people, and we believe that everyone should live in peace. If our sons are guilty of this, they should be punished. They weren't raised like that. They're educated and should know better. We only want to make sure that, if found guilty, they'll not receive the death penalty."

"We can't assure you of that, but I believe that our good word on behalf of your sons, because of your intercession, will go a long way in keeping them off of death row. However, if bombs go off here tonight, I believe they'll both be dead by morning. That's all I can say, but there's always hope." *There's always hope.*

ल्क्ल

All third shift employees had to be at the front desk by 11:45 p.m. to go through security and then to their lockers. They wore uniforms and name badges identifying themselves as to their job, grade, and where they were allowed to be in the building at any given time. They'd change the color of their badges, depending on the day, to identify where they were cleaning that night. Pawel Wysocki and Tomasz Symanski walked through the front door at exactly 11:45 p.m. They came in with Axmad who dropped them off near the facility. He'd pick them up later, after their job was done.

"Cutting it short, guys?" the guard said. "One more minute and you'd have been barred from your shift. You know the rules."

"Sorry, we were held up," Wysocki said.

They passed through security and headed toward their lockers. As they turned the corner to make a left down the hallway armed security guards stopped them.

"Gentlemen, please follow me," said the head of security.

Wysocki and Symanski looked at each other and Wysocki lifted his chin. "What's up, sir?"

Four armed guards in addition to the chief of security surrounded them.

"Please follow me, gentlemen."

The four guards took each man by the arms, two per man, and moved them toward the conference room. Both of them now looked a little concerned but didn't let on.

As they moved down the corridor and into the room, Tomasz Symanski looked at the two men sitting in the chairs next to Joe, Frank, Mark, and Trinity. "Dad? What're you doing here," he said.

Pawel looked at his father as well. "Father, what're you two doing here?"

Both fathers looked at their sons and quietly shook their heads. Joe spoke for the first time. "Mr. Pawel Wysocki, and Mr. Tomasz Symanski, please take a seat. If you attempt to escape, you'll be shot. Please don't make these men shoot you in front of your fathers."

Joe waited for them to comply. "You won't be arrested as American citizens and prosecuted under normal law," he continued when they'd taken their seats. "You're being secured under the Patriot Act for so many crimes that I need to read them to you. You won't be Mirandized. There's no need at this point. Both of you are charged with the murder of a police officer, Mr. Archie Higgins, and in the attempted murder of officers, Lenny Bannister and Fred Stein. You're charged with the terrorist attacks on three churches and the murder of Leon Jenkins, the maintenance man at the First Baptist Church of Orlando. You're charged with aiding and abetting an escaped murderer and with the attempted murder of thousands of unnamed individuals now working at the Naval Air Warfare Center Training System in this University of Central Florida Research Park. I could come up with a dozen more felony charges but why bother?"

"We'd nothing to do with anything you're talking about," Wysocki said.

Symanski simply kept his mouth shut. Joe knew who was leading whom in this event.

Joe looked at the two fathers, as if to say, "Well, why are you here? Are you going to help or not?"

Martyn Wysocki turned to his son and slapped him across the face. The son was startled. He then turned to Tomasz Symanski., "My son is dead to us, now. Save yourself. You were seduced into this by my son, Pawel. Were you not? Stefan, talk to this man. My son will be terminated one way or the other." He turned to Stefan Symanski. "Have your son tell them what they need to know. Now!"

Pawel stared at his father in shock.

Joe turned to Mark, Frank and Trinity. "Let's give them ten minutes. We've got a little time left. It's just after midnight."

With that, they got up. The guards once again, completely patted the two sons down and then turned to the fathers and did the same thing. The fathers were a little shocked but understood. If they had anything that could be used as a weapon, the sons could turn on them, or the officers could believe that they'd help their sons. That wouldn't be the case.

Joe and the crew came back into the conference room and looked at the two sons. "Well?"

Tomasz spoke first. It looked as if he was finally empowered. He stared right at Pawel and began to speak. "Axmad will be meeting us at the back door at 1:00 a.m. He dropped us off in a stolen car. He said he'd pick us up exactly at 3:00 a.m. down about a half mile at the bus stop. We've got the keys for every room in this section, including the alarm for each of the doors. We were told that we could unarm one door a night so a few of the scientists could go out and have a smoke. They never believed that anything would ever happen here. He'll hand us ten burner cell phones and ten chlorine bomb components that we need to place in the assemblies in the air conditioning ducts. We placed those over the last several weeks and hid them down where they couldn't be found. They're made of ceramic that wouldn't be picked up as we went through security."

"We found one bomb already," Joe said. "Are any of those other nine armed at this point?"

"No. We were going to do it tonight. We've got two hours to arm all ten and then take off out the back door. We'd meet Axmad after we left the building through the rear door and he'd dial up each number, twenty seconds apart until all ten were set off. Then we were to leave with him and head to Mexico after meeting with Hamzah and his crew."

"Do you really believe that he'd let you live after this? Do you really believe that he'd take you with him and the others? We believe that you two and the imam would be immediately killed after the release of the chlorine gas. We now believe after talking to the others that Hamzah was meeting with the imam and would take him out. You three were the only ones, other than the cell members, who knew what was going on."

Joe glanced at the fathers whom were now in shock as well.

"Will this save their lives, at least?" asked Martyn.

"We'll do our best," Joe said. "They were planning on murdering a thousand-plus people who work here on the midnight shift. All would be done in the name of Allah. Gentlemen, who were you supposed to take the handoff from? Jawarski?"

"Axmad was going to give the cell phones and armed components to Pawel at the back entrance at 1:00 a.m.," Tomasz said.

"We will cooperate with you out of respect for our fathers," Pawel said. "We'd rather die than fail, but we will cooperate with our parents' wishes. We just spoke to our mothers as well during our brief meeting alone with our fathers."

Joe left the room to talk to the rear admiral. His team would be set up on the perimeter of the property at all four corners. The sniper would be set up with his M24 Sniper Weapon System, which was the military version of the Remington 700 rifle. It was a system because it consisted, not only of a rifle but also a detachable telescopic sight and other accessories. It was equipped with a Leupold Ultra M3A ten-by-forty-two-mm fixed-power scope with an elongated-shaped mil-dot wire reticle. He'd stay way back and would be vigilant from 12:45 a.m. through 1:15 a.m. and then would step down if no one showed. After Jawarski opened the door, handed the explosive units to Pawel, and then closed the door, the sniper would take him out, if he had a clear shot and the suspect was alone. If he had others with him, he'd be taken down and then they'd be taken out as well.

Joe was worried that Jawarski would already be in place after dropping them off before they entered the building. He probably parked down the road and had binoculars to keep an eye on the perimeter. There was no way he could see the back of the building unless he was already there. From the camera angles, it didn't look like he arrived yet.

Joe didn't think he'd be holding a bag of bombs and cell phones for longer than he needed. He'd probable get in place around 12:45 a.m. and get to the back door just as it was to be opened by Pawel.

Game on..

CHAPTER 33

As it got closer to 1:00 a.m., everyone started to stare at the clock on the wall. Pawel was staring at Tomasz as if to stay "You betrayed Allah."

Tomasz stared right back. If Pawel wouldn't open the door for Axmad, then he would. It was just starting to hit him that his life would be over either way. At least he'd be alive, and if he helped, at least his family wouldn't suffer any consequences.

Tomasz looked around the room at his father and uncle, the armed guards, and at the men he was just speaking to. Pawel was very quiet.

Tomasz said to him in Chechen, " If you help Axmad after all this, I'll kill you in prison myself."

Joe turned to Tomasz and said in Russian-infused Chechen, "You won't have to, because he'll be dead by the time the door closes."

The two fathers and their sons looked at Joe incredulously. "Sir, you speak Russian? And Chechen?" Martyn Wysocki said.

"Very little Chechen although both languages are similar. All four of you are fluent in Polish, Russian, and Chechen, are you not?"

"Yes," Martyn said. "You understood everything we said since we got here, haven't you?"

"Pretty much," Joe said in Russian.

"Then you know that my son, Pawel, led his cousin into this don't you?" he said back in Russian.

"Pretty much. I believe that you and Mr. Symanski and your wives are innocent of any wrongdoing that comes out of this. It's a shame that someone was allowed to brainwash your sons into murder. How could you've not known what was happening? Didn't you see what was going on?"

At that point, both fathers bowed their heads. "We can only apologize for their actions. Honestly, we didn't know. We were happy that they were religious after seeing young men their age, and even in our own mosque, become secularized because of the freedoms they now enjoy," Stefan Symanski said. "Trust us. We will bring this up to the elders of all ten mosques in Orlando, and we will fight terrorism until the day we die. I promise you that."

Martyn Wysoski nodded in agreement.

It was now two minutes to 1:00 a.m. Joe and Pawel headed to the door. The rear admiral came back at the same time to tell them that his men were in place. Tomasz seemed suspicious of Pawel and moved in ahead of him to get to the door. He raised his hand to Joe to tell him to move Pawel back. There was a distinct knock on the door, two times. Tomasz had his cart partially blocking the door so Jawarski couldn't come in if he wanted to. Tomasz opened the door and Jawarski handed him the package with the chlorine gas and cell phones. Jawarski quietly asked Tomasz where Pawel was because he was supposed to open the door instead of Tomasz.

At that point, Pawel shouted out in Chechen, "Run, Axmad. They know." Mark and Frank grabbed Pawel and tackled him to the ground, placing their hands over his mouth and covering it with duct tape. They duct taped his hands and feet and ran him into the wall to slow him down. It was as if he was a caged animal waiting to attack. The two fathers were dumbstruck at Pawel's efforts to warn Jawarski. Tomasz had the materials in his hand and closed the outside door tight. He shook his head at Joe.

Immediately, after the door was closed, there was a shot fired and a sound of "Ugh." Joe knew at that point that the sniper probably hit Jawarski in the chest where he was aiming from his hiding place a hundred yards away. They then heard shouting and running. Joe quickly opened the door to see what was happening. The guards at the corners had closed in but evidently the sniper didn't take Jawarski out after Pawel shouted to run. Jawarski was probably stunned but not hurt because he must have been wearing a vest that saved his life. There was no doubt that he was in a fight for his life. He'd run to the east side of the rear of the building, holding his ribs, and immediately opened fire with an automatic weapon, taking out the two guards on that side. He ran through the back fence where he'd cut it to get in to bring the bomb materials.

Joe could see an outline of a man running about a hundred yards away. He and Trinity ran to the front of the building to get to their vehicle. Frank and Mark did the same. Frank was driving and had parked right in front of Trinity's vehicle, so they had to wait for them to move. Both had left their keys in the ignition. They were in front of a federal installation and never thought they'd need their cars or that anyone would be crazy enough to take them. It was a good thing they didn't have to fumble around to open the doors and start their engines.

Frank pulled out leaving rubber on the road. Joe and Trinity looked where they were headed and, in the dark, they could see rear brake lights a block away, east of the facility. Frank was headed that way and Trinity was right behind him. *Thank God*, Joe thought. *I hope her driving ability is better than mine.* He was a notoriously bad driver on the best of days. He hadn't driven much over the last fifteen years because he was always driven places by someone else or was on a ship. She was hitting sixty miles an hour coming out of the driveway past the guard shack. Frank was about a half a block ahead.

Trinity glanced at Joe. "I got this, Joe. Don't worry. I

know what I'm doing. I took the full FBI course before I signed on to the Orlando Police Department. Bet you didn't know that, huh?" she asked with a smile. "I almost joined the FBI."

"I didn't know that, Trinity. But this is as good a time as any to tell me."

Trinity had been up to FBI headquarters after she got her first degree from the University of Central Florida. She was thinking about joining them, but in truth, she always wanted to be the new chief of the Orlando Police Department. She didn't want to be the first African American chief. Cal Roberts earned that title. She wanted to be the first female chief, not the first African American female chief. The first female was good enough for her.

Trinity had taken the full FBI operational skills training. This concentration included everything from defensive tactics to surveillance, from physical fitness to tactical driving. Defensive tactics training focused on boxing and grappling, handcuffing, control holds, searches of subjects, weapon retention, and disarming techniques. Safe driving techniques were provided at the FBI Tactical Emergency Vehicle Operations Center at the Academy. Trainees also received more than ninety hours of instruction and practical exercises focused on tactics, operations planning, operation of cooperating witnesses and informants, physical and electronic surveillance, undercover operations, and the development and dissemination of intelligence. At Hogan's Alley, trainees conducted interviews, planned and carried out an arrest, performed day and nighttime surveillance, and put to use street survival techniques taught by their instructors. Real-life exercises included a bank robbery, a kidnapping, an assault on a federal officer, and both compliant and armed and dangerous arrest scenarios. Trainees used paint guns to test their tactical skills.

At the FBI Operations Center, she learned how to conduct a before-operation inspection of a vehicle; negotiate a motor vehicle through seven mandated driving courses; set-up, supervise, and score students on the seven mandated courses, that included serpentine, fixed radius curve, precision, off-set lane maneuver, evasive action, emergency response, and pursuit. They were now in pursuit mode and, as Joe looked at Trinity, her focus was like a laser beam on the road ahead.

Jawarski was a pretty good driver himself. He went through every red light and never stopped. He made evasive maneuvers, going through side streets and alleyways. Frank was losing ground and was now in Trinity's way as she hit the gas, doing about eighty, hit the brakes, and took the right hand turn on two wheels. Frank kept on going straight, missing the turn. It looked like it would be Joe and Trinity heading east in hot pursuit.

While driving, she handed Joe her radio and told him where they were and to call for police cars to go ahead about a mile or two and to get in place and block the main roads. At this pace, they'd be there in about two minutes. If those roads were blocked, Trinity could flush him out. She knew all the one-way streets. Jawarski did not. He would only get so far.

God, she's good. I hope we make it out alive.

"Joe, there he is ahead about a block up. He's headed right into our road block." As she said it, Jawarski took a left turn into a narrow street, which was the back entrance to one of the large hotels. As he turned, Trinity sped up and caught up with him half way down the street. She hit the gas and clipped Jawarki's vehicle from behind, hitting the left rear bumper, spinning his car around, and she plowed right into him.

Thank God we have our seatbelts on.

As badly bruised as Jawarski was, he quickly got out of the vehicle and started to shoot at their car with his automatic weapon. Trinity opened the door and rolled across the road, coming up firing at Jawarski. He couldn't shoot at both of them at the same time.

While she was unloading her gun, Joe was right behind

her at the passenger door and he, too, was unloading on Jawarski.

Before Jawarski ran around the corner, he fired at Joe, missing his head by inches. The bullet hit the wall behind him. A chuck of cement came flying off the wall and hit Joe right behind his left ear. He was knocked unconscious. Trinity looked for Joe and called him but he didn't answer. She couldn't let Jawarski go. She knew that Joe wanted her to catch him. She didn't think Joe'd been shot because the bullets seemed to go wide of him. She thought he might have slipped and fallen.

Trinity ran to the corner that Jawarski just took. He was still firing. He must have had several clips on him. At least it felt that way. Once again, her training kicked in. His footsteps had stopped, and she heard nothing. She wondered if he got hit. She heard sirens coming toward them, but it would be too late and Jawarski would get away if she didn't do something quickly.

She counted to three in her head and ran to the right of the wall, dropping in the dark and started to fire as soon as she saw a flash from what appeared to be a gunshot. His shots were close but not close enough. She had already reloaded behind the wall before, and as soon as she hit the ground, she started firing with everything she had. There was no one else around, at least she hoped not. Even the bums should be asleep by now unless they were woken up.

She heard a gasping sound and something hitting the ground. She then heard a gurgling sound. As she slowly crept up the street, crouched low, she saw a man with his back against the wall and his legs spread apart on the ground as if he was trying to get up. He was under the dim streetlight, halfway down the street. She'd shot him in the throat and the left shoulder. *So much for vests.* It served him well behind the naval facility, but not now.

As she approached him, she saw his gun dangling from his fingertips. She kicked it out of his hand. She took out her phone and starting taking pictures immediately and then turned on the recorder, in case he was able to speak. She looked him in the eyes. She said into the recorder, "Mr. Jawarski, you're under arrest for the murder of Archie Higgins and a whole bunch of other crimes." She then read him his Miranda rights into the recorder.

He looked at her with hate in his eyes and was obviously on his last breath. He said something to her in Chechen and then died. Trinity checked his pulse to make sure he was dead, and he was. She got up and ran back to the car when two police cars pulled up and hit the brakes. She had her badge high above her head. She was a police officer but she was driving a wrecked unmarked police vehicle and she was African American. It was going on 2:00 a.m. in the morning, with a white guy on the ground in front of her, obviously coming out of being knocked out. She dropped her gun on the ground and put her hands on the vehicle. "I'm Detective Trinity Hightower of the Orlando Police Department. Call Chief Cal Roberts right now please and tell him we got Jawarski."

One of the officers knew Trinity because he graduated with her from the police academy. He was also African American. "Trinity, it's okay. It's Mack Davis. You're okay now."

The other white officer looked a little relieved. "Detective what happened?"

"I'll tell you later. Call an ambulance. Lieutenant Joe Traynor has a gash on the back of his head and probably has a concussion. He wasn't shot, at least not from his appearance. It looks like he got hit with a chuck of something and went down. Still hurts the same, right, Joe?" She smiled at him and placed a handkerchief on the back of his head. "Our terrorist, Axmad Khan, or as you know him, Bronislaw Jawarski, is dead half way down that street."

Within minutes, Frank and Mark showed up and about ten other police cars. The local television stations were starting to swarm. Evidently, someone made a call for everyone to arrive here on the police radio that was followed by anyone with a scanner. At least the ambulance got through. Joe was placed on a gurney and would be taken to the trauma center. He'd be rushed into the same center where the two mothers were waiting for their sons to show up. *How ironic*, Trinity thought.

She was covered in grime and muck and had abrasions on her elbows, arms, and legs from hitting the car and rolling on the ground to avoid being hit. They told her to hop into the ambulance for the same ride. Cal Roberts showed up and started to take charge until Homeland Security and the FBI got there to sort everything out. At least the two sons back at the naval facility were in jail, with one of them facing the death penalty. He could have saved himself but his calling to Allah was too great. What a tragedy for a very nice family. Somebody would be sorting this out for a long time to come.

CHAPTER 34

They got to the Orlando Regional Medical Center in minutes, and Joe was rushed into the trauma center, followed closely by Trinity as she walked behind his gurney. The staff had been waiting for them and prepared for anything. They checked out Joe but he looked worse than he was. Blood from a head wound looked ten times worse than it was. In fact, if Joe hadn't been knocked unconscious, Trinity was probably in worse shape.

The emergency doctor attended to Joe's head wound caused by the flying cement. He really was lucky that the bullet didn't ricochet instead. They gave him a tetanus shot and six stitches to close up the wound after shaving the area around the cut. He was now fully awake and concerned about Trinity who was standing by his side. She wouldn't leave until she knew he was okay. The nurses grabbed Trinity by the elbows and told her to sit over on the other bed. They cleaned all of her cuts but she didn't need a shot or any stitches. She'd be hurting tomorrow, though.

"Joe, are you okay?" Trinity asked.

"I think so. Julie's is going to kill me. Now I'm bald behind my left ear. Some haircut for the wedding, huh?"

"That's the least of your worries."

Before the chief arrived, along with all the head honchos who were standing in line to take credit for the capture of Jawarski and the stopping of mass murder at the navy facility, Trinity played her tape recorder for Joe. "Joe, these are Jawarski's last few words before he died. I took pictures of him in the alley, the gun, and all the spent shells so we could match them to those that killed Archie and wounded the other officers and the two navy guards that he took out. I called the rear admiral at the facility to tell him that we got Jawarski and he didn't make it."

She played the tape from the very beginning until she checked Jawarski's pulse and said into the tape that he was dead. "Joe, what did he say? Was that in Russian?" she asked.

He listened to the tape several times, just to make sure, and turned to Trinity. "His last words were, 'We'll be coming back soon' in Chechen."

"Well, I'll guarantee you that he won't be coming back soon from where he's headed, Joe."

"What he meant, I believe, is that they targeted Orlando and all the military facilities down here. They must have done research to target this navy installation. I didn't even know that it was the 'think tank' for naval weaponry. We better make sure everyone is on full alert from now on. They were lucky that we stopped the mass murder attempt. Outside security was way below par, and to be able to turn off the alarms on individual doors is unheard of, especially for the cleaning crew. Allowing them to smoke outside the backdoor was ludicrous. There was a good reason why the rear admiral was nervous. He should have been nervous. He also should have been more alert. Terrorists are landing in the United States every day, and we're wide open for attack."

Mark and Frank walked into the room and were concerned until they saw Joe sitting up in the chair while they were cleaning up Trinity.

"Where the hell did you learn to drive like that?" Mark asked Trinity. "That was quite impressive."

Frank nodded sheepishly in agreement. After all, she blew by him doing eighty, hit the brakes, and took a corner on two wheels, all the time telling Joe to get the roadblock in place.

"I took FBI tactical driving training a few years ago," she said. "When I blew by you, I was able to hit Jawarski's left rear panel perfectly to spin him around. Otherwise, I'd have run into him doing at least sixty by that point. It gave us enough time to shoot back after he quickly got out and started firing. But I don't want to do that too often. My heart is still racing."

Homeland Security, the FBI, and the chief were all there at the same time. All of them wanted to get everything down in writing immediately. It was a good thing that Frank was still left in charge.

"Hold on, guys," he said to all assembled. "This is my show. We will get everything recorded and transcripts will be made for each and every one of you. Right now, let's let them come down from this high. Give them an hour, at least, and then we will all be debriefed."

Joe told them that first he needed to call Rear Admiral Jake Barnes. He was sure that the navy had already been informed by the facility commander, so Joe didn't want Jake far behind. He was the contact for Washington for the Coast Guard, Homeland Security, and the FBI.

"Jake, it's Joe. We're done. We got our guy. He's dead and we stopped the bombs from going off. The Chechen cell has been rounded up with the imam and pretty soon there will be a bow tied around all the cases. They were responsible for killing Archie Higgins, wounding the two police officers, the murder of the maintenance man in one of the three church bombings, and the attempt on this naval facility.

"The two sons were heading for mass murder but one helped us at the end, due to the father's intervention. The other can be tried and executed for everything, right along with Jawarski but he's dead. Unfortunately, two naval guards were killed in Jawarski's escape from the facility. I'll have to give you the full details when I get back. Jake,

I've got a headache. I was knocked cold when a bullet hit behind me and a chuck of cement knocked me down. I've got a mild concussion. Trinity was unbelievable but don't go for a drive with her."

"Hurt again? Are you okay for the wedding? If this didn't kill you, Julie will for screwing up the wedding plans in Key Largo. When's the wedding, a week from now?"

"I'm fine, other than this funny haircut with a bald spot on the back of my head behind my left ear. We'll only take pictures from the front and the right side. Got to go, Jake. I'll tell you all about it later. Please let everyone know we're okay and everything came down well."

"Will do. I'll see to it that Trinity gets a commendation from the Coast Guard, Homeland Security, and the FBI. You can't do better than that."

"I'll tell her. Thanks, Jake." Joe turned to Trinity. "Hey, Trinity. Are you up for some hero worship over the next couple of weeks? It will happen, if you want it to or nor, so enjoy the ride. I have to call Julie and let her know I'll be home in a day or so, permanently."

Everyone started to clear out of the hospital. The two fathers arrived to meet the mothers who were still there. Neither mother would be pleased that their sons would be incarcerated or that one would receive the death penalty for their actions. At least Mrs. Symanski would know that their son, Tomasz, did the right thing at the end. Joe would put a good word in for him if the fathers made good on their promise to help fund and rebuild the churches that were burned to the ground and compensate the family of Leon Jenkins, who died at the Baptist Church bombing.

Just as they were ready to leave, Trinity's family and her boyfriend arrived. Evidently the chief had called them to come to the hospital and let them know that she was all right and a national hero. Joe shook hands with Trinity's father Marvin, hugged her mother Mavis, and shook hands with her two sisters and Kiki, her niece and goddaughter.

Joe, Mark, and Frank were introduced to Gene Whitcomb, Trinity's professor boyfriend. Joe thought he was a very nice guy. As they were all gathered in the hallway, Joe called Julie. It must have been around 6:00 a.m. because Julie answered the phone immediately. That was the time she got up for school, and she kept the same hours even on summer recess.

"Julie, Hi. Everything's fine. We got Jawarski. We stopped the bombing of the naval facility, and I'm coming home tomorrow or the next day, as soon as I can. Trust me. This was my last investigation, ever."

"How are you? You sound a little groggy."

"I'm fine. I got hit in the head with a chuck of cement and got a few stitches but I'm fine. Need some rest that's all. We've been up all night. I love you. I'll call you later today after I rest."

"Love you too. Are you sure you're all right. Joe?"

"I'm fine." *I'll be fine until she sees the back of my head.*

CHAPTER 35

Chief Roberts decided to hold an early meeting at 8:00 a.m. After getting back from the hospital to the hotel, they only had time to shower and change their clothes. Joe, Mark, and Frank grabbed a breakfast sandwich and a cup of coffee on the way out of the hotel. Once again, the staff let Frank place his vehicle near the front lobby. The staff knew that they'd be leaving for an early meeting and then coming back to checkout, hopefully for the last time.

They arrived at police headquarters and walked through the front door a few minutes before 8:00 a.m. The chief told them that the meeting wouldn't be long and they'd head back, get some sleep, and then head home after having their own telephone conference with the rear admiral, Homeland Security, and the FBI in Washington. It was clear to Joe that what really went down would probably never come out to the public. He needed to convey that message, loud and clear, to those assembled in the chief's office.

Chief Roberts began the meeting by praising everyone for stopping a mass murder attempt and for catching Jawarski and the others involved in everything that had happened. He asked Trinity to summarize all the events to date. She did.

She told the assembled team about the capture of Jawarski and the two young men at the naval facility, and how the murder of Archie Higgins and the shooting of the other officers all tied in together. She touched on the burning of the churches and the subsequent death of the maintenance man at her father's Baptist Church. She went into how they found the perpetrators through a scratched off landfill sticker and how a sleeper cell was found. She didn't go into the mosque or the imam nor how much money they gathered up from all the sources. She turned to Joe and asked him to speak.

Joe had already spoken to his rear admiral and the brass in Washington. He told the gathering, "You'll all be asked to sign a document before you leave the meeting that states that you'll never disclose what happened during this investigation. It's classified, a matter of national security, and those higher up than me don't want the public to panic." He waited until the shock and murmuring died down and then continued. "They're concerned that having a naval weapon facility on a national university campus would be held up to further scrutiny, and that isn't about to happen. They're also reluctant to discuss mass terrorism in the land of theme parks, and that isn't going to happen, either. They also want to put to rest that white supremacists were burning down African American churches. They want to stop the burning and looting that had just started in Orlando because of those accusations."

He told them that Jawarski and his cell started those bombings as a diversionary tactic and it caused uproar in the African American community just like they knew it would. That allowed them the time to target their real enemy— soldiers and weaponry and the planned slaughter of those at the facility.

One of the deputy chiefs asked Joe what would happen if someone didn't sign the release or actually let it leak?

"That's not up to me," Joe said, "but I know for certain that under the Patriot Act, and this certainly falls under those parameters, if someone doesn't sign or leaks the information, they too could be held accountable without access to an attorney or a trial and could be held by Homeland

Security, indefinitely. I don't think it's worth the price you'd pay. I'm just saying."

Everyone went very quiet. This was real. They'd never been in this situation before. Joe thought, before they left the meeting, they'd all sign. He wasn't sure what would happen later, but he knew the Washington spin machine was up and running.

He pulled out a piece of paper. "This will be reported in the Orlando newspapers and in all the media and social networks. Sergeant Beverly Fitch will be making the presentation at 11 a.m. this morning. Beverly, do you want to read the release?"

"Certainly," she said. "'Last night at approximately 2:00 a.m., Mr. Bronislaw Jawarski was killed while being pursued by Orlando police officers. Mr. Jawarski, a Polish citizen, was responsible for the murder of Officer Archie Higgins and the wounding of Officers Lenny Bannister and Fred Stein at the Orlando International Airport. His two compatriots, Arzu Dudayev, age forty, and Elbek Shishani, age thirty-two, were killed in that incident. They were also from Poland and had lengthy criminal records in that country. We believe they were connected with a crime syndicate from that country, trying to start an operation here. We believe it failed.

"'In addition, a white van was seen at the last church bombing and that van was discovered abandoned. After a thorough examination of the vehicle, DNA samples from all three of these men were found inside the van. It was obvious that the bombings took place after the two men were killed, so that Mr. Jawarski was solely responsible for these three subsequent church bombings. There are no indications as to why they were bombed but it puts an end to be rumors that white supremacists were involved. To our knowledge, they were not. We believe that the sole perpetrator of those bombings was Mr. Jawarski.

"'These churches will be made whole by our community. The Orlando Police Department and the mayor's office of the City of Orlando will start a fund raising campaign to help rebuild all three churches. We've already received over a million dollars from an anonymous source to start the campaign. Your donations may be mailed directly to the 'Church Rebuilding Fund,' care of Sergeant Beverly Fitch at the Orlando Police Headquarters on South Hughey Avenue. Thank you.'"

"Well, that concludes our meeting, ladies and gentlemen," said Chief Roberts. "Please sign your document before leaving and present your ID and badge number, which will be attached to the document along with your picture."

That was suggested by Joe, in case there was anyone who though they could bypass the procedure on the way out.

The chief would personally check every signature to make sure it belonged to the identified individual. He was trusting, but after having a bad cop in Jim Butler, he was a lot less trusting these days.

"Joe, where did the million dollars come from to start the campaign?" Beverly asked.

"I can't say, Beverly, but trust me, it's already in the bank in a new account established this morning by Jack Forest, our guy in Virginia. He opened the account at 9:00 a.m. as we were speaking. The money was wired from my office in Islamorada by Warrant Officer Joan Talbot to the new account."

"How did she get the money?" Beverly asked, pushing for an answer.

"Beverly, did you sign your document after the meeting?"

"Yes."

"Good. That's all you need to know. Chief, can I speak to you for a minute?"

"Sure, Joe. What's up?"

They walked into the chief's office and Joe closed the door. "I can tell you but no one else, not even Trinity. Do we understand each other?"

"Yes, of course, Joe. You do trust me, don't you?"

"More than most but never one-hundred percent," Joe said, and he meant it.

"I guess you've seen more than me. I never saw Jim Butler as a murderer, either. So, you have me there," the chief said.

"Jack Forest uncovered almost five million dollars in cash, between Hamzah Umarov, the owner of the furniture store and leader of the sleeper cell, and Imam Abu Malik. The mosque had over a million in identified funds in cash and the imam had over five hundred thousand in his account in the Cayman Islands, all transferred from Chechnya by Hamzah's family. They're very rich and support terrorists, obviously. Hamzah had over two million in securities and cash in the local bank and another million spread among the ten Chechen associates in the cell working at the store. The two fathers of the bombers, Wysocki and Symanski, also pledged a half million total to the kitty. They'll send quarterly payment of $125,000.00 over the next year to meet their pledge.

"The churches will be rebuilt, state-of-the-art, with technology, video, and solar energy so they'll never have another electric bill. The total bill will be around two million for the three churches. They aren't that large but we will build them bigger and better. We'll leave one-point-five million to do so, matching the million already transferred into the new account. By the way, chief, you're the administrator of that account and only signee. Let me know if you're not feeling well, and we'll get it changed," Joe said, laughing.

Cal laughed as well.

"Also, there will be a donation to the families of Archie Higgins and Leon Jenkins. Mr. Higgins's funds will go to the school at the cathedral and Mr. Jenkins's funds will be given directly to the support of his family. There will be about a million left over to divide up for costs of the operation. We can decide that later. If not me, since I won't be here nor will my rear admiral, it will be someone else. I don't know who it will be at this point."

"When the hell did you have time to think about this?" said Cal.

"Well, this didn't just jump into my head. Do you want to see my daily notes that I kept? It started the day I got back from my honeymoon. I thought it would be only a matter of time before we'd find out exactly what was going on. It had to be financially supported or nothing would have happened. The more elaborate the scheme, the more money they needed. Trust me, this was a very elaborate scheme that didn't start yesterday. From what we found out, it started the day Hamzah came to Orlando and the funding never stopped. They bought a lot of patronage to do what they did. You may want to take a much deeper look into the community to see who was paid off, when, how, and we know why. It doesn't take a genius to know this plot was bought and paid for. Hamzah wasn't the 'Businessman of the Year' without a lot of grease. You know that."

"You're saying it's not over, aren't you, Joe? I think you're right. We need to follow the money and sit down with all the leaders of the mosques and see what we can do to help each other to keep the peace. Terrorists are coming to America. They came here. We kept a lid on it for now, but if something else happens, this will all surface and come back on us. Won't it, Joe?"

"Yes it will. But, you aren't alone, Cal," Joe said.

With that, he walked out of the office to give Trinity a kiss and a hug. His job, Mark's job, and Frank's job were done. Cal's job wasn't done and wouldn't be for a long time. Today, Joe didn't want to be in the shoes of the guy in charge of the naval facility. Rear Admiral Stephen Slater would have a very short career, starting tomorrow.

CHAPTER 36

Mark, Frank, and Joe went back to the Embassy Suites, packed, and got a few hours of sleep before they headed south to Miami. The rear admiral was expecting Joe at his office no later than 5:00 p.m. If they left at noon, they'd just about make it after dropping off Mark at his house in Dania Beach. They said their goodbyes to the hotel staff and tipped them all generously. They never knew when they'd be back and it never hurt to be nice. Joe thought it would be his last official trip to Orlando, but you never knew.

Frank drove. Joe and Mark got some more shuteye along the way. They stopped for a break about halfway down the Florida Turnpike and got a quick bite to eat, drink, and hit the bathroom. Joe changed into his dress uniform. It was the last chance he'd have before hitting Coast Guard headquarters in Miami. Frank and Mark stayed in their civilian clothes. Joe knew that he'd be seeing both of them and their families on Saturday down in Key Largo for the wedding, so they simply dropped off Mark without saying hello to Louise, Jennifer, and MJ.

Frank pulled up in front of headquarters about 4:45 p.m. and let Joe out. Joe grabbed his bag and uniform garment bag and shook hands with Frank. "See you on Saturday, Frank. As usual, thanks for everything. I'll be sure to let Rear Admiral Barnes know about your contribution. Remember, you were in charge of this operation."

"Sure, Joe. Whatever you say," Frank said with a smile. "We know how true that statement is. Don't we?"

"Frank, thank your guys for me, too. See you Saturday. Be on your best behavior. The rear admiral and his wife will be there as well. No uniforms, and I mean it. This is a non-military event. Jake knows as well, and I'll politely remind him."

Joe headed up the stairs and asked the guard if they could get someone to pull his car around to the front so he could head out immediately after the meeting. They said they would. They had the keys already.

Joe walked into the outer office for the rear admiral and spotted his administrative assistant, Al Cummings. Joe thought that Al had been a lot nicer to him lately. That fact that he wouldn't see Joe anymore probably had more to do with it than anything else. Joe nodded, dropped his bag and garment bag. and walked into Rear Admiral Barnes's conference room.

He wasn't expecting a full room of VIPs and simply shook his head. "Hi."

He took a seat at the opposite end of the table from Jake Barnes. Jake's direct reports were all there and greeted Joe as he sat down.

"A little tired, Joe?" Jake asked.

"A lot tired, sir. The wedding is coming up Saturday. I could sleep the next three days around the clock and I'll still be tired but I'd better not. I've got a ton of stuff to do with Julie before the wedding on Saturday."

Jake nodded. "Let's make this as painless as possible, and quick, so we can get you out of here. I also want to see you privately after the meeting. Please tell everyone exactly what you just went through."

Joe did. It took about a half an hour. No one had any idea about this mission that Joe just completed. There were a few questions but, mostly, the assembled staff was spellbound, listening to Joe tell how they found Jawarski and broke up the sleeper cell. As they left the room, each member of the staff shook Joe's hand, thanked him for his service, and wished him well in his new job at the community college. Joe hadn't even accepted the job yet but evidently it was a given that he'd take it and that the rear admiral had announced it. Joe went into the rear admiral's inner office and closed the door.

Jake smiled. "Nothing major, Joe. As you can see, I told everyone about your next assignment at the Florida Keys Community College and about your PhD candidacy at Barry University while assigned there. They all thought that was great. I told them they were probably meeting the next superintendent of the Coast Guard Academy in five years. That's if you're still with us, Joe."

"Hopefully, Jake," Joe said. "I have to hit the road. I promised Julie that I'd be home no later than 8:00 p.m."

"Well, you're technically still on your honeymoon, even though you're having another wedding Saturday. What's up with that?"

"You ask Julie, Jake. See what her response is. She doesn't even have to answer you if she doesn't want to. Maybe she'll tell your wife so she can let you know why."

"Please, no thanks. By the way, I know you aren't accepting wedding gifts for this pending event, and we already got you a present for the New York City wedding, but, the admiral in Washington and the brass at Homeland Security and the FBI, along with the Coast Guard, want to present you with this check for $20,000.00 as our gift to you and Julie for a job well done. The check is made payable to the St. Justin Martyr Catholic Church to be used for the food bank and second hand store. That's the least we can do, Joe. Thank you. What you're doing for your community, with your wedding gifts, is wonderful."

Joe was lost for words. He had a tear coming from his eye as he looked up at Jake. "Thank you, Jake. It's greatly appreciated. Please thank all those who contributed. Life has been good to me now that Julie is with me. I couldn't be happier, and this gift will help a lot of people that Julie and Tillie love in the community. I can't thank you enough."

With that, he reached out and gave a hug to Jake. Joe hadn't hugged anyone other than his brother and Julie in a very long time.

೪ോെ೪

Joe headed south to Tavernier. Door to door it took him a little over two hours, just making it under the wire for 8:00 p.m. As he pulled into the driveway, Julie greeted him with a big hug and a kiss. He turned and saw Tillie holding hands with a little girl. *Must be Bella.* There was a man standing next to Tillie that he didn't recognize. *So, this must be the beau.* He got his bags out of the car and started for the door.

Julie laughed. "Nice haircut, Joe. New look?"

"Like it? Looks good. Doesn't it? I'm glad it's only this bad," he said.

Julie just shook her head and looked at him.

"I'll be all right. Thanks for asking."

She shook her head again. "Joe, this is Bella. She's staying with us for the night. I hope that's okay?"

"Of course. I'm tired and very glad to see everyone."

Tillie introduced him to Ed Lansing and they shook hands. Joe was sure he'd hear more about Mr. Lansing in a little while. He turned to Bella and, in Spanish, said, "Bella, what a pretty name. You're beautiful. Tell me all about yourself. Will you?"

She answered him back in Spanish and smiled from ear to ear. He'd made a new friend. Joe kind of knew what Julie's intentions were toward Bella after the introduction but he'd wait for her sales pitch. They had a wedding and a short honeymoon coming up in Key West. Would Bella be coming with them? How was her mother doing? Probably not good, he thought. There was a lot going on and he needed to decompress. Just as he started to think he was getting overwhelmed, Julie handed him a Sam Adams Oktoberfest, ice cold from a cooler she'd set up on the back patio. New house. New wife. New daughter? New Grandfather-in-Law? Joe needed a good night's sleep before he'd tackle any one of those questions.

"Julie, Jake said to say hi to you and Tillie, and I guess to the rest of you as well." He handed her the check and her eyes went wide.

"What's this, Joe?" she asked.

"It's a check from Rear Admiral Barnes, from his Coast Guard account, for $20,000.00 for the food bank and second hand store as their wedding gift. Read the attached letter from the admiral in Washington expressing their gratitude and thanks for a job well done and honoring our vows with this contribution to a very worthy cause."

"Wow. I can't wait to give this to Pastor Schmidt. He'll be so pleased." She turned around and showed the check to Tillie and Ed who nodded with approval.

"Joe, I bought subs. I hope that's okay? I wasn't sure what time you'd be home even though you said 8:00 p.m."

"That's great. Thanks."

He turned to Bella and started to talk to her in Spanish and English and Julie noticed a big smile on his face. Her mother wasn't doing well. She took Bella for the night and her friend, Jan, who taught fifth grade at the Key Largo School, would pick Bella up tomorrow and take her to the Mariner Hospital where Juanita was in intensive care. Jan had told Julie that Juanita's brain cancer was now affecting her every day activities, and it looked like it was only a matter of time before she'd succumb.

Julie had made the call to Jack Forest to see if they could find the father but they'd had no luck so far. Juanita was Cuban and she never said how she made it to the Keys. Julie thought that maybe the father never came along when they landed. She wasn't sure if she was undocumented because it never came up in any conversations that they had. Cubans had special landing privileges so they could enter the country legally if they touched land. Also, any child could attend school whether documented or not, so that wasn't a problem. The problem would only come up upon Juanita Lopez's death. There would be no one to take care of Bella, and she'd probably have to go to Child Protective Services for placement.

Julie didn't want that to happen but was unclear on how to approach Joe. After all, if it weren't for Tillie, her grandmother, Julie would be in the exact same position, only a few years older. No child should ever be left alone and unloved. She knew Joe had a good heart and would approach him after Saturday, maybe while they're in Key West on their short honeymoon. They'd meet Cal and Estelle Roberts for dinner one night but she'd have plenty of time to approach Joe on this decision she knew she had to make.

"Joe, after your shower and after I put Bella to bed, I want to tell you about my latest call from Marcia Manning from Burbank. They've just made me an offer that I don't think we want to reject. It could set us up for life, Joe. I'm closing in on finishing the *Early Years* of the trilogy and I now know where it will head, and I can see the light and a movie could very well be on the horizon. She said they'd make it right here in Key Largo. Go take a shower and I'll tell you all about it later."

"Nice haircut, Joe," said Tillie.

"I thought you'd like it, Tillie. I was going for a new look for the wedding. What do you think?"

"I'd keep looking if I were you, Joe," she said, smiled, and walked away.

CHAPTER 37

After rehearsal Friday night, everyone headed over to Bentley's Restaurant, right on Overseas Highway, which was made available for the wedding party. Bentley's was Joe and Julie's favorite place and it was where Joe had taken her and Tillie when he was only nineteen and a new member of the Coast Guard. The place held a lot of memories for them.

Locals in this wedding included Jan Marino and her husband, Tony. Julie's principal, Gary Myers, and his wife dropped by just to say hello. They weren't in the wedding. Mark and his family were there. Jack and his girlfriend had arrived from Virginia. Trinity and her boyfriend, Gene Whitcomb, and her niece, Kiki, arrived as well. Trinity was in this wedding along with the Talbots. Young Jeff was in charge of the beer kegs but had other plans for this night. He'd come down from Miami in the morning with his girlfriend.

Also in the wedding party, and now in Key Largo, were Jane Swanson and her husband, Dr. Nick Snyder; Claire Murphy and her husband, Brian; Joe's father, John; and his brother, Pete and his girlfriend Tanya. Mike McGreevy was flying in from San Diego, would meet the Malone family at the airport, and they drive up to Key Largo together. Sean O'Neil came down by cutter from New London, where he was stationed at the Coast Guard Academy. Dan Simmons and his girlfriend, Samantha, flew in with Johnathon Mills and his wife, Francine, from Albany. Tillie was with Ed Lansing and the whole atmosphere seemed strange to Joe. Julie had made sure that no one bought special dresses for the event. Those who were in the wedding up in New York City were wearing their outfits but the men in the Coast Guard were to wear civvies at Joe's request. Trinity, Jan, and Jane could wear what they wanted.

"Joe, are you all right? You seem a little on edge," Julie said.

"Not exactly on edge, Julie, but this place, Bentley's, brings back a lot of memories and it seems unreal to me. I don't know. I guess I'm just caught up in memories. Did you ever think that this is where we'd be, together, after all these years?"

"Yes, Joe. The day I met you, a long time ago. Ask Tillie. She'll tell you. I couldn't be happier. But you're right, at this moment, looking around at our friends and family, how could we not be happy? We have a house that I always wanted. You're getting a new job that you seem to want. My books are being published and I love working at the school. I've never been happier, Joe."

"Well, I feel the same but I guess I need to relax. I've been on edge for so long, I think I forgot how to do that. But I'll try," he said and kissed her. "I guess when I stop looking around for flying bullets, perhaps then I'll be all right."

"Forget about everything, Joe. This is our time."

Just as she said that, Jimmy Smith came by on the team bus from Coral Shores High School with all the girls from both the track team and the cross-country team. Twenty girls hopped off the bus. It was a total shock to Julie. This surprise visit was set up by both Jimmy and Lucy. All the girls would be at the wedding tomorrow as volunteer servers and they wanted to stop by tonight to give Julie a gift from the high school students. They collected over a thousand dollars from all the students, unbeknownst to Julie and Joe. The collection took place around Julie's schedule so she would never know. Lucy handed Julie the check and there wasn't a dry eye at the party.

"What do I call you?" Lucy asked, laughing. Is it now Mrs. Traynor? Is it Julie my babysitter? Is it Coach Chapman like always?" she asked.

All the girls were wondering.

"Today and tomorrow, it's just plain Julie and Joe. In school, it better be Mrs. Traynor or Coach Chapman or whatever. You're confusing me, Lucy."

Everyone laughed. Julie and Joe gave each of the girls a hug and kiss and told them thank you for everything, especially for helping out tomorrow for the fundraiser and wedding.

"We really appreciate it, girls," Julie said.

She gave Jimmy a big kiss and hug and told him that she would see he and his wife tomorrow. They hopped back on the school bus and left.

⚜

In anticipation of a large amount of guests coming to the wedding from out of town, Julie had already booked twenty-five rooms at the Key Largo Marriott Beach Resort, exactly two miles from St. Justin Martyr Church, on the Overseas Highway. The hotel was right on the water. She also made arrangements for guests to be transported by the hotel to the church and then picked up at several different times during the day so that those guests could come and go as they pleased. Julie didn't want a formal affair. This was for friends and family. After all, a bishop, a cardinal, and her own priest, in Saint Patrick's Cathedral in New York City, had already married Joe and Julie, only a month ago. *Boy, does that seem like a long time ago*, she thought.

After the rehearsal dinner broke up around 9:00 p.m., Julie headed to Tillie's apartment, which was only a block from the church. Joe was staying at their house in Tavernier this night and would arrive at 11:15 a.m. tomorrow, forty-five minutes before the ceremony. Mike and Sean, the only two bachelors alone for the wedding, went with Joe. They promised Joe that they'd hit the sack by 1:00 a.m. at the latest. They're tired and came a long way for this. They didn't want Julie's wrath if they screwed up Joe for the ceremony. God knew, they'd had enough drunken times together over the last fifteen years to last a lifetime.

⁂

The church grounds were fully decorated with tents galore, beer kegs, food setups, beverage stations, and church volunteers ready to work as soon as the wedding was over. Everyone at the church pitched in to help. Not only was it a wedding of one of their very own getting married, but also it was the largest fundraisers in the history of St. Justin Martyr's Church. They knew that with all gifts going to the food bank and second hand store that the total could reach almost $35,000.00, that included the $20,000.00 check already received from Joe's military friends. There were several large screen televisions set up under the tent for the workers to watch the wedding through closed circuit cameras set up throughout the church. The overflow crowds would still be able to watch the entire ceremony from outside. This was a big event in the lives of the parishioners of St. Justin Martyr's. Church.

The music began, taped from the ceremony at Saint Patrick's Cathedral, as Julie walked down the aisle with Jeff and Joan Talbot. Mark and Louise were in the wedding standing right behind their daughter and son, Jennifer and MJ, who were the flower girl and ring bearer. Following were the friends from the New York City wedding and the new friends including Sean and Mike, Trinity and Gene, Claire and Brian Murphy, and Jan and Tony Marino. Little Bella was with Jan for the day, so she stayed in the aisle with Tony and their kids. She would go with the Marino family after the ceremony and cookout were over. Her mother was too ill to see her now. They would bring her to the Mariner Hospital on Sunday to see her, even if she was weak. They didn't know how much time she had left. Bella needed to see her at least one more time. It was heartbreaking.

Julie looked stunning, once again, in her bridal gown and train. Joan bent over several times to help her make adjustment as they proceeded up the aisle. Joe, Mark and Pete met her at the front of the aisle as Father Schmidt proceeded to start the official Catholic ceremony, including Mass and Holy Communion. No one counted, but it looked like the church was packed with friends, family, parishioners, and other members of the community that knew Julie and Tillie and wanted to make a contribution to the fundraiser. Also attending, just as regular guests, were the mayor, a few local judges. town council members, and other church officials. Doctors and nurses from the Mariner Hospital, that took such good care of Tillie, attended as well. This was more than a wedding. This was a ceremony celebrating life in a joyous occasion that everyone could share in and contribute to.

"It was a happening" as Lucy Talbot mentioned.

The ceremony ended with Joe kissing the bride, and then they walked hand in hand down the aisle to the front of the church. The group picture was not of the wedding party but of everyone who attended the ceremony, including those left outside watching the monitors. The pictures were of Joe and Julie, Tillie and Joe's family and their friends, surrounded by 250 other people. The photographers and videographer had to move back over 100 feet to get everyone in the picture. Everyone laughed and said it was great.

Joe and Julie walked over to the cake and cut a slice so that everyone could eat whatever they wanted, when they wanted. Joe and Julie and their friends went into the church hall bathrooms and changed for the biggest cookout in the history of Key Largo. People from around the neighborhood, who weren't at the wedding ceremony, came to the cookout as well. One thing they did have was plenty of food, drink, and wedding cake. The church ladies all helped bake the largest cake they'd ever seen.

Joe and Julie danced the first dance and then Julie danced with Joe's father, John. Joe danced with Tillie to the same music they had at the Waldorf Astoria. Everyone else joined in. By 5:00 p.m. most people were worn out. Julie and Joe and all the guests helped pack up everything so as not to interfere with church Mass on Sunday. All the leftover food was placed in prearranged containers and picked up by local shelters and food banks. The tent company had everything down by 7:00 p.m. and hauled away.

A lot of the guests were now sitting on the church steps having a drink. Jake Barnes and his wife came over. "That might be the two best weddings I've ever attended and they were for the same two people," Becky said to them both. "The wedding in New York City was a fairy tale wedding and this one today was all about friends and family. Can I ask you how much you raised today for the food bank and second hand store?"

"At last count, including Jake's generous donation, we raised over $40,000.00, and they're still counting," Joe said. "It might just hit $50,000.00 when all is said and done."

Julie looked at Joe. "Really?"

"Yes, Julie. Really."

"That means over $30,000.00 was raised by everyone here today, not counting the special gift from you, Jake. That's simply amazing. I'm so happy."

"Well, if we're going to make Key West by 10:00 p.m., we better start heading out." Joe turned to address everyone. "We're packed and ready to go. Sean and Mike are going to bunk at the hotel tonight. Can someone get them there in one piece? They knew they had to stay sober last night or Julie would kill them. But, today, they said they'd make up for it."

Everyone said goodbye and Joe and Julie headed out to Key West. Cal and Estelle Roberts had left about an hour earlier for their mini-vacation in Key West. Joe and Julie were meeting them the next night for dinner at Estelle's favorite restaurant, *La Trattoria*, located in the center of Duval Street. It had been honored numerous times with the People's Choice Award as one of Key West's favorite Italian restaurants and as the best romantic dinner where the locals eat. Julie concurred.

Joe booked their favorite Key West hotel, Southernmost Hotel, which was on the very end of Duval Street, right next to the southernmost point buoy at the corner of South and Whitehead Streets. They were on the main street that housed most of the activity in Key West. This was where they stayed when Joe took Julie down for a weekend a while ago to look at wedding rings. It was about a two-hour drive, door-to-door. They had four days to themselves and then on the way back, Joe had to stop at the Florida Keys Community College and meet the college's president for the first time. He'd give Joe and Julie a tour of this beautiful campus and speak to Joe about his pending duties, which would be coupled with his PhD program from Barry University.

CHAPTER 38

Joe and Julie met Cal and Estelle at *La Trattoria* the following night. They spent most of the evening together and went their separate ways back to their hotels around 10:00 p.m. Everyone was still tired, not only from the wedding itself but from all the activities leading up to it for the last month. Joe was just starting to relax, had a few beers too many, and was smiling at Julie. They walked hand in hand down Duval Street.

Key West was packed for a Sunday night in June. It was hot and muggy but there was always a breeze coming in from the ocean that helped. They stopped at the Shores Bar at the hotel, the Southernmost on the Beach. It had a beautiful outdoor setting overlooking the Shores Bar's pool and the Atlantic Ocean. They each had the famous Shores Bar Key Lime Colada and toasted each other until closing at 11:00 p.m. As soon as they got to their room, they collapsed into each other's arms and were fast asleep until morning.

They got up around 9:00 a.m., showered, and headed to the Beach Café, only steps from their room. When they arrived late Saturday night, they made love enough times to keep them satisfied for some time. Joe thought perhaps, after a nice breakfast, there would be a little activity when they went back to their rooms before heading out to see the sights. Julie ordered the lobster benedict, consisting of poached eggs, lobster, spinach, and key lime hollandaise on a toasted croissant with specialty house potatoes. Lobster was her favorite meal. Joe could never resist the corned beef hash, eggs, toast, and a bloody mary. He was Irish after all.

"Tell me about Ed Lansing," he said. "He seems like a very nice man and it certainly looks like Tillie is impressed. Are you?"

"I've only met him twice but Tillie has talked about him on several occasions to me," she said and told Joe what she knew. "As Tillie said, she never expected to find male friendship at this stage of her live," she concluded. "She then told me, 'never say never.' So I'm happy for her, and I think he's a good guy. Time will tell."

"He seemed nice and I hope it works out for both of them. Are the daughters coming down to visit any time soon?"

"He said they were planning to come down for Christmas with their husbands and the kids, so we can meet them. They sound like normal people, for a change." Julie thought this might be as good a time as any and said to Joe, "I'm really concerned about Bella, Joe."

"I thought you were, Julie. Is that why she was at the wedding?"

"Well, yes, of course, but I really do love her, Joe. I got to meet her over the last year working with Juanita after school on our technology grant. They're both special to me and I'm afraid of what's going to happen to her if Juanita doesn't make it. So far, Jack couldn't find her father. I've a feeling he's somewhere still in Cuba. How and why Juanita made it to the United States, I don't really know. What happens if Juanita dies and we can't find Bella's father? I'd hate to think what happens to her if she has to go with Child Protective Services. Foster care only works if the child gets a loving family and support. It doesn't always happen. I see it at the Key Largo School, Joe. We have several foster kids, and they aren't treated as well as you may think. Some fall through the cracks."

"I know you're concerned, Julie. I can see it written all

over your face. I know you have flashbacks of what happened to you. I hope your interest in Bella isn't just based on what happened to you. You can't build a relationship with a child based on worry. If Juanita doesn't make it, we could consider taking her, at least for the rest of the summer or through early fall. I'll be in a new job, and I won't be around as much. It's eighty miles door-to-door, both ways, every day, to the college, and I'll be taking courses for my PhD. Can we play it by ear? It's a hell of a responsibility. We just got married a month ago and, of course, two days ago, as well," he said and smiled. "She's a very nice little girl, and I just met her but I know where your heart is, Julie. We'll work it out, somehow."

"Thank you, Joe. You've got no idea how relieved I am. Jan can only take her for so long, and I was worried about what would happen. I don't think Juanita has much time left but let's hope for the best. I'm sorry to ruin your breakfast. I really am."

"Julie, I love you more than anything, and if this makes you happy, then fine. I'm thirty-four. I've been thinking that if we're going to have kids, I'm not getting any younger. I just didn't think about a ready-made family just yet. You know?"

"I hear you. I love you very much, and thank you."

"Let's finish and go back to our room for a while."

"Payback?" she asked with a smile.

"Maybe a little."

❧❧❧

Wednesday morning, they had a leisurely breakfast. Julie had the same lobster benedict. They had a late checkout for noon. They'd walk around for an hour or so and then head up to the Florida Keys Community College so they could meet the president, Morgan L. Hennessy, PhD, and take a tour of the facilities. The meeting was scheduled for lunch at 1:00 p.m. and was only five miles away, heading north on the Overseas Highway toward Key Largo to 5901 College Road.

They strolled around for a while, and it began to rain lightly so they headed back to their room, packed, and checked out. They had an hour to get to the college so Joe wanted to drive around the facility first before heading to the president's office. Both Joe and Julie brought their professional clothing. Joe didn't wear his uniform because he didn't want Dr. Hennessey to think he was only a military officer filling in for a job as a resume builder.

He wanted to talk to him about the PhD program as well and how he could work everything out while serving as the head of the military education division and serve as vice president for Institutional Research and Funding. Joe read all about the PhD program which was picked by the admiral in Washington or at least by Rear Admiral Barnes. Joe would receive a Doctor of Philosophy in Leadership and Education Specialization in Higher Education Administration. This was the degree he'd need if he was selected as the next superintendent of the Coast Guard Academy. The superintendent position was the same as president of a college or university. This doctoral program was centered on the student and not the faculty. He'd then be more in tune with the everyday enlisted man and woman, and education wouldn't be top down but aimed at a new generation of learners who'd been weaned on technology, the Internet, and social media.

He read from his material that this PhD in Leadership and Education was a specialization in Higher Education Administration, diversified in scope and would prepare the candidate for teaching and administrative positions in community colleges, four year colleges, and universities, or a career path in the industry. This doctoral program would prepare Joe to positively contribute to areas such as research, policy development, law, history of education, and the teaching and learning process. Joe would be exposed to leadership theories, dynamics of change, and the integration of a cybernetics framework and prepare him to work toward a research platform and teaching agenda that complemented the higher education context.

Joe had read that in the brochure and wanted to better understand what that meant from Dr. Hennessy's perspective. He had to accumulate fifty-four credits, produce a dissertation, which he'd already planned, and had to go to Miami to Barry University once a month to meet with his mentor, all during the program. Joe wasn't going to have a lot of time, so he was going to ask if the mentor could come to the Keys.

They pulled up at the president's office, parked in the reserved spot as a guest of the president, and he and Julie walked in to meet with Dr. Hennessy. They shook hands and Dr. Hennessy brought them to his private dining room for lunch. He explained that he was relatively new at the college and that this was his first presidency. He was rather young at forty-two but had the pedigree. He had a PhD in Education from Brown, the same university where Julie got her MFA. They had a lot to talk about. He'd heard about Julie's book and asked if she was interested in a teaching position. She said she had more than enough to do at Coral Shores High School with her grants and counseling and with a new book and a potential movie in the works.

He was duly impressed. Joe had given him his resume by mail when the rear admiral first mentioned the position as head of the military division. Dr. Hennessy was unaware of Joe's military background and fluency in Spanish and Russian. They only had a sixteen percent Hispanic student population and the president wanted to increase that along with other minority populations. The Keys didn't have a large African American population and the college reflected that at only six percent.

Joe told him of his background working with at-risk minority students in Albany. The college only had 1,200 students and half of those were military related which would fall under Joe's auspices. Wives of military personnel went full time at the college and represented twenty percent of the student base. Joe got very excited over the potential that this small community college held. It was the most southerly college, south of Miami. Fifty-eight percent of the college students were women.

Joe asked him several questions about his affiliation with Barry University and his PhD program and asked if the mentor could alternate at least every other month to come down to the Keys. Dr. Hennessey said he didn't see why not because he'd pick a PhD mentor that also taught in Key West. Joe was very happy.

After the tour, they all shook hands and said goodbye. Joe and Julie headed home.

EPILOGUE

During the trip, Julie told Joe more about her telephone conversations, in detail, with Marcia Manning. "I told her that I'll be finished with the final book by September and it will be ready for edits. I called Sarah Atwood and she wants me to come to New York City for a few days as soon as I'm through. School starts in early August, so I'll have to take a few personal days after Labor Day and a few days for Maddy's wedding. Do you want to come with me, Joe?"

"Of course, I'm going to Maddy's wedding but I can't go to New York City with you. I have to take off a few days as well. I wish I could, Julie, but I have to be at the college at the same time that you're starting. My first classes for my doctorate will be in late August up in Miami. I have to meet the dean and the staff and get totally acclimated into the program before I start down at the Florida Keys Community College. Then it will be full time, full steam ahead for the next two years, at least. You know that, right?"

"Of course. I wasn't sure of your schedule. We haven't seen a lot of each other, you know? Marcia and the studio are offering me some concessions. The money stays the same at $600,000.00 for the movie rights for all three books, now taken as one, for movie purposes, which is fine. They're giving me two percent on all gross sales over ten million dollars, plus I keep the $600,000.00 for just signing, which seems very fair, according to Jane. Jane has already reviewed the new contract and she insisted that I have a say in the final script. If there was an issue, it will go to a neutral arbitrator. Jane's boss, Sidney Clyne, put that clause in the contract. Clyne, Roberts, and Lynch have gone above and beyond for me, Joe, as you know," Julie said. "Also, in the contract, all the filming will be done in or near Key Largo. They said they'd try to use some students at Coral Shores High School in the production, either in the film or working with the crews. I'm going to recommend Lucy for a small part in the film if she's up to it."

"That would be terrific. So, it looks like you're going to do it. When do you have to sign the contract?"

"I've got until the first of September to sign. I think I'd be crazy not to do it, Joe. It could set us up for life. I don't know where my writing will take me after the trilogy is done. I could stay in the nonfiction arena, which in essence is autobiographical, try my hand at fiction, or even go to my first love, children's and young adult books. After all, my three books are aimed at middle school, teens, and young adults. I can see myself staying with that genre. Don't you?"

"I can see you heading in any direction that makes you happy. You'll be successful anywhere you go."

"By the way, I just got a notice from Sarah that the first book is doing even better than the previous quarter and with the second book coming out, it could mean a lot more money. If it's a lot, I'd like to give some of it back to the high school for scholarships for some of our poorest students. Joe, as you know, starting with me, poor doesn't mean a dead end. If I could set up a scholarship with $50,000.00, to start, for ten students a year and then see if we can get a match from all the local businesses, I think anyone who wants to go to college from Coral Shores could then have a way to do so."

"Julie, I know you believe it's our money, but it's yours and you can do anything you want with it. As a matter of fact, when I start at the college, I'll ask Dr. Hennessy if we can apply for some grants as matching funds or flat out give two scholarships for Coral Shores High School students who otherwise wouldn't be able to go to college."

"Joe that would be great. Thank you."

❦❦❦

Joe pulled up to Tillie's apartment a little before 5:00 p.m. They took their time coming home. It was a beautiful day and an easy commute straight up the Overseas Highway.

Tillie opened the door and gave them both a big hug. "Welcome back."

"Hi, Tillie, how're you? We came so I could pick up my dress and veil and all the other stuff I left here. We're heading home or we'd stay for dinner. We'll pick something up on the way. We had a great time, Tillie, and thank you for everything."

"Julie, come in for a minute. You as well, Joe. I've something to tell you. Please sit. Unfortunately, Juanita passed away last night. I debated calling you because I knew you'd be home later today. I wanted to tell you but I didn't want to ruin your last day or your meeting at the college, Joe."

"That's terrible, Tillie, just terrible. I knew it would be sooner rather than later, but I didn't expect it to happen while we were away. I just wish I was there to say goodbye. I feel so bad. How is Bella doing? How is she taking it? It's got to be so hard for a five-year old. It certainly was hard for you and me, Tillie, when my mother died."

"We don't know how Bella is doing. Jan called this morning. As soon as Juanita died, someone at the hospital called Child Protective Services, and they came and got Bella from Jan's. We don't know why someone called, but it must have been someone who felt self-righteous."

"I'd love to find out who it was and give him or her a

piece of my mind," Julie snarled. "That poor child, she's all by herself and her mother's dead. At least I had you, Tillie" She sighed. "Who'd do such a thing? Everyone at the hospital's intensive care unit knew Juanita had friends taking care of Bella and people stopped to see her every day."

"They showed up at Jan's house because someone at the hospital knew she was staying there while you were away for a few days. The official who showed up wouldn't tell Jan anything, including where they were going to take her, other than to Miami. Evidently there are no foster parents available right now in the Keys. They flashed their IDs and then they were gone."

"Did Jan tell them that we'd take her?"

"She didn't feel comfortable telling them that, Julie, so there was nothing she could say or do to stop them."

"Joe, what can we do? We have to find her."

"We will, Julie. Let's take a breather for a minute. It's after 5:00 p.m. right now so I doubt anyone in charge would still be there. We can go home, unpack, and start making calls. We can head up to Miami as soon as we know where she is," he said.

"Julie, the nurse who took care of me, Audrey Kenny, dropped by this afternoon and gave me a letter written by Juanita to you. It was sealed. This was given to her yesterday afternoon before she died. Audrey was Juanita's assigned nurse, and Juanita asked Audrey if she'd give the letter to you if anything happened to her." Tillie handed the sealed letter to Julie. Julie looked down on it and began to weep. Tillie hugged her. "Audrey is Detective Mike Kenny's wife from the Monroe County Sheriff's Department. Perhaps you can call her and see if she knows anything that's going on."

Joe nodded. "That a great idea, Julie. Read the letter and you'll feel better. We can call her from here if you want before we go home. Is that okay? We can go see her tonight as well."

"Yes, Joe." With that, she took her time to open the letter. It was in Spanish. Evidently, Juanita wanted it to be in her native language so there would be no mistakes. "Joe, it's in Spanish. Can you read it to me?"

"Certainly." Joe read the letter to himself to make sure he understood her Spanish. His was Mexican infused but the Cuban dialect and writing were very similar, other than a few idioms here and there.

"Joe, what's it say?" Julie asked.

"I'm translating in my head, Julie. Hold on one minute. I just want to make sure what it says so there's no confusion." He read, "'Dear, Julie. I want to thank you for everything you've done for Bella and me. I love you for that. People have been kind to us here, but you've gone out of your way to help both of us. I know how much you love Bella. I need to ask you a very big favor. I know I don't have much time left. I'm writing this now that I'm clear headed and I'm not under any pain medicine at this time. I'm writing in Spanish because I can't write very well in English. Forgive me.

"'If I die, would you please take care of Bella for me? I know it's a very big favor but I don't have anyone else. I arrived in Florida on a small fishing boat, landing in Key West. I was six months pregnant at the time. I delivered her at the Lower Keys Medical Center in Key West. As you know, she's now five and her birthday is in October, just like yours. I checked.

"'We moved up to Key Largo when I filled in as a night cleaner at the school. We've been here ever since. Bella is an American citizen and her birth records are at our apartment in my dresser in a metal box. As a Cuban national, I was allowed to stay in this country with the US wet hand dry hand policy. Thank God.

"'Bella's father still lives in Havana and we were never married. As a Catholic, I regret that to this day but I can't change that. When I told him I was pregnant, he abandoned us. That's why I left on a fishing boat to Florida. I borrowed the money from my family. I made it but very few did. When I landed, I had nothing, I was pregnant, and finally went to the officials who allowed me to stay. I wasn't sure if they would, but being Cuban, meant I could stay.

"'Julie, when I pass, please take Bella and love her as your own. I'll be forever in your debt and I know Bella will love you like she loves me. Nurse Kenny signed the bottom of this letter so you'll know it's real. She doesn't read Spanish but she watched me sign this letter. With love and thank you. Juanita.'"

"Can you read it again, slowly, so I can write it out exactly in English, Joe?"

"Sure."

And he did. After she finished, she put her writing and the letter back into the envelope. Tillie gave her Audrey's phone number. Audrey had told Tillie that she'd expect a call from Julie just to verify that she actually signed the bottom of the letter.

"Tillie, did they say if there was a wake or a funeral?" Julie asked.

"While you call Audrey, I'll call the hospital," Joe said. "If she's at the local morgue, we can call your friend at the local funeral home to pick her up. They may not have even moved her from the hospital yet. We'll pay for her wake, funeral, and burial. Tillie can you call Father Schmidt to make sure we can have a funeral Mass for Juanita? She said she was Catholic in the letter. We can give Father a copy just to be safe."

Tillie picked up her phone on the kitchen table. She still had a landline. She wasn't used to cell phones and only carried one at Julie insistence while they were away. She called Father Schmidt to tell him what was going on. Father said he'd call the funeral home and have Juanita's body delivered to them and prepared for the funeral Mass. He said he'd set aside a burial plot in the newer section of St. Justin Martyr's cemetery, down the street from the church. He said he'd take the cost of the plot out of the fundraiser. Tillie said that wasn't necessary, that they'd pay for all Juanita's services. Tillie wanted to help as well. She fell in love with

Bella the day she saw her with Julie at their new house.

Tillie had wondered what would happen if Juanita passed. Now she knew. She knew in her heart that Julie loved that little girl just like Tillie loved Julie all these years. A mother could tell. Joe would make a wonderful father and, with his grasp of Spanish, he could help Bella more and help Julie give Bella an ethnic understanding of her heritage. Joe knew more about that heritage than most people of Hispanic ethnicity.

e∞o

"Audrey? Hi. This is Julie Traynor. We just got back from our honeymoon, and Tillie gave me Juanita's letter. Thank you so much for being there for her at the end. I feel terrible that we weren't there. I didn't realize that you're Mike's wife. We know him very well from when Tillie was hit by the car."

"Hi, Julie. Yes, I'm so sorry about Juanita. She spoke highly of you. She explained the content of the letter to me before I signed as a witness even though it was in Spanish. She went quietly. At least that was a blessing."

"It was a blessing but I think we now have several problems to deal with. Joe is calling the hospital to have her body released to the funeral home so she can have a proper Catholic wake and funeral and burial in St. Justin Martyr's cemetery. The other problem is that Bella was picked up by Florida Child Protective Services at Jan Moreno's house this afternoon. They wouldn't tell Jan where they were taking her. We just got back a few minutes ago, that's why we're calling now. Can we speak to Mike for a minute? I'll put us on speakerphone. Joe is just finishing up with the hospital."

"Mike, it's Julie and Joe."

"Hi, guys. Congratulations on the wedding. The second wedding, I understand. That was a great thing, giving all the proceeds to the food bank and second hand store. Everyone in the Keys is talking about it."

"Thanks, Mike. I take it you heard about Juanita Lopez's passing from Audrey?"

"Yes, it's a shame and so young. She was only thirty, wasn't she?"

"Yes, but brain cancer can take anyone at any time, so, thank God for every day," Julie said.

They could hear Audrey in the background voicing her agreement. She was a nurse, caring for the most sick in the intensive care ward, so she saw death every day. She took care of Tillie all that time while she way hanging by a thread before they took her out of the induced coma and then saw her improve over several weeks before she was released.

"Mike, what do you know about Florida's Child Protective Services unit down here in the Keys?" Joe asked. "They came in and scooped up Bella and didn't tell anyone what's going on or where they were taking her. Do you know anyone who can get to the bottom of this?"

"Mike," Audrey said, "can they just do that right after the little girl's mother died?"

"They think they can do whatever they want and justify it as being good for the child," Mike snarled. "If they have a judge wrapped around their fingers, they *can* pretty much do anything they want. As chief of detectives, I can file a BOLO and an Amber Alert. All I know is I received a call that a child was taken, and they don't know by whom. That way, when the Amber Alert hits, they'll have to call us and tell us that she was, in fact, taken by Child Protective Services, and they'll have to tell us where she is, and we can go and see if she's all right. That's the law. Tell Jan Moreno that I overheard the conversation, Julie, that she was not sure who they were who took her. They flashed something but didn't give her time to look at it, and they were gone. Julie, it was Jan who called me, okay?"

"Yes, sir. It was Jan who called you. She just called us to

tell us what happened and we called you because we knew you. Is that correct?"

"Yes, that's correct."

"Thanks, Mike. We owe you a big one. Audrey, after reading the letter and we already discussed it, Joe and I will immediately call our attorney and apply as foster parents or we'll just outright adopt her. According to the letter, her father is still in Cuba and abandoned Juanita when he found out she was pregnant. I know that relations with Cuba are relaxing but not happening quickly yet. Mike, do you think that Juanita's dying written declaration and witnessed by Audrey would be enough to get her back?"

"It should be, but if Child Protective Services doesn't want it to happen, it could take forever. They may want to place her with a Cuban family if they have a chance. However, Joe you're fluent in Spanish, aren't you? I saw you interrogate the Russians but I wasn't sure about the Spanish."

"Yes, in both. I just read the letter to Julie from Juanita in Spanish. I've been fluent for over fifteen years and speak and write like a native so that might help."

"I'll let you know what I find out, guys. In the meantime, say a prayer and get Juanita's body over to the funeral home. All these personal efforts will bode well, if it comes down to how well you knew the mother."

With that, they hung up. Joe and Julie would head home and wait for the call from Mike. The Amber Alert and playing dumb was a great idea. Julie would call Jan from the car and tell her what Mike said. If Child Protective Services could be that cavalier with a small child, all bets were off, and Joe and Julie would do everything in their power to get the child back.

തരു

After they got back to Tavernier, Mike Kenny called.

"The Amber Alert worked, guys. We just got an indignant call from the managing director of the Miami office of Child Protective Services. The lady said that when her staff picked up the child, they flashed their badges and picked up the girl. They were supposed to get Jan's signature on the release form that they were taking the child. Putting it politely, Joe and Julie, they messed up. She said no one had ever questioned her staff in doing their jobs. She said she was sorry, but that's the way it stands. I told her it was an illegal pickup, and I had a judge's signature on a release form, and that I'd be picking her up at 8:00 a.m. tomorrow morning at her office at 401 NW Second Avenue in Miami. I will need a judge's release form before we leave in the morning, so you'll need to get that. It's about sixty miles to where we're going, so I'll be leaving at 6:00 a.m. to make sure we're at her front door by 8:00 a.m. You're coming, right? I'll pick you up at 6:00 a.m. at Tillie's apartment. Is that all right?

Julie cheered and hugged Joe. "All right! Mike, you're a Godsend. Thank you. Thank you. Thank you. I'll call my attorney, Jane Swanson, to see if her firm has anyone who specializes in child-related issues."

"See you tomorrow."

Julie called Jane at home and told her about Juanita and Bella. She'd already privately discussed the situation with Jane when she knew that she might be able to get Bella if Juanita died. She hadn't told Joe at that point because it was premature. It was her secret with Jane, who honored her secrecy. She was Julie's attorney. It wasn't premature now and she needed Jane tomorrow, along with the expert, if they were to get Bella out from under Child Protective Services. Jane told her to call her local judge who was at the wedding.

The Honorable Bonnie Garcia was in charge of family court for the Sixteenth Judicial Court, located at the Upper Keys Government Center in Tavernier. She and Julie met at a high school function. She was also a fan of Julie's book and offered to help her in her duties as guidance counselor for the Coral Shores High School. Julie was trying to place those most at-risk into college to be the first in their families to receive a degree. Bonnie told her that she was very familiar with the poor in the area because that was whom she worked with the most. They were in and out of family court, and she knew most of the students Julie was trying to place. Julie made the call.

"Judge, I'm sorry to call you at home so late. It's Julie Chapman, now Traynor, as you know since you just attended our rather peculiar fundraiser and wedding extravaganza. I've a major problem that I have to get fixed tonight. I'm so sorry to bother you."

"You wouldn't have called if it wasn't important, Julie. What can I do for you?"

Julie told her the entire story about Juanita death's and Bella being physically removed from Jan' Moreno's house just this afternoon while Julie was coming home from her honeymoon.

"What time are you going to be in Miami tomorrow?"

"Eight a.m., Bonnie."

"You can come over in a half hour to my house. I understand you bought a house in Tavernier. I only live a few miles from you. Here's my address. You can pick up my decree that will give you temporary custody of Bella Lopez, daughter of Juanita Lopez, deceased. I'll need the death certificate by tomorrow, and I'll file it here in my family court. You'll have thirty days to become her full legal guardian and, when that process is completed, you can apply for adoption or as full foster care, whatever you want to do at this point. Is Joe on board with this?"

"Yes, very much. Mike Kenny brought up the fact that she might have been taken because of lack of Cuban foster parents in the region, but I think you know Joe's background. He's fluent in Spanish and will be starting at the Florida Keys Community College in September as vice president for institutional research and grants as well as director of the military division of the college. He's getting his PhD from Barry University and has an MBA from RPI. You know about my background."

"You don't have to sell me, Julie. Any child would be fortunate to have you two as parents. See me in half an hour and I'll give you the decree that you can hand her. In addition, in case it gets misplaced, I'm forwarding a PDF of the document to the head of Child Protective Services in Tallahassee. They can't say they never received that. I'll have coffee on. Did you eat yet?"

"No, you want a sub?"

Bonnie laughed. "Sure, ham, provolone, sweet peppers, and olives. I should get something out of this. Bring some beer too. I'm out."

Julie turned to Joe. " I think by tomorrow we're going to be parents to the cutest little girl you've ever seen. I'm heading to Bonnie's. I have to pick her up a sub and beer. Want anything?"

"Great minds think alike. I'll have the same. I'll unpack and shower. We should hit the sack early. It's going to be a long day. We should stop at Bella and Juanita's house on the way home with her tomorrow to get her documents, including Bella's birth certificate, Juanita's green card, Bella's clothes and her toys and dolls. I'll get the guys at the Islamorada station to help clean out their apartment and bring the stuff here. I'll get the key from the landlord and pass it on to the crew. I'll call Joan and let her know that we're expecting a girl, about forty pounds and three and a half feet tall."

Julie laughed and hugged Joe again. "Thank you from the bottom of my heart, Joe."

જીજી

They were standing outside Tillie's apartment when Mike showed up. He had his cruiser. "We can make better time heading out of the Keys with the strobe light flashing, guys."

Audrey had taken the day off and was sitting right next to Mike.

Julie had a broad smile. "At least I'll have someone to talk to on the way up. Hi, Audrey. Thanks for coming. The more the merrier. My friend, the attorney, and her expert will meet us at the front door to the facility at 8:00 a.m."

"Can I play with the siren?" Joe asked as he handed Mike a coffee and two glazed donuts for the trip.

"A man after my own heart."

Julie just looked at the two of them. "Behave. We've got a child to bring home."

"Yes, ma'am," they both said at the same time.

Audrey stared into the rearview mirror at Mike as if to say, "behave."

"Mike and Audrey, do you know Bonnie Garcia?"

"The judge?"

"The one and only," Julie said. "I bribed her with a foot long sub and a six-pack last night, and we've legal papers giving us temporary guardianship of Bella for thirty days and then we can either file for foster care or adoption. Joe knows which one I want."

"That's awesome," Audrey said . Mike agreed.

They arrived at 7:20 a.m. and stopped at a Dunkin' Donut right down the street from the Child Protective Services offices. The women hit the ladies' room while the guys ordered breakfast sandwiches, coffees, and muffins for the ladies. They parked in front of the building while Mike put a placard over the steering wheel that stated, "Monroe County Sheriff's Department."

The four walked in and in the lobby was Jane Swanson and a partner in her law firm who dealt with children and family services and immigration issues. Jane knew that Bella was a US citizen but Juanita only had a green card. If there were any issues, he'd handle them. Julie handed the judge's decree to Jane. They walked in to the managing director's office. The secretary seemed to be expecting them.

Sitting on the floor playing with a doll was little Bella. She turned, saw Julie, and screamed with joy. "Julie. You came for me. My mommy said you'd take care of me because she was sick. The lady here said my mommy is in heaven. Can I see her?"

Julie broke down in tears. Audrey and Jane grabbed her shoulders because she was so shaken. Julie bent down and opened her arms for Bella. Bella ran across the room, jumped into Julie's arms, and gave her a hug. Julie couldn't let go. Her tears were streaming down her face.

"Don't cry, Julie. Why are you crying? I'm happy to see you. Can you take me home? Can I see my mommy?"

"We came to get you, Bella. We will never leave you again. I promise." Julie took Bella's hand just as the managing director's door opened and Jane handed her the judge's orders.

"I really don't think you had to call my boss's boss to come get her. We did what the law requires. We follow the law to protect the children. You had no reason to do what you did. I'll be filing a complaint over this," the director said.

Julie glared at the woman. "Bella is ours. It was requested as her mother's dying wish that we take her and raise her as our own. I'll honor that wish until the day I die. You have no idea the lengths we will go to make sure that happens. Don't start a war you won't win. I'm warning you, as God is my witness. Standing here is my husband, the most honorable man I know. Also here are two attorneys that I trust implicitly, and a detective and his wife are here as well to make sure that the right thing happens. We're leaving with Bella. Please get her belongings."

The woman stared at Julie, turned around, went into her office, and brought out Bella's bag. Not one word was said. Julie scooped Bella up into her arms and they all walked out the front door.

Jane turned to Julie. "You were awesome."

Audrey went over and gave Bella and Julie a hug and hugged Jane as well. "I've never seen anything like that it my life. That was awesome."

Julie said goodbye to Jane and her partner. Julie, Joe, and Bella hopped into the police car. Julie sat in the back with Bella still in her arms. Audrey sat in the back as well with Bella's bags in her arms. Joe sat quietly in the front and wiped away a tear from his eyes. It was a guy thing where he thought he might have a speck in his eye and he was trying to remove it. Mike turned to him and smiled. He never said a word.

They were back in Key Largo by noon. Mike dropped them off at Tillie's to get their car.

"This might be one of the best days of my life," Audrey said to them. "I won't forget today for a very long time. Bella is so lucky to have you two, and you're lucky to have such a beautiful little girl. Julie, call us and let us know about the funeral arrangements if you will."

"We will, and, if it wasn't for you two, none of this would have happened. We thank you from the bottom of our hearts. Audrey, I'll call you tonight and let you know what's going on. Thanks again."

❧❦❧

They went to Juanita's apartment and picked up all the documents and Bella's clothes and toys. They headed for Tavernier with Bella to an entirely new life.

They had the wake two days later and the funeral Mass the following day after that. They buried Juanita Lopez in a grave in St. Justin Martyr's Church cemetery. Father Schmidt said a few words at the gravesite. Bella came to the funeral parlor, the funeral Mass, and the graveside ceremony. Julie explained, as best she could to a five year old, that her mother was in heaven watching over her. It would take a long time for Bella to get over this. But, as Julie remembered, she had Tillie when her mother, Annie, died and now Bella had Joe, Julie, and Tillie. Although, it would still never replace Juanita's love for her child.

Joe was fully on board and fell in love with Bella the night they brought her home. She sat in his lap and fell asleep as they watched The Disney Channel. Julie took a picture of the two of them. She'd develop the picture and would keep it in her purse forever.

Bella started to become acclimated to Joe and Julie. They were a family in everything they did. School started in late August and Julie or Joe brought her every day to her first grade class at Key Largo School. Julie would bring her home. They pulled her out of school for a few days so that Bella could go with them to Maddy's wedding up in Massachusetts. Julie had never flown before she had attended Brown University and Joe's mother's funeral up in Troy. Bella was only five years old for her first flight. When they landed at Logan, Maddy, who had picked them up, was shocked that Bella was now part of Joe and Julie's family. She quickly asked Bella if she would be their flower girl. Everyone fell in love with Bella.

Joe had to go to Miami for a week to start his PhD at Barry University. He started his job at the community college the Tuesday after Labor Day. Julie went to New York City to meet with her editor, Sarah Atwood. It went well and she had now finished her Trilogy. They discussed what direction she'd head in next, especially now that she was the mother of a five-year-old. While there, no one could believe that she was the mother of a five-year-old until she brought out her little girl's pictures.

Tillie came to stay with Joe and Bella to babysit while Joe went to work at his new job. Her new beau, Ed Lansing, came over a few times during the week when Julie was gone. He was old fashioned. He left when he felt he should and was very deferential to Tillie. He was good to her. As Tillie had said, "Never say never."

Joe and Julie could someday have another family member in the future.

In late September, Joe and Julie had to attend the retirement party for Rear Admiral Jake Barnes, who was like a second father to him. Jake and Becky were thinking of moving to the Florida Keys. Joe was trying to talk him in to teaching at the college. Time would tell.

Julie came home from New York City, flying into Key West International Airport this time, instead of Miami, all paid for by her publisher. Joe and Bella were waiting for her in the luggage concourse area as Julie came down the ramp from the plane and then down the stairs to the luggage area.

Bella went running to Julie, hollering, "M-O-M-M-Y!"

Julie grabbed her up into a big hug and gave her kisses all over her little face.

Joe thought that he was now the luckiest man alive.

The End

About the Author

Daniel J. Barrett was born in Rutland, Vermont, and has lived his entire life in Troy, New York, ten miles north of Albany. He is a graduate of both Siena College in Loudonville, N.Y. with a BS in Finance, and from Rensselaer Polytechnic Institute in Troy, NY, with an MBA in Management. He has had a varied career, first as a commercial banker, then as the chief accountant and manager of financial and strategic planning for a large division of a major international corporation. He has extensive international experience, traveling worldwide.

Barrett has also served as the first executive director for economic development for a county in New York State, and as the first lay director for a Catholic shrine in Massachusetts. For the last twenty years, he has served as a financial, strategic planning, and educational consultant to corporations, non-profit organizations, colleges and universities, and government agencies.

Currently, he serves as a grant writing, development and strategic planning consultant for many non-profit organizations in the Capital Region of New York State and Vermont. Barrett continues to live in Troy and has been married to his wife, Sandy, for forty-six years. They have three children, Sean, Eileen, and Ryan, and four grandchildren, Shannon, Caden, Megan, and Declan.

An avid reader, and inspired by numerous authors, Barrett has read over 1,900 books in the last eight years. He continues to work, as a consultant, serving those most at risk in the Capital Region, and is now working on another novel.

www.ingramcontent.com/pod-product-compliance
Lightning Source LLC
Chambersburg PA
CBHW072156130726
47910CB00010B/525